By Jennifer Ryan

Stand-Alone Novels
THE ME I USED TO BE

Wild Rose Ranch Series
RESTLESS RANCHER
DIRTY LITTLE SECRET

Montana Heat Series
TEMPTED BY LOVE
TRUE TO YOU
ESCAPE TO YOU
PROTECTED BY LOVE (novella)

Montana Men Series
HIS COWBOY HEART
HER RENEGADE RANCHER
STONE COLD COWBOY
HER LUCKY COWBOY
WHEN IT'S RIGHT
AT WOLF RANCH

The McBrides Series
DYLAN'S REDEMPTION
FALLING FOR OWEN
THE RETURN OF BRODY MCBRIDE

The Hunted Series
EVERYTHING SHE WANTED
CHASING MORGAN
THE RIGHT BRIDE
LUCKY LIKE US
SAVED BY THE RANCHER

Short Stories
CLOSE TO PERFECT
(appears in SNOWBOUND AT CHRISTMAS)
CAN'T WAIT
(appears in ALL I WANT FOR CHRISTMAS IS A COWBOY)
WAITING FOR YOU
(appears in CONFESSIONS OF A SECRET ADMIRER)

RESTLESS RANCHER

JENNIFER RYAN

RESTLESS RANCHER

Wild Rose Ranch

AVONBOOKS

An Imprint of HarperCollins*Publishers*

First Avon Books mass market printing: December 2019
First Avon Books hardcover printing: November 2019

Print Edition ISBN: 978-0-06-295264-6
Digital Edition ISBN: 978-0-06-285184-0

FIRST EDITION

19 20 21 22 23 LSC 10 9 8 7 6 5 4 3 2 1

United States Army Lieutenant Colonel Monica Looney,
badass sister of my heart, this one is for you.
I infused some of your strength, beautiful heart, and sass into Sonya.
I also borrowed that kickass saying about the 3 S's you taught me.
Told you it would end up in a book.
Love you, sis.

RESTLESS RANCHER

Chapter One

Austin stood in front of the small mirror he'd hung on the stable wall and drew the razor down his jaw, scraping away shaving cream and two days' worth of whiskers. He rinsed the blade in a bowl of lukewarm water, ran it down the last section, then wiped his face clean with a damp towel. His hair could use a trim. A comb would do it a hell of a lot of good. Eyedrops would erase the red from his eyes. But not even the four ibuprofen he'd taken an hour ago could eradicate the headache raging through his skull.

Until two weeks ago, his sleepless nights occurred courtesy of a bottle of whiskey. But he'd put the bottle down and was on the cusp of piecing his shattered life back together.

One of those broken pieces from his past walked in through the barn door that hung off-kilter on one hinge like a drunk propped against a bar.

He'd been that guy. But not anymore.

"Lookin' good, Austin honey." Kelly's voice evoked a lot of memories. Not all of them good.

Her gaze swept over his chest, down his abs, and landed on the button on his jeans. "You are a sight to behold." Her tongue swept over her red painted lips. For a split second he remembered how those lips used to wrap around his cock.

But not anymore.

Lust turned to resentment and set his back teeth to grinding.

Wearing a pair of worn jeans barely hanging on his skinny hips and nothing else, he felt naked under her lascivious gaze. He'd lost some weight these last many months drinking and living hand to mouth, hoping he came up with enough money to pay for groceries.

Yes, he'd been humbled, going from living large with money overflowing his bank account to scraping by. He'd taken any odd job he could find without his father finding out and retaliating against the person who'd graciously hired him. Most everyone in these parts wouldn't dare cross Walter Hubbard. Not when most of them did business with Hubbard Ranch or worked for Blue Mining. Those few brave souls who hired him did so because they wanted to take Austin down a peg or two.

After his grandfather died and left Austin this ranch, his father fired him from the family business and kicked him out of his home. His father wanted the ranch with a passion and vengeance Austin never saw coming.

But he held on. The ranch was the one thing that was still his, though the money ran out and so did Kelly. This dump wasn't the home Kelly imagined they'd live in after getting married. She expected the same kind of life he'd lived at his father's place, Hubbard Ranch, where the good life and their future seemed so easy to imagine.

Here at his grandfather's dilapidated place, you needed a fantastical imagination to see its potential.

He also needed an investor willing to take a chance on someone who'd hit rock bottom but dreamed big.

He still had a few people who believed in him, like his best friend Noah's girlfriend, Roxy, who thought he could make this place great again. She was an amazing woman with a huge heart and an even bigger bank account. He didn't know what he'd done to deserve it, but Roxy wanted to partner with him and turn this pile of dirt and rotten wood back into a modern working ranch.

Kelly had walked away because she didn't believe in the dream or him.

She never gave him a chance to turn this place into what she wanted. What he'd promised her. Abandoned by his girlfriend and disowned by his father in a matter of weeks, beaten down by his father sabotaging his chances for work, yeah, he'd given up and slowly drowned in a bottle and his going-nowhere life.

"What are you doing here? Last time we spoke, you said you'd never step foot on this shit pile again."

Kelly pasted on a pretty pout, not an ounce of regret in her eyes about what she'd said to him. "I wanted to see how you're doing. Can't I come by to check on a friend?"

"You think we're friends?" When he lost everything, he found out just how many friends he truly had, and she wasn't one of the few who stuck by him.

"Don't be like that. How can you still be angry at me? I wanted you. I wanted a ranch and family of our own. You refused to see that this place wasn't going to be our place. All I wanted you to do was sell it and give your father what he wanted. Put a stop to your feud. We could have bought a new home, got married, and had the life we wanted. It was stupid to hold on to this place out of spite and nostalgia. It's just a piece of land."

That last part struck him like a gut punch. "To you. Not to me." They'd had this same argument dozens upon dozens of times. "My father took away everything from me because he wanted to take the one thing that actually belongs to me. This land belonged to my mother's father, and his father before him. I won't sell it."

"Everyone knows you don't have the money to save it." The pity look pissed him off.

"He's made sure of that." Bitterness filled his words and every fiber of his being.

"So you lose it to him anyway. It's useless and stubborn to keep holding on to something when it's already lost."

He didn't want her or his father to know about his new partnership with Roxy. Let them find out when the work finally began and he had his operation up and running. He'd show Kelly, his father, everyone that he could rise from the ashes and rebuild this place. He had the skill, the drive, and the money if Roxy came through the way she'd promised.

"Did you get dressed up and come all the way out here just to call me names and tell me how stupid I am again?"

He appreciated her sexy legs sticking out the bottom of that flouncy white skirt and the way her breasts rose above the low-cut dark blue top.

He'd bought her the brown boots with the embossed roses on the sides when he'd had money to burn. Her blond hair was curled into thick rings and was tousled to look like she'd just been tumbled good in bed.

He'd messed up her perfectly styled hair and wrinkled her clothes in all sorts of ways when they were together. He wondered if she'd come here to rekindle the old fire. Before his brain had time to process what a bad idea that was, she stepped up close, wrapped her arms around his neck, pressed her soft breasts against his bare chest, and kissed him with a slow sexy sweep of her tongue along his bottom lip.

She knew how to tempt him. He'd been living in a sexual drought for a good long while now. So he didn't move and enjoyed the brief moment of feeling desirable and wanted.

She'd burned him in the past, so had many others, and a subtle alert went off in his mind.

She kept her body plastered to his and leaned back to look at him. "What's wrong, honey? You never used to hesitate to take what you wanted." She nudged her belly against his neglected, but eagerly growing dick.

He was always ready to bed a beautiful woman, but something didn't feel right.

Kelly had never been this . . . calculated.

Why come back now?

Nothing had changed in his life or with his circumstances.

Unless she'd found out about Roxy partnering with him. But he hadn't told anyone, and Roxy wanted to keep things quiet. She didn't need everyone else in town gossiping about how she used the money she earned from the notorious Wild Rose Ranch brothel she owned outside of Vegas.

"Why are you here now? I'm still broke and you still don't want to live here."

She leaned in and kissed him again. He tried not to get sucked in by her familiar scent and lush curves pressed against him.

"This hasn't changed. I want you. You want me."

His body wanted the release and relief, but the passion and need he once felt for her didn't rise up and drive him to fill his hands with her soft breasts and thrust his aching cock into her welcoming heat.

Her hand slid over his hard stomach, dipped into his jeans, and ran down the length of him. She gripped him in her hand and stroked up and down, her mouth planting hot, wet, openmouthed kisses down his neck and over his chest. "You know you want more."

She hooked her leg around his hip and used her free hand to take his and slide it up her thigh and under her skirt to her bare bottom. All that silky skin at his fingertips made him grab a handful of ass and press her closer.

She undid his jeans and freed him. "That's it. Give it to me."

His body wanted to give her a good hard fucking right here, standing up in the dusty barn. But his mind started adding things up. One and one still equaled two, but her and him doing this right here, right now didn't add up to anything good happening after the deed was done.

She never showed up to any of their dates with no panties and I-can-paint-your-dick-red lips. She flirted but never took an aggressive lead with him for sex. He'd had to talk her into making love on a picnic blanket under a tree on a secluded spot on the ranch. She'd been afraid someone would see them.

All this shot through his mind and his hands went to her hips as one final thought blared in his brain. She always, always insisted on a condom because she didn't want to have children until they were good and married. So a split second before she encased him in her slick core, he set her away and zipped his jeans.

"What the hell is going on here?" His mind identified the clues, but he didn't see the whole picture.

"Why did you stop?" Her cheeks flushed pink. She took a step toward him, her hand reaching for his neck.

He sidestepped before she backed him into the wall and faced her, standing just out of her reach.

Her gaze dropped to his thick erection, then back up to his face. "You still want me."

"My dick's not broke the way I am. I don't have a dime to my name. Seems to me, you cared more about that than fucking me anymore, so why don't you tell me why you're all of a sudden all hot and bothered over me to the point you haven't insisted I wear a condom."

"I'm on the pill."

"Bullshit. We had this talk a long time ago. You can't use the pill because it messes up your system so bad. Try again."

She huffed out a breath and flipped her long blond hair over her shoulder with a careless flick of her hand. "I can't believe you remember that."

"Important talks like that kind of stick with you, especially when *you* made it clear no kids before marriage."

She pressed her lips together and eyed him before the stiffness left her shoulders and they slumped. "I want to get pregnant." Her lips tilted into a lopsided frown. "We want a baby."

"*We*." For the first time, he saw the diamond ring on her finger. How he'd missed the dime-sized rock, he didn't know. He'd been too stunned to see her and distracted by her attempted seduction to take in the details that had helped set off that alarm in his mind.

"I've been seeing someone. He's good to me. He loves me and wants to give me everything I ever wanted." Her eyes pleaded with him to understand. Like it wasn't personal she loved someone else now.

Despite what happened between them, he wanted her to be happy. "If that's the case, why the hell are you here cheating on your fiancé?" His stomach soured with the thought of touching someone else's woman. He didn't do those kinds of things. He believed in being faithful and telling the truth, even when it hurt and meant the end if you wanted out.

"He wants another child but he had a vasectomy years ago. He had it reversed but the doctors told him his low sperm count would make it difficult to conceive a baby. We talked about alternative ways to get pregnant and he encouraged me to see you."

IVF. Surrogacy. Sperm donor. Adoption. Take your pick of available options. But send your fiancée to another man?

No man who truly loved his woman would share her with another man.

That alert he got earlier turned into a full-on alarm in his head. His chest tightened with a weight he didn't want to carry because he suspected where this was going and he didn't want to believe it. It couldn't be true.

"Why me?"

"*We* have a history. I always thought we'd make beautiful babies. We're not together, and things for you haven't exactly worked out the way you wanted. I'm ovulating. I thought we'd have one last good time."

"And what? You'd never tell me about the baby?" Every breath made him ache more.

"With the way your life is now, you can't take on that responsibility or financial burden."

He didn't know this callous, calculating woman.

"My fiancé and I would love and care for the baby. He'd want for nothing." She moved closer and put her hand on his chest. "Please, Austin. You know how much I want this."

He slapped her hand away. His heart thrashed in his chest and his mind screamed, *No.* This could not be happening. It couldn't be as bad as it appeared. But he had to know the full truth and what she'd planned to keep from him as long as she could before it all came out. Because secrets like this always came out.

"Who put that ring on your finger?" His mind screamed, *You don't want to know.*

Her gaze dropped to his boots. "We've kept our relationship quiet."

He pointed to her hand. "Astronauts can see that ring from space. You really think you're being discreet?"

"Austin, who I'm with doesn't change the fact this is what I want. You don't have to take responsibility for the child. Ten minutes and your work is done." A plea filled her eyes. "I know that sounds insensitive, but men get women pregnant all the time and don't have anything to do with the child."

She sounded like a lunatic.

"And you think I'm that kind of man." It hurt that someone would believe that about him.

"I want a baby, Austin. This is the most expedient way to get one. You and I care about each other, which makes this easier. You're a good guy. You want me to be happy. So please, help me have a baby."

Despite what she thought of him and the hurtful words, though she really had no idea how much they stung, he did want her to have everything. Maybe some guys would see the upside of having sex with a beautiful woman and walking away. But he would never turn his back on a child the way his father had turned his back on him. That she didn't see that hurt more.

"No."

Surprise filled her eyes, but his rejection didn't squash her determination. "I'll pay you."

The desperate words slammed into him with the force of a knife plunging into his chest. "Not only no, but fuck you. I'm not some stud for hire." The thought sickened him.

For the first time, he understood how Roxy felt when people accused her of being a prostitute.

"Ten thousand dollars." She clasped her hands in front of her like she prayed he'd accept. But her desperation spoke of more than her desire to have a child.

She *needed* him to say yes.

He wouldn't play Kelly's whore for any amount of money. And he wondered, like the ring, where she got that kind of cash. "Who is your fiancé?"

She shook her head and backed up a step, too afraid to tell him.

And that's when the rage exploded inside him as fast as the truth lit up his mind.

He shot forward, tilted her chin up with the tip of his finger, and made her look at him. "Who is it? Say it," he dared her.

Tears filled her eyes. Her gaze strayed over his shoulder and she whispered, "Your father." Those two words blasted through his mind and constricted his chest. He couldn't breathe for trying to contain the fury burning inside him.

Before he lost his head, he released Kelly and turned his back on her.

His own father had taken up with his ex-girlfriend and wanted Austin to sire a child that he'd raise. The thought turned his stomach and sent bile to the back of his throat.

Over my dead body.

"He wants *my* child." He spit out the vile words.

"You two are so stubborn. You won't sell. He refuses to leave his estate or the companies to anyone but family."

"So long as that family isn't me."

"Do you blame him?"

Austin spun around to face her. "Yes! Why do I have to bend and give up what's mine? Why do I have to do what he says because he demands it? Why can't I have what's mine and make something of it? I busted my ass working for him. I did everything he wanted from the time I was a child to running the operations. But this one thing he can't let go of. Why?"

Kelly held her hands out and let them drop to the sides of her thighs. "I don't know. I tried to change his mind, but he won't let it go."

"Instead, he doubles down on humiliating me by seducing my ex-girlfriend, then sends her here to fuck me for my baby. He hasn't taken enough, he wants my child, too!" Anger stung his throat as those ridiculous words burst out his mouth.

"The child would be his grandson. He'd get everything."

"And that's all that matters. You get what you want. He gets what he wants. What about what I fucking want?" He yelled so loudly he was sure the rickety rafters overhead vibrated with his rage the way his whole body shook with it. "I would never—EVER!—give up my child. Anyone who thinks that of me doesn't know the real me. And that includes you." He took a menacing step toward her, his body rigid and begging for a fight it wouldn't get. "How could you come here with his ring on your finger and think I'd ever want to touch you, let alone have a baby with you? I don't even want to look at you. Get out."

She reached for him again, but he stepped back. The thought of her ever touching him again sent a shiver of revulsion through him.

"Get out!"

This time he was sure his fury would bring down the roof.

She spun on the heels of the boots he'd bought her, her skirt flaring out, showing off a lot of thigh. She'd come here hoping he'd knock her up without a second thought and she'd walk out with his child and raise it with his father.

He didn't think Kelly or his father could hurt him more than they had when they abandoned him, but this twisted deception they'd tried to pull over on him hit hard and cut deep.

He waited for the sound of her car to fade before he walked out of the barn and headed for his pathetic bed on the porch of the hoarder house he couldn't stand to go in and the bottle he'd left under the cot and hadn't touched in two weeks.

He needed a drink.

Or ten.

There might not be enough whiskey in Montana to make him forget what just happened.

His life couldn't get any worse than this. Right?

Chapter Two

Kelly slammed the front door and threw her purse on the console table, knocking over a vase filled with giant white mums. Water spread across the table and dripped onto the marble floor, spreading toward the expensive rug. She cursed and stomped her foot, her hands fisted at her sides.

Nothing went her way today.

The office door to her right opened and she inwardly cringed. She hated to disappoint Walter. He'd blame her for not getting the job done.

She didn't like hurting Austin. It tore at her heart, because she still cared about him. She always would. But she wanted a baby to please Walter and earn his praise. She wanted to feel that light of appreciation and acceptance he'd made her feel when they started seeing each other. It had waned recently with the stress of trying to get pregnant.

She hoped to change that today but she had failed miserably.

"Kelly. You're back." Surprise filled his eyes and words. He held up his hand. "Look."

She stared at the golf ball–sized raw sapphire surrounded by several smaller ones in his palm. His eyes were alight with sheer elation. He didn't look at her the way he did his coveted sapphires with that much enthusiasm.

"They're great."

"There's more where this came from." And he looked like he couldn't wait to go back where he found them and dig for more.

He finally focused on her and studied her face. "So that was quick."

She didn't respond. She didn't know what to say.

"Well?"

Embarrassment and humiliation swept through her once more, heating her face, but this time a wave of disappointment and defeat came with it. "He turned me down."

Walter looked her up and down, his displeasure evident in his cool gaze and tense jaw. "I hope not for lack of trying."

When they'd first discussed using Austin to get pregnant the plan seemed so easy. She got the baby and the man who could give her the home and life she wanted. Sleeping with Austin again intrigued her because they'd always been great together in bed. And she'd spent countless hours thinking about their life, future, and children. If she couldn't have that life with Austin, having his child would give her at least part of that dream and make her memories of him even sweeter.

But things hadn't gone as planned and she left Austin feeling like someone she didn't recognize. She didn't use people. She didn't lie to Austin. She didn't cheat.

And that Walter had asked her to lie, cheat, and steal left her shaken and disturbed, wondering how she'd allowed herself to be talked into treating Austin with callous calculation.

Walter continued to eye her, staring hard and waiting for her to explain, like he couldn't believe she'd failed, when failure was not an option. He expected her to get it done so they could move on and have their family.

She tugged her skirt down an inch in a futile attempt to cover her legs. "I thought I had Austin right where I wanted him."

"And?"

She didn't want to go into detail, wanted to spare him—and her—the . . . uncomfortable play-by-play. "He stopped just before . . . you know."

"Why? What did you do that made him stop?"

She brushed her hand against her thigh, feeling the echo of Austin's hand on her. It washed away with the memory of the scorn she'd seen in his eyes. "I didn't do anything. He just stopped and thought about what we were doing and why." She touched her fingers to the diamond ring that seemed heavier to carry today. "He figured it out."

"Figured what out?"

"That I wanted to get pregnant."

Walter tilted his head, but his intense gaze never wavered from her face. "How did he possibly arrive at that conclusion?"

"I didn't insist he use a condom."

Walter stared down at her clasped hands. "And you didn't think to take off my ring."

She clasped her hands. "I guess I was too preoccupied with seducing your son."

Walter stuffed the gems in his pocket, then reached out and jerked one of her hands free. Shocked by the abrupt move, a wave of adrenaline shot through her system.

He pulled her toward the stairs and she trudged after him, unsure of his intent. "Well, since neither of you got the job done, I suppose it's up to me to do it right."

His attempt to make that sound seductive and not like an insult fell flat to her ears. Especially after what she'd done, his readiness to send her to Austin in the first place, and his reaction to the news she hadn't slept with his son.

At the foot of the stairs, he stopped and pulled her close. His hand slid down over her hip. His fingers gathered her skirt, pulled it up, then slipped beneath and brushed over her thigh. His soft kiss eased her fast-beating heart and drew her back into the connection they shared. He cupped her bottom, his fingers an inch from her warming core. "I will always give you everything you need, everything you want."

She settled into him and the hypnotic and seductive way his fingers traced circles on her soft skin, infinitesimally moving closer to her building heat.

"With me, everything is possible." He dipped his hand lower and thrust two fingers into her slick core. The intrusion shocked her and sent a wave of lust through her throbbing system. "I will never leave you wanting."

As he played her body to his tune, for the first time a niggling suspicion rose to the forefront of her mind. Did he want to please her and give her everything *she* wanted, or was he using her to get what *he* wanted?

Chapter Three

Sonya stood over the man she'd come here to help. She held a pitcher of water in one hand and a cup of coffee in the other. Austin snored like a snorting pig who'd wallowed in a bottle of whiskey. The putrid stench coming off him wasn't much better than a team of swine, or the smell coming out of the packed-with-crap-to-the-rafters house. Lying on the cot, one booted foot on the ground next to the discarded food container, his dingy gray shirt stained with fried-chicken-grease streaks from his fingers wiping across it, Austin slept like the dead.

The noisy dead.

Her sister Roxy warned her Austin wouldn't be an easy project, but Sonya didn't expect she'd have to save a drowning man from the bottom of a bottle.

Roxy thought Austin was on board with this crazy venture. She claimed he'd cleaned up his act and quit drinking.

He should have been expecting Sonya.

Well, he wasn't expecting this.

She dumped the cool water over his face and chest.

"What the hell?" Austin sat up, sputtering. He wiped his hand over his drenched face and raked his fingers through his oily hair. He squinted his bloodshot eyes against the bright morning sunlight, twisted, and stared up at her. "What the hell?"

"You said that already." She stared into his striking blue eyes. The anger faded to pure male appreciation when his gaze dipped from her face and traveled down her body. She didn't want to feel the warmth that look spread through her system. "Drink this." She handed him the steaming paper coffee cup. "The trucks are here."

As if on cue, the Dumpster trucks turned into the drive, followed by the crew she'd hired to help clean out the house. Another truck would arrive later today to haul away anything worth donating.

"Who the hell are you?"

"Sonya. Roxy sent me. Remember?"

Austin rubbed the heel of his hand into his eye socket. "Vaguely. She said Tuesday."

"It is Tuesday."

Austin gazed up at the sky, checked his watch, then patted his pockets looking for something. Probably his phone to confirm the date. "Seriously?"

"Comes after Monday and right before Wednesday."

Austin glared up at her, but she didn't miss the way he tried not to let the right corner of his mouth sneak up just a fraction of an inch.

"Time to get to work."

"So much for getting to know you."

Sonya cocked her hip and glared down at him. "I quit my job and moved here to make all your dreams come true."

"I can think of a dozen ways you can do that, sweetheart."

Sonya fumed. "I'm not your sweetheart or honey. I'm not here for you." She wasn't quite sure why she agreed to do this for Roxy. She should have stuck it out at her accounting firm, made them take notice and give her the promotion she deserved. "While I'd like to toss a stick of dynamite into this dump and call it a day, Roxy says this place means something to you and we need to clean it out. So get your drunk ass up and get to work."

She walked down the steps and headed for the driver of the first Dumpster truck to instruct him where to unload the large bin. Feeling Austin's gaze on her, she turned back. "Stop staring at my ass. You want off that cot and into a real bed"—she looked around the yard—"inside. Well, we're going to have to be able to get through the front door."

Austin grinned and poured the last dribble of whiskey into his coffee. "By all means, sweetheart, if you want me in a bed, let's get started."

Cocky son of a bitch.

This time, she hid the smile tugging at *her* lips. "Roxy said I'd have my hands full with you. You will *not* have your hands full of me."

Austin raised one eyebrow and gave her a wolfish grin. "Challenge accepted."

"The only thing you need to accept is that one word from me and Roxy pulls out of this misadventure. As I see it right now, Roxy would be better off leveling this place and starting over."

Anger replaced the mischief in Austin's eyes. "People always want to toss out the old and bring in the new. This place has a history. It's solid. The fireplace is built from rock taken from this land. My grandfather hand hewed and carved the mantel. That barn was raised by good men, neighbors who helped out and didn't ask for anything in return. While the house might smell like shit, it holds a lifetime of my grandfather's memories. Somewhere in that mess is my mother's childhood. She was happy here. My grandfather was happy here. With simple things and a good life. He left it to me, and I'll be damned if you or anyone else is going to toss it in the trash or burn it to the ground. So move your ass, sweetheart. We've got work to do." Austin walked down the bowed steps and headed for the truck backing in the Dumpster.

Taken by surprise by his connection to this place, she accepted this wasn't just a down and dirty clean-out job. Austin had a deep sentimental attachment she'd never felt for anything or anyplace she'd ever lived. To let him know she was on board for the job ahead, because they needed to work together, she said, "I've slept in worse places."

Austin stopped in his tracks and stared at her, the house, then back to her. His gaze filled with disbelief and sorrow that at one time her life had taken her to some scary, dark, disgusting places.

Chapter Four

Austin wiped his hand over his drenched shirt and shook his head, disgusted with himself. Not exactly the way he'd like to be woken up by a beautiful woman, but he didn't blame her. He had a vague memory of someone tapping his shoulder and nudging his chest several times trying to get his attention. With as much as he'd drunk last night, he was surprised the near drowning actually worked.

Not exactly the best way to meet his new partner.

Disappointed in himself for drinking away his troubles instead of letting what happened with Kelly go, he swore now he'd get his act together. Nothing was more important than putting the past in the rearview mirror and starting his business.

Roxy, his best friend Noah's new—and probably forever—woman, had offered him the moon. A chance to rebuild the ranch from the ground up. She offered him the money and banked on him doing the hard work.

He didn't blame Roxy for sending her sister Sonya to oversee her investment. He'd made a mess of his life.

The dilapidated house was filled to the rafters with everything his hoarder grandfather ever owned. Austin managed to make a path from the disgustingly gross kitchen to the mildewed and musty bathroom where he'd found a trash can overflowing with toothbrushes and disposable razors. The toilet worked but water trickled incessantly. He couldn't get into the spare bedrooms. The doors had been blocked long ago by stacks of stuff that might be trash, or simply items his grandfather thought he might need again someday.

He wouldn't cook anything in the kitchen to save his life. His grandfather had long ago lost all the silverware, dishes, and glasses somewhere in the house. He'd found a fork sticking out of the sofa cushion where his grandfather spent his last days. He wondered how many times his grandfather poked his ass on the fork tines. It made him cringe to think his grandfather simply stored it there in between meals.

Except for his grandfather's spot, the rest of the couch overflowed with newspapers, discarded jackets and shirts, and plastic TV dinner trays that had crusted over and stank up the place.

How his grandfather survived living in that house—with that smell—astounded Austin. Ten minutes inside and he'd give his left nut to get out, which was why he'd been living in the stables.

He waved his hand and guided the truck driver into the spot where the Dumpster would be close to the house. The daunting task ahead made his already throbbing head pound even more. The bass drum tempo reverberated with his heartbeat.

The pain served to remind him nothing good came from the bottom of a bottle. Drinking numbed his brain, but he only woke up with the same anger and resentments.

It wasn't simply cleaning out the house, but facing his past. How he'd been so self-centered while living with his own father that he'd allowed his grandfather to wallow and deteriorate in this place. Austin had offered no help. Anytime he'd even attempted to go inside, he'd backed down when his grandfather shouted, "This is my house. These are my things. Leave it be." Desperation and fear had laced those words.

Austin had let it go, but he'd carried the weight in his chest of the shame he saw in his grandfather's eyes.

After Austin lost everything, he'd seen that same humiliation in his own eyes in the mirror and felt the guilt he carried about his grandfather turn into shame.

Pride kept his grandfather living in these terrible conditions instead of asking for help.

Austin's stubborn streak made him wallow in self-pity and hold on to his vow that he'd never sell this place no matter the cost.

He'd held on longer than his father anticipated, but even Austin had grown tired of looking at this place, seeing what it could be and what it was, and holding on for no other reason than to spite his father. But every time he thought about giving up and selling, he thought about his deceased mother and grandfather and how much they'd loved what had been their home. He wanted to turn it back into the house they'd loved.

Then, there'd been love and happiness here.

He wanted that for himself.

A hand settled on his shoulder. "You okay? You look like you're about to puke up your lungs and you lost your best friend."

Austin stared at the four men pulling on coveralls, heavy-duty gloves, and respirator masks.

"My grandfather never wanted anyone to see inside that house. I should have made him let me in. I shouldn't have let it get this bad. I should have done something."

She squeezed his shoulder, her grip steady and strong. "He wouldn't want you sleeping in the cold, holding on to his baggage. He couldn't let it go. It's time you did it for him."

Those words eased the band around his chest and renewed his sense of purpose.

Sonya put him back on track. "So I've laid out two tarps. One is for items to donate. One is for items to keep. The truck with the slightly smaller recycle bin just pulled in. The large Dumpster is for garbage.

"We'll go room by room, sorting. Everything comes out of the house for now. You will oversee the men, directing them as to what category every item falls under. From what I've seen, there are bills and papers interspersed throughout the house. Let's gather that all together. I'll go through it and determine what we need and what can go. If you don't mind, I'll start in the kitchen. I'll set up a couple tarps in back and keep things you'll need and donate what you don't. Sound good?"

"Yeah. I'm not that great a cook. I imagine you'll do a better job setting up the kitchen. The fridge needs to be replaced, but I did clean it out, so it's not that bad. The microwave doesn't work. I mostly use the toaster oven. I think my grandfather had a massive fire in the oven. Only one burner works on the ancient stove."

"Roxy and I spoke about some of the needed renovations. We'll gut the kitchen. I've got cabinet and countertop guys scheduled for the day after next. Electricians and plumbers will be here with the kitchen guys. I've got a contractor lined up who will oversee the repairs and painting. We have two full days to empty the house before they get here, so I need you to sort quickly. If you're not sure about an item, put it in the keep pile. We can go through it out here later."

Austin gulped his cooling coffee, needing the caffeine to get through this day. Hungover and feeling the weight of being on the cusp of a new and better life, he needed to finally step up and take charge. The daunting task ahead would take more than muscle. He needed to get past his sentimentality and do the job.

He needed a safe, clean place to live. He'd wanted to tackle this project for months. Now was the time to get it done so he could move on to getting the stables, barn, and land ready for business.

His skinny ass wouldn't survive another winter in the barn. Even the thought of it made his body shiver.

He didn't like the idea of taking money from Roxy, but if he could get the place in shape, start working the ranch, he'd put all his blood, sweat, and tears into making it a success so he could pay her back every cent.

Sonya held up the empty bottle of whiskey he'd left on the porch. "Ready to get started?"

Austin took the bottle, walked over to the recycle bin, and pitched the bottle into the back corner, smashing it to bits of flying glass.

Something inside him shifted. For the first time in a long time, he let himself believe everything would be different now. He didn't need to drink away the pain because he had a purpose and a goal that he could actually achieve. He could make a go of this place. He could prove his father wrong.

Chapter Five

Sonya left Austin staring at shattered glass. She hoped it symbolized the break of the hold booze had on him. She grabbed two garbage bins and headed to the back door that opened into the kitchen. Despite the worn and neglected look of the house, it reminded her of the cottage she shared with her sisters. The wide porch offered a view of the beautiful land and arching trees shading the house. Right now, the dusty yard offered up more weeds than wildflowers, but with some new plantings, it could be bright and welcoming. The perfect spot to sit after a long day on the ranch, enjoy a beer and quiet contemplation of all that had been accomplished and needed to be done the next day.

She should order some rocking chairs and a small table.

Maybe she could pot some pretty flowers and line the steps. Their sweet scent would drift on the wind through the screen door and into the house that would be a cozy retreat when she finished with it.

She stopped just outside the back door and stared at the chipped and weathered siding on the wall. Enthusiasm turned to disappointment. This wasn't her house. Not her home.

She didn't have a place of her own.

She didn't really belong anywhere.

The loneliness she carried with her stopped up her throat and made it ache.

Yes, she and her sisters had their cottage at the Wild Rose Ranch, but that had been more Roxy's place. She'd taken Sonya, Adria, and Juliana into her home when their mothers started working at the Ranch. It had been a good place to finish growing up. Better than living with her mother's pimps and boyfriends who promised her mother everything and gave her nothing but hell.

Fear had been her constant companion.

The Ranch had been the first place Sonya ever felt safe. The Madam, Big Mama, took care of Sonya's mother, June. No one beat her anymore. No one used her. No one forced her to do things she didn't want to do.

Her mother lived a happy life at the Wild Rose Ranch. She didn't have to think about the past anymore.

As for Sonya, she thought about the past and future far too much. Analyzing things from every angle kept her stuck in a loop, anxious, and unsettled.

When Roxy asked her to quit her job and work for her, Sonya had nearly given herself an ulcer weighing her options and fretting over giving up a steady salary and a career with a real future. She'd worked so hard to earn her degree and become a respected accountant.

Numbers made sense to her. Everything lined up.

People, the things they did, their capacity to hurt others and inflict such cruelties, boggled her mind.

Doing the books for Roxy for the Wild Rose Ranch didn't take much more than what she did at her job. But taking on this project with Austin, starting a business and running it, that had been outside her wheelhouse.

Roxy begged her to help. Sonya balked, but then the accounting firm passed her up for a promotion that would have set her up to become a partner. They gave it to Dave, the guy who came to Sonya all the time for help. And stupid her, she'd done the nice thing and helped him—right into the position that should have been hers.

Roxy always told her Sonya played things too safe. Coming from Roxy, who never did anything that might make people think she was like their prostitute mothers, that was saying something.

After Roxy's father died, she'd changed her whole life and moved here to Montana with only a hope and a prayer that things would turn out fine working on her father's ranch and raising a teenage sister. When the town found out Roxy owned the Wild Rose Ranch, they hadn't been kind or welcoming. But Roxy found her place, the home she always wanted, and a man who loved and accepted her.

That took courage.

Sonya agreed to the job, the move, accepted the challenge of getting this ranch up and running and working with a man she knew nothing about, except he'd fallen on hard times and into a bottle.

Not very promising.

But Sonya didn't give up and she didn't let obstacles get in her way.

She had a job to do and she'd get it done even if Austin stayed drunk and stupid while she did it.

This may not be her house, her business, or the future she wanted but couldn't define anyway, but she'd get to it and figure out what came next when the job was done. Maybe it was time to step out of her safe world and take a chance on something new.

She never expected to start with this project. She wrinkled her nose as the stench of rot and filth wafted out the back door. Ten feet away, it hit her in the face like a wave. She'd made the coffee this morning, but feared drinking any of it. Who knew what kind of germs and toxins were in the air in this place. She had no idea how Austin could stand it, but he'd been scraping by for months.

No one should live like this.

And with that depressing thought in mind, she pulled on her respirator, set the two trash bins side by side at the back door, and walked into the horror that should be the heart of the home. Looking around at the sheer volume of stuff, she vowed she'd restore this kitchen if it was the last thing she ever did.

She started at the door, pulling newspapers, bottles, cans, and empty cereal and food boxes from the counter and tossing them into the recycle can. Trash, like the broken can opener, disgusting food containers, the dead mouse she found in a drawer of beer bottle caps, and the eight, nine, ten . . . no, eleven boxes of expired graham crackers stuffed into the pots and pans cupboard, went into the other bin.

She filled them quickly, dragging them again and again around the house to the front and emptying them in the Dumpsters. Each trip gave her a glimpse into how things were going with Austin in the rest of the house. The Dumpsters filled quickly. The tarps held items in reasonably good shape to donate and keep. Surprisingly, the pile to donate grew faster than the keep.

After dumping her last load in the recycle bin, she pulled off her mask and sucked in some much-needed cool clean air.

"Why three new packs of glass Christmas ornaments? There's no place to put a fucking tree in the house." The anger and frustration laced with disbelief in Austin's voice made her smile. He set the silver, green, and red balls on top of a laundry basket filled with plastic hangers. "There are six new photo frames and thirteen pairs of reader glasses so far. Why?"

"Why the drawer filled with coupons he clipped but never used? The oldest one I found expired in 1971 for Folgers instant coffee."

"Who the hell drinks that stuff?"

"Not him. Based on the progression from bottom to top of the piles, I'd say he started out a Maxwell House drinker, went through a Yuban phase, then recently started drinking Seattle's Best. He started with the Portside Blend, but abandoned a third used bag inside one of the hundred rocky road containers I tossed and discovered he was a Very Vanilla kind of guy."

"Are you shitting me?"

"Nope. Your grandfather turned in his manly black coffee for a sweet vanilla treat in the morning."

Austin planted his hands on his hips, hung his head, and laughed. Before it tinged with hysteria, he sucked in a ragged breath and stared up at the sky. "I really don't understand."

"Stop trying to understand the crazy in that place and look at what that man really cared about." She held her hand out to the keep pile. "Pictures of, I presume, your grandmother and mother. I'll bet the frames were for that stack of photos. Empty hangers. A pile of men's clothes, but not women's. Maybe it hurt too much to see his dead wife's clothes hanging in the closet. A pristine set of china is stashed in a cupboard in the kitchen with a million wadded-up paper towels. I guess to keep them safe. The family of mice I discovered living in them didn't get the message that those dishes meant a lot to your grandfather. So much so, he tried to protect them from getting broken or damaged by what he'd done in the rest of the house. I found the silverware secure in a wood case stashed in the pullout drawer under the oven. All by itself."

"My grandmother used those dishes at every birthday, holiday, and special occasion."

"Look past the arbitrary stuff and you'll see what really mattered to your grandfather." She waved him to follow her around back.

Like her, he stepped over the piles of dishes, kitchen utensils, cups, and glasses she'd sorted out of the mess to the piles of pictures she'd left on the steps. She picked up the colorful stack of construction papers and handed them to Austin.

"I imagine he kept every drawing you ever doodled for him."

Austin sat on the step and sorted through the fifty or more crayon drawings of horses, cowboys, and houses with bright yellow suns and fat trees with stick figure people. Some just Austin and his grandpa. A few with Grandma included. Others Austin with his mom and dad. A plane with Austin waving out a window.

"I wanted to be a fireman." Austin held up the bright red fire truck on yellow construction paper.

She smiled down at it. "I like the purple puppy and green kitten one the best."

He pulled it out of the stack. "My father wouldn't let me have a pet. I loved coming here to Grandpa's ranch. I played for hours with Rumble the cat and Copper, the German shepherd my grandfather adopted, just so I could play with him when I was here." Austin shuffled to a picture of a white, brown, and black pony. "He taught me how to ride Bandit." A grin tugged at Austin's lips as he stared at the picture. "He used to get out of his stall and raid the grain bin. My grandfather said he was just as naughty and up to mischief as me."

"I believe it." Something about the boyish glint in his eyes made her want to ruffle his hair. She held back. They didn't know each other that well. They'd barely spoken today after she woke him up in a not-so-nice way. Still, she felt something for him and the memories of this place and his grandfather that meant so much to him.

She had no such memories. From what her mother told her of her grandfather, she was better off never meeting him.

She set aside her baggage about her fucked-up family and asked, "Uh, why Rumble for the cat?"

"Purred as loud as thunder. He'd curl up with me at night and that purr would put me out like a light." Austin glanced up at her. "Did you have any pets growing up?"

"I fed the mouse who hid behind our refrigerator for a week when I was like four or five."

"Why only a week? Did he run away?"

"No. My mother's pimp threw his knife and stabbed him. He flicked the mouse off it out the door and into the gutter. No more pets."

Roxy had her horses at the ranch. Sonya was a proficient rider. She'd competed alongside her sisters and won. But she'd never forgotten the lesson about the mouse. The horses were Roxy's, not hers. Loving them meant she'd have to leave them because where Roxy went, so did her beloved horses.

Austin stared at her, stunned.

Not exactly the happy memories he had of puppies, kittens, and ponies. He grew up with money, privilege, and possibility.

She started her life in poverty, believing that nothing in her life would ever change because challenge was met by force to suppress and control. Thanks to a hand up by Big Mama and the Wild Rose Ranch, she learned that opportunity could change your life if you were willing to work hard. And she had, because no one handed her anything.

Despite the state of the ranch, he'd been given a piece of land worth a lot of money. He wanted to keep it, but if he had to sell, he'd have the means to do anything he wanted.

"Your life's not that bad." She walked up the steps and back into the kitchen.

Sharing personal stories wasn't really her strong suit. Better to stick to business. She wasn't here to be Austin's best friend. Her job was to keep her eye on the money and get this place up and running. Not that she knew all that much about buying horses and cattle. She'd leave the purchases to Austin so long as he stayed on budget.

But that was for later. Right now, she needed to tackle the rest of the kitchen and the piles of stuff clogging the archway into the living room.

The men she'd hired worked diligently trying to clear out the space. They'd made a good-sized dent from the front door into the room toward the hallway. Eventually, the small path leading into the kitchen would open up. And now, with doors and windows open, the overwhelming smell had dissipated.

She stood in the 60 percent cleared kitchen, her feet sticking to the dingy cream-and-gold-plaid linoleum that cracked with every shift of her weight because it was so brittle, and tried to picture what it would look like all cleaned up.

If they widened the casing into the living room, they could add an island and stools, open up the space and make it more practical. They could . . .

Wait. Not they. As much as she loved the idea of turning this cesspool into a warm and welcoming home, the minute she finished the task she'd be out of here.

Roxy offered to let her stay with her and Noah. No thanks. As happy as she was for her sister, she didn't want to intrude on the lovebirds. Her short stay with them last month showed her how happy Roxy was and how empty Sonya's life felt.

She'd lived with Roxy, Adria, and Juliana since she was thirteen. When Roxy moved out, Sonya resented that she'd broken up their quartet, but that just masked the fact that Sonya wondered how long she'd cling to her sisters and the only safe place she'd ever had in her life before venturing out and finding the life she wanted for herself.

She thought she needed the degree and the job, the stability they both offered, but deep down she wanted what she'd never had. A real family. A chance to make memories with someone special and a life for her children that she'd only dreamed about during her own lonely and sometimes ugly childhood.

She didn't understand how anyone, Austin's father included, could turn their back on their child and not do everything in their power to give them a good life.

"Hey, sweetheart, you okay?"

Sonya snapped out of her head and focused on Austin standing in the narrow opening between the kitchen and living room still crammed with crap.

"You've been standing in that spot for, like, three minutes."

She lifted one foot, then the other, showing Austin how her hiking boots stuck to the floor. "It's easy to get stuck in this place."

Austin stared down at her feet. "I didn't remember the color of the floor. Seeing it now, that funky yellow, I wish I could forget again." At least he'd found some humor to help ease his frustration with the state of this place.

"Not to worry, the floors are being redone." She looked around at the massive job still left to do. "As soon as we uncover the floors."

Austin ran his gloved hand over the back of his neck. "I, uh, didn't get a chance this morning to say thanks for coming to help."

"So you forgive me for pouring a bucket of water on you?"

Austin held back a smile. "Probably the only way to wake my ass up. And I'm sure it cut the stench. It's hard to make myself walk in here and use the shower. It's usually me and the hose by the barn sometime during the day."

Sad. "You smelled a hell of a lot better than this place."

His eyes clouded with pain and regret.

"In a few days, this will be a memory, Austin. I may not be your go-to girl for the ranching part of this partnership, but I can clean up this mess and turn the house into somewhere you not only want to sleep but show off."

"I never expected Roxy to fix the house beyond cleaning it out. I can work on the repairs and painting and stuff a little at a time once I've got the ranch up and running."

Sonya shook her head all through that guilt-ridden statement. "Roxy knows what it's like to live in a place that's unhealthy and makes you feel as sad as the place looks."

"You do, too, don't you?"

"Roxy and I have a lot in common." She glanced around the dismal room. "Roxy has the means to give you a hand up. Take it. And when you have the chance to do it for someone else, do it."

"Are you always this serious?"

"Yes." Cautious. Steady. Boring. Her sisters constantly tried to get her to loosen up. "Now get back to work." She cocked her head toward one of the guys in the other room. "Looks like they found another buried treasure."

Austin turned and stared at the sterling silver box, tarnished by time. "My grandmother used to keep the jewelry case on the dresser in her room."

"Looks like your grandfather hid it in an old apple crate filled with dish towels."

"Where else would one keep it?"

She liked the sarcasm far better than his earlier anger and frustration over what his grandfather had done to the house and his memories. "I found a Cheerios box filled with ketchup packets."

"I guess you have to store them somewhere," he quipped.

"He stuffed it behind a paper bag filled with other folded paper bags."

Austin shook his head and rolled his eyes. "Trying to figure him out makes my head hurt."

"I'm pretty sure that's the massive hangover."

He frowned, but nodded his reluctant agreement. "There won't be any more of those."

If he said so.

"We're making progress. Keep at it." Just like every other daunting task in her life, that's all she could do. One step at a time until the job was done. But like every other time, in the back of her mind, she wondered what happened next. Where was her life headed? With every achievement, was she moving closer to what she really wanted?

Or simply going through the motions because she didn't really know where she fit or belonged.

Chapter Six

Austin woke at the crack of dawn. During the winter, sleeping in the barn had made his bones ache in the freezing cold, but now the Montana days grew warmer with spring taking hold.

After working all day yesterday, his whole body rebelled against the slightest movement. His muscles clenched every time he even thought about getting up. He didn't know how many times he'd dragged the large trash cans out to the Dumpsters yesterday, but it was enough to tell him he was getting old and soft. If nothing else, all this hard labor would get him ready for the ranch work ahead.

Before he let his mind spin out on everything he needed to do to bring animals onto the ranch, he focused on what needed to be done today. He and the guys Sonya hired had cleared the main living space. It shamed him to let anyone see the place in such dire conditions. But what they did in one day would have taken him two weeks or more on his own.

He turned his head and stared at the piles of stuff on the tarps out in the yard. At first, he'd wanted to keep every little thing. A lot of the stuff had barely been used, if ever.

He found a vacuum cleaner in the box. Why? There wasn't a square inch of floor you could use it on. Until now. He found other cleaning supplies and flattened boxes. Signs his grandfather had at least wanted to try to clean out the house, but like Austin, he had probably taken one look at the mess, gotten overwhelmed, and simply ignored it rather than do the hard work.

Austin had spent too long putting things off for later.

He'd put his whole life off for later.

Not anymore.

His muscles still protested, but he rolled up and turned to sit on his uncomfortable and too-small cot. Across the yard and next to her truck, Sonya stood on a mat in tight black pants and a pink long-sleeve T, her arms stretched up to the sky. She bent at the waist and planted her hands on the mat, her sweet round ass pointed right at him.

Damn. He'd spent most of yesterday trying not to notice the beautiful dictator. From the minute she arrived, she'd been in charge, telling him where to start, what to do, when to take a break, when to eat, when to quit for the day. She set up all the workers and contractors. She made the decisions for the updates to the house. He'd gone along for the ride because he'd been too hungover to think let alone keep up with her.

Today would be a different story. He didn't need her to get the place in order. He could oversee the workers. She was supposed to write the checks and make sure he didn't squander Roxy's money. He wished she'd stick to that and stay out of his way. Because she was a distraction he didn't need or want.

His aching morning wood didn't heed his wishes. It wanted to nudge itself right past her round bottom and bury itself deep inside her.

But that would end in disaster.

She was Roxy's sister. The last thing he wanted to do was give Roxy any reason to back out of their deal.

Besides, he didn't have the money to take her out on a proper date and still fill the gas tank in his truck.

So he'd kept his head down yesterday and tried to keep up with the guys helping out.

Didn't mean he didn't notice Sonya's boundless determination, her strength, and the way she defused his anger and frustration when it came to this place and how he'd let down his grandfather. The woman didn't bat an eye at the mess, the roaches scurrying from one hidey hole to the next, or the rodents squeaking their displeasure at having their homes disturbed. She voiced her opinion about the atrocious smell, but never demurred when it came to cleaning unidentifiable grunge and droppings.

He'd had a moment when he stood in the middle of all that filth and disarray and thought he should just get a bulldozer and level the place. But with every memory he uncovered—the rocking chair his grandmother read him stories in, the paint-by-numbers floral painting his mother did in high school that hung proudly over the fireplace, cans of his favorite Hershey's hot cocoa he used to sip by the fire while playing cards with his grandpa—he wanted to return the house to what it was for him: a home where he'd been safe and loved. Where he'd been enough.

Sonya moved into a deep lunge, arms overhead, then falling sideways as she stretched. Maybe he should join her and loosen up, though he doubted anything would untie the knot in his gut that pulled taut every time he looked at her. He tried not to look into her eyes. Every time he did, he saw something deep inside her. A longing and wanting.

Not the way he wanted her in his bed. It had been a long time since he'd satisfied the itch she exacerbated with every graceful move she made as she worked out in the soft morning light. No, she wanted something deep and meaningful.

How did he know that? He'd seen the way she looked at the house and talked about how his grandfather buried his memories. A life he'd lost with the death of his wife and daughter.

Austin felt their loss keenly. Yes, he'd lost his mother, but did that kind of pain even come close to losing a beloved wife and child? The ache in his chest had intensified with every recollection of the good times he'd had here with his family.

Granddad must have found the memories unbearable to have buried them deep in the chaos he'd created in the house.

Unwanted and unloved by his own father, Austin finally understood why he'd been drinking himself into oblivion. He missed his mother, his grandparents, and the love they'd given him unconditionally and wholeheartedly.

Their loss had hit him harder and more profoundly than his father firing him from the business and disowning him. At the time he'd thought Kelly would stick by his side. She didn't get his connection to this place. She said he loved it more than he loved her. Well, he'd kept the land and let her go. If she didn't get it, he didn't need her.

That's what he told himself.

But the long lonely nights always made him second-guess himself.

After what Kelly did the other day, he had no doubts he'd made the right choice. Her deceitfulness and calculation cut deep and showed him just how little she cared. Who could do something so despicable to someone they claimed to love?

Sonya rolled up her mat, set it in the truck bed next to the inflatable mattress where she'd slept last night, picked up a toiletry bag, and headed for the back door.

He stood and stretched his back. His foot knocked over a beer bottle that toppled two more. Sonya stopped and stared over at him. She didn't show any outward sign of disapproval, but he felt it all the same.

She thought him nothing better than a drunk. Well, she'd had the barbecue and beer delivered last night for him and the crew, though three beers was nothing compared to what he'd been drinking lately.

He didn't need to forget and numb his body and mind anymore. He had things to do, a business to start. He deserved a couple of cold beers at the end of a twelve-hour day.

She didn't know anything about him and what he'd been through.

I'm arguing with myself.

Fuck.

He didn't care what she thought.

To prove it, he grabbed his stuff and headed for the kitchen. They'd left the doors and windows open to air the place out last night. It only smelled half as bad as it did yesterday. They didn't need the masks in the kitchen. The bedrooms they needed to clear today remained to be seen.

Sonya stood at the sink brushing her teeth. He set his bag of stuff next to hers, took out his toothbrush and paste, spread some on the bristles, and started to brush. She didn't say anything about him standing so close. She spit in the sink, turned on the water, leaned over to drink from the faucet, swished, and spit a couple of times. She left the tap on for him to do the same while she raked her fingers through her long dark hair, drew it into one hand, then used the band around her wrist to tie it up in a ponytail. She cupped her hands under the water and splashed it on her face. While droplets dripped into the sink, she squeezed some liquid soap onto her fingers, set the bottle down, lathered the soap on both hands, then scrubbed her cheeks, chin, and forehead. She rinsed, then used the small towel draped over her shoulder to dry off.

"That stuff smells good." Like the apricots pictured on the label. "Can I use some?"

She handed him the bottle. While he washed his face, she spread lotion over hers and massaged it in. When he finished rinsing his face, she handed him her towel.

"You're quiet in the morning."

"I need coffee." The pot slowly dripped on the counter in front of him. "I'm sure you do, too."

For some reason, that sparked his anger. "I'm not hungover. I had a few beers after a long day. Shoot me."

She held her hands up in front of her. "Hey, I'm not your babysitter. Do whatever the hell you want. I only meant if you're as tired as I am, it's going to take a lot of caffeine to get through this day. You want to get smashed, be my guest. You're the only one who can ruin this deal. I just work here." She grabbed her stuff and walked out, leaving him feeling like a complete asshole and still holding her towel in his fist.

He pressed it to his big mouth, smelled her, and tossed it on the counter she'd cleaned along with two mugs. The rest of the dishes she'd salvaged from the cupboards and piles in the house were stacked and spread out on a tarp out back.

She'd worked her ass off yesterday, fed him and everyone else, then made the coffee this morning. He had no doubt she'd work just as hard today. For him. For this place he couldn't let go. And he'd snapped at her because he was angry at himself for the way he'd been behaving this past year, not because she'd in any way reprimanded him the way he deserved to be.

Disappointed in himself for hiding in a bottle and treating the few people left in his life like shit, he vowed to do better and be better.

He rinsed the mugs in the sink just to be on the safe side, then filled both with hot coffee. He carried them out the back and found Sonya standing at the lowered tailgate of her truck. He handed one mug to her.

"Thanks."

"You're welcome. And I'm sorry about snapping at you. Drinking to avoid my problems was beyond stupid. I want this project to work, and I'll do whatever I have to do to make it happen. I don't need a drink, I need this business to succeed, and I know that only happens if I'm on my game."

She stopped studying the papers in front of her and turned to him. "Keep your shit together and work harder than you did yesterday." Sound advice. She gave no quarter. He didn't deserve any. But her direct manner still annoyed the hell out of him. "What do you think about opening up the casing into the living room and putting in an island?"

Back to business. "I think it will cost a lot of money I don't have."

She pinched her lips. "I think it's just what the house needs." She picked up her phone and tapped a button. "Ask the cabinet guys to add an island to the order."

"How many messages did you record for yourself yesterday?"

"It took me twenty minutes to go through them last night and write them up on my various lists."

He cocked his chin toward the phone. "Is that how you keep track of everything?"

"It's easy and convenient. I don't have to stop what I'm doing and find a piece of paper or my notebook." She set her phone aside. "It may take an extra day or two for the cabinet guys to do the island. I sent them the final measurements for the kitchen last night. If you need the kitchen sink for anything, I'd do it this morning because I'm tearing out the old cabinets and sink today." She opened the lid on a plastic bin and pulled out samples. "This is the floor I chose. Wide planks to match what's in the living room."

Sonya held up a white square. "I went with marble countertops. Classic. Because the floors are dark, I ordered white cabinets with brushed nickel nobs. They come in standard sizes, which is why I could get them so quickly. I'll match the kitchen cabinets in both bathrooms with undermount sinks and brushed nickel faucets. Roxy suggested wood-look tile on the floors." She pulled a sample from the bin and set it on the tailgate. "She also chose the rectangular shower tiles." Sonya showed him the light gray tile sample that had a soft texture that added depth to the pale color.

"I knew she wanted to redo the kitchen, but both bathrooms, too. That's going to take time and a hell of a lot of money."

"We talked about it and agreed that doing it all at once when the house was gutted was the best time. Once you're working the ranch and busy with other things, you'll never find time to do the improvements."

"I take it the 'we' you're talking about was you and Roxy plotting and planning my life."

"I don't see how redecorating is plotting and planning your life, but we did save you from picking tile and floor samples. If you want to change something, then say so."

"I don't want any of this. Yes, I wanted the house cleaned out, but I don't want to be beholden to Roxy for all this money. She said she'd help me with the ranch. Okay. Let's focus on that."

"I'm sorry, Austin, but there is no way in hell Roxy is going to allow you to live like you've been living here. She grew up in some terrible places. She knows what it's like to go to sleep and hope the cockroaches don't cart you off in the middle of the night."

"Roxy knows? Or you know?"

She stared into her coffee mug. "Roxy has a kind and generous heart. She wants to do this for you. It's happening. Make my life easier and just go with it."

"I heard you quit your job and gave up a huge salary and a chance at a promotion."

"The promotion went to a coworker who did half the work and was a quarter as smart as me, but he had a couple years on me and the same equipment as the guys running the place, so despite my being the better employee, he got a job he'll suck at and no one will do anything about it because he's part of the boys' club. They didn't bat an eye when I gave my notice. But I'm still getting emails asking for help on accounts."

"I hope you told them to fuck off."

"If only. I might need a reference, so . . ." She shrugged and pulled more tile out of the bin. "What do you think of this for the kitchen backsplash?"

He gave up his objection to the renovation. Apparently he couldn't win that futile battle.

Black, white, and light gray tiles in different sizes were held together by string or something. "I like the random pattern. The colors will go with the marble. It might be nice to have some color."

Sonya dipped her hand into the seemingly bottomless bin and pulled out a sheet of dark blue glass tiles. "What if we pulled out some of the black and added in the blue?"

"I like green better. Maybe a dark and light shade added to the pattern. Green goes with everything, right?" He spread his hands out to indicate the massive fields around them. "Let's bring the outdoors in."

"Green it is. Any other requests?"

He didn't want to add to the bill, but . . . "What about the appliances? I can live with a coffeepot and toaster oven, but an upgrade might be nice."

A glimmer of a smile tilted her lips. "Everything new in stainless steel. They'll be delivered in four days. So you'll have to rough it a few more days."

"I can't believe you've got this all set up and ready to be done in such a short amount of time."

"Yeah, well, it will be a few extra days to get the bathrooms done. But once they are, you'll be thanking me. Well, Roxy." She put away all the samples and folded up the blueprint of the house she'd drawn up. "Sun's up. Let's get to work. The crew will be here in about an hour, but I'm sure you and I can make a dent in the hallway to the bedrooms."

"Drink your coffee first. I want to go through the donate and keep piles, see if there's anything I want to switch."

"Okay. I'll drink my coffee and sort dishes. There's so many random items and multiples of things that I need to see if there's actual sets of things that make sense and donate some of the extra items. I mean, how many potato peelers do you need?"

"Two. One for me to help and one for whoever's actually doing the cooking."

She chuckled under her breath and smiled. This time a real one that brightened her eyes.

"You should smile more. It makes your beautiful face kind of sparkle."

Her head dipped and she turned toward the house. "How many orange juicers do you want to keep?"

"None. Juice comes in a carton."

He thought he caught the whisper of another laugh on the breeze as she turned behind the back of the house.

He dove into the piles of stuff he'd tossed on the donate tarp. At first glance in the house, he hadn't thought he needed any of it, but now, thanks to Sonya making him see what the house could be, he took a second look.

Instead of looking at the place as his grandfather's house, he needed to see its potential and what it would be as his place. Green glass tiles on the backsplash, a new kitchen island, and all. So he picked up the brand-new boxes of Christmas ornaments and put them on the keep tarp. He picked out the cream bath towels that still had the tags on them. A little dusty and dirty, but they'd wash up nicely. The black wrought-iron lamps would look good in the living room. He pulled the dirty shades off them and tossed them in the trash. He'd have Sonya add new shades to her growing list of items they needed to buy on their next trip into town. He saved a carved wood horse and an hourglass with deep blue sand to use as decorations in the living room. It felt good to look at the items and think of how he could use them in *his* house.

He lost track of time sorting the two piles and making sure everything he kept would have a place and purpose in the house. He'd have to buy some new furniture, but the mix of new with old would make for a good place to come home to after a long day working the ranch. Some of it he'd keep for sentimental reasons. Other items for pure practicality. But by the time he finished, he had a sense of what worked for him and it wasn't the overpriced underused stuff he'd lived with under his father's roof.

The apartment over the garage had been his getaway and as far as he'd managed to move out. He'd told himself it was because he'd worked for his father and needed to be on the vast property most of the time. While he didn't miss his father, he did miss the 800-thread-count sheets on the massive king size bed he used to sleep in. But when his father kicked him out, it had been with his clothes and not much else.

He stared back at the house and hoped the bedrooms weren't as bad off as the front of the house had been. If he could salvage some of the bedroom furniture and the bed frames, in a few days, he could buy a new mattress and he might actually get a good night's sleep.

Sonya had probably already thought of ordering a mattress. He'd never met anyone so efficient and thoughtful. She'd arrived and hit the ground running. From what he'd gathered, she and Roxy had spent a lot of time planning what needed to be done. Sonya had set that plan in motion. And despite his objections, things were moving forward whether he liked it or not.

He had to admit, he couldn't wait to see the house restored.

"Hey, man, where's the hottie?"

In a flash his blood boiled with anger. He turned to Chris. Josh and Mark, the other two workers from yesterday, looked very interested in their work boots. Chris didn't catch the warning when Austin took two menacing steps toward him, barely able to contain his temper.

Austin took another step and crowded Chris so he had to look up, catch Austin's narrowed eyes, and step back before Austin grabbed him by the shirt and shook some sense into him. "Sonya, your boss, is around back. I expect you'll get your head out of your ass and remember to address her by her name with a hell of a lot more respect than you showed thirty seconds ago."

Chris held his hands up and took another step back. "Hey, man, I didn't know you two were a thing."

Austin didn't correct him. Chris should respect Sonya whether they were "a thing" or not, but if these guys thought they were together, they'd steer clear of her.

"Grab the empty trash cans we left by the Dumpsters last night and let's get started."

The men headed over to grab as many plastic garbage cans as they could carry. Austin turned back to the house and spotted Sonya standing on the wide porch watching him. He didn't know if she'd heard the exchange, but something in the way she stared at him made everything inside him still and take notice. She didn't shy away from looking right at him. He stared right back. With a nod that didn't tell him a damn thing about what was going on inside her head, she walked down the steps and approached him.

"Do you have a sledgehammer?"

He cocked up one eyebrow. "Why?"

"Demolition." The glint in her eyes told him how much she wanted to destroy something just for the fun of it.

"Garage probably." He waved his hand out toward the two-car garage that stood twenty feet on the other side of the house. She walked beside him, quiet as usual. He grabbed the handle on the pull-up door but hesitated. "I haven't been in here in a long time. Step back just in case whatever he's got crammed in here comes down in an avalanche and buries you."

Sonya took a few steps back. Austin pulled up the door and stepped back all at the same time, prepared to fend off anything that fell forward.

Sonya busted up laughing at his angry growl.

"All this time you've been camped out on the porch and the garage is empty."

Everything stood as he remembered it as a child. The workbenches, toolboxes, tools hanging on the walls, every damn thing in its place and perfectly in order.

"Fuck me."

Sonya swallowed another round of giggles and stared up at him with all innocence and anticipation in her bright eyes.

Austin shook his head. "I don't get it. The house is crammed with shit. The barn and stables are ready to fall down around me. But the garage is in perfect order."

Sonya touched his arm. The heat from her touch shot up his arm and spread through his whole system. The last woman to touch him left him repulsed in the end. Sonya ignited a wildfire. Though he knew she wanted to comfort him, he had other ideas about how she could go about doing that for the next couple of hours. Days, tops.

Sonya squeezed his arm and let him go. "I'd have thought it was crammed to the rafters, too."

Austin missed her touch. "Maybe, but ten seconds later you would have checked to be sure. I was so pissed at my dad for kicking me out and spent every dime I'd saved to hold on to this dump, I just assumed and threw up my hands in defeat."

"It's okay, Austin. We can use this space to hold the boxes and bags you've got on the porch from your move here and some of the bigger items we need to clean up before we put them back in the house. I can restore the dining table and chairs, paint that cute little bureau, and probably recover the ottoman with those gorgeous swirled spindle legs."

He didn't think, just pulled her into his arms and hugged her with his cheek pressed to the top of her head. "You never criticize. You just come up with a plan and do what needs to be done."

For a second, she pressed her hands to his back, then stepped out of his arms, her cheeks pink with embarrassment. "To do that, I need a sledgehammer."

He'd enjoyed the moment they'd shared and he meant what he said, but he let it go because she didn't want to make things personal between them. Like when he'd asked about her childhood being a lot like Roxy's, she'd shut him down.

Sonya didn't let many people close. But for a second there, he'd felt her let out a breath and draw closer to him. It was a start.

Of what, he didn't really know because they still had one hell of a job ahead of them. And he was still broke as shit. And Roxy and Noah might kill him for dating her. As if that was even a possibility.

He walked over to the stand that held the shovels, rakes, and other assorted tools. He pulled out the sledgehammer and handed it to her just to see what happened.

The second she took the weight, her arms fell and she nearly dropped the heavy tool.

She glared at him. "You did that on purpose."

"I love that you think you can swing that thing again and again to get the kitchen cabinets down, but you need the right tool for the job."

"And what's that?"

"Me, swinging this thing." He tried not to smile, he really did, at her open hostility that he thought her, a woman, incapable of doing the job. She could do damn near anything. It really wasn't her gender but the simple fact that she didn't have the strength to swing the heavy head more than half a dozen times before she dropped it or hurt herself.

He'd never let that happen. When it came to a job that required brute strength, she'd have to let him handle it. "Don't get mad. I've got some thing for you, demolition junkie." He went to one of the toolboxes and pulled out a heavy-duty hammer that despite its weight he thought she could handle and not get hurt.

She tested the tool in her hand and the control she'd have swinging it with the shorter handle.

"Ready?"

The smile she beamed up at him said she was looking forward to it.

Before they headed back to the house, he grabbed a couple pairs of leather gloves and safety glasses from the workbench and handed her a pair of each.

"This is a well-appointed workshop."

"Grandpa always said to put the tools back in their place, that way you know where they are when you need them." The absurdity of it boggled his mind.

"I guess he meant it."

Austin rolled his eyes. "Except he didn't keep anything in its place in the house."

"Let it go, Austin."

"I'm trying, but it's damn hard to look at those two huge bins filled with garbage and the damage to the house and furniture and not feel it all the way to my soul."

"They're just things. Not as important as the memories you hold of how much your grandfather loved you. That's worth more than any broken plate, scratched table, or smelly house. It's more than some people ever have to hold on to."

"It makes me sad when you say things like that, because I know you're talking about yourself."

She scrunched up her face into an incredulous look. He hoped because she wanted to cover the fact that on some level he got to her, because in a very short time she'd grown on him. Her steady presence and thoughtful insights made him feel closer to her. He especially appreciated her easy way of letting him do and say what he needed to before she reminded him to move on.

And then ordered him to get back to work.

He was getting used to that, too.

Sonya tried to play off his comment. "Don't cry for me, *sweetheart*. My life's not that bad."

"Anymore." He added the qualifier she didn't say out loud but he heard all the same, because she didn't like talking about her past despite the little hints she dropped.

The snarky *sweetheart* was meant to make him back off and let him know she didn't like it when he so casually called her that yesterday.

But he didn't want her to dismiss what her life used to be. She'd gotten an up-close and gross look at his. All he wanted to do was get to know her the way she so easily seemed to know him just by paying attention. He wanted her to know he had his own insights into her life because he listened not only to what she said, but what she didn't.

She held up the hammer. "Let's go pound some shit. We'll both feel better." She walked away like she always did when things got too personal.

He followed her to the house and into the kitchen. She handed him a mask and put one on herself. He checked out the sink she'd already disconnected from the water source.

"I say we start with the countertop."

Austin went with her suggestion, held the sledgehammer with his hands spread wide on the handle, swung down, then up into the corner of the Formica countertop, dislodging it with one shot on one end. Adrenaline burst through his system with the satisfaction that one swing made him feel. Four more satisfying thwacks and the entire counter came loose and lay haphazard on the cabinets that were already falling to pieces in some areas with the vibration from each swing.

At his side, Sonya opened the top cupboard doors, swung the hammer, and knocked them from their hinges. She stacked the latest one with the others she'd already taken down by the door.

She set her hammer on the floor and took one side of the countertop. He took the other. They held it upright and walked out the back door and tossed the heavy piece in the Dumpster. Without a word, they headed back into the kitchen and spent the next thirty minutes bashing the cabinets to smaller pieces and dragging them out to the trash. Austin got one of the guys cleaning out the hallway to help him dump the old stove. By the time they entered the kitchen again, Sonya had most of the walls down to the studs, old wires and pipes exposed.

"We're not taking the whole house down to the studs, are we?"

Sonya pulled her mask off and coughed from the dust floating in the air. "No. But I anticipated there'd be some water damage from leaks of years past." She pointed to the discolored floor where the sink used to be and the oddly repaired white-and-black pipes that connected to metal. "We'll probably encounter more of the same in the bathrooms. Best to take care of it now, replace rotting wood and old pipes with new while we have the chance. The wiring doesn't look that bad to me, but I'll leave that to the electrician. I also asked him to look at the main panel, see if we need an upgrade."

"We?" He cocked up an eyebrow just to rile her.

"*You* have one electrical panel servicing the house and outbuildings. If I've learned anything from HGTV renovation shows it's that the wiring always needs to be fixed and upgraded. You want to run a modern ranch, you need power for water pumps, refrigerators in the outbuildings, computers in the office."

"And a flat-screen TV," he suggested. "I miss TV."

She gave him one of those reluctant smiles. "Upgraded lights in the stables. A new stove so you can eat." She raised her thumb and pointed back over her shoulder. "A washer and dryer for the mudroom to replace the rust bucket you've got out there now."

He'd stopped letting himself get overwhelmed by the daunting task and number of new things coming to this place. "I'll have one of the guys help me move those out."

"I'll scrape the linoleum off the floor, then join you in the back to do the rooms. We get those done today, we'll be on schedule and ready for the contractors tomorrow."

Austin raked his hand over his head. "I can't believe how fast this is moving."

"I'll take over the house once the contractors are done here. You'll be busy with them repairing and adding on to the stables and barn. Once that's done, it's auction time."

"I assume you mean cattle and horses."

"Can't have a working ranch without them. Two, three weeks, we'll be up and running."

His hand went over his head again and he held the back of his neck. "I can't believe it's really happening. And this fast."

"I find it's best to focus on the task at hand instead of the whole thing. Makes it easier to stay on course and not get overwhelmed."

He stared at her. So practical. But this was his life. His dream.

He'd had an easy life growing up. When it all went away and he had nothing, everything seemed so hard. He didn't trust that they'd keep chugging along on the house and ranch and everything would work out fine.

"Trash the washer and dryer, then on to the bedrooms," she ordered, getting him back on track.

"Chris," he yelled. "I need your help in here."

The worker poked his head into the kitchen and asked Sonya, "What can I do for you?" The suggestive tone made Austin glare.

Sonya pretended she didn't hear anything and walked out the back door. Chris's gaze followed her every move.

"I'm not paying you to stare at her ass."

"I'll do it for free." Chris tapped him in the chest with the back of his hand like they were buddies picking up chicks in a bar.

Austin shoved him by the shoulder to point him toward the mudroom. "Get to work."

He felt old. When did he turn into the guy who passed up fun and jokes to get the job done?

The last many months had truly changed him.

He hoped for the better.

Chapter Seven

They formed a line from the hallway into the living room, Austin at the lead, Sonya at the back of the three guys who were far more interested in her than doing the job. It took an hour to clear the hallway and unblock the doors to the two spare rooms.

Austin opened the door on the left. "Office." He stood back and let her stare past him.

"It's not that bad." Once the mail and papers piled up on the desk and chairs and books and junk overflowed the bookcases, Austin's grandpa simply closed the door and never went back in. Now dust coated every surface. "I'll get one of the shop vacs and tackle this room. I'd like to go through the inside of these filing cabinets and papers. I'll figure out what to keep and what to shred."

"I can go through the paperwork," Chris offered. "You probably don't need to keep anything past the last couple of years."

Sonya shook her head. "I'll do it. You guys head into Grandpa's bedroom. We need to get that cleaned out so I can redo it for Austin."

"I don't mind doing the office," Chris persisted.

Austin shut the office door. "Stick to the heavy lifting. The office can wait. I'll need to go through all the old paperwork and make sure my grandfather didn't have any other assets or leave something undone."

Sonya waved her hand down the hall. "Go help the others box up the clothes."

Chris sighed and did as she ordered.

She didn't blame him for wanting a break from the overwhelming mess in the house. The office would be hours of sorting papers and figuring out what was still relevant and what could be tossed. She didn't want to leave the task to someone unfamiliar with business paperwork. She also didn't want anything sentimental ending up in the trash.

Chris joined the other men at the end of the hall.

Austin went to the door opposite the office, put his hand on the handle, and hesitated.

"What's wrong?"

"This used to be my mother's room."

Sympathy welled in her heart. She and her own mother had a complicated relationship, but their love ran as deep as the love she saw in Austin's sad eyes.

Drawn to him, she put her hand on his back. His muscles tensed, then relaxed at her touch. She tried not to be aware of his height, lean build, the hint of her apricot soap, or the strength emanating off him. This house, his grandfather, and mother, they meant so much to him. He couldn't hide his emotions, not when this place made him raw.

She wished she had even half the good memories of childhood he did.

They hadn't spent a lot of time talking about themselves, but she felt how hard this was for him, how the sweet memories conflicted with the sour reality of the state of this house. He wanted the room to be exactly as he pictured it in his mind. Untainted. Filled with his mother's memory and love.

"Just remember she's not in that room. She's in your heart."

He stared down at her for one long intense moment, his gaze boring into her soul, letting her know her words meant something to him.

He turned the knob and pushed the door wide, revealing a room that probably hadn't been touched since the last time his mother entered it. Dust covered the antique dresser, floor, cream-colored bedspread, and night tables. The drapes were drawn but threadbare from years of sunlight and use.

Austin walked in and went to the dresser. He touched his fingertips to the silver-backed brush, leaving a shiny trail, his fingers coated in grime.

He stared at the hazy pictures tucked in the mirror along with the blue ribbon hanging from the top of the frame.

"She loved to ride. She was a champion barrel racer."

"Me, too."

Austin tipped his head and smiled. "The infamous Wild Rose riders."

"We Ride Hard." The motto they'd printed on their T-shirts. Yes, to be provocative, but also to let others know they'd come to compete. She let the pride show in her smile even though her proclamation made him chuckle.

"I bet you do."

She got the innuendo, but appreciated that under that he really did believe she could ride with the best of them. Which most of the time was her sisters, Roxy in the lead. Most of the time.

"Noah raves about Roxy and how she trains and rides the horses."

"They were always her babies. She taught me and our sisters to ride. It was our thing."

"From what I heard, you guys didn't have a lot of friends growing up."

"We had each other." The Wild Rose Ranch was located in a small town outside of Las Vegas because prostitution wasn't legal in Clark County. Everyone in town knew who worked at the brothel or was associated with it. The brothel brought money to the small town, but that didn't mean everyone liked it, which made growing up there hard. Kids could be cruel to those they thought were different. In most cases, kids took on their parents' disapproval and hate and lashed out at her and her sisters. They were teased, bullied, and ridiculed. So they stuck together and didn't give many outsiders a chance or the benefit of the doubt.

She walked into the room for the first time and looked around. "This won't take long to clean up. You could probably sleep in here tonight."

"With the number of rodents and bugs in this place, I'm going to say no until we get new mattresses and disinfect the place."

"Good call. Still, the furniture is great. I'll take the spread to a cleaner who will handle it with care."

"I think my grandmother made it."

The intricate needlework on the quilt showed swirls circling open flowers with a spray of leaves. "It's beautiful."

She smiled at the stuffed bunny propped against the pillows and the picture of the pigtailed girl sitting atop a fence rail in the photo by the bed.

Austin moved around the room behind her. Something crinkled.

She turned as he bent, picked up a crumpled piece of paper at the end of the bed, and stood, pulling the sides of the paper wide to spread it out.

"At least there's only one piece of trash in here."

"It's a letter."

Something in his rough voice drew her closer. She peered over his arm and read . . .

Daddy,

I'm sorry it took me so long to see the truth. You were right. I should have listened to you, but by the time I saw what was right in front of my face, it was too late. I believed his excuses and lies until I couldn't justify what he was doing any longer. I've done what I can, but it's not enough. I need you to watch over him. Protect him. Make sure he gets what his father stole from all of us.

If Austin isn't told, he'll never know. He needs to know.

I thought I found a way out, but his threats are far from empty. We both know that all too well.

I'm sorry, Daddy, for everything. I wish it didn't end this way. I've run out of time, but my love for you and Austin is infinite. I'll be watching over both of you.

All my love,
Annie

"What does this mean, Austin? What did your father steal?"

Austin stared at the words on the page with glassy eyes. "I don't know."

"She talks about your father threatening them."

His lips drew back into a line. "He likes to do that."

She put her hand on his arm. "It kind of sounds like—"

"It's not a suicide note." His words were clipped and filled with rage.

She pressed her lips together and turned to leave to give him privacy.

He snagged her hand and pulled her back. He didn't let go. Instead, his fingers linked with hers. It seemed more intimate than it should. The connection beyond physical, it vibrated all around them. "She died years ago. Cancer. I was by her side when she passed." His solemn voice held a richness that went deep into her heart. "I don't know exactly what this note means, but I know she and my father were angry at each other. You could feel it in the deafening quiet. My father likes to control everything and everyone. When she says he threatened her"—he waved his free hand—"for whatever she implies in this letter, you can bet he meant it."

Austin stared down at their joined hands. "After my grandfather died, my father called me into his office. My grandfather's lawyer was there to tell me I'd inherited his humble estate." Austin sighed. "The house may be a wreck, but the land is worth something. The lawyer said it's mine. My father ordered me to sign it over. My way of buying into the business."

She eyed him. "If the business is owned and operated by your family, why would you have to buy in? You'll inherit."

"My father takes my carefree attitude and sometimes wild ways for stupidity. But I know when he's doing that thing where it seems like he's giving me what I want but I'm paying for it in some way. I told him I'd been thinking about getting my own place. He came back with an offer to buy the place for a modest price so I could buy someplace suitable."

Sonya tilted her head. "He showed his cards. He wanted *this* place."

"Or he didn't want me to have it."

"Why?"

"Beats the hell out of me." He held up the letter. "What does it have to do with whatever he stole? 'From all of us.'" Austin repeated his mother's words. He stared at the bed and bunny that blankly stared back at him, giving no answers. "They were happy. I remember them that way. At least, I thought they were until my mother got sick."

"You have a lot of memories of being here."

"We visited Grandma and Grandpa all the time. My mother would sleep in that bed, me with her when I didn't build a fort between the couch and coffee table in the living room and sleep with Rumble."

She squeezed his hand. "Your father wasn't here?"

"Why? We only lived fifteen minutes away."

She countered, "Why stay here at all if you lived so close?"

One side of his mouth drew back. "Damn. I was just a little kid who loved riding Bandit and playing ball with Copper. I thought it was fun to stay the night and play with the pets."

"But your mother came here to get away from your father."

Austin's gaze grew distant. His hand squeezed hers to the point it hurt. She covered their joined hands with her free one. "Austin, what is it?"

"I remember once seeing him slap her. Her head snapped to the side. She covered her cheek, then glared at him with tears streaming down her face. Then she noticed me and turned her back on him and ran to me. She scooped me up into her arms and held me close. She ran out of the house and put me in the car. We came here." He finally focused on her again. "We came here a lot."

She held on tighter to him. "It doesn't mean he hit her all the time." But her words rang hollow.

"How can there be so much happening right in front of me and I don't see it? I didn't stop it."

"You were a child, Austin. Your mother was protecting you from seeing those ugly things. She wanted you to grow up happy and loved. And you did. Your grandfather and this house, he didn't let you in because he wanted to protect you from his demons. He didn't want you to see this place the way it became but the way it was in your memories. They loved you so much. That's everything, Austin. That's all you need to remember."

She let him go and went to the door. "Take all the time you need in here. I'll go help the others with your grandfather's room." She turned to leave, but stopped when he called to her.

"I haven't thanked you for everything you've done. I've never known anyone who's worked as hard as you do."

"It's my job."

He walked toward her. It took every ounce of courage she had to stand still and not back up from him and the intensity in his gaze. He reached out to her and still she remained rooted to her spot in the door frame—not inside the room with him, not away from him, but on the brink.

He slipped his hand over the side of her neck, his fingers deep in her hair, caressing her skin. "You listening. You understanding. The compassion you show in how you do this job and treat me falls outside the job. I appreciate it more than you know."

He leaned in.

She held her breath.

He kissed her softly on the forehead.

He stared down at her, his thumb softly brushing over her cheek. "Thank you for being here."

Her heart beat faster and filled with an emotion she couldn't wholly identify, but his words touched her deeply because he meant them. And after she'd given up her safe job to take on this project for Roxy with no plan for what she'd do once the ranch was up and running, it made her feel like her contribution mattered. She wasn't just an employee. Her hard work and attention to the details hadn't gone unnoticed. The heart she put into getting the job done but doing it with Austin's best interests in mind meant something to him.

For a split second he seemed like he wanted to say or do something, but then he released her and walked away, leaving her feeling a tug to go after him, like the moment they'd shared had created a bond that tethered her to him.

As much as she wanted to dismiss the need to go after him, for what, other than needing to be close to him, she didn't know. But she couldn't deny the attraction. Not anymore.

But she also didn't dare pursue it. They had to work together. And once she finished this project, she'd go back to the Ranch. Why? She didn't know. She didn't have a job to go back to.

Working for Roxy meant she had more freedom.

If only she knew what she wanted to do with it.

Chapter Eight

Sonya stood by the front door and inspected the living room floor. She'd spent the last hour scrubbing it on her hands and knees. The hardwood shined, clean for the first time in God knows how many years. Despite the years of neglect and crap piled from floor to ceiling in places, it hadn't suffered more than a few dings and scratches. She'd bought some stain pens for the scratches and used some floor shine to give it a new finish.

She sucked in a deep breath and let it out, hoping it eased the ache in her shoulders and back. No such luck. Her arms felt like limp noodles. She needed a full-on body massage to work out all her sore muscles.

She wouldn't mind Austin putting his big capable hands to use on her.

But mixing business and pleasure had *bad idea* written all over it.

Jumping the man she was supposed to help . . . not a good idea. But a great fantasy. A few that had woken her in the night breathless with her heart jackhammering and her hands itching to get ahold of him.

Austin wasn't in a good place right now. She didn't want to make things worse for him or complicate their working relationship when they still had so much to do.

Like refinishing the floor. She'd give her abused body a break and do it after dinner. The crew had left for the day and Austin should be back any minute with food. After another long day, she was starving but satisfied they'd gotten the entire house cleaned out and ready for the contractors to come in and do their thing tomorrow. They'd even spared a couple hours this afternoon to bug bomb the house and kill whatever was left after the cleanup. In a few short days, this place would be transformed into a beautiful home.

The sound of a car coming down the drive made her stomach growl with anticipation. She set the mop on the porch and leaned it up against the wall, then dumped the bucket of dirty water into the tall grass at the end of the porch.

The car engine approaching didn't match the rumble of Austin's truck. A prickle of unease teased her nerve endings. Alone on the isolated ranch, she didn't take any chances. She set the bucket aside and picked up the shotgun among the four other rifles and over a hundred boxes of ammunition they'd found in Grandpa Alan's bedroom and laid out on the porch. She tucked two shells into her pocket. Just in case.

She stood on the porch, highlighted from behind by the house lights, with the gun lying beneath her hands on the porch railing. Not an outright threat, but there if she needed it.

The Mercedes sedan stopped in the yard in front of her and two men got out. The older one wore khaki pants, a pearl-button navy blue shirt, black polished cowboy boots, and a big gold watch that screamed *I've got money.* The younger guy in black jeans and T-shirt, dusty boots, and a well-used cowboy hat was obviously the help. Or muscle, judging by the scowl on his face. She hoped he kept the knife sheathed on his belt and didn't pull it and make her shoot him.

The older guy approached the steps, his gaze going from her face to the shotgun on the railing, and back.

The muscle glowered and fisted his hands, looking tough and threatening. Totally wasted on her. She didn't intimidate easily.

Especially when she recognized the older man. The resemblance pegged him as Austin's father.

The man had accosted Austin and Roxy at some ranchers' dinner. He'd demanded Austin sell the ranch to him and let Roxy know he thought little of the "whore" who'd come to town to disgrace her father's family.

For that alone, Sonya should fill him with buckshot. No one called her sister a whore and got away with it.

She hid the smile that came with memories of Roxy retelling how she'd put this asshat in his place.

"You're on private property. What do you want?"

"I'm Austin's father."

"Walter Hubbard. Owner of Blue Mining, so called for the vast amount of sapphires you mine every year. You're one of a handful of mining businesses that has a heat treating operation. Separately, you run Hubbard Ranch. According to public records, though lacking exact figures, your two businesses have been profitable with modest increases each year, signaling the companies are well managed."

Walter cocked his head and studied her, obviously surprised she knew a lot about him and his businesses, but savvy enough to keep his reaction in check. He didn't hide the pride he took in how well the companies did. "As a privately held company, we don't disclose dollar amounts, but yes, we do all right."

"Oh, I bet what you put out for public consumption about Blue Mining is just enough to let your competitors know you're a player, but the actual figures are much higher, the profits probably well insulated from what you actually report. After all, you could simply hold the assets in the very ground you pull them from. Riches upon riches you hoard while your son lives in squalor."

His face flushed red. His eyes filled with rage. He mistakenly took a step forward.

She shifted several steps to stand at the top of the stairs and swung the shotgun up and casually draped it over her left arm, her right hand holding the stock, index finger safely above the trigger. "I'll remind you once more, you're trespassing."

"You're not going to shoot me. That thing's probably not even loaded." He took another step forward.

She pulled the gun up and into her shoulder and pointed it right at his chest. "Want to find out?" She gave him a smile to let him know she was happy to oblige.

The sound of Austin's truck in the distance caught their attention.

Mr. Hubbard eyed the oncoming headlights, let out a frustrated sigh, and spoke quickly. "I'm here to gather my father-in-law's paperwork and see what needs to be done next."

Austin pulled into the drive.

"With what? Austin inherited the ranch from his grandfather. Judging by the state of this house and your relationship with your son, you washed your hands of this place and him long ago."

Austin's presence frustrated Mr. Hubbard to the point he lashed out. "Listen, I know you work for Roxy. One doesn't have to guess in what capacity."

Sonya laughed at that. "Do you seriously think Roxy sent me here to be your son's whore?"

Austin slammed the truck door on those words. "What the hell is going on here?"

"Tell her to let me pass," his father ordered.

"No." Austin stared up at her. "Do you know how to use that thing?"

She gave him a cocky lopsided grin and stared down the barrel at her target. "Shoot. Shovel. Shut up."

Austin busted up laughing. "Damn, sweetheart. That's badass."

Mr. Hubbard fumed. The muscle took a menacing step forward.

She eyed him. "I can dig a hole deep enough to fit you, too."

Austin moved forward and waved for her to put the gun down.

She didn't. "Your father wants to take the paperwork from your grandfather's office." She held Mr. Hubbard's infuriated gaze. "I guess your guy didn't get his hands on it, so you came yourself after Chris told you Austin left the property to run errands in town."

Mr. Hubbard didn't flinch at the accusation, but she read it in his eyes. He despised her for uncovering his plot to use one of the workers she'd hired to get his hands on whatever he wanted from the office.

Chris had been just a little too pushy to get in there.

She'd let it go. Until now.

"I don't owe the likes of you an answer to that absurd statement."

"Well, see, I do work for my sister Roxy. I'm an accountant. In my last job, I specialized in forensic accounting. You know, finding money, property, whatever people try to hide in the numbers. What's there can sometimes tell you what's missing."

"Alan didn't have much. What he had went to Austin. I'm here to make sure everything pertaining to my wife is accounted for and returned to me."

She pointed the barrel of the shotgun to the boxes with Annie's name printed on them stacked on the keep pile. "Your wife's things. She didn't leave much here, just clothes and old blankets. Mementoes from her childhood. Pictures. I'm sure you have no use for sentimentality, but I bet Austin would let you go through them and take what you want."

Austin waved his hand out to the boxes. "Take a look if you want."

"That's not what I came for."

Sonya wondered what Grandpa Alan had that Mr. Hubbard wanted. Obviously, something he didn't want Austin to see. "Austin is perfectly capable of sorting through his grandfather's statements and records. If he finds something related to his mother, he can share it with you, but at this point, I don't see the relevance as she's passed."

"He doesn't know what's relevant and what's not. My relationship with Alan and Annie goes back before Austin was ever born. And it's not for you to decide what I can and cannot do when it comes to my father-in-law."

Austin walked up the steps and stood beside her. "It's my call. I own this place. You kicked me out and cut me off. You wanted nothing to do with me so long as I held on to this ranch. As guilty as I feel about the state of this place and how Granddad was living, you're just as responsible. You didn't do a damn thing to help him."

"He wasn't my responsibility."

"He was Mom's family. She was your wife. Didn't you owe it to her to look after him?"

"Your mother turned her back on me long before she died. She ruined our marriage and destroyed any kind feelings I had when she took Alan's side and—" Mr. Hubbard clamped his jaw shut so tight the muscle in his cheek ticked.

"And?" Austin, vibrating with anger beside her, prompted his father to continue.

"Always so stubborn. Why can't you just do what I tell you? Your continued stubbornness is what has put us on opposing sides."

"I'm stubborn? You're pissed because I won't sell this place to you. Why? You've got your own land, the mines, wealth, everything a person could want and more than most ever dream of having. Why isn't that enough? Why do you have to take the only thing I have left of her and Grandpa? Why can't I have this?"

"Because it was meant to belong to me! She ruined that, too."

Austin's shoulders slumped and his head tilted. "Yeah. She died before she inherited. How dare she!" The words came out bitter and filled with scorn for his father. "How dare I get what you thought should be yours. But here's what you don't get. I will never sell this place. It's my birthright. I'm Grandpa's blood. I love this place the way he loved it. This is my home. The same home Mom ran to when you treated her like shit and she wanted to get away from you."

"You don't know what you're talking about."

"With everything I uncover in this house and the memories that come back to me, I'm getting a clearer picture of the past. She protected me when I was little. As I grew older, I was too busy and self-absorbed to notice what was going on between you two. But when she got sick, I saw the way you ignored her. You never even tried to comfort her. She wasted away, miserable and unhappy and so angry that she didn't have more time. She resented you." Austin's lips drew back in a half frown. "No, she hated you. How could you turn your back on her when she needed you so badly?"

"She wanted out. But no wife of mine was going to leave me. I wouldn't allow it."

Austin turned and stared down at her, the question with no answer—*Do you get it?*—in his eyes. She shook her head, feeling his pain.

Mr. Hubbard had no heart. And without a heart, he had no kindness. He wanted what he wanted and demanded it from others without giving anything back. The more Austin refused him, the more Mr. Hubbard hated his own son for defying him.

No, it didn't make any sense.

Nothing Sonya said or did would make it right for Austin. And she wanted to make it right because no one should feel the kind of pain Mr. Hubbard inflicted on his son with every callous word out of his mouth.

Sympathy, the kind that makes you want to protect and vindicate and ease someone's pain, rose up and tensed her muscles for a fight she could only wage with words.

She dropped the gun barrel and stepped down to the tread below Austin. She faced off with Mr. Hubbard and let him have it. "You wouldn't allow her to leave and instead made her life an even bigger misery to her dying day. Getting this land because you think it's owed to you because you married Annie means more to you than your only child. Be careful. You don't have the land. If you continue to alienate your son, you won't have him either. Last I checked, sapphires weren't warm and loving."

"Sentiment from a whore."

She swung the barrel up, but Austin caught it in his hand and shoved it down. "This is getting old. You don't get your way, so you start calling people names. You belittle me, Roxy, and now Sonya. You're nothing but a bully who lashes out like a child."

"I don't hear you defending her."

"She doesn't need me to defend her against your lies. She's got you on the wrong end of a shotgun. She doesn't care what you think of her. Why would she? You aren't worth her time or consideration."

"Her time will cost you," Mr. Hubbard shot back.

Over the years, she'd grown numb to those kinds of taunts and insults.

Austin tensed and stopped breathing for a second before he let out a ragged sigh. He still had a grip on the shotgun barrel and pulled it from her grasp. "Get off my property and don't come back, or I'll shoot you myself."

Mr. Hubbard opened his mouth to speak, but Austin shook his head, stopping him with a deadly look. "I don't want to hear anything you have to say. You have five seconds to get in your car or I'll start shooting."

Mr. Hubbard, his face contorted in anger and frustration, spun on his heel. The two men walked back to their car.

Mr. Hubbard hesitated before getting in. Standing behind the open door, he stared Austin down and tested his patience and resolve once more. "This isn't over."

Austin set his shoulders. "There's nothing here for you. You wanted me out of your life. You got it."

Walter glared and pointed his finger at Austin. "You brought this on yourself."

Chapter Nine

Austin seethed at his father's parting shot. Every muscle in his body felt rigid. His hand ached from gripping the shotgun so tightly. He never expected his father to show up here now. He hated that for a split second he'd thought his father had come because he wanted to share in his mother's memories, that maybe he wanted to help with his grandfather's house despite having done nothing while Granddad was alive.

Nope.

Austin should have known his father only came because he wanted something.

He still didn't know what his father thought he'd found in the house. Something he wanted or something he didn't want Austin to find?

Sonya's hands settled on his shoulders. "Are you okay?"

He turned, coming nearly face-to-face with her standing up a step from him. He reached up and cupped her soft cheek in his free hand. "I'm fine. Are you okay?"

"Your dad's an ass."

"Tell me something I don't know."

"The shotgun isn't loaded."

Austin stared up at her, then burst out laughing. A full-on belly laugh. He couldn't remember the last time he laughed about anything. "Damn, sweetheart. What if they'd tried to get past you?"

"Swing it like a bat and knock some sense into them," she suggested, not missing a beat again.

He wrapped her in a hug. “You continue to surprise me.” It took him a second to realize she’d gone completely still in his arms. Then his whole body became aware of her pressed down the length of him, her breasts against his chest, arms around his shoulders, and her hair tickling his cheek. The wave of heat that swept through him coincided with the overwhelming urge to hold her closer and kiss her.

She leaned back and stared at him, her eyes wide with the same surprise catching him off guard. No doubt he was attracted to her. But the intensity of having her this close burst through him. He saw the same desperate desire reflected in her eyes and it was all he could do to stop himself from taking everything he wanted.

He found the strength to go slow and lowered his head until he was a breath away from her tempting lips, and then her phone rang. She jerked and caught herself before her lips actually touched his. She stepped back, but her gaze never left his as she took the call.

“Hey, Mama, everything okay?”

He noticed she assumed her mother had a problem and wasn’t just calling to say hi.

The heat in Sonya’s eyes took on a whole other meaning when her body went rigid and anger vibrated off her. “Where are you?” She listened for another few seconds. Her lips drew into a tight line. “Are you hurt?” Tears filled her eyes and one cascaded over her cheek.

Austin stepped up and took her by the shoulders, wanting to offer comfort, but unsure what to do.

“Which one of them?” The answer only seemed to make her angrier. “Both of them.” The haunting way she said that tightened his gut with the same dread filling her eyes. “Hang up and call the cops.” Sonya shook her head too many times to count as her mother spoke. “I don’t give a fuck what people will think.” Her eyes narrowed and her mouth pressed into a tight line again. “Mama, if you don’t report them, they will keep doing this.” Sonya’s head fell back and she stared up at the stars, tears welling up in her eyes. “Please don’t cry, Mama.” She looked back at him, but her shoulders sagged with the weight of whatever happened to her mother. “How much did you give them?” Sonya swore at the amount. “All right. I’m sending help.”

Sonya kept her mother on the line and held her hand out to him. "I need your phone."

He pulled it out and handed it to her. "What can I do?"

"Nothing. This is my problem."

She used that same direct, do-what-I-say tone telling him what to do the last couple days on the job. It grated then, but pissed him off now. She'd helped him through all his emotional shit, but she wouldn't let him return the favor.

"Let me help you."

"You can't."

Frustrated, he backed off, trying not to take her dismissive tone personally. But it wasn't easy, because he really wanted to make her feel better and put the smile back on her face.

In her I-can-do-anything manner, she dialed and put the phone to her ear. "It's Sonya. Get me Big Mama right fucking now."

Big Mama? He could only guess that was someone at the brothel.

Sonya barely contained the rage shaking her small frame. "How the fuck did Roger and Fred take my mother off the property?" Sonya held the other phone with her mother on the line and pressed the back of her hand to her forehead as she listened to Big Mama explain.

This up-close view into Sonya's life blew his mind. She had a mom who worked in a legal brothel. Until now he hadn't given that much real thought. Whatever happened meant she had to call the manager to protect her mom.

The pain in Sonya's eyes was a real reminder that, despite what her mother did for a living, she was a person with real feelings and in a desperate situation. Scared and apparently hurt, she'd reached out to her daughter for help.

He didn't understand exactly what happened, but Sonya's side of the conversation implied the situation was dire and this wasn't the first time something like this happened.

Even stranger was the fact that Sonya's mother paid whomever hurt her instead of being the one who got paid.

"She's not supposed to go anywhere alone," Sonya snapped. "She's too vulnerable and easily manipulated. They took her. They hurt her again. How many times are they going to get away with abusing her?"

The fight went out of Sonya. Grief sent her collapsing onto the steps, her butt hitting hard as her knees went limp. “Send two security guards to go get her at the coffee shop in the Riviera. Call the doctor and be sure he’s at the Ranch when they bring her back. She says it’s not bad, but you know it is. Keep me posted. I’ll be there on the next flight.” Sonya listened for another minute, the tears streaming down her face. “It is my fault. I wasn’t there to stop it.” She hung up, handed him back his phone, sucked in a deep breath, hit the button to unmute her phone, then put it to her ear. “Hey, Mama, you doing okay?” She wiped the tears from her cheek and collected herself. “The guys are on their way. They’ll take you back to the Ranch. Big Mama is waiting for you.” She shook her head. “No, Mama, no one is mad at you. I’m glad you called me. I’ll stay on the line with you until the guys arrive.” Sonya stood, took the steps down to the yard, and paced in the dark just outside the light spilling from the house. “I heard you went shopping today. Did you buy anything pretty?”

Austin gave Sonya the space she obviously wanted and went to his truck to get the pizza he’d picked up in town. He doubted Sonya was hungry after the disturbing call, but she hadn’t eaten for hours and had worked her ass off all day. She needed something to eat before she took off.

The unhappy thought of her leaving stopped him halfway up the steps. He turned and stared at her back. Long dark hair pulled into a messy ponytail. One hand braced on her hip as she stood staring out at the dark pasture. Too thin, her tiny waist barely flared out at her hips, but she had a great ass and long slim legs. He smiled at the jeans bunched up at the top of her work boots that looked too heavy and cumbersome for her to move in all day.

But under that slight frame a core of strength and steely determination kept her composed and ready to take on anything. Even a call that made her cry but not fall apart. She’d held it together for her mother, who obviously counted on Sonya to take care of her.

Who took care of Sonya?

She’d run home to put the pieces back together for her mother, but who ran to Sonya’s side when she needed someone? It had to be Roxy. Her other sisters. But they couldn’t do that full-time.

She’d been by his side through this whole process of sorting out the house and cleaning up his life. She'd comforted him when his guilt over letting things get this bad for his granddad became too much to bear and when they found his mother's letter. She'd stood up for him against his father.

They'd shared a moment right before she got that call. For a second, she'd let her guard down and almost welcomed him in.

The need to kiss her still raged through his system.

He wanted her in his bed with a desperation that grew the longer they worked together and the more he got to know her. But more than that, he wanted her to trust him and let him into her world.

He wanted to understand her relationship with her mother, the way she grew up, and what she wanted for her future.

He wanted to wipe the worry from her eyes and ease the pain in her heart.

He'd never wanted to be there for someone, other than Noah, the way he wanted to make things better for Sonya.

She gave up her job in Vegas. Did she want to stay here in Montana?

Roxy lived here now. Why not start a new life near her sister and help him with the ranch?

He could do the paperwork and finances for the ranch, but in a very short time, he'd gotten so used to her being here. Yes, it had been a lonely year. But it went deeper than that. He wanted her to stay and help him. It might be nice to share the burden. Especially when getting the business started would be the hardest part. They still had work to do on the stables and pastures. Once the animals were on the property, he'd be busy taking care of them and maintaining the ranch; it would be nice to know someone else was watching over the business and sharing the load.

Sonya was strong, more than capable, and so independent.

Kelly had wanted him to take care of her, which hadn't been a problem when he worked for his father. But she bailed when things got tough.

Sonya wasn't like that at all. She'd stand by whoever she loved. She'd be a true partner. Adversity challenged her, it didn't back her down.

He liked her even more for that kind of resolve and dedication to the ones she loved.

If only she'd widen that circle to include him.

Sonya turned and spotted him staring at her. "I'll see you tomorrow." One side of her ruby-red lips dipped into a lopsided frown. "I don't know how long I can stay. I'm working on a big project." She nodded. "We'll see. Go with the guards. I need to book a flight. I'll be there soon. I love you, Mama."

Sonya closed the distance between them. He stayed in his spot and let her come to him. Why? He didn't really know, but he wanted her to want to be near him. He wanted her to think of him as a friend, someone she could count on. And a hell of a lot more.

"Sorry about all that."

"You just fended off my father with a shotgun and you're sorry about taking a phone call from your mom? Don't be. Is she okay?"

"She will be. It'll take time. Sadly this has happened so many times, she's learned to cope in a bizarre way that I don't get but works for her. I want to rage and kill them for what they did." She sucked in a breath, trying to dispel the fresh wave of anger that tightened all her muscles. If she held the phone any tighter, it would shatter in her hand. "She'll go quiet for a while. She'll find solace focusing on simple things like a beautiful sunset or the flowers in the garden. She won't let herself think about what happened. She'll romanticize her job and . . ." She caught herself.

"I'm not judging, sweetheart. I'm trying to understand."

Sonya raked her fingers over her head, pulling even more strands from the ponytail. "I don't even understand how she can be so innocently sweet and childlike after the cruelty she's suffered."

"What do you mean?"

She threw up her hands and let them fall. "You don't think women become prostitutes because they came from happy loving homes, do you?"

He didn't answer the rhetorical question. "I never thought about it."

"Men don't think about how women ended up twirling around a pole or giving ten-dollar blow jobs in the front seat of a car. They just see them as an itch scratcher. Someone there to give them what they want. Like they aren't people with feelings and dreams."

She didn't imply it, or say it outright, but he didn't like even the implication that she lumped him in that group. "Not all men are like that. I'm not. I've never even been to a strip club or paid for sex."

For a split second, disbelief filled her eyes, but it quickly disappeared. "I'm sorry. As you can see, dealing with my mother riles me up, and I'm taking my anger out on you."

If it helped her, he could take it and a hell of a lot more because this had nothing to do with him and he wanted her to feel better and put this ugly business behind her. But she wouldn't because it was too personal and heartbreaking to know your mother hurt and you weren't there to help. "Who are Roger and Fred? And what did they do to your mom?"

She exhaled so hard he pictured a cartoon bull blasting out a breath in a huge cloud and kicking up dust.

"They're my mother's uncles. You think your father is bad, you have no idea how cruel people can be."

That thought kicked in all his protective instincts. He wanted to keep her away from them and any kind of danger. "What did they do?" He softened his tone, hoping it encouraged her to open up.

"What they've done my mom's whole life. Beat her and took what they wanted from her."

"When the cops pick them up, they'll get what's coming."

Sonya narrowed her eyes and shook her head. "She won't call the cops."

"Do it for her." He gave the order this time. "They can't get away with hurting her."

"They always do, because she can't bring herself to face what they've done, to let everyone know the depths of how they destroyed her." Sonya brushed her hand over her head, pulling the rubber band free and releasing her disheveled hair. She shook it out, but she didn't shake off her anger. "I've tried to protect her since we moved to the Ranch, but just when I think they've given up and will leave her alone, they come back and pick at her soul like vultures feasting on carrion." She sat on the step and tapped at her cell screen. "She gave them five thousand dollars," she mumbled under her breath. "They deserve five thousand bullets."

Unsure what to do now that she'd shut him out, he sat behind her, pulled her up so she sat on his thighs, wrapped his arms around her, and held her close to his chest, his cheek pressed to her head. Her whole body went rigid at the surprise of him taking her into his arms, but she settled in and crossed her arms over his, her hands holding on to him as tightly as he held her.

He didn't say anything. He just hugged her, because he didn't think anyone had ever held her through the bad times.

Her I-can-do-it attitude and tough-girl exterior made people think she didn't need it. The hard shell on the outside hid her soft center. But this thing with her mother put a crack in it. And he looked deeper. The way she'd done with him.

And so he gave back to her what she'd shown him. Kindness and empathy and a hug he meant.

The quiet night surrounded them. House lights behind them. The stars above them. No words, just two people living with the consequences of their pasts, sharing a closeness he'd never felt with anyone.

This might possibly be the most intimate thing he'd ever shared with a woman.

Certainly the most honest thing he'd ever experienced.

Sonya wiped the silent tears from her face. He rubbed his cheek against her head to let her know he was there. She snuggled back into him and relaxed in his arms. "I need to book my flight."

He pressed the side of his face to her soft hair. "I know you have to go, but I don't want you to."

Her breath caught for a second before she exhaled and settled into him again.

"If you want me to go with you, I will."

"Why?" Surprise and wonder and suspicion filled that one little word.

"Because I want to be with you." The honest confession didn't faze him the way he thought it might. The words were out there. He didn't want to take them back. He didn't usually show his cards this openly to a woman. Then again, Sonya wasn't just any woman. She'd shown him strength and compassion and he wanted to give it back to her. "You probably don't need my help with your mother." Lord knows she'd put everything to rights. "But I could be there for you."

She opened her mouth to say something, closed it, took a breath, then found her words. "I appreciate the offer." She tightened her hold on his arms. "And this. More than you can possibly know. But I'll deal with my mom." She turned her head and rubbed her cheek against his. "I'll be back soon."

He slid his hand away from her belly and moved it up along her neck and jaw. He brushed his thumb over her soft skin and stared into her fathomless hazel eyes. "Maybe this will make you hurry back." He leaned in, his gaze locked with hers, and brushed his lips against hers. When he settled his mouth over hers, her eyelids slowly fell, and she pressed into him. He drew back. She sucked in a surprised gasp that he'd leave her, but he kissed her again. He closed his eyes, savored the sensations rushing through him: warmth, pleasure to wallow in, and a sense of peace that everything would be all right. He hadn't felt that way in a long time.

His body begged him to dive in and take more. Something else inside him told him to savor the quiet intensity of the moment. So he did, keeping the soft, light, undemanding kisses an exploration of her and the way she made him feel.

When his body couldn't take any more restraint without the release it demanded, he kissed her one last time, his mouth pressed to hers, his hand on her cheek, holding her to him. He ended the kiss and laid his forehead to hers but didn't open his eyes. "Damn, sweetheart. I really don't want you to go."

"You gave me a hell of a reason to stay."

He opened his eyes and leaned back a few inches so he could see her clearly. "I can live with that for now." He brushed his thumb over her cheek.

She leaned into his touch. "I don't know how long I'm meant to be here."

He appreciated her honesty and marveled at the thought that maybe she was meant to stay. He'd fallen and settled into a hole of despair because he didn't see a way out or a reason to claw his way up to something better.

Roxy offered him a hand up. Sonya gave him a reason to want to be his best.

"We were ordered to work together. I never anticipated or expected that we'd actually *work* together." When nothing much else did in his life, they made sense. "I've been so angry about what happened in the past, I haven't thought about the future. I'm thinking about it now. What this place could be. What's been missing in my life." He tightened his arm around her to let her know he meant her, even if he couldn't come right out and say it.

"Because of school, work, my own hang-ups, it's been a while since I allowed anyone in. Once this place is up and running, my responsibility will be to solely oversee Roxy's interests and the financial aspect of the business."

"You'll go from renovation to spreadsheets."

"Numbers make sense. I'm not sure we do. I still have obligations back home."

"So does Roxy, but she lives here with Noah. I'm not asking you to move in," he quickly added, "but stay. Spend time with your sister. Give us a chance to see if this adds up the way one and one makes two do."

A soft smile tilted her rosy lips. "Well, I still need to finish the house and stables, get some animals roaming on this patch of weeds, and see that you're a rancher worth betting on."

"So Roxy gets her money back, or you know that I'm more than the drunk you tried to drown the day you arrived?"

She smiled. "You deserved that."

"Yes, I did."

"You're not a drunk. I've seen true alcoholics. They *need* a drink. You just wanted an escape."

"Now I don't need one." He kissed her softly. "You woke me up yesterday in more ways than one."

She tilted her forehead back to his. "It's not fair what your father did to you."

"If he hadn't, I might not have met you."

Sonya leaned back and stared at him. "I don't know. Roxy still would have moved here. I'd come to visit. You're Noah's best friend. Eventually we would have met."

"But would I have gotten to know you the way I have working here with you? Would I have seen the way you issue orders like a drill sergeant? Would I know that you make lists for everything? Maybe you'd still laugh with me, but would we have gotten this close this fast because of all the memories I've shared with you, all the raw stuff you've seen me go through here? Would you have seen the real me you saw when I lost it over this place or when I found my mother's letter? Would I have let you see deeper, or simply tried to impress you with only what I wanted you to see?" He didn't think so.

"The attraction has been there from the start, despite how hard we both try to ignore it because we have a job to do. I'm connected to Roxy. You're now connected to her because of the partnership, but also because she's your best friend's girlfriend. That complicates things."

He agreed. "But it doesn't make them impossible."

"No, but it does mean we go in with our eyes open and understand that things could get messy if this ends badly."

"I'm tired of my complicated and messy life. This is the first time I've felt like something could be simple and easy."

"Because of Roxy and the business, it's not simple." She pressed her fingers to his lips when he tried to protest. "But it does feel easy for me, too. You were such a wreck when I arrived—"

"Thanks." The small word held every ounce of sarcasm inside him.

She touched his face the way he'd held hers earlier. "You're a gorgeous guy."

He smiled at that, because somehow she'd seen past his drunk-ass haggard appearance and seen what he'd look like clean, sober, composed, and working hard to turn his dream into reality.

"But let's face it, Austin, you were broken and vulnerable and disillusioned. I've seen you come out of it and believe the future you want for yourself and this place is possible. I've seen you work harder than everyone on-site to make it happen. And because you put that first over flirting with me, I could be myself. You could have any woman you want. Me included, I'm embarrassed and crazy to admit to your face, because I'm not usually so forward or easy. I've never been attracted to someone the way I am to you."

Stunned, he stared into her earnest and, yes, embarrassed gaze, and took in her pretty pink cheeks. "I thought you might be interested, but I had no idea . . ."

"I was sure I made a fool of myself gawking at you all the time."

"You're so beautiful. You killed me this morning when you were doing yoga, bending over and stretching and looking so damn sexy I want to jump you."

She smiled and pressed her forehead to his chin. "That's just it. We've let this thing simmer." She leaned back and stared up at him. "I'm afraid if we leap, we'll screw it up by going too fast."

He had a hard time not picking her up and taking her to the nearest comfortable spot and laying her out beneath him so he could make love to her the rest of the night. Knowing she was willing and wanted it as much as he did didn't help one damn bit. But . . . "I agree. We should take our time." He couldn't believe those words came out of his mouth, but he meant them. He'd been flying by the seat of his pants this past year. Now he had a chance at being with someone who not only made him want her more than he'd ever wanted a woman, but who also challenged and supported him.

"You're okay with taking things slow?"

"I'm not saying it'll be easy." He shifted, rubbing his achingly hard cock against her hip. No way the woman hadn't noticed that all this time she'd been sitting sideways in his lap. "But it's been a hell of a night and you're on your way back to Vegas in the morning." He tangled his fingers in her hair. "All bets are off when you get back. I can't tell you what I'll do when the house is finished and there's an actual bed in our vicinity."

She deserved better than his cot or her air mattress.

Sonya giggled and he held her closer and whispered in her ear, "I shouldn't tell you this, but . . ." He pressed a kiss to her soft earlobe. "Wherever you lead, I'll follow."

He wanted her to know that despite her admission that he could seduce her into his bed, she had control of when and if that happened. Not that he wouldn't tempt her to want to be there sooner rather than later. When they took that next step, it would be because it was right for both of them.

It wouldn't be easy. He wasn't used to denying himself a willing woman. But they both understood what was at stake if they screwed this up. He could take the heat from Roxy and Noah, but he didn't want to damage Sonya's relationship with her sister, especially when they'd only had each other growing up at the Wild Rose Ranch where their mothers worked and they looked out for each other.

He needed to get this ranch up and running so he could make some money of his own and take her on a proper date. She deserved at the very least a night out for all the hard work she'd put in here. He wanted to give her candlelight, good food, wine, and all the romance she deserved.

Right now, thanks to her inheriting the Wild Rose Ranch from her father, Roxy was footing the bill. He wanted Sonya to know he could take care of her without anyone's help.

As much as he wanted to hold Sonya for the rest of the night, he nudged her to stand up, but kept his hands on her hips. "Make your plane reservations. I'll heat up the pizza and get us something to drink."

"I could use a beer, or three."

He squeezed her hips. "Coming up." He stood and stepped up to the wide porch.

"Shoot." She frowned at the open doorway.

"What?"

"I forgot. I need to put the finish on the living room floor."

"I'll take care of it. Book your flight. I've got the house covered while you're gone."

"But the cabinet guys and contractors are coming and—"

"Sonya, the lists and plans you've drawn up are so detailed a kindergartener could follow them. Focus on your mother. Everything will be fine."

She sighed and studied him. "I hate to leave you in the middle of this mess."

"I hate you leaving me at all, but having so much to do will make the time go by faster."

"It's sweet that you're trying to distract me from being obsessed with the project."

"I'm telling you the truth. I already know there's nothing that will keep you from fixating on work." He turned to go grab the beers from the cooler and a couple of paper plates from the table she'd set up with snacks, water, plastic cups, and utensils, and other things they used for their camping-style meals since they didn't have a kitchen anymore.

"I'll be thinking about you, too," she called out.

He turned and stared at her, his heart pounding in his chest. Some wild possessive thing burst inside him. He wanted to go to her, kiss her, make love to her to show her what she said meant something to him. But he'd just told her they'd take things slow.

She made it damn hard to keep that promise.

"Make your reservations, sweetheart." The words were the exact opposite of what he wanted to say. Not "go away," but "come here." Now.

Now that's an order he'd follow every damn time if she said it to him.

She must have read it in his eyes, how close he was to going after her and showing her how much he desperately wanted and needed her. She held up her phone and walked over to the other side of the porch and sat in one of the kitchen table chairs she'd stored there.

He tried to dial down his hyperawareness of her and focus on what had to be done before he finally got to sleep tonight, but she took up his every thought and his body wanted to act on them.

They ate together, though she spent most of that time making travel arrangements and updating her lists for the contractor and cabinet and tile guys. She made him a detailed to-do list. Second to the last item was, "Think about Sonya." He drew lines with arrows pointing in between each of the other items and held it up for her to see he'd be doing a lot of that.

Her smile warmed his heart. The kiss she laid on him had him thinking of his own to-do list for when he had her naked and in his bed where he'd be thinking of nothing but her and figuring out all the ways she liked to be pleased.

When she called to check on her mother, he gave her some privacy and went inside to put the finish on the hardwood floors. Sonya planned to get the living room done tonight. He started at the back rooms and worked his way through the two bedrooms, office, hallway, and the entire living room. Might as well get it done while the rooms were empty. They'd be dry and ready for the painters to come in and do their job tomorrow.

He walked out of the house only to find Sonya asleep on the porch. She'd moved the air mattress out of the back of her truck along with some of her bags and placed them next to his cot.

She'd fallen asleep with a pen in her hand, several pages and lists scattered across her stomach, and her cell on her chest. He'd heard her listening to the recorded reminders she made herself throughout the day so she could make notes for tomorrow.

He leaned down and gathered everything up and set it aside on the floor. Tired, his back sore and throbbing, he brushed his hand over her hair. He wanted to kiss her good-night, but couldn't bend over that far after mopping the floors with the refinishing stuff that left them gleaming and him aching.

The beautiful sleeping woman in front of him gave him a different kind of ache.

He didn't want to disturb her, but he'd give anything to lie down beside her.

With a heavy heart, he went to his narrow cot, sat, pulled off his boots, stood and swapped his jeans for comfy sweats, and laid himself down, careful of his tight muscles. Every little movement seemed to send them into spasm.

He should have taken a couple ibuprofen, but they were in the bathroom on the opposite side of the room he'd backed out of as he mopped his way to the door. The floor wouldn't be dry enough to walk on for at least an hour.

He punched up his pillow and tried to get more comfortable, but his big frame didn't exactly fit the short, slim cot. He wanted to plant his foot on the floor to keep him from rolling over and off the cot in the middle of the night, but Sonya had stuffed her bed between the cot and porch railing.

He shifted again and involuntarily let out a moan when his back protested.

Sonya rolled over and touched his arm. "Your back?"

"Is screaming at me," he confirmed.

"Come down here. Share the air mattress with me. You'll be more comfortable."

I doubt that. Lying beside her would be a whole other kind of torture, but he'd take that over another uncomfortable night on the cot. He could go and sleep in a sleeping bag in the hay in the barn, but he didn't want to leave her alone out here. Not after his father had come by and threatened them. Not that he really thought his father would do anything besides issue more threats and say nasty things, but he didn't want to take the chance.

And he wouldn't give up an opportunity to be close to Sonya.

It took some maneuvering to roll off the cot and settle in next to Sonya when the air mattress dipped with his weight and Sonya slid into his side.

"You take up almost the whole damn thing," Sonya complained, trying to get comfortable beside him.

He stopped trying not to touch her and give her some space. She'd offered him a comfortable place to sleep, nothing else. But this was ridiculous. The full-size mattress barely fit the both of them.

"Stop squirming and come here." He rolled to his side, hooked his arm around her waist, drew her backside to him, stretched his other arm out beneath her neck, and nuzzled his nose in her soft hair. "Better?"

She snuggled back, then instead of remaining facing away from him, she shifted over so she lay mostly on his chest and in the crook of his shoulder. It made it easier for him to stay on his back and ease the tension in his abused muscles.

"Is this okay?"

He kissed her temple. "It works for now. Go to sleep, sweetheart. You've got an early flight tomorrow."

She relaxed next to him. He listened to her breathing even out and marveled at how quickly she fell into sleep with him this close.

She trusted him.

He liked having her beside him in the quiet cool night.

He kissed her head, rested his face against her soft hair, and closed his eyes and slept like the dead.

He woke up to the smell of sugary pastries, Sonya saying, "God, that's good," and Roxy leaning over his face, her golden eyes dark with a threat he didn't understand until she said, "Get your hand off my sister."

Chapter Ten

Austin turned his head to Sonya lying beside him, chewing a mouthful of chocolate-glazed doughnut, her eyes wide with surprise and a spark of heat. Sure enough, he had a handful of Sonya's breast. His fingers contracted just a fraction with the knowledge of exactly where his hand ended up while they slept last night.

Just to rile Roxy and give him an extra few seconds to feel Sonya's soft flesh and erratic heartbeat, he looked back at Roxy and said, "Only if you've got coffee to go with those doughnuts."

Noah came into view above Roxy and held out a take-out coffee cup.

"Well, damn, that ruins my morning." Austin ignored Noah's narrowed gaze and reluctantly reached for the coffee. He glanced over at Sonya, who stopped chewing. "Sorry. I was sleeping. My hand had a mind of its own."

Sonya didn't say anything, but leaned her head way back over his arm to stare up at Roxy and Noah standing on the porch behind them. "What are you doing here so early?"

Roxy handed Sonya a cup of coffee. "Austin texted last night and said you needed to go home to see your mom. He needs the truck, so I came to take you to the airport. What happened with June?"

Sonya sat up, giving his arm a chance to let the blood flow to his fingers again. They tingled back to life, but he barely noticed. Sonya avoided looking at Roxy. Instead she turned to him, her eyes sad. "Why did you tell her?"

"You were so upset last night. I thought you'd like to talk to your sister. I wanted to do something for you, so I asked her to bring you something sweet for breakfast before you left. You, sweetheart, have a major sweet tooth." He couldn't talk to her lying on his back, so he sat up and faced her. "I'm sorry if you wanted me to keep it quiet. If it helps, I didn't tell her about you holding a shotgun on my dad."

"What?" Outrage mixed with fear in Roxy's voice.

Austin smiled at Sonya, who rolled her eyes. "There. I changed the subject."

She planted her hand over his face and shoved him back down onto the mattress. Thank God his coffee had a lid, or he'd be scalded.

"What happened with your dad?" Noah asked.

Austin sat up again, shifted, and leaned his back against the porch railing. "He stopped by to issue more threats and insist I do what he wants. Or else." He took a sip of the coffee and tried not to stare at the woman he'd slept beside all night and wanted to sleep with again tonight.

"I take it he backed down."

Austin smiled at Sonya. "She was fantastic. And sexy as hell when she's pissed and armed."

"Are you sleeping with my sister?" Roxy demanded to know, her gaze darting back and forth between them as Sonya quietly finished off her doughnut.

Austin didn't miss a beat. "Well, that's none of your business, but since you asked . . . we're taking our time getting to know each other. She's fierce and sweet. She had mercy on my poor back last night and let me share her soft bed. Best sleep I've ever had." He sipped his coffee again, but didn't miss Sonya's surprised gaze. Her eyes softened as he continued to stare at her, letting her know he meant it. They may not have made love last night, but sleeping with her had strengthened the connection between them. Maybe even more than if they had had sex last night. He'd never really been a patient man, but he found taking his time with Sonya heightened the anticipation and made him want to know more about her all at the same time.

Roxy and Noah didn't miss the sexual tension crackling between them. Austin certainly couldn't ignore it. Not when it made every nerve in his body spark to life.

Sonya turned to Roxy and held out her hand. “Let it go.”

Roxy pulled Sonya up to her feet, which made Austin sink deeper into the squishy bed.

“Fine. What happened to June? Austin said she got hurt but is okay. Big Mama didn’t call me about anyone getting hurt last night.”

“It didn’t happen at the Ranch. Roger and Fred rolled into town and squeezed another five grand from Mom.”

Roxy planted her hands on her hips. “How the hell did that happen? She’s not allowed to leave the property alone.”

“Is that true for all the women who work there?” Austin honestly wanted to know, because it didn’t seem right.

“No,” Roxy snapped, her eyes filled with distress that something happened to June.

“So *June* went out alone. What’s the big deal?” Austin wanted to understand.

Sonya raked her fingers through her long hair and held it away from her face. “While my uncles are a danger to her, they don’t often leave Kentucky unless they’re broker than broke. They can make that five grand last.” Frustration and rage tinted Sonya’s face red. “It’s more that my mother is easily taken advantage of and flighty. She loses track of time and likes to go exploring and the next thing you know, she’s lost. She can leave whenever she wants, I just prefer she takes someone with her to keep her grounded and make sure she gets back okay.”

Roxy laid her hand on Sonya’s arm. “So your uncles came to town and took her from the mansion? Where the hell was security?”

“They know they’re banned from that place after what happened the last time.”

“What happened last time?” Austin asked, concerned this happened at all, let alone more than once.

Sonya ignored his question and focused on Roxy. “She went shopping alone. Usually she takes one of the bodyguards. My uncles must have been watching the place, waiting for their chance, and followed her.”

Roxy frowned. “How long did they hold her?”

Sonya’s gaze held Roxy’s. “Long enough to do what they do.” Her voice shook with those words. “I need to see her.”

Roxy pulled Sonya into a tight hug. “Okay. Let’s go.”

Sonya stepped back. “You’re coming with me?”

“You’re my sister. She’s your mom and my responsibility now, too.”

Sonya’s lips scrunched. “This doesn’t have to do with the Ranch.”

Roxy brushed her hand over Sonya’s head and grabbed a lock of her hair and held on to her head. “It has to do with you. Adria and Juliana are with her now. They’re waiting for us.”

A single tear traced its way down Sonya’s cheek to her jaw, then dripped onto her bare skin above her T-shirt. She didn’t wipe it away or even acknowledge it was there. She simply stared into Roxy’s eyes, a thousand words said between them without a word spoken.

Austin felt left out. He wanted to know all the details Sonya held back and didn’t have to say because Roxy knew Sonya’s life the way he didn’t.

Austin glanced up at Noah, wondering if he knew what they were so carefully not saying.

Noah shook his head, oblivious like him.

Sonya turned to the front door and pushed it open. She gasped and looked back at him. “It’s gorgeous.”

He smiled up at her. “You were right. They look brand-new.”

Roxy stared past Sonya. “I can’t believe what you guys have accomplished in just a few days.”

Austin rolled up to his feet and groaned as he stretched. “My back sure feels it.”

“It’s better than being hungover, right?” Roxy studied his eyes, looking for any sign he’d been drinking. After she found him in the same bed with Sonya, he didn’t blame her for sizing him up to see if he’d keep his shit together and treat her friend right.

Sonya deserved a good guy. Someone who could take care of her.

“She works me so hard I’m too sore and tired to lift a bottle. Besides, thanks to you, I’ve got better things to do with my time.” He looked at Sonya. “And a reason to stay sober.”

Sonya shared a look with him filled with the awareness of the building attraction and connection between them.

Roxy eyed her, then him.

Sonya lightened things up. "Yeah, because if I catch you passed out again, I'll dump another pitcher of water on you."

Roxy laughed. "You didn't."

Sonya nodded, her own bright smile lighting her eyes. "I did. Then I put him to work. He was green most of that first day, but he got through it without complaining. Well, about the hangover, not about the mess in the house."

"The smell alone had to have made you sick." Roxy showed the first sign of sympathy for him.

"I puked twice in the bushes." He gestured with his thumb to the clump of brush by a nearby tree.

"Oh God, why didn't you say anything?" Regret filled Sonya's soft voice.

"Because I deserved it." He didn't want to dwell on the past anymore. He wanted to move forward. "Go on, sweetheart, you can walk on the floors. Get ready before you miss your flight."

Sonya grabbed the bag she left on the porch and headed inside to the bathroom. Later today, both bathrooms would be gutted.

"The place really does look a thousand times better."

Austin nodded in acknowledgment but pushed Roxy to tell him more about Sonya. "What isn't she telling me about her mother? Is it worse than she said?"

Roxy pulled her bottom lip between her teeth, glanced at Noah, then back to him. "We don't talk about our mothers with other people."

"*I'm* other people." He glanced over at Noah.

"Don't look at me. I don't know anything."

He pinned Roxy with a glare. "Is it safe for her to go back to the Ranch?"

Roxy reached out immediately and put her hand on his shoulder. "Oh God, yes. It's fine. Yes, her uncles hurt her mother, but they never stick around long enough to get caught."

"She said her mother wouldn't go to the cops because June was too ashamed to tell what happened. It's not her fault those bastards roughed her up and stole her money, so why keep it a secret?"

Roxy's gaze fell to the floor. "I can't tell you that."

"And you expect me to just let Sonya go, not knowing if something might happen to her."

Roxy cocked her head and studied him. "You really are worried about her."

"Hell yes, I'm worried. I saw the way she looked when she spoke to her mom last night. I don't know what she said to put that devastated look in Sonya's eyes, but I saw how it broke her heart."

Roxy placed her hand on her chest like knowing Sonya hurt broke her heart, too.

"Tell me what she left out about what happened."

Roxy shook her head. "I can't." She glanced into the house and at the closed bathroom door. "You're asking me to reveal something deeply personal and traumatic. If she didn't tell you, it's because she doesn't want you to know and think less of her."

"Are you kidding me? She's amazing. Everything about her blows my mind."

"Who are you talking about?" Sonya stepped back out onto the porch wearing black jeans and ankle boots and a pink top that draped softly around her hips in a feminine flutter.

Damn, she looked fantastic.

"You," he admitted.

"Ready to go?" Roxy held her hand out toward the truck. "We need to get on the road."

Which meant he wasn't going to get an answer.

Roxy went into Noah's arms and kissed him several beats longer than a simple kiss goodbye.

Austin envied his friend's close deep relationship. Austin had been living alone with nothing and no one.

The sting of Kelly leaving him after his father kicked him out didn't hurt as much as it should have because he hadn't felt about her the way Noah felt about Roxy. She'd only be gone a few days tops, but Noah kissed her like he'd never see her again and it killed him.

Austin stared at Sonya and wondered that after only a couple days he could relate.

Uncomfortable with his steady stare, she fell back on work. "Cabinet guys should be here in half an hour."

"Got it."

"Contractors and painters are scheduled three hours after that." Nerves infused her words. "Make sure the contractor starts on opening up the kitchen archway while the painters do the back rooms."

"Got it."

"I left the paint swatch details for you on the clipboard with this week's schedule. Make sure they don't mix up the colors for the inside and outside."

He cupped her face and kissed her hard to shut her up because he loved her help but he wasn't a complete idiot. Not that his little control freak thought that. Not like his father did. "I've got this."

Her hands clamped around his wrists. The dazed look in her eyes made him smile. "If you need anything, just call me. I'll have my cell."

He brushed his thumbs over her cheeks, amused that she couldn't let go of control of the project. "Everything will be fine. Go. Take care of your mother. I'll take care of *my* house."

She gasped. "The hay and feed delivery will be here day after next. There's that big space at the back of the stables. We can organize bins along the wall."

He rolled his eyes and smiled because her kind of crazy made him chuckle. They'd already discussed this in detail. "What would I do without you?"

Her gaze softened. "I know, you know, it's just that I hate to leave in the middle of things. Especially when all the contractors are finally coming."

"I used to run a mining operation. I think I can manage a renovation."

Her mouth scrunched into an adorable pout.

He kissed it right off her lips.

She'd put a lot into this project and wanted to see it through.

He couldn't blame her for that. "When you get back, this place might actually be habitable."

"Yeah." Not much enthusiasm filled that word. "It'll be nearly done." Which meant she wouldn't need to be here all the time.

The thought didn't sit well with him either. He looked down into her worried hazel eyes and offered something he hoped eased her mind and made her hurry the hell up and get back here. "We're just getting started."

Chapter Eleven

Sonya thought she'd gotten away without having a conversation with Roxy about her relationship with Austin. Apparently, only a plane full of people who could overhear them made Roxy hold her tongue, because the moment they walked in the front door of their cottage on the Wild Rose Ranch property and Roxy shut it behind them, she didn't hold back. "What the hell, Sonya? Are you seriously seeing Austin?"

Sonya rolled her eyes and let the sarcasm fly. "Every day since I arrived in Montana."

She didn't want to have this conversation. What she and Austin shared, it was . . . different. Maybe even special. She wanted to hold it close for a while and not let anything touch it or mess it up.

Roxy huffed out a frustrated breath. "What's the plan?"

Sonya set her carry-on suitcase next to the wall near the hallway and walked into the kitchen to get a soda from the fridge. "I don't have one."

She liked that being with Austin seemed natural. Easy. Just the way it was without overthinking it.

Roxy left her bag in the entry and came after her. "*You* don't have a plan. I don't believe it."

Sonya downed two huge gulps. She couldn't believe how not knowing where this thing was going didn't send her into a tailspin of worry. Just knowing she was going back to see him eased her mind. He'd made it clear he wanted her back. Immediately. It did her ego good to know he liked her enough to lay it out there like that. "You heard what Austin said. We're just getting started."

"I found you in bed together with his hand on your—"

"It's none of your business. It's my life." Her breasts went heavy just thinking about how good it felt to have his hand on her. She wondered what it would feel like to have his mouth on her, too.

"You work for me on this project."

That stopped her train of thought from chugging too far into Dirty Town and set off her anger. "I've done my job. You work with Noah. You're partners. Don't sit there and judge me for getting involved with Austin when you did the same thing."

"That's different."

Sonya cocked her head. "Really? How is it different?"

"Once you're done getting the house and ranch set up, I'll need you back here. What are you going to do, have a long-distance relationship?"

"I didn't realize I was at your beck and call. I guess when I quit my job to work for you I should have read the fine print that said you get to dictate how I live my life and who I get to see." The thought of being away from Austin for any length of time made her stomach sour and her anxiety soar.

Roxy leaned back against the counter and softened her tone. "I'm not saying that."

"No? You get Noah, a new home, and a new life, but I'm supposed to stay here and watch over what you left behind, so you can have your bright shiny future. You told me to come work for you so I'd have more time for myself instead of working sixty hours a week. You wanted me to have time to figure out what I wanted for my life, because yours is so great and you wanted me to find that for myself. But not in your backyard. Not with Austin. You want me, Adria, and Juliana to stay put, so you can have your life there without having to worry about us anymore." The words, and that they might be true, hurt her heart and constricted her throat.

Roxy rushed forward and wrapped her in a tight hug. "No. Stop this. That's not what I meant at all. I love you. I love having you in Montana.

Yes, I want you to be happy. I want you to find someone who sees how amazing you are and wants to spend his life making you happy. But Austin . . . he's barely been able to take care of himself this past year. I think he's coming around and taking charge of his life now, but the project is barely off the ground. Who knows what he'll be like once the real work starts and he's running that place mostly on his own until the business can afford to hire help. I don't want you to get hurt."

Sonya put her hands on Roxy's waist and set her away so she could look her in the eye. "I know you're worried. We talked about your concerns before I ever met Austin. But then I did meet him. I see how much he loves that place, how dedicated he is to making something out of it and himself. His father tried to destroy him over that stupid piece of land. But Austin sees the chance he's been given as a means to start over and do it right. I'm not worried about whether or not he can make that place profitable." She pointed a finger. "You shouldn't be either. He's got the experience of working his family ranch and the mining business. When it was all taken away, yes, he didn't know how to handle it or what to do when he sank all his money into keeping that place. But that stubborn streak of his won't allow him to fail now that he's got the means to make a go of the ranch."

Roxy squeezed Sonya's arm. "And what about the two of you? As I understand it, his last relationship fell apart when his father kicked him out and he's indiscriminately played the field since. How much of that had to do with his drinking?"

"Aside from having a beer or two with dinner after he'd put in a twelve-hour day, I haven't seen him overindulge. I don't particularly care what happened with those other women. I've seen the change in him from the man you described to me, to the person I've seen him be *with* me.

"He's treated me with respect and kindness and shown his appreciation for my help. He didn't take advantage of my attraction to him. He recognized, like I did, that there was something there worth exploring and we decided because there is a lot at stake to take things slow and get to know each other. That's not a guy out to take what he wants. That's a man who knows what he wants and is patient enough to work hard to get it because the prize is worth the effort." She was worth the effort. No one had ever made her feel that way. And she didn't know what to do with all the feels that burst from her heart knowing that.

"You didn't tell him what really happened with your mother."

Yeah, she'd held back some of the details instead of dumping that kind of baggage and trauma on him. "You didn't tell Noah right away about your mother. When you did, look what happened."

"We fixed it."

"Well, Austin knows what my mother does for a living and that she's had a rough life. For now, that's enough to unload on him. If we become more than friends, I'll tell him more."

"If you stay in Montana, you'll have to make frequent trips to keep the books on the Ranch. Is it enough for you? You're such a go-getter. I hired you so you could help me and quit that company because they overlooked you and took you for granted. I thought you'd look for a better job and find someplace that treated you right. What are you going to do on Austin's ranch to fill the hours and give you the satisfaction you found doing the work you love?"

Sonya wondered about that, too.

"I just don't see how this will work out in a way that will make you wholly fulfilled."

"Maybe it won't, but I like him. He makes me laugh and think and want to get to know him better." Just because she didn't have everything figured out didn't mean she had to give up Austin until she did. "He didn't judge my mom. He wanted to know how he could help. He offered to come with me just so he could be here in case I needed cheering up."

"He did?"

"He's a nice guy, Roxy. He's got a good heart. It's been a long time since I felt this connected and attracted to and excited about a man all at once. Maybe it won't last through the project taking off. I don't know. But so far I've found a lot of reasons to be with him and nothing that makes me willing to walk away without thinking I made a mistake and regretting it later." She shrugged and gave up trying to explain herself or convince Roxy she knew what she was getting into and had faith it would all work out.

Sonya had the same reservations as Roxy about work and her life.

Right now, she liked what she was doing, even if in the back of her mind she knew eventually she'd want more than just a boyfriend and doing the books for the Ranch.

Maybe she dug in her heels because Roxy warned her away, but Sonya had already made up her mind to see where things went with Austin. She liked him. And yeah, the guy wasn't just good-looking, but built like a delectable soccer player, all lean sculpted muscle. Waking up in his arms this morning gave her all kinds of ideas about how good it would feel to get her hands on him and feel his body move against hers.

She liked his golden hair and blue eyes and the way he looked at her. She liked the way he opened up and let her in. She wouldn't say the last few days had been easy, but they'd been at ease with each other.

"I need to see my mom."

Roxy grabbed her arm to stop her from leaving the kitchen. "I like Austin, too. If I didn't believe in him, I wouldn't have sunk a fortune into helping him. But the business is separate from him dating my sister."

Sonya got that. Roxy had always looked out for her.

Roxy sighed. "I don't want you to give up what you worked so hard to achieve just to be with him."

"I'm not doing that. If another job opportunity comes up that I really want, I will consider it, even if that means reevaluating my relationship with Austin. But let me remind you, we're just getting to know each other. I don't know how things will be or change over the next couple weeks."

Roxy touched her arm. "I don't want you to get hurt, but I also want you to be happy. I saw the way he looks at you. I'm not surprised he sees how amazing you are."

She remembered Austin's words and hope bloomed in her heart, letting her know how much she cared about what he thought of her. "He was talking about me?"

"Yes."

It made her ridiculously happy. Which told her how much she liked Austin and wanted to see him again.

Roxy let her arm go. "I'm worried about what happens if things don't work out and how you'll work together in the future. I'm worried about how it will affect my relationship with Austin and his with Noah. But if

I set aside those worries, I can see you two happy together. I want that for you, Sonya. You deserve it and so much more. It was hard for me to believe I would ever find someone who didn't get hung up on my mother and this place. If Austin is that person for you, great, but you need to tell him the whole truth."

Keeping secrets only lasted so long. They always found a way to come into the light. "It's a little early to spill my guts."

Roxy eyed her.

"I see how being completely honest brought you and Noah closer. If Austin and I make it to actually going out on dates and things heat up, I'll tell him." Not an easy conversation, but holding pieces of herself back would only drive a wedge between them.

"He's already curious."

"Who wouldn't be? My mother is a prostitute with a twisted past. I told him my great-uncles attacked my mother and extorted money from her."

"That's not the whole story." Sympathy and fierce determination to put a stop to it lit Roxy's eyes. "Let me call the cops, hire an attorney, and make them pay for all they've done."

"I'll speak to her again, but you know her answer. She won't testify against them. She can't take the shame of it."

"It's not her fault. She's already living with the shame."

Sonya didn't have to speak her agreement. They'd had this conversation among themselves and with her mother. Nothing helped. Nothing changed. Without her mother's cooperation, her great-uncles got away with their heinous acts.

Sonya set all that aside again. "Are you coming up to the mansion?"

"Later. I want to check on the horses and talk to Adria and Juliana. They should be home from school soon."

Sonya headed out the door and across the pasture to the big house where men came to play out their fantasies. Well, she had a few of her own she'd like to satisfy in Austin's arms. She hadn't had sex in a long time. And she wanted to with Austin. She didn't need Roxy or anyone else making it so complicated.

Why couldn't they keep things simple?

He liked her. She liked him.

What they did or didn't do didn't have anything to do with anyone else.

Except it did, because their lives, the business, touched other people's lives.

She walked up the steps to the side door, rang the bell, waited for security to buzz her in, then went inside and up the back stairs to her mother's room on the second floor.

Big Mama and a man in tan slacks and a blue dress shirt stood in the hallway outside her mother's door.

"Ah, here she is." Big Mama held her hand out toward Sonya. "Dr. Wilson just checked on June again."

"How is she, Doctor?"

"Better than I'd expect from someone who's been through what she's been through."

Yeah, well, June had been down this road many times. "My mother is very resilient."

"I'm concerned that she's compartmentalizing. She needs to face what happened, talk about it, so that she can heal. This environment will only traumatize her more."

Sonya and Big Mama shared a look. The doctor meant well, but he didn't know June the way they did.

"Thank you for taking care of her, Doctor. In any other case, I'd say you are correct, but it's taken me a long time to understand my mother. She only knows this life because she was raised to believe this is what she was put on this earth to do."

Shock widened the doctor's sympathetic eyes. "Well that's just not true."

"That's *her* truth. It's what she's been programmed to believe. What happened yesterday only makes her believe it more."

The doctor tried another tactic. "She refuses to report the incident."

"That's her choice."

"But the police can't do anything without her cooperation."

"I know." Sonya touched the doctor's arm to comfort him. "Thank you for caring."

Big Mama hooked her arm through the doctor's and led him out.

Sonya put her hand on the doorknob, sucked in a breath, plastered on a fake smile, and walked in to find her mother sitting in a chair by the window. Gorgeous legs poked out of the slit in the pink silk robe tied at the waist and draped over her full breasts. Her mother didn't feel the need to cover herself or hide behind layers of clothes. She'd been taught long ago that her body was something for others to use.

The sadness threatened to overwhelm her, but she kept the stupid smile on her face and tried to be strong for her mom. June didn't need her sympathy, rage, or assertions that she knew what was best.

June endured, the way she'd always done, because it's the only way she knew how to survive.

"Hi, Mama." Sonya's voice barely made it past her lips. She hated seeing the bruises on her mother's thighs and around her wrists where her great-uncles' tight grips left their mark.

June's head slowly turned from the view of the back garden and pool. The vacant look in her mother's eyes brightened with recognition. "My sweet Angel, what are you doing here?"

"I told you I was on my way."

"I told you it wasn't necessary for you to come just for this."

Like what happened to her didn't matter or merit Sonya dropping everything to come and comfort her mother.

Sonya stood two steps away and held her arms out wide. June's eyes filled with tears that streamed down her pale cheeks. She stood and rushed into Sonya's arms and cried like a child who hurt and wanted everyone to know it.

Sometimes Sonya felt like the parent. By fourteen, her mother had simply stopped maturing. She'd been raised by a mother too afraid to stand up to her husband, a father who didn't spare the rod, uncles who took what they wanted by force, bending June's will to their liking. Even her grandmother, who blamed and punished the child instead of the men she raised but couldn't control.

June had come into this world like every other child, filled with possibility. But her life had been shaped by pain and disappointment. Her sweet nature had been used against her. Her need to please and be accepted made it easy for her uncles to manipulate her into doing their bidding.

Sonya hated them for abusing a sweet girl without an ounce of remorse or regret.

One day, they'd get what was coming to them.

And she hoped it was excruciating.

Because holding her crying mother broke her heart and shredded her soul. It killed her to stand there, knowing she could do so much more, but not without hurting her mother further.

June picked her head up off Sonya's shoulder and wiped at her red-rimmed eyes and runny nose. "It's silly to cry about such things. It's not like I don't have sex all the time."

Sonya contained her rage. "Mom, you know it's not the same, so don't make excuses for what they did." It should surprise her that they had to have this talk at all, but it didn't. She'd spent her whole life understanding that sex between consenting adults was normal and shouldn't be judged. Yes, people had their hang-ups, but that didn't mean you put your insecurities on others for indulging in what they enjoyed.

She didn't like what her mother did, but it was June's choice. No one forced her to be here. She had the money to leave anytime she wanted to go. Sonya had encouraged her to do so many times to no avail. June simply found this to be the best alternative to what she'd known her whole life.

June stepped back and wrapped her arms around her chest. The first sign that what her uncles had done affected her deeply enough she felt the need to protect herself in some way. "I'm not making excuses. I hate what they did. I hate it!"

Shock froze her with her mouth dropped open. June never raised her voice. Ever. Not even when Sonya deserved it.

"I let them." Her eyes narrowed with anger. "I always let them."

Sonya didn't like seeing her mother's anger directed at herself. "Mama, it's not your fault. You were scared. They hurt you."

June hugged herself harder. "Don't you get it? I'm always afraid. I'm always hiding."

Sonya closed the distance and rubbed her hands up and down her mother's arms. "It's okay, Mama. I'll make sure they never come back. Security won't let them in. When you go out, one of the guys will go with you."

"So I'm to be a prisoner again."

Sonya tilted her head, surprised by her mother's statement. "You can leave here whenever you want. Say the word, I'll move you out of here immediately."

"It's not about this place. Though I know you disapprove and hate it here."

Sonya chose her words carefully because the last thing she wanted to do was shame her mom. She'd done that as a child and had grown to learn it only broke her mother's heart to think her only daughter thought so little of her. Sonya loved June with everything inside her. Her mom had sacrificed and always put Sonya first. Maybe there'd been times they'd gone without, but Sonya had always been loved.

"They kept me prisoner as a child. Now they keep me prisoner here. I'll only be free of them when I'm dead." June's gaze darted around the room like she was looking for a way to make that happen.

Scared and unsure about June's state of mind, Sonya tried to see just how far her mother was willing to go to be rid, once and for all, of her uncles. "That's not true. You know what you need to do if you want to keep them away for good."

June shook her head. "Everyone will know." Her voice shook and her lips trembled. Fresh tears poured from her eyes.

Sonya gentled her tone, because shouting at June only made her feel worse. "If you truly want to be free, stop hiding, stop lying, stop worrying about what people will think. The truth is on your side. You did nothing wrong. Others will have compassion for what they put you through."

Her mother reached out and brushed her hand over Sonya's head and pushed a lock behind her ear before cupping her face. "I never wanted what they did to touch you. If I tell, people will know how I got you."

Sonya had always assumed her mother was too embarrassed and ashamed to come forward. She'd never imagined she stayed quiet to protect Sonya.

She held her mother's shoulders. "Above all else, I want you to be happy and free of them no matter the cost. I don't care what anyone else thinks about me, you, or what happened. I love you. You have always loved me one thousand percent. As long as I have you and my sisters, that's enough, Mama. Please. Don't let them get away with this again. Once was too many. It's grown to too many times to count. Maybe they stay away longer this time. Maybe they never come back. But do you want to spend every day wondering when? I don't want that for you, Mama."

June kissed her on the forehead and hugged her close. "I'll think about it, Angel. I'm upset. I need some time."

"The longer you wait the harder it will be." The more likely the chance her great-uncles would return because they believed they'd get away with it.

They always got away with it.

And that bitter thought spawned a million ways she'd like to hurt and kill them.

June let her go and went back to her seat by the window. "Come. Sit. Tell me about this project you're doing with Roxy." Her mother rolled her eyes. "You know, Roxy's mom is impossible now that Roxy owns this place. Candy thinks she can do whatever the hell she wants."

Sonya didn't have to imagine how impossible Candy had become. June and Candy had little in common. Yes, they both worked at the Wild Rose Ranch, but Candy loved it in a way June didn't. Candy was up for a party and a good time. June wanted to pretend someone loved her, even if it was for an hour or two.

June had created her own fantasy world here. She played it out day after day, happy to immerse herself in the illusion because then she didn't have to deal with the pain in real life. She could live the lie so she didn't have to face the truth.

"You know Roxy and Noah run the ranch in Montana together. Well, Noah's best friend, Austin, inherited this huge piece of property from his grandfather. His father wanted the land, but Austin refused to sell it to him."

"Why does his father care, so long as it stays in the family?"

"Exactly, but Austin's father seems to believe it should have gone to him. When Austin refused to sell, his father fired him from their family ranching and mining businesses and kicked him out. Austin spent every last dime he had to pay off his grandfather's debts and the taxes on the land so he could keep it. He's been sleeping on the porch and in the stables when it's too cold because his grandfather had turned into a hoarder and the house was too overcrowded and disgusting to live in. Land rich and cash poor, Austin fell on hard times and started drinking."

June frowned, even as she listened intently. "Not a good way to solve a problem."

"He was too proud to accept help from his friends." She eyed her mother for having that in common with Austin. "Roxy wanted to do something good with the money she inherited, so she went to Austin with a proposition. He dreams of turning his grandfather's old place back into a prosperous ranch."

June's eyes brightened with the idea of dreams coming true. June wished for her own monster-free fairy-tale life. "So she gave him the money."

"They created a partnership. Roxy fronts him the money, Austin runs the business, and they split the profits."

June's eyes filled with admiration. "She's such a good girl."

"Roxy hired me to oversee the partnership. I'll do the books for the business once it's up and running. Right now, I'm helping Austin renovate the house and stables so he can live and work there."

Her mother clasped her hands at her chest. "Wonderful. You'll help him get back on his feet."

She'd planned the project and lent him a hand and sympathetic ear, but . . . "He's doing that all on his own. I'm just there to oversee the contractors and painters and make sure the plans Roxy and I came up with are done right."

"Well, I have no doubt you'll have that place in order in no time."

"Thanks, Mama. He really loves it there. He has so many happy memories of being with his mother and grandparents. I can't believe his father turned his back on him. He's mean and vindictive for no reason. It's not like he needs the land. He's got a thriving business of his own."

"For some people, there is never enough. They always want more."

The pieces of her mother's soul, the money her great-uncles stole, no, it was never enough. Her great-uncles were always coming back for more.

"I want you to want more for yourself, Mama."

"I have you, Angel. You're all I need." And that right there showed how sweet, kind, and loving her mother remained even after all the trauma and heartache she'd suffered.

Her mother leaned forward, elbow on her knee, chin cupped in her hand, eyes locked on Sonya. "Now tell me about *you* and Austin."

The blush heated her cheeks instantly. She'd never been able to hide anything from her mom. "You'd like him. He's really nice. Truthfully, after Roxy told me about the drinking, I didn't expect much. But from day one, he stepped up and has worked harder than any of the people I hired to help. I can feel how much he wants the ranch to be a success, but more than that he needs it. No one will ever take something from him again. He won't let it happen because he knows what it's like to have nothing and he's not going back."

"He sounds tough."

"With a big heart. He blames himself for not helping his grandfather when he spiraled and the house became too much for him to fix. Austin lost his mother several years ago. He found a letter from her. The grief and love I saw in his eyes . . ." Even now, her heart ached for him.

"Are you sleeping with him?" Sex had always been an open subject, especially after they moved here to the Ranch. Her mother simply thought making sex a secret or something that should be whispered about only gave power to those who used sex as a tool or weapon.

"No." Sonya held back some of what she felt from Roxy, but with her mother, she opened up because June didn't judge others since she knew how much it hurt to be judged. "But it's been hard to keep my hands to myself. Sometimes, I just want to hug him. Most of the time, I want to rip his clothes off and lick him."

Her mother gave her a knowing smile even as she wrapped her arms around her middle and sat back.

"I know it's not a good idea. We have to work together. But the pull I feel is different than what I've felt for other men."

"You learned what you didn't want from them. He shows you something different."

Sonya nodded. "I want something different for you, Mama. Would you consider talking to someone? A psychologist or counselor. Maybe if you talked about what happened, you could heal and decide what you want to do."

"I wish you had a family like the ones you see on TV." June grew up dirt-poor. No TV. She only knew the world inside the walls of her home and the boundaries of her small town. She thought all little girls grew up the way she did, until she left and TV showed her what a family could be like.

Sonya laid her hand on June's knee, careful not to touch any of the angry bruises. "I need you to be safe and happy and loved."

June found a smile for her. "You love me."

Sonya wanted her to have more. "Do you ever think about getting married and growing old with someone?"

"I dream about it all the time." Her gaze drifted out the window to the garden she loved, then snapped back to Sonya's when she slid her hands over her thighs and winced. "But reality is a harsh reminder that some dreams aren't meant to come true."

"It could happen. If you didn't work here . . ."

June shook her head and turned to stare out the window, unwilling to listen to a bunch of if-onlys she'd been cruelly taught were not for her.

Sonya laid her hand on her mom's arm. "I believe you can do and have anything you want, Mama. You deserve to be happy."

June didn't turn from the window, but smiled softly and whispered, "Seeing you grow up happy and loved and living your life the way you want to makes me happy. I didn't want you to have a life like mine."

"You don't have to live this life anymore, Mama. I know you're brave and strong. You don't have to do it alone. I'll help you."

June placed her hand over Sonya's. "I'll think about it." She settled back into the chair and watched the world outside. "I'm tired."

Sonya wondered if her mother meant far more than physically.

Had her great-uncles finally broken her mother?

Sonya hoped not. She wanted her mom to use the strength that had gotten her away from them and saved Sonya from a life of poverty and abuse and finally stand up for herself.

She wanted her mom to want more for herself, to believe that any dream she imagined could be a reality if only she reached for it. Her mother had instilled that in her, even if she didn't believe it herself.

Sonya wished for a way to show her mom she could have it, too.

Chapter Twelve

Austin and one of the crew shouldered a heavy beam into place above the new case opening between the kitchen and living room. He loved how it opened up the space, but his back protested the heavy lifting. Four construction guys lifted the other end into place, secured it, then came to brace and secure his side. Sonya's great ideas were taking a toll on his body. And when she got back, he hoped she'd help ease some of his throbbing pains.

He missed her.

The ache in his chest flared. Nothing but Sonya coming home would erase it.

He couldn't look anywhere in the house and not see her. Though he hadn't moved any furniture back into the house, the empty kitchen now had a brand-new hardwood floor that matched the rest of the house. A wall of cabinets hung on each side of the window. She was right, the lighter color made the room feel brighter and bigger.

The tile guy put up the backsplash with the green accent tiles Austin requested. And even that made him think of her and how she'd chosen every little thing but had no problem incorporating what he wanted. She made it easy because she'd made some excellent choices and coordinated everything. If he'd done it, he'd have gone with the most basic choice and not thought to tie the tile to the countertops to the cabinets. It probably would have looked bland as hell.

She'd picked out a soft, light beige that wasn't really yellow or tan but somewhere in between for the rest of the house. Neutral, she called it. He had to admit he liked it better than sterile white walls. The dark floors and warm walls gave the place a cozy feel and they hadn't even brought in any furniture yet.

Noah walked in the front door and stood in the entry. "I can't get over the transformation."

"It takes some getting used to, but it's going to be amazing when it's done." Austin stepped down the ladder and joined Noah in the living room. They stood back and watched the dozen men working on different aspects of the house in choreographed chaos. Everyone had a job and worked around the other men.

Noah tapped him on the shoulder. "The kitchen. The island and bigger opening . . . Man, that's nice."

"Sonya added that once we cleaned out the house. It changed the feel of the place."

"How are the bathrooms coming?"

"We gutted them yesterday. Showers and drywall are in. Tilers are finishing the floors. They should be done tomorrow."

Noah gestured behind them with his thumb. "Way better than the portable restroom outside."

"Tell me about it. But I've been roughing it a long time." Austin sighed and took a moment to really appreciate how his life would change in the next few days. "I can't tell you how excited I am to finally sleep in a real bed." He stretched from side to side, easing the persistent ache in his back.

Noah cocked up one eyebrow. "Will you be alone in that bed?"

Austin walked out the front door to the porch and pulled out two sodas from the cooler. He handed one to Noah, cracked his open, and took a long swallow.

Austin eyed his best friend, knowing where this was going, but asking anyway. "Something you want to say?"

Noah eyed him. "She's Roxy's sister. You work together."

"You didn't seem to have a problem making things personal between you and Roxy when she came to work with you at the ranch."

"That's different."

Why did people say that to justify them doing essentially the same thing?

Austin spoke the truth. "Why? Seems to me, it was more complicated than Sonya and me because of what was at stake if you two didn't make it. She'd have lost her share in the ranch and your sister Annabelle would lose a guardian. You both thought it was worth the risk to see what happened. Sonya and I want a chance to do that. Sonya and I don't work out, she goes back to Vegas and never has to see me again."

"Why her? Why now? You're starting from scratch. Is it a good time to start seeing someone?"

"Is that your way of saying I'm dead broke and have nothing to offer her?"

Noah huffed out a frustrated breath. "I didn't say that."

"Not in so many words. You're right, though. I have nothing but myself to offer her. Is that enough? Probably not. She deserves a hell of a lot more. But I like her. She's different. Direct, honest, insightful, smart as hell. And tough. She pulled a shotgun on my father." He tapped his fingers to his chest. "I can't tell you how damn sexy that was and how it hit me deep. Just like Roxy did at the ranchers' dinner, Sonya sized him up, didn't back down from his threats, and stood up for me and this place. Like me, she sees the potential here and in me. She sees the man I want to be."

"It's not potential, it's who you are, Austin. Up until your father fired you, you were a damn fine rancher and businessman. That's what Roxy invested in. Not this place. She believes in you, and so do I."

His chest tightened with those heartfelt words. He appreciated his friend more each day, because in the past he'd taken Noah for granted. They'd been buddies forever. That's just how it was and how it would always be. And having lost everything, he came to realize what was really important in his life. Noah topped that short list.

Austin conceded. "And because I owe Roxy everything for what she's done, I know what's at stake with Sonya."

"You like her that much."

He didn't really know how to explain it. "When you met Roxy, did it just hit you?"

Noah reluctantly nodded. "I knew there was something there."

"When Sonya dumped that pitcher of water on me, she woke me up in more ways than one. The second I saw her, something sparked inside me. I thought it was just attraction, a good healthy dose of lust, something I'd felt with other women all the time. But it's quickly turned into something different. I can't explain it. And I sure as hell don't want to screw it up. I don't know . . . I don't want to hurt her. I want to take that sadness she hides so well I see deep in her eyes and make it disappear."

Noah held out his soda can. "Good luck, man."

Austin tapped his can to Noah's. "Thanks. Lord knows, I need it." Austin drank with Noah. "Did Roxy send you here to warn me away from Sonya?"

"No. From what I gathered, Sonya told Roxy to back off."

"Well, that's something." And eased his mind, because the last thing he wanted was for Sonya to take a step back before this thing ever really got started. "When are they coming home?"

"Not sure. June is doing better, but Juliana got into some trouble, so Roxy and Adria are handling that."

"What kind of trouble?"

Noah tightened his jaw, making the muscle in his cheek tick. "How much do you know about Sonya, Adria, and Juliana's mothers and how they were raised?"

"I know the girls grew up together in a cottage on the Wild Rose Ranch property. Their mothers work at the Ranch. Adria and Juliana are twins and a couple years younger than Roxy. Sonya's the oldest."

"Roxy's mother, Candy, is a party girl. Sonya's mother came from an abusive background. I guess you could say there's abuse in all of their mothers' backgrounds. Adria and Juliana's mother was a junkie before Big Mama met her at a women's shelter. She was about to lose her twins."

"Big Mama took her in, cleaned her up, gave her a job, and saved the girls."

"Yes. Addiction runs in families. Roxy, Sonya, and Adria have stayed away from that path, but from what I understand, Juliana has merrily skipped her way down it. She's got a wild streak Roxy and the others have tried to tame. Adria usually talks her sister into doing the right thing, but lately, Juliana doesn't listen to anyone. She's over twenty-one and the party is just starting."

"Maybe it's nothing more than a rebellious stage. That scene gets old fast once the initial fun and excitement wear off and all you're left with is a massive hangover."

"Yet some people keep repeating it." Noah gave him a pointed look, his mouth scrunched into a frown that said, *I'm talking about you.*

"You have to want to stop or have a reason to quit. I had both. Maybe Juliana will figure out what she wants more than a good time before it takes over her life."

"I hope so. Roxy is really worried about Juliana. And Sonya." Noah's tone said more than the words he spoke.

"You said her mom is okay after those fucking uncles roughed her up."

"She is." Noah amended that statement. "Physically. A bruised and battered body heals faster and easier than the mind."

"That's for sure. Anything I can do?"

Noah held his hands up and let them drop. "Make Sonya happy. That will keep Roxy happy. Which makes me happy, too."

Austin smacked Noah on the shoulder and grinned at his best friend. "You really have it bad," he teased.

"I see it in you. I hope it works out with you and Sonya."

"Well, I wouldn't want to make Roxy unhappy and, in doing so, make you unhappy." He meant it, even if he infused a little sarcasm in his words.

"Oh, I'll have to kill you." Noah's lopsided grin took some of the sting out of the deadly glare he leveled on Austin.

Noah slapped him on the back and walked down the porch steps to his truck, got in, waved goodbye out the window, then took off, leaving Austin standing there questioning whether or not this thing with Sonya would work out or get him killed.

Chapter Thirteen

Sonya parked the truck in the hardware store lot and stared up at the big blue sky. The same sky she saw at the Ranch in Nevada, but so much different here in Montana. She loved the wide-open spaces, hills that rose to mountains in places, and the crisp clean air.

The quaint little downtown area had storefronts with overflowing pots of flowers in their doorways and pretty window displays. The coffee shop, restaurants, and specialty shops tempted customers with their yummy treats. Some even had tables and chairs out front to enjoy the warmer spring days.

Black poles topped with white dome lights lined the streets.

No neon lights promising all-you-can-eat buffets and girls, girls, girls.

Not on this little all-American main street.

She understood why Roxy wanted to leave the Vegas area and the Ranch behind and stay here.

It had a lot to do with her sexy cowboy, but not all. This place just felt good.

June pushed her to come back to Whitefall and finish the job. Of course, June gave the gentle order with a wink that what she really meant was *Go get your cowboy crush*. Her mother wanted her to be happy. Maybe she could be with Austin, living here on a ranch near her sister with a man who made her want things she thought only other people without all her baggage found and managed to hold on to for a lifetime.

She needed to stop thinking like her mother and believe anything was possible.

Okay, so maybe she and Austin were nowhere near the point it even looked like forever, but she'd like to see if they could take the open and honest conversations they'd had, turn the heat up, and at least take this thing to the next level—where she got her hands on him, while he was naked and kissing her stupid again and again.

"You've got that look on your face again with what looks suspiciously like a smile." Roxy grinned at her. "You're thinking about Austin, aren't you?" Roxy pestered her.

"Shut up." She might not be able to deny it, but she didn't have to outright confirm. That led to questions and more of her sister's teasing. She didn't want either right now.

"Come on, Noah texted that they just finished paying. They'll be walking out any second. Noah kept our homecoming a secret so you can surprise Austin. We can catch up on what's been going on at both ranches and have lunch before we head home. I can't wait to see the progress at Austin's place."

Sonya's stomach tightened with anticipation. She couldn't wait to see the house, but she really wanted to see Austin. "That house is going to look amazing when it's done. You really did a wonderful thing for him, Rox."

Roxy touched her arm. "We know what it's like to have nothing and no one. Well, you have June on your side always, but you know what I mean."

"I do. Austin's father is truly something else. He really doesn't care how much he hurts his only son." It pained Sonya's heart to think how deeply that cut Austin after growing up thinking his father loved him and wanted him to be a part of the family business and legacy. It seemed when Austin's mother passed things changed, but then they took a drastic turn when Austin's grandfather died and Austin inherited the broken-down ranch.

She needed to think more about that.

Something niggled in the back of her mind. She just wished she could figure out what really bothered her about the whole land thing.

"Looks like he's at it again." Roxy pointed to Mr. Hubbard with a beautiful, young blonde on the other side of the street just outside the restaurant they were supposed to go to after they surprised Austin that they were back.

"Who's that with Mr. Hubbard?"

"Austin's ex."

Sonya couldn't help noticing all the differences between herself and the woman Austin used to date. Her styled hair, polished clothes, confident air, makeup that perfectly enhanced her pretty eyes and bowed lips, and a figure that had all the right curves and proportions that didn't match Sonya in any way. Sonya hadn't done her hair since she took on the project. She wore it up in a ponytail. In jeans and a T-shirt, she didn't have the same sophistication she'd mastered working at the accounting firm with her smart suits and silk blouses. While Sonya had soft curves, her lithe body showed off her firm, toned muscles, especially after all the physical labor she'd been doing lately.

Physically, they seemed so different.

Had he really fallen in love with her?

Was it really over?

Austin and Noah walked out of the hardware store. Noah pushed the cart filled with items to update the stables' bathroom and office. Austin rushed ahead and jogged right past her and Roxy without even a glance and headed across the street and stopped right in front of his ex. He gave his father an angry glare, then settled his gaze on the beautiful blonde with a look Sonya couldn't read because it was a mix of quickly changing emotions. Anger. Disappointment. Sadness. Other things too fleeting to comprehend beyond the fact she affected Austin deeply.

Did he still love her?

Sonya's heart sank and settled like a stone in her gut.

Was he hoping now that he was back on his feet they'd get back together?

AUSTIN DIDN'T THINK. He saw red and rushed across the street to confront his father who had walked out of the restaurant with Kelly on his arm. Her diamond engagement ring twinkled in the afternoon sunlight.

He spoke to Kelly because no doubt his father would lie through his teeth. "After what he asked you to do, you stayed with him. What the hell is wrong with you?"

Kelly sighed and held her handbag in front of her. "Hello, Austin. You shouldn't throw stones when your glass house has cracks."

"What the hell does that mean?"

"It's all over town. You've hooked up with some new partners. You were so angry about my using you as a stud, yet you went into business with those women."

Austin cocked his head and one eyebrow shot up. "The Wild Rose women?" Everyone in town knew about Roxy and that she owned the notorious brothel. Apparently they'd all heard about Sonya coming to town and working with him. No doubt, the gleam in his father's eye meant he'd spread that bit of gossip.

"Yes. Them."

"Jealous?" He didn't really care if she was, because he wanted to rile his father.

She scoffed and sputtered, "You have lost your mind." Not really a straight answer, but it seemed she couldn't come up with anything else.

"Why do you care what I do? Once the money ran out, so did you."

"That's not what happened." She pouted and he regretted restarting this same old argument yet again. "You refused to see reason and a way out."

"You mean selling out to him." Austin cocked his head toward his father, but didn't look at him.

"If not that, then at least finding something else to do with your life."

"If you'd stuck around long enough, you'd know I tried. He cut off every opportunity. No one wanted to hire me because he'd made it clear anyone who did would suffer his wrath. With his clout, business relationships, and the number of people and families dependent on him, no one wanted to take a chance on me."

Kelly gave his father a sideways look. She didn't know that part.

Oh yes, his father had torn apart his relationship with Kelly along with his life.

The second his bank account hit rock bottom, their relationship deteriorated to fights that were all about what she thought he should do and how much he felt like a failure. He'd gotten himself into a damn hole he couldn't climb out of because his father kept digging it deeper.

Then he came back for more, trying to trick Austin into sleeping with Kelly—the woman his father now slept with every night—and trying to rob Austin of his future child.

"I did no such thing," his father lied right to Kelly's face.

She turned to Austin for an explanation.

He didn't even try to convince her that he was telling the truth, not Walter. "I finally have a chance to build *my* ranch into what I always wanted it to be."

"Is this how you want to do it? You refused my offer, then turned around and used money that came from prostitution." Kelly's blue eyes filled with censure, though he rejected it because she was the one who made that despicable proposition.

The rage he felt then came back in a rush he couldn't contain. "Hell yes, I refused. You wanted to trick me into getting you pregnant and not tell me about it all while you're engaged to my father." He lashed out when he should hold his tongue. "Let's face it, sweetheart, you came begging for more because we both know who the better man is."

His father took a step forward.

Kelly stepped in between them and shoved Austin back a step. "Stop this. People are already talking."

"Yeah, how long before they're talking about my ex and my dad hooking up?" He looked past Kelly's shoulder, directly into his father's eyes. "You're so concerned about how bad I made the family look, yet you go after a woman who is half your age and used to sleep with your son."

"What bothers you more? That she prefers me? Or that I can provide for her the way you never could and never will?" That hit too close to how he felt about taking care of Sonya. "That ranch will never make a dime. You know it and I know it. That slut—"

"Watch it."

The warning didn't stop his father from speaking his mind right over Austin's words.

"—will back out if she's got a brain in her head."

"She knows a good thing when she sees it." As intended, his cocky tone only riled his father more.

Austin didn't want to talk about how grateful he was to Roxy and Sonya for all they'd done for him. Neither of these self-centered people would understand how much it meant to him that his friends had his back when his very own family conspired against him at every turn.

He needed Roxy's help now, but he would pay her back. "It's a business transaction. That's all. Once I pay back the loan and am making a profit, it will all be legit. I'll have everything I wanted and I'll run that place better than I ever did Hubbard Ranch. Once I've got the horses and cattle and everything is up and running, it's all me. The Wild Rose women will have nothing to do with it then." He couldn't help but try to make them see he'd be a success despite how hard his father tried to bring him down.

"One of them is out there living with you," Kelly pointed out.

Why the hell did she sound jealous when she'd walked out on him?

"Only during construction. Once the initial start-up is on its way, she'll go back to Nevada." Unless he convinced her to stay. But neither Kelly nor his father needed to know his plans for Sonya and seeing where they could take their intense attraction.

She was supposed to be home soon. He couldn't wait to see her.

He didn't want his father to know how much Sonya meant to him, because then, he might go after her.

That thought turned his stomach. Sonya stood up to him once. That was enough.

His father folded his arms over his chest and eyed him. "Someone like her doesn't belong here. People like that get what they deserve. Just look what happened to her mother."

Another one of those alerts went off in his head. "How do you know about that?"

"After she pulled a shotgun on me, I looked into her. Easy enough for my man to get one of those Wild Rose whores to talk for a little cash, and she had a lot to say. Prostitution leads to a lot of nasty consequences. Johns beating up whores and leaving them in seedy motels."

Kelly frowned again. "It's terrible what happened to her mother, but not unexpected given what she does. Is that the kind of woman you want in your life, Austin, representing your business and making you look bad?"

"Her life has nothing to do with my ranch."

Kelly frowned. "Yes, it does, Austin. You know it matters. Just look how people changed their minds about Noah when he started seeing John's daughter. John knocked up a prostitute. People don't forget things like that. Take Walter's offer. Sell the ranch to him, take the money, and start your own ranch on your terms."

Austin pointed at his father. "He's using you to get to me. Don't you see that? You are just a pawn in his game."

Kelly shifted to his father's side and took his hand, standing by her man and unwilling to believe the truth even when it was staring her right in the face.

His father pasted on his wounded mask and tried to impart some fatherly wisdom to prove to Kelly he had Austin's best interests at heart. "Listen to her before you have nothing, not even the tatters of your good reputation."

All Austin heard was, *Give me what I want, or else.*

"I'd rather be in business with a bunch of whores than sell that land to you."

The gasp behind him startled him, but the victorious smile on his father's face twisted his gut. He turned, knowing who he'd find behind him and wishing with every fiber of his being he could turn back time and take back his careless words.

He didn't mean it. He just wanted his father to know anything was better than being under his father's thumb.

With Noah, Roxy, and Sonya behind them, he and Kelly hadn't seen them standing there watching this scene play out, orchestrated by the man he used to love but now despised.

He played right into his father's hands and jeopardized his shot at a relationship with Sonya and his partnership with Roxy. Judging by the way Roxy held on to Noah's arm, he'd pissed off his best friend, too, who looked like he wanted to kill him.

Austin didn't know which one of them to address first because he didn't want to lose any of them, but the thought of Sonya leaving him tore his heart to shreds. He was both so happy to see her and unbelievably sorry she'd overheard this conversation. He'd held back what he really thought and felt about her and Roxy. Now they both had the wrong impression.

"Sonya, let me explain."

"You may think I'm a stupid whore, but I've been enlightened. You made yourself perfectly clear." She glared at his father. "They get what they deserve." She nailed Kelly with eyes ablaze with rage. "My mother should have expected what happened given what she does?"

Her gaze came back to him and filled with a heartbreak and pain he felt in his chest and all the way to his soul. The sheer force of the pain threatened to drop him to his knees.

"How can you possibly think *anyone* deserves to be raped and beaten? Why? Because she was born to a mother too weak to defend her against an abusive father? Because her two uncles started molesting her when she was four and continued to do so even after she turned twelve and they started sharing her with their friends? For a price, of course. Yeah, sure, she deserved it. Her mother couldn't help her. Her father turned a blind eye, too busy trying to put food on the table, getting by on minimum wage jobs that came and went because of his temper and drinking.

"When she worked up the courage to tell her grandmother at age seven what her uncles were doing to her, her grandmother told her she'd asked for it, flirting and being all cute in front of them. What did she expect?

"That little girl deserved it," she spat out, glaring at all of them.

"When she turned up pregnant at thirteen, well, that was all her fault, too. Her father beat her and told her he wasn't going to be responsible for another mouth to feed. Her uncles told him she'd been making money behind his back, whoring it out to all the high school boys and dirty old men in town. Well, her daddy wanted his cut in exchange for letting her keep the baby.

"With a seventh grade education and no idea what the hell she was doing, she gave birth to me at fourteen in a dirty shack with no doctor, no drugs, no understanding of what was happening, and a wish and a prayer that she and I didn't die.

"But she deserved that kind of soul-crushing pain and fear, too, right? She deserved to be treated like a thing, made to do things she didn't understand at four and hated when she was fourteen and just wanted to love her little girl and give her the childhood those bastards stole from her.

"Who cares about her hopes and dreams of getting out of there and having a better life? She should have expected what she got because of what she did to survive.

"She may not know if my father is one of my great-uncles or some random john forced on her, but I know who she is, and she doesn't deserve what she got or you all standing around talking about how she did and should have *expected* it."

She looked him dead in the eye. "Fuck you. You're not working with this whore ever again." She turned to Roxy. "Do whatever the fuck you want with the business. I'm out." The hurt in her eyes was only eclipsed by the pain he couldn't stand to see in their depths. It went soul deep.

She walked away without looking back, leaving Austin standing there reeling from her words and the pain of losing her and knowing that he didn't deserve her, but he had to get her back.

He took two steps forward but came up short when this time Roxy released Noah's arm. His hand shot up and slammed into the center of Austin's chest. "Leave her alone."

"I need to apologize and explain." He glanced past Noah's shoulder to Roxy. "You know I don't think anything bad about you guys. And I don't think her mother or anyone deserves to be hurt."

"*I'm* hurt by what you said. You devastated *her*."

"Roxy, you know how much I appreciate what you've done for me."

"I thought I did. But then I heard what you said and saw you break my sister's heart." Roxy turned and walked away.

Noah shoved him back, gave him a furious look that said how much he wanted to beat him into the ground, then turned and ran after Roxy.

"Sell me the land before you have nothing left."

Everyone he cared about just walked away from him. His father orchestrated this whole thing and provoked him into saying exactly what he did so Sonya, Roxy, and Noah would overhear and turn their backs on him.

He wanted Austin isolated and desperate.

Roxy stopped in the middle of the street, stood there for a couple of beats, then turned back. She must have overheard his father.

A glimmer of hope sparked in his heart. He hoped she didn't blow it out because right now that tiny light was the only thing in his dark world that gave him hope he could fix this.

Roxy glanced from him to his father and back, sighed so hard her chest rose and fell. Her lips pressed into a thin line, but then her gaze softened. "I'll come by tomorrow to check on the progress on the house and make sure we're still on track with the stables and the livestock delivery." She turned on her heel and kept on walking. Noah hooked his arm around her shoulders, drew her close, and kissed her on the head.

Austin turned on his father and Kelly. "Don't ever fucking come near me again."

Without a plan, or a ride because Sonya left in Roxy's truck and Roxy took off with Noah and the truck they'd driven into town, he left his father and an astonished Kelly at his back, pulled out his phone to call a cab, and started thinking about what he'd say to Sonya when he caught up to her.

Chapter Fourteen

Sonya sat behind Big Mama's desk going over the night's receipts and entering information into the spreadsheet on her laptop. The busy-work didn't keep her mind off what happened yesterday.

It didn't make her heart stop hurting or her insides feel less raw.

She'd made the last plane to Vegas. She'd held it together over the long drive to the cottage. Barely. Then she'd walked past Adria and Juliana with nothing more to say than, *I'm home for good*, before she slammed her bedroom door, fell on her bed, and cried off and on for hours until her throat ached and her eyes were swollen and red.

She woke up this morning wrung out with puffy eyes and a broken heart.

Others had disparaged her mother. It always hurt, but she'd learned to brush it off. But hearing the callous way Austin spoke to his ex and father and let them say those things about her mom, it broke something inside her.

She'd thought . . . Well, what did it matter what she'd thought about her and Austin? They weren't a thing then. They weren't going to be anything now.

Her phone buzzed with another text. She wanted to ignore it, but wondered what Roxy had to say this time. Her curiosity got the better of her.

She picked up her phone, saw the text from Dave, and slammed her phone facedown on the desk. He'd gotten the promotion back at the firm, but still asked her to do the work for him. She'd taken Austin's advice and stopped answering him. Dave resorted to begging at this point, but she simply didn't care. She was done letting people take advantage of her.

Maybe she'd saddle one of the horses and go for a ride. Clear her head and figure out a way to ease the pain in her chest that just might turn into a real heart attack if she didn't let go of some of this pent-up anger.

She needed to figure out what to do next.

Until then, she worked on the Wild Rose books.

Only two minutes later, distracted by her thoughts and the hurt that wouldn't go away, she entered the wrong figure into her spreadsheet for the third time, huffed out a frustrated breath, fell back into the chair, and stared out the office door in stunned disbelief when she spotted Juliana leading Austin down the hall and straight for her.

He was here. At the Wild Rose Ranch. What the . . .

He walked in and sucked all the air out of the room. His presence took up the entire space. He stood there looking devastatingly handsome in the same black T-shirt and worn blue jeans he wore yesterday and bone-weary tired all at the same time with a huge bouquet of roses and lilacs in his hand.

Her heart leaped but her anger ruled. "What the fuck are you doing here?"

"You swear a lot when you're angry," he casually pointed out, his eyes roaming over her like he hadn't seen her in weeks.

She turned on Juliana, who stood next to him, smiling like a crazy person as she held her hands clasped together in front of her. Her heels beat up and down on the carpet with her nervous energy. She acted like a five-year-old waiting her turn to hold a puppy.

Sonya studied her sister more closely. Was she wearing the same clothes as last night? "Did you just get home?"

Juliana's eyes went wide, giving Sonya a better look at her dilated pupils. "Are you high?"

"I delivered your guy. I'm out of here." Juliana rushed for the door and didn't stop, despite Sonya calling out, "Juliana, come back here."

Austin glanced over his shoulder at her retreating sister. "She said she was Adria."

Sonya scrunched her mouth and tried to breathe. "She does that sometimes. It's a childish game she refuses to give up."

"I don't give up either."

That drew Sonya's attention back to him. "Then let me be clear. Get the fuck out."

Austin sighed out his weariness. "So you want to do the whole fight thing."

"I don't want to do anything. I don't even want to fucking look at you."

Austin took three steps closer. "You're swearing and getting angrier."

She barely held back a snarl as her ears burned with rage. "I have nothing else to say to you."

"Good, then listen. I'm sorry."

"Me, too. Sorry I ever met you and thought you understood about Roxy and me. But that was all bullshit—"

"No it wasn't!"

"—so Roxy would invest her money and I'd help you get *your* business up and running. As soon as you get what you want, you'll dump her, too, because we're just a bunch of fucking whores!"

"I don't think you or Roxy or your sisters are anything of the sort. But I wasn't about to stand on the street defending you and me and what we're doing together to a man who could give a shit what I say and only wants to hurt me. And he'll hurt you to do it if he thinks you're important to me."

"Yeah, well, we know what you really want—"

"I want you!"

"—is me back in Nevada, Roxy out of the picture, and the ranch to yourself."

He raked his fingers through his disheveled hair and grabbed a fistful. "Damnit, I want you, with me, the fucking business be damned."

Sonya rolled her eyes. "Right. I'm supposed to believe that after what you said because you feed me some bullshit 'I'm sorry' and bring me flowers."

He held up the bouquet. "These are for your mom."

She leaned forward. "Do you seriously think I'd let you anywhere near her after what happened yesterday?"

"Either you introduce me, or I plop my credit card down and hope that I haven't spent every last dime I have on the plane ticket here so I can apologize to her."

Sonya stood and planted her hands on the desk and leaned forward. "I don't know what you think you're playing at, but you fucking spend one cent to spend time with my mother and tell her about the vile things your ex and father said about her, I'll kill you."

"They said those things. Not me. You heard what I said and what I glaringly left out. Which is what I really think. Do you seriously believe I'm such a callous asshole that I don't care what happened to your mom? That I think she deserved what happened to her? Which you lied about."

"I didn't lie. I told you what happened."

"You left off the part about your uncles raping her. Why? Because you thought I'd think she deserved that because of her job? What the fuck, Sonya? Didn't our time together show you who I am? Or do you just believe what *he* wants you and everyone else to think about me?" Austin collapsed into the chair in front of the desk and rubbed his hand over his face. The flowers dangled from his other hand. His big frame slumped in the chair and his eyes filled with misery. "You've been there for me through cleaning out my grandfather's house and finding that letter from my mom. Didn't you think I'd be there for you when you found out your mother had been violated like that? I can only imagine how devastated and scared you must have been for her. I saw it in your face when you got that call. I would have come here with you, held and comforted you, done anything I could to ease that pain the way you did mine with just your presence and understanding."

Her anger dissipated and her heart warmed but she still had some questions. "What did you mean when you said she propositioned you?"

His head fell back and he stared at the ceiling before he turned and looked at her again. "Remember the first day you showed up and found me passed out drunk on the porch?"

"Hard to forget how we met." The humor of it failed to alleviate her anger at the moment.

"I spent the night before trying to drink away the memory of her coming to me, acting like she wanted me while she wore his ring. But all she wanted was a heartless stud." Austin stared up at the ceiling, sighed, then faced her again. "My father sent her to me. Because I'm such a disappointment, he needs a new heir, but apparently he's shooting more blanks than bullets."

"So she tried to seduce you so she'd get pregnant, then she'd pass the child off as your father's."

Cold-blooded, devious bitch. What the hell was she thinking?

"If he can't have another son, why not raise his grandchild and groom him to take over?"

"And they never intended to tell you the child is yours?"

"Why? She thought the same thing you do, that I'm such a heartless bastard I'd turn my back on my child, or simply just give him up."

"I think no such thing," she snapped. "After what your father put you through, you'd never do that to a child, a friend, anyone. You know how much it hurts."

"Lucky for me, I figured out her game before things went too far. When her plan didn't work, she offered to pay me ten grand to do it and walk away. That's why she made the reference to me being just like you. Neither one of us is who they think we are, and while I didn't defend you, I know exactly how you feel when someone thinks that you'd sell yourself." He held up his hand to stop her from saying anything. "I'm not saying that people who do are bad or deserve whatever terrible things happen to them. I'm just saying that's not you." He sighed out the weight of his anger, grief, and resignation that what happened comprised a whole lot of convoluted drama with his father, his ex, working with Roxy and what that implied to others, and her.

"For what it's worth, he set me up. He knew you all were standing there and steered the conversation so I'd say those things or not say what I really felt so you, Roxy, and Noah would hate me. Then I'd really have nothing left. Not even my friends." He glanced up at her again. "Or someone who could have been a hell of a lot more." He leaned forward, propped his elbow on his knee, and dug the heel of his hand into his eye socket, then rubbed his hand over his head and looked up again. "I came here to tell you I'm sorry. I despise him, but I hate myself more for making you think for one second I thought you were anything less than amazing. I thought we had something good going, but . . . Never mind. He ruined it just like he's ruined everything else. You really are the smartest, strongest, kindest woman I've ever met." He set the flowers on the desk. "Please give those to your mom and tell her I hope she feels better real soon. I wish you both all the happiness you deserve."

He stood, gave her one last forlorn look, and headed for the door.

"Austin." Fear that he'd actually leave and she'd never see him again seized her heart.

He stopped but didn't turn around to face her. Every muscle in his back and shoulders tensed in anticipation. She could only imagine what he thought she'd say to knock him down even harder than his father had already done.

But she couldn't let him walk away. Not without asking herself every day of the rest of her life if she'd let real love walk out the door.

"My mother loves flowers. Roses and lilacs especially. She'd like to meet you."

He turned slowly and studied her face. "I'd like to meet her." One side of his mouth drew back, making the corner of his eye crinkle. "I have to confess, Roxy told me about the flowers."

Sonya held up her phone. "She's been texting me nonstop."

"She already explained what happened?"

Sonya nodded.

"You knew I was coming."

She shook her head and dropped her gaze to the series of texts lighting up her phone.

"You weren't sure I'd show. You really were surprised to see me when I walked in."

She glanced up at him. "My life hasn't been as rough as Roxy's, but I have my own trust issues." She put her hand on her opposite elbow and held herself.

He nodded. "You needed to hear it from me."

She needed to see it in his eyes. "You've been open and honest from the beginning. You say what's on your mind."

"So when I didn't stand up for you, your mother, and tell them to go to hell, I made you doubt what I really think about"—he looked around—

"this place and the women who work here. You doubted how I really feel about you."

She pressed her lips tight, feeling the sting of his words again. "You acted like I was an employee who'd be back here the minute the project ended."

"And in my mind all I thought about was seeing you again and figuring out a way to get you to stay longer that didn't involve sabotaging the renovation or burning the place to the ground."

She held back a smile. He really was determined to be with her. He'd used every dime he had to come after her.

Who did that?

Someone who cared deeply. Someone like Austin.

Still a little skeptical about his feelings for the Ranch, she tried to make him understand what she expected. "I don't need you to agree with what goes on here. But I need you to remember these women are human beings with the same feelings we all have and lives with history that sometimes is filled with abuse, trauma, and violence. Show them the same kindness you would any other woman. They aren't hurting anyone or doing anything illegal."

"At the risk of pissing you off again, I don't care what goes on here, or what anyone back home thinks of me working with you and Roxy." He came around the desk separating them and cupped her face in his big hands and looked deep into her eyes. "I want you to come back. I want to get to know you better. I want to get the ranch up and running. And I'm hoping that when I do you'll stick around because you want to, not because you work for Roxy."

"What else do you want?"

"You. And I desperately want to kiss you." He gave her time to pull away if she wanted to before his lips touched hers in a soft caress.

Sonya rose up on her toes, wrapped her arms around his neck, and took the kiss deeper, slipping her tongue past his warm lips and tasting his restrained need for her.

Maybe after all that happened, they needed this quiet, intense moment to recharge their connection. And it felt good to be held and kissed like it was a relief and a pleasure to simply be this close again. She wallowed in it and let time slip away. The tightness in her chest eased. His shoulders relaxed under her arms and she sank into him as he pulled her closer.

She ended the kiss and laid her chin on his shoulder. Embraced in his strong arms, she sighed. This was where she belonged.

His hand came up and cupped the back of her head. "Well, we got our first fight out of the way. I have to say, seeing you angry and disappointed in me isn't my favorite thing."

"Then you should let me be right from now on."

His chest vibrated against hers with his laugh. "My mom used to say, 'You can be happy or right.' I think in order for her to be happy, she let my father be right even when he wasn't. He's so used to getting what he wants, he can't take it that I keep saying no."

"You want to be right, too."

"Are you trying to start another fight?"

She leaned back and tipped her head to look up at him. "No. I get why you held on to the land and what it means to you. I don't understand your father's compulsion to get it from you."

"Maybe it ties to my mother's letter and whatever he stole."

Sonya's gaze turned thoughtful. "What did she and your grandfather want to tell you?"

"Sonya."

She turned toward her mother, though Austin didn't let her go. "Hi, Mama. There's someone I'd like you to meet."

Chapter Fifteen

Austin stared past Sonya, amazed by the pretty, petite woman before him. Makeup hid most of the bruising along her swollen jaw and on her neck. Her dark hair hung in spiraling curls and stopped just above her shoulders. Her big brown eyes were filled with childlike innocence. The simple white blouse and lace skirt that stopped several inches above her knees, where even more bruises disappeared up her thighs, emphasized her youthful look. His gut tightened with anger and his heart sank with sorrow for all she'd endured and survived. Brown sandals showed off her cotton candy–pink painted toes. But her shy smile held his attention. The same smile he'd gotten used to seeing on Sonya's face.

"Who's your friend?" June asked Sonya, still eyeing him holding her daughter in his arms.

Austin reluctantly released Sonya, picked up the flowers, and walked over to June. He stood a couple feet away. He didn't want to crowd her after what she'd been through.

Her gaze sharpened on him and her hands clasped together in front of her.

"Hello, Miss June. I'm Austin Hubbard. I've been working with Sonya on the ranch up in Montana. These are for you."

"Why?"

He gave her a sheepish smile. He'd never tried to win over a reluctant mother. "I thought you might like them."

"They're beautiful." She eyed the flowers with appreciation.

"So are you."

June blushed and her eyes went soft with gratitude. Finally, she reached out for the flowers and held them to her chest, bent her head, and inhaled their heady scent. "Thank you."

"You're very welcome. Thank you for sharing your daughter with me. I couldn't have gotten through the renovation on my house without her."

Suspicion clouded her brown eyes. Her gaze darted from him to Sonya and back. "What are you doing here if your business is up north?"

"I didn't treat Sonya with the respect she deserves."

Sonya jumped into the conversation. "Austin, you don't have to explain."

He glanced back at her. "It's the truth." He faced June again. "Arguing with my father has a way of making me angry and say stupid things without thinking. I hurt Sonya and I'm sorrier than I can say. So I came here to apologize to her in person and bring you those."

June looked past him to Sonya. They didn't say anything out loud but carried on a whole conversation with one long look. Satisfied, June smiled softly. "I've got lunch set out by the pool. Would you like to join us?"

Austin looked to Sonya to know if she wanted him to stay or go. He held his breath and waited to see if she'd crush him or keep him.

She walked to him, linked her arm through his, and tugged him to come along. "You're here, you might as well eat, though I warn you, I have no idea what's going on at the pool right now."

June giggled and held her flowers like a precious gift against her chest.

Adria—no, Juliana had brought him in through a side door, not the brothel's main entrance. He didn't know what to expect or how to act walking through this place with the woman he wanted and her mother who worked here. It felt unreal and as normal as meeting his girlfriend's mother could be under the circumstances.

He kept his eyes on the floor and let Sonya lead him down the hall into a large living room filled with soft sofas and tall plants that gave each section the idea of privacy. A man sat in the corner of the sofa, lounging back against the cushions, his dress shirt open to midchest, a whiskey in one hand, cigar in the other, and a woman wearing a skimpy purple dress kneeling between his legs, her big breasts spilling out of the dress and filling his lap as he stared down at her and they spoke in quiet tones.

Austin shifted his gaze to the French doors that led out to the back patio. Sonya squeezed his arm. He glanced down at her and she smiled and shook her head, silently teasing him for getting caught gawking.

"It's not a sin to look." June gave him a smile that matched Sonya's and held the door open.

"Uh . . ."

Sonya patted his arm as they approached a wood table laden with a platter with strips of medium-rare steak, tomatoes, lettuce, cheddar cheese, a bowl of fresh fruit, and a basket of sliced bread. A pitcher of iced tea with sprigs of mint sat behind three glasses, plates, and sets of silverware wrapped in linen napkins.

June planned this lunch for three.

He bet Juliana had not only brought him to Sonya but gone to June to let her know he'd come to see Sonya.

He held a chair out for June, nudged Sonya over to the chair across from her mother, and helped her sit, then took the chair between them. With his back to the woman sunbathing nude in the lounge chair behind him and the couple making out in the pool who looked like they were ready to take things all the way any second, his view remained on the two beautiful women sitting with him and a stone wall covered in a vine with bright pink roses blooming in profusion.

Sonya tried to hide her smile, but failed miserably at holding back another giggle at his expense.

June laid out slices of steak on a piece of bread to make a sandwich. "Austin, how long will you be in town?"

He took a plate from Sonya and began making his own lunch. "Unfortunately, I've got a lot of work on the ranch and am booked on the evening flight home." He stared at Sonya. "I know Sonya wants to be here with you, but I'm hoping she'll consider coming back to work soon. I've come to rely on her."

"She's so good at what she does," June agreed. "I don't know where she gets all those smarts with numbers. Me, I can barely keep my checking account register straight. It's better to let her handle the accounts."

"I agree. Which is why Roxy put Sonya in charge of the project. But she's good at more than numbers. You should see the house. It's better than I hoped. And she can swing a hammer like Thor. She likes demolition."

June laughed and eyed Sonya with appreciation. "There's nothing my girl can't do. Though I wish she'd let me help once in a while. She wouldn't even let me pay for college."

Sonya set her glass down and stared at her mother. "You need that money to settle somewhere when you leave this place."

June squished her mouth into a pout. The two really did have a lot of the same mannerisms. "I can support and take care of you."

"You did, Mama, when you came here."

June turned to him. "She means when I got away from my family and the two pimps who weren't much better than them. Those were some bad years." June fell silent for a moment, lost in her nightmares. Fear and regret shined in her expressive eyes. "But now we live here. A beautiful mansion, good food, and kind friends."

And that's when he understood why June ended up working in a brothel. She'd been taught all she was good for was sex and doing what a man wanted. Uneducated, her self-esteem ground right out of her, she didn't see any other options. She wanted to take care of her daughter and found that here she could give Sonya a beautiful home, a family of sorts with her sisters, and food and money to keep her safe and happy. Simple things everyone wanted. Maybe June went about it in a different way, but it was the only way she knew how to achieve it.

"Sounds like you turned those rough times into a good life for you and Sonya. Her love for you and her sisters shines through when she talks about all of you. I don't have any siblings, but as a kid, I'd always wished for a brother or sister."

June stared at Sonya, but spoke to him. "I was always here for her, but it was best that she stay with her sisters. She needed that kind of stability and home life. I wasn't any good at helping her with her homework. With my hours, I slept well past the time she needed to be up and out the door to school. But we spent time together in the afternoons. I loved our shopping trips and going to the movies. I used to go to her school functions, but then I stopped. People can be cruel. They whispered about the girls, us, this place. I didn't want to shame my daughter."

"Mama . . ."

"Don't make excuses or say it didn't bother you. I embarrass you."

Sonya held her hand out over the table.

June took it.

"You amaze me, Mama. I know who you are. Strong. Resilient. Kinder than anyone I've ever known. You love me with everything inside you. You sacrificed and fought hard to give me a good life. Others would have given up or sent me away after going through what you've been through. Not you. You held on. I love you. End of story."

Austin reached out and brushed his hand over Sonya's hair and laid it on her shoulder, squeezing softly. "You're sweet." He glanced back and forth between them. "I miss my mom. I wish I'd told her more often how much I loved her."

Sonya squeezed her mom's hand and released it. "Is there a way to reconcile with your father?"

He sat back and sipped his tea. "Maybe if I understood what happened. I thought everything was fine before my grandfather died. He's never been an easy man, but there was a respect between us as father and son. When I wouldn't sign over the land or sell it to him, everything changed in the blink of an eye."

"Your grandfather ran cattle on the ranch back in the day." Sonya set a bowl of fruit in front of him. "Do you know if the land has any gems or minerals worth mining? Your father wants it for a reason."

"I've thought of that, but haven't been able to find the records." He sipped his tea, hoping the caffeine would wake him up. "I wanted to hire a geologist but I used up the bulk of my money paying the property taxes and settling my grandfather's debts."

"I'll look into getting the property records at the county courthouse. We can get a geologist out there to survey the land and take some samples."

He leaned forward and propped his forearms on the table edge. "Does this mean you're coming back?"

"Who else is going to keep you on schedule and on budget?"

"If anyone is going to bark orders at me, I want it to be you."

"I don't bark." She leaned toward him, planted her elbow on the table and her chin in her palm, and gave him a wicked smile. "But you might like my bite."

He side-eyed June to gauge her reaction, which was nothing short of amused. Sonya flirting relieved the last of his fear that they wouldn't work out their issues and find their way back to being friends and a lot more.

He leaned in and kissed her. "So far, I like everything about you."

"You two are adorable together." June popped a fat red grape into her mouth and chewed, smiling the whole time. "You should call and get a reservation to go back on his flight."

Sonya hesitated, waiting to see what he thought of that.

He picked up her phone and handed it to her. "Please come home with me." He didn't know what she thought of the way he phrased that request, but he'd said exactly what he meant.

She sat back and started typing on her phone.

June waved her hand toward his plate. "Eat. Tell me about the house. What have you done so far?"

He told her about the renovation, his plans for the stables, and his anticipation of getting the horses and cattle on the property and finally running the ranch the way he'd always wanted. Lunch flew by with easy conversation and a better understanding of June and Sonya and their complicated but loving relationship.

He went back to the cottage with Sonya and stood in her bedroom doorway with his shoulder propped against the frame as she packed for their flight. Like Sonya, the room was perfectly put together. No clutter. No fuss, no muss. She liked things neat and tidy, cool soft blues and white for the bedding. Warm wood dressers and night tables. Gleaming glass lamps. Pictures of her with her sisters in silver frames. Black framed photos of her graduation from high school and college. Sweet photos of her and June. A picnic under a tree on a checkered blanket. June teaching her to swim in the pool. June smiling proudly up at Sonya sitting atop a horse holding a championship barrel racing ribbon.

Sonya zipped her suitcase closed and looked around the room to be sure everything was in its place and she'd left nothing behind she'd need in Montana.

"You had a good life here." He notched his chin toward the photo of

Sonya and her sisters back when they were little girls eating ribs and corn on the cob, their faces smeared with sauce and butter and smiling big, happiness in their eyes.

"I was luckier than Roxy. My mother loved me. She came to see me all the time. Adria and Juliana's mother isn't as bad as Roxy's mom, but she can be selfish, too." She traced her finger over the picture frame. "After the terrible places we'd stayed, this place truly was heaven. Peaceful. A chance for a normal life. It may have been different than the way other kids grow up, but I was happy here. My mother was safe. No one ever hurt her at Wild Rose Ranch. Big Mama and the security guards made sure of that. That's all I wanted. When I knew she had it, I don't know, I could breathe."

Austin went to her and wrapped her in a hug and kissed her on the head. "I want you to be able to breathe when you're with me."

Her hands slid up his back and she buried her face in his shoulder and held on.

He gave her a minute and just held her close, letting her know from now on, she was safe with him, because somewhere deep inside her was a little girl who'd never truly felt that way.

She tilted her head back and looked up at him. "I'm glad you came."

"Nothing and no one could have stopped me." He met her on the way up and leaned down and kissed her. He lost himself in the feel of her body pressed to his, the taste of her on his tongue, and the way his heart eased having her this close. "Come on, sweetheart. We don't want to miss our plane." And if he kept kissing her, he'd have her laid out naked on the bed beside them and he wouldn't let her go until he'd satisfied his need for her.

If that was even possible.

They held hands in the car, through security, and at the gate. When they boarded the plane and he realized they weren't sitting together, he left his seat and approached the guy sitting next to her. "Hey, man, you mind taking my aisle seat two back so I can sit next to my girlfriend?" He notched his chin toward Sonya. For a split second her eyes went wide when he called her his *girlfriend*, but then she smiled up at him.

The guy looked at Sonya like he'd be sorry to miss getting to know her during the flight, but grabbed his bag out from under the seat, and stood. "Sure. More room for me."

Austin stood back while the lady sitting on the aisle let the guy out. He took the middle seat next to Sonya. "Hey, sweetheart." He put his hand on her thigh and squeezed.

She put her hand over his. "Hey."

Scrunched in the middle, he tried to maneuver his seat belt on without bumping shoulders with the annoyed lady beside him. Sonya unbuckled and put the armrest up between them. "Switch with me." She stood and he slid over. He held her hips as she lifted her legs over his and took the middle seat.

"Please get settled and buckle your seat belt," the flight attendant advised. "We're almost ready to go."

He and Sonya buckled in. Sonya surprised him and took his arm, settling his hand between her thighs. She leaned into his side and snuggled against his arm. He kissed her on the head and settled in for an uncomfortable flight with his hard cock pressed against his fly the way the beautiful woman beside him was pressed against his body.

"Were the furniture and mattresses I ordered delivered to the house?"

Great. Now all he could think about was the king-size bed in his new room. "Yes."

"That's good."

Was that more flirting in her voice?

He glanced down.

Her gaze shifted from his lap to his face. "Are you uncomfortable?"

"Very."

She smiled. "Me, too."

He squeezed her leg and she clenched her thighs around his hand. Yeah, she was hot for him, too.

"I can't wait to see the house."

He leaned down and nuzzled his nose at her ear and whispered, "I can't wait to be alone with you."

Chapter Sixteen

Sonya walked in the front door ahead of Austin, flipped on the lights, and stopped short and stared in disbelief at the transformation. The contractors and cabinet guys had performed a miracle in an amazingly short period of time.

Austin set aside her suitcase and stood behind her. "What do you think?"

Overhead canned lights had been added in the living room and kitchen. The hardwoods gleamed. In this light, the wall color looked like a creamy subtle soft yellow. The stone fireplace had been brushed of cobwebs and dust and washed down so the colors in the stone shined with multitoned grays with white-and-black veins. The opening into the kitchen had been widened and trimmed in stained wood that matched the baseboards and window casings and contrasted with the white crown molding. The white cabinets in the kitchen matched the island. The marble countertops gleamed white with gray-and-black veins. The dark hardwood floors that ran through the house were perfectly matched in the kitchen.

"It's better than I imagined. The green tile you wanted in the backsplash is gorgeous."

"They matched it in the guest bath shower." He took her hand. "Come see."

He pulled her through the living room to the bathroom and turned on the light. They stood together and studied everything from the marble counter on the white cabinet, brushed nickel sink faucet, the black-and-white tile floor, and the gorgeous new shower with the same kitchen backsplash tiles in a band around the shower to add interest to the wide, rectangle, white tiles. All of it worked and gave the house a brand-new feel that made her think of those transformations on the home and garden shows she loved to watch on TV.

But did Austin like all the choices she and Roxy had made for him? "Are you happy?"

Austin stared down at her. "Are you kidding me? This is more than I ever expected. I don't think I would have come up with the design and how it all ties together the way you did."

"Roxy helped."

He touched her face and swept his thumb over her cheek. "Don't think I don't know how many changes you made to the plans because you were here and got to know me and what I'd like."

"The point was always to make the house your space." She put her hand on his chest. "That's what your grandfather wanted."

"It's getting there. Once we move the furniture and other belongings still out in the front yard on tarps into the house, it'll start feeling like home and not some project. Want to see the master bath? It's even better than this with the double sinks and the huge shower."

Sonya headed down the hall with him.

"The office and guest room still need work," he admitted. He probably would have gotten to them if he hadn't gone to Vegas to see her. "I moved all the office stuff back in for safekeeping."

The office door remained closed. Only the antique bed with a brand-new mattress sat in the middle of the clean spare room. Once they brought in the furniture, it would be a lovely guest room.

"I need to buy new sheets, blankets, and pillows for the beds."

"I'll get started on this room and the office tomorrow. I'll make a list of what we need to buy for the bedrooms and kitchen, though I think you can get by with what I salvaged of your grandfather's dishes and utensils."

"I bet you've got a list in your head or on your phone for each room."

They entered the master bedroom. Austin turned on the newly installed black overhead light with the mercury glass lightbulb covers.

She barely noticed it. Both of them stopped and stared at the beautifully made bed in the center of the otherwise empty room.

"Uh, I didn't do that."

Sonya smiled and shook her head. "Roxy did it."

Austin put his hands on her shoulders. "Except for the green blanket instead of blue, it looks a hell of a lot like your bed at the Ranch."

"Yes, it does." Roxy's way of making her feel at home here and hinting that this is the bed she belonged in with a man who refused to let her go without a fight and came after her because she mattered to him. Austin declared her his girlfriend because that's what he wanted her to be. And she wanted to be that in every sense of the word.

Right now, she wanted to dive in headfirst and let the current of this thing between them sweep them away, taking them wherever they were meant to be.

She turned to Austin and spread her hands wide on his chest. "She went through a lot of trouble to make that bed all nice for us."

Austin didn't speak. He just nodded once.

"Want to mess it up with me?"

He caressed her cheek with his thumb again. "Are you sure? I can crash in the other room."

"Is that what you want?"

He leaned in close. "I want you."

His words thrilled and excited her. "Show me how much."

He didn't hesitate to unleash his need and kiss her with a passion he'd obviously held in check the last few times he'd kissed her. She recognized the feel of his lips against hers and the taste of him. But the kiss held an exciting intensity that promised what came next was going to be like nothing she'd ever experienced.

He didn't rush, but kept the kissing going so they could both learn what the other liked and they had time to settle the initial rush of lust to a level that made it easier for them to explore and savor. She slid her hands up and down his hard chest and around his back. Sculpted muscles pressed against her palms, her fingertips mapping every dip and rise. His hands sank from her shoulders, down her sides, and around her waist to settle on her bottom. He pulled her closer, pressing his hard length against her soft belly.

The contact made him growl low in his throat. She smiled against his lips.

"You like that." He dipped his head and kissed his way down her throat and over her chest. He nipped her hard nipple through her T-shirt and bra. She gripped his golden hair and held him to her. "You like that better."

"Stop teasing." Her fingers threaded through his hair as he stood, bringing her shirt up and over her head, making her let go of him. She reached behind herself to undo her bra. He dipped low and licked her breast above the cup, then took her nipple into his warm mouth and sucked and slid his tongue over her heavy breast.

With his mouth at her other breast, her bra a mere memory on the floor, she slid her hands down his back, gripped his T-shirt in her fists, and pulled it off. He left her breasts only long enough for the shirt to clear his head and for her to toss it away. His hands worked on the button and zipper on her jeans. He kissed his way down her belly as he lowered the jeans to her ankles. She toed off her tennis shoes and then kicked off the jeans.

He sank to his knees and traced his fingers over the vine and roses tattoo that wound around her thigh and up over her hip on her right leg. "Noah said Annabelle's been bugging him to get the same tattoo all of you have." He kissed each of the four roses. "You and your sisters."

She brushed her fingers through his silky blond hair. "We are all connected to each other and to that place, though we made a small part of it ours."

He nodded, then laid a trail of kisses over her belly and worked off her socks. His hands slid up and down her legs in soft caresses until they came up and cupped her bottom. His fingers hooked her panties' waistband, the palms of his hands pressed to her ass. He looked up at her, his eyes alight with a burning desire that made the blue look like sparkling crystal. "God, you're so soft and beautiful."

She didn't know what to say when the whispered words held a reverence that made her eyes glass over and her heart swell and melt all at the same time.

She cupped his rough jaw in her hands and stared down at him. "Austin."

His name made the fire in his eyes flash. Her panties disappeared as fast as his mouth found her center. His tongue stroked her soft folds, and then he sank into her heat. He hooked one arm under her thigh and propped her leg over his shoulder. Her head fell back and she gave herself over to the amazing feel of his mouth on her wet center, his tongue plunging deep and sweeping over her clit. She wanted him so bad she didn't last long and came with his name on her lips and his mouth pressed hard against her.

Her legs wobbled and threatened to buckle, but she didn't have to worry. Austin wrapped his arm around her waist, lifted her up, kissed her hard and deep, and walked to the bed and laid her out on the cool cover. They sank into the new mattress. Austin broke the kiss and levered himself up on his hands and stared down at her. "You're . . ." He swept his gaze over her face and down her body between them and back up. "Damn, sweetheart, I want you so bad." He pressed his forehead to her shoulder and sucked in a deep ragged breath to cool down.

He leaned back and slid off the end of the bed. She watched him staring at her as he undid his belt, button, and zipper at his waist. His hard length strained against his black boxer briefs. He yanked off his boots, then dropped his jeans and everything else to the floor. He stood before her, his manhood hard and smooth jutting out toward her.

He held up the condom to let her know he had it.

"Come and get me."

He crawled back up the bed and her body, drawing out the tension and increasing her need for him to finally touch her and lay his big body over hers so that they lay skin to skin.

When he finally lowered himself between her legs and his chest pressed to her and he kissed her again, her body reached for his. Her arms went around his back. Her legs wrapped around his strong thighs, and she kissed him like her life depended on it. Her hips rocked forward trying to find him, but he kept his head and rubbed his hard length against her wet center and that sweet spot that made ripples of bliss spread through her whole system.

Austin broke the kiss long enough to tear open the condom, roll it on, then cover her again. His lips met hers. His tongue swept along hers. And she took him into her body and deep into her heart with one powerful thrust that joined them and made her whole body tighten around him.

He stopped. For a second, they both held their breath and held on to the moment for a heartbeat that seemed to freeze time.

"Oh God, baby, this is where I've wanted to be since I met you." He pushed in deep and rocked his hips against hers, creating a sweet friction against her clit. She couldn't get enough. Of that. Of him.

She swept her hands up his back to his shoulders and spread her legs wide and tilted her hips up to meet every one of his powerful thrusts. As his body stroked hers, his breath whispered against her ear along with a dozen sweet sentiments.

Her nails scored across his back as she held tight and met his need with her own. "Harder. Show me how much you want me."

Instead of heeding her plea, he knew what she really wanted and pulled out and pushed back in with a steady, long, deep push and pull that drove her up to the edge and sent her flying over it. With one hard thrust, he followed her, his body pulsing within hers.

She held him close and went limp into the mattress when his body relaxed on top of hers.

Their breathing seesawed in and out and filled the quiet night. The light blazed overhead, spotlighting them on the bed. She loved the feel of him lying between her legs and draped over her.

She found the strength to softly rub her hands up and down his smooth strong back. She liked his weight on her, the feel of him pressed against her and inside of her. The possessive way he had one hand under her neck, the other under her hip, and his face buried in her hair at the side of her head.

"If you keep doing that, I'm going to fall asleep on top of you."

"Did you sleep at all last night?"

"No. I had two stops before my plane finally landed in Vegas this morning."

"You didn't pack a bag or anything."

He'd simply come after her. No change of clothes. Nothing but a hope and a prayer that she'd forgive him and come back.

She hugged him closer because it meant so much to her.

He leaned up on his forearm and stared down at her. "I just needed to see you. I needed to apologize and make you believe I'm not cold and calculated like my father."

"You could never be like him. You have a good and kind heart, Austin."

"It's you. I've never even thought about going after a woman the way I went after you. I saw how much what happened hurt you. Even if you didn't forgive me, I had to know that you were all right."

"Right now, I'm fantastic." She rubbed her hands up and over his shoulders and drew him down for a kiss. "Let's put what happened in the past."

He rubbed his nose against hers, then nuzzled it across her cheek to her ear. "Want to see the shower now?" His tongue swept over her earlobe.

She giggled. "I'd love to see your shower." She gave him a suggestive look that only ignited that crystalline blue fire in his eyes again.

Chapter Seventeen

Sonya ran out of the bathroom to grab her ringing phone on the bedside table. She held the towel wrapped around her at her chest, raked her damp hair away from her face, and stared down at the caller ID.

Fed up with Dave calling her all the time to help him with his work at the accounting firm, she answered and gave him a piece of her mind. "I quit the firm weeks ago, Dave. You got the promotion that should have been mine. It's about time you figured out how to do your job on your own. I don't work for you. And I'm done covering for you and helping you keep what should have been mine, you incompetent ass. Don't call. Don't text. I helped you when I worked there because it was good for the firm, but I'm not your lackey anymore. I don't care if I don't get a favorable reference."

"You don't need one, Miss Tucker," the female voice announced.

Sonya held her breath. She'd seen the firm's name on the caller ID and assumed . . . Oh God, what had she done?

"Um . . ."

"I apologize for calling so early. I wanted to catch you before you headed out for the day. This is May Mathis."

Oh shit. VP of her old department.

"Ms. Mathis, how can I help you?"

"Well, you confirmed many of my suspicions about Dave, his work, and his character. It's come to my attention that he's . . . ill suited to his new position. While looking into some questionable account matters, I happened to notice since you left he's sent you over a hundred emails. Based on how you answered this call, I assume he's called you numerous times as well. As for the emails, most of them you responded to with detailed instructions on what he should do to handle one matter or another. In addition to your blunt statements that a person at his level should know how to do those things, you made it clear in your responses just how inept he was at his job and that, in fact, you are more qualified. As you stated, the promotion should have gone to you. I was not involved in the decision to give it to Dave, but I believe in promoting talented, smart, dedicated individuals like yourself. I believe the job should go to the most qualified *person*."

In not so many words, Ms. Mathis let her know she was that person and Dave had indeed gotten the job because he was a man with seniority, but not a proven track record.

"In my position, I think it's my responsibility to look out for other women coming up the ladder rungs behind me. I'm sorry I was unaware of the circumstances of your departure from the company. I apologize that you were made to feel like you weren't an important member of the team. I'll work hard to make sure that doesn't happen again."

"Ms. Mathis, what are you getting at?"

"Dave has been fired. The job is yours if you want it. With a significant pay raise and yearly bonus."

Sonya's head spun. "I didn't expect this. I don't know what to say."

She'd worked damn hard to get that promotion.

But did she want to go back?

"I understand. I sprang this on you. Take a few days to think it over."

"Uh, yes. I'm in the middle of a project that I would like to see through, but I will take your offer under consideration and get back to you with my decision as soon as possible."

"Great. I truly believe you are an asset to the company. I appreciate that after what happened, you're willing to consider coming back. I hope to hear from you soon."

"Yes. You will. And thank you, Ms. Mathis. I appreciate the call and the offer."

Sonya said goodbye and sat on the edge of the bed she'd shared with Austin last night.

She truly didn't expect the situation with Dave would turn into this. She'd been ready to put a stop to the calls and leave the accounting firm behind her.

But now, they'd offered her the very thing she thought she wanted more than anything in life. She'd worked hard to get the recognition for her contribution and expertise.

This thing between her and Austin was so new. If she left, would the spark they'd ignited into a fire last night fizzle out?

Long-distance relationships were hard. Especially when she'd be expected to work sixty-plus hours a week again.

Did she want to go back to that kind of grind?

Was the money and promotion worth it?

Did she have to give up her chance for personal happiness with Austin to have the dream job?

Was the job worth all the hard work and losing Austin?

She liked being with him every day. She'd missed him terribly the few days she'd been in Nevada.

Her mind spun out with questions and possibilities. She didn't know what to do because she never saw this coming.

She really would need every second of the next few days to figure out what she wanted to do.

She stood and stared down at the rumpled bed. Echoes of making love to Austin pulsed through her body. More than that, she remembered how she felt in his arms. Safe. Protected. Even loved.

She felt like this is where she belonged.

To have one, did she have to give up another? Could she find a way to have both, a job that mattered and the man she cared about more each day?

AUSTIN WALKED INTO the bedroom, smiled at the bed he and Sonya wrecked last night, and went to the open bathroom door. Sonya stood in front of the mirror, brushing her hair into a ponytail. Gorgeous. Her pale skin glowed against her dark hair. He knew every inch of her lithe body and wanted her again even though he'd made love to her an hour ago and twice last night. He thought his need for her would calm once he'd finally gotten his hands on her. But it only grew with every tempting touch and look she gave him, showing him in a way he'd never experienced with a woman that she enjoyed being with him as much as he did with her. She didn't hesitate or shy away from letting him know what she wanted and how she wanted it.

He had to admit, her eager participation only made it easier and more comfortable for him to let go. The experience had given him a freedom to explore her and the limits of what she liked and didn't without feeling like he'd overstepped. It just gave him another avenue to explore.

The way she wanted him patched up the broken pieces of his ego and gave him the confidence to prove to her she'd made the right decision coming back and giving him a second chance.

"Are the contractors here?"

He handed her one of the cups of coffee he'd brought with him and took a sip of his own. "Setting up outside to get to work on the stables. The painters should be here soon. I'll help you move in the furniture for the guest room and office as soon as they're done in there."

"That would be great." She took a sip of her coffee, then grabbed the zippered bag on the counter. "Let me clean this up. I'll meet you in there so we can decide how we want to set up the furniture."

Lotion, hair spray, her brush, toothbrush, toothpaste, and some other miscellaneous stuff sat spread around the sink. "Why are you putting that all away if you're just going to pull it all out later when you shower again?"

She dropped the floss container in the bag, then glanced at him and looked away again.

"Sonya?"

"I don't live here, Austin."

Ah. She wasn't sure where they stood as far as them working together and being together. He hadn't given it a lot of thought. He'd had a lot of other things on his mind last night. And her in his hands, which shut off his mind to anything but making her want to stay in bed with him.

"You had no problem sleeping here before last night."

"Sleeping in the back of my truck or on your porch isn't the same as sleeping in your bed."

"In my bed is a hell of a lot better, I can tell you that."

"The house is livable now. I'll have it finished by end of tomorrow. I can get a room in town or stay with Roxy." She nodded to herself in the mirror like it was settled.

"Why?" He liked rattling her and putting that confused and hopeful look in her eyes.

"Because you didn't bring me back here to be underfoot every second of the day."

"Why do you think I brought you back here?" He hadn't really thought about it past the fact he wanted her with him.

Overall, it seemed simple. The details were complicated.

"You need me to help you finish getting this place set up."

"What happened to the woman who came home with me last night and knew exactly what she wanted and had no trouble telling me? I'd like her back."

Sonya picked up the lotion, then let it drop on the counter. "Austin, I don't know how to do this."

He gave her a break. "Do you want to stay here with me while we get this place up and running, or do you want your own space?"

"I want to know what you want."

He cocked an eyebrow and waited for her to answer his question.

"I'd like more of last night." She spoke to her bare toes sticking out the bottom of her jeans.

After all they shared last night, he didn't like that she couldn't look him in the eye and say what she wanted to say. "It'll make it easier to give you that if you stay."

Her head came up. "Do you want me to stay?"

"Yes." He set his mug on the counter and closed the distance between them. "I don't know how to do this either." He'd never lived with a woman. He wasn't thinking that's what this was. He just didn't want her to leave.

Yeah, he copped out on that thought. But this was new and he didn't want to think too hard about it. “Leave your stuff on the counter. Or put it in the cabinet. I don’t care. You and me, we work together. And that has nothing to do with business. As long as we work, stay. Because if you leave, I’m coming after you until I convince you to come back again.” And that was new, too.

He let his relationship with Kelly fall apart without a fight. He and Sonya had only been friends a short time and he’d crossed several states to get her back.

He thought of how bad Noah had it for Roxy and recognized it in himself. That driving need to protect Sonya the way Noah had done for Roxy. The way Noah had seen Roxy in a way no one else did.

After seeing Sonya with June, he understood her on a deeper level than he’d ever known any other woman.

The sultry smile he remembered from last night spread across Sonya’s face. “So you don’t care if I mess up your bed, your bathroom, or your life?”

“You’re beautiful and a dream come true in my bed. I could give a shit about the bathroom. As for my life, you made it infinitely better when you walked into it and dark as hell when you left.”

He snaked his arm around her waist and drew her close. His words and the move had taken her by surprise. He kissed her long and deep, telling her without words that he meant it. He ended the kiss with a brush of his lips, pressed his forehead to hers, and stared into her bright hazel eyes. “Stay with me.”

Part of that plea came from deep in his heart because he lost the only two people who had really loved him: his mother and grandfather. But it mattered a hell of a lot more than not wanting to lose another person who cared about him.

He didn’t want to lose *her.*

“Austin, I don’t know what to do with all that.”

“Let it sink in. Hold on. That’s what I’m trying to do.”

She wrapped her arms around his neck and hugged him tightly enough to nearly choke him. He didn’t care. He held her close. He didn’t know what happened next, how long she’d stay, or if this thing would last or fizzle out, but right now, he had everything he could ever want.

She let out a heavy sigh, then sucked in a deep breath. "My old company called this morning and offered me a job."

Austin went still. He'd just convinced her to stay, and now she was telling him she might leave again. "What did you say?"

"Nothing. They gave me a couple days to think about it." She unhooked her arms from his neck and stepped back, but not out of his light hold on her hips.

"Are you going to accept? Is that what you want?" He barely got the words out of his tight throat. He didn't want to lose her, not when they were so close to having what he thought they both wanted.

"I thought it was." Yet she hadn't snatched the opportunity the second it was offered.

Because she wanted a life with him more? God, he hoped so.

She laid her hand on his chest, over his thrashing heart. "I want what we have and more. More with you. And more for me. Does that mean taking the job, or finding something else?"

Maybe she'd find something here that satisfied her need to be productive, in charge, and challenged.

"I don't know right now. Everything seems so up in the air." Frustration lit her eyes. She wasn't used to being indecisive. Sonya went after what she wanted.

He liked that about her. He would never stop her from doing what she wanted, but he hated the idea of her living in Nevada instead of here with him. "You and me, we're solid again, I hope."

"Yes, we are. I want to be with you. That is perfectly clear."

That made him feel a thousand times better.

"How we do that going forward remains to be seen."

That made his confidence falter. "You've got time to decide. Think about it. We can talk more about the job later. Right now, just know that I want you to do what makes you happy. If that means taking the job, it doesn't mean you lose me. We'll find a way to make it work, because I want you in my life."

Sonya found a halfhearted smile. "Are we going to have all our deep conversations in the bathroom?"

"I'm too busy worshipping you in bed to talk," he teased, gave her another hug, then set her away, but not before he kissed her one more time.

"Okay, I'll stay and think about the job, but you need to remember one thing."

"What's that, sweetheart?"

She picked up her coffee and sneered at it. "I like milk in my coffee."

He laughed and tugged her ponytail. "I know that. The fridge is empty."

She walked out of the bathroom with him, headed for the living room. "Once I get the painters working, I'll drive into town for groceries and the other things we need here."

"Want me to go with you?"

She shook her head. "I know you're dying to get started on the stables. The auction is only four days away. We need to be ready to bring the horses back."

Austin rolled his eyes. "I've got to get to the south hay field, too."

"You do that. I'll take care of the house."

"You sure?"

She nodded. "Everything is moving forward. We're on track."

He hoped she meant between them as well. He didn't know what she'd decide about the job, but he'd already decided he wanted to keep her even if that meant he had to take a plane to see her. He kissed her again. "Yes, we are."

They parted ways on the porch. She waited for the painters to haul their gear inside. He walked across the yard and up the drive to the stables where the contractors unloaded new beams and piles of wood.

He set aside his worries about her taking the job she wasn't even sure she wanted anymore. Right now, she wanted to be with him, here on the ranch. He rode the buzz from that thought, which echoed the one he'd woken up with this morning and had nothing to do with drinking and everything to do with the woman lying down the length of him in bed.

He could get used to a high like this.

He liked being drunk on her.

Chapter Eighteen

Sonya stood in front of the refrigerated dessert case and tried to decide among the triple chocolate cake, éclairs, or creamy New York cheesecake. Or all of them. She'd earned the extra calories working on Austin's house and in his bed last night. The memory of it sent a hum of anticipation through her body. Her heart melted all over again when she recalled his words this morning and how much he wanted her to stay at his place.

"He hates chocolate, and if you put strawberries on the cheesecake he'll end up in the emergency room." The familiar voice killed her Austin buzz.

Sonya stood taller and faced Kelly standing on the other side of the case holding a shopping basket filled with fruits, vegetables, and a bag of chocolate chunk cookies.

Sonya tried to be polite and play it off that it didn't sting when Kelly knew those things about Austin and she didn't. "Good to know. Thanks."

Austin walked out of the aisle behind Kelly and stopped when he spotted them. Sonya wondered how he got here and why he came at all instead of calling her if he needed something. She'd left him working with the contractors in the stables.

"So, not the chocolate cake or éclairs."

Austin shook his head.

"Cheesecake with raspberries?"

Kelly didn't blink at the way she posed it as a question for Austin, who stayed out of sight behind Kelly.

Austin nodded and she put the dessert in the cart and started to walk away to get the raspberries in the produce section.

"What is it about you?"

Sonya stopped and turned back to Kelly.

Austin eyed Kelly and went very still.

Okay, polite went out the window. They were doing the whole jealous ex-girlfriend thing. Well, she could do snark, too. "Maybe he swore off blondes after dating you."

Kelly cocked her hip. "The whole Snow White thing is cute, but come on . . ."

The comparison didn't surprise her. She did have dark hair, red lips, and pale skin. What could she say, she stayed out of the sun. Not for vanity, but because she'd spent the last few years in a classroom or office.

"You're stick thin."

Austin shook his head.

Kelly glanced down at her chest. "He likes curves."

Austin's gaze roamed over Sonya in an appreciative sweep. He looked her in the eye and nodded his absolute approval of her modest attributes.

"Austin likes a hell of a lot more about me than what I look like."

Austin smiled broadly.

"I don't know what it could be when all I see is an inbred slut."

Austin moved so fast she couldn't stop him before he spun Kelly around to face him. "Apologize."

"Austin." Kelly pressed her hand to her chest. "I didn't see you there."

"Is that why you think it's okay to say something so vile to my girlfriend?"

Sonya put her hand on Austin's shoulder and tried to make him take a step back, but he wouldn't budge. "Let it go."

"No one talks to you that way and gets away with it." He pinned Kelly with his glaring gaze. "Apologize."

"Why? It's the truth. She admitted it herself."

"She didn't have a choice in who her father is, but you have a choice whether you take the rape of a child and use it against Sonya. I thought you'd hit a real low when you tried to use me to get pregnant and steal my child from me, but this . . . To use what happened to her poor mother to hurt Sonya because you're jealous . . . You disgust me."

"I didn't mean it like that."

"No? You didn't mean to hurt her with that slur? Or you didn't think about what you were saying because you didn't think about your words and what they mean? You've got no compassion or empathy for her, her mom, anyone, because you only think about yourself. What *you* want. What *you* think you deserve. Fuck everyone else."

Kelly's eyes filled with tears.

A small crowd of people stopped in the bakery area and stared.

Sonya put her hand on Austin's back. "That's enough. Let's go."

Kelly looked up at Austin with watery eyes. "How could you say no to me and choose her?"

"Because you continue to prove I made the right decision. You don't really care about me."

"I love you."

"You loved what you thought we could be and what we could have, but it was just an empty dream because the second I had nothing to offer you but myself, you walked away."

He glanced at Sonya. "You know what the house and that piece of land mean to me. Why it's important I hold on to it. I have nothing else to my name."

Sonya ran her hand up and down his arm. "I have my own things, Austin."

He turned back to Kelly. "Things aren't what keep people together. Why her? She's everything I ever wanted in my life that I can't buy or touch or define and explain. I woke up happier than I've ever been because she was beside me. I know I can talk to her about anything and count on her to have my back no matter what. If I'm lucky, I'll wake up every day feeling that way and knowing those two things.

"Can you say the same about the man who put that ring on your finger and ordered you to get knocked up by his son? If you think so, you're a fool. When you can't give him what he wants and he tosses you aside, don't say I didn't warn you."

"Austin." Sonya tugged his arm. "I know you're angry, but that's enough."

Kelly dropped her basket and ran for the exit with her hand over her face, shielding her tears and embarrassment.

Austin glared at the onlookers, who quickly dispersed, leaving them a semiprivate moment to regroup.

Austin pulled her into his arms and held her close. "Are you okay?"

"I kind of feel bad for her."

He held her away at arm's length. "Why? After the horrible thing she said to you and trying to steal a child from me . . ."

"She's lost, Austin. Obviously your father's influence in her life has changed her."

"That's for sure. I actually can't believe she fell for him."

Sonya didn't want to think about Kelly saying she loved Austin. He didn't seem to believe it, but Sonya saw it in Kelly's eyes.

Sonya didn't sense any jealousy from Austin. He didn't like Kelly seeing his dad, but he didn't want her back either. After the fast one she'd tried to pull on him, he was over her.

"I have a feeling your father targeted Kelly. He played up the fact you couldn't give her what she needs and deserves, but your father could and then some. She wants a baby. He used that against her, too, and humiliated her in the process by taking what she wants most and making it so the only way he'd give it to her was if she seduced you back into her bed and left you and handed the child over to him."

Austin stared down at her. "Can you believe those words came out of your mouth?"

"No." She laughed under her breath. But she sympathized with Kelly. She must have been really desperate to do what she did. "But I wonder if he really wanted the child, or if he just wanted to torture you with the fact he married the woman who was once yours and left you wondering if the child was yours on top of it. It's not enough for him to fire you and kick you out of your home. He wants to take everything away from you. That's some truly reprehensible psychological torment."

He squeezed her shoulders. "If he thought marrying her would hurt me, he's wrong. That's why when she came to me, I didn't fall into her trap. I was over her already. If she can't see he's using her, then I don't know what to do. I don't want to see her get hurt. But if I keep trying to get her to see reason, I'm afraid it will only give her false hope there's still something between us."

She put her hand on his chest to reassure him she didn't believe that. "I think you made it clear there isn't."

"Everything I said was the truth."

She brushed her hand up his arm to his shoulder and stared up at him. "You make me very happy, too."

"Good. Let's be happy together, finish up here, and go home so I can show you again how much I want you."

Before she went back to her cart, she snatched the éclairs from the display.

"I thought you were getting the cheesecake."

She pointed to the cart. "I did. But I think it's a two-dessert night."

He eyed the chocolate-covered éclairs. "I only get one."

She smiled up at him. "You get me."

He hooked his arm around her shoulders. "Lucky me. You're my favorite thing in the whole world."

She leaned into him and pushed the cart toward the produce aisle to grab the raspberries before they checked out and headed home for dessert night.

Chapter Nineteen

Sonya woke up to a slice of sunlight cutting across her face and Austin peeling her panties down her legs. One annoyed the hell out of her. The other made her hot all over.

"I know you're awake, sweetheart."

The purr in that *sweetheart* rippled over her skin like a heatwave. "I'm still sleeping."

Austin's hand glided up and down her thigh. "I'll have to try harder to get your attention." He slipped his hand between her legs and brushed his fingers feather light over her soft folds. Her thighs fell apart without her really thinking about it.

"Even when you're not awake you want me."

She rocked her hips into his wandering fingers. "I always want you."

"Do you want me here?" He slipped one finger, then two into her slick core.

"Yes," she sighed out.

"Do you want this?" He circled his tongue around her tight nipple, then sucked it into his warm mouth.

"More."

"You're greedy this morning."

She'd show him. She rolled on top of him, straddled his hips, and took him in with one long press of her body down his. She'd felt his condom-covered length against her thigh while he teased her. She wasn't the only eager one this morning.

"You started it."

His wolfish grin matched his mischievous mood.

His hands clamped onto her hips and he guided her up and down his hard shaft in a rhythm that wasn't too fast or slow, but just right for waking up her whole body. She planted her hands on either side of his head and leaned down for a sultry kiss that mimicked the push and pull of their bodies. He wrapped his arms around her, drew her close, and clamped his mouth over her nipple as she rocked her hips against his, finding that sweet spot that had him pumping into her as she moved against him.

"Damn, sweetheart." He hissed, then licked her nipple and took it into his mouth again. The sweet torture sent a bolt of heat down to her core. He thrust deeper, harder, taking her up to the edge and driving her right over it. He lifted and slammed her down on his hard length one more time. Her body quaked around his pulsing shaft. Ripples of pleasure faded with the burst of release in both of them.

She collapsed on his chest, her face buried in his neck. His arms wrapped around her back and held her close and warm against his big body heaving with his deep breaths.

"Morning, honey." She smiled against his warm skin.

"Mmm. Sweetheart, I think you're trying to kill me."

"You take your chances when you wake me up."

His chest rumbled with his laugh. "I have to get up. I have horses to feed."

"They're beautiful." And nothing had been more glorious than seeing his face when he led the six of them out of the trailer and into the completely repaired and refurbished stables.

They'd worked hard this past week to finish the house and stables and finally start bringing the animals to the property.

"I can't believe how far we've come in the past couple weeks."

She didn't know if he meant with the ranch, or their relationship. They'd grown closer, to the point they did everything together. Including making decisions for the ranch, which horses to buy, and the things they needed for the house. He asked her what she'd like, though they hadn't agreed she'd stay longer than it took to have the ranch up and running with the cattle and a couple of workers to help him with the daily chores.

When she first arrived, she'd never thought about staying. In fact, she'd wondered what she'd do with all her time back at the Ranch. Now she couldn't see doing anything else but living here with Austin.

She'd let her firm know she needed a little more time to decide about the job. Austin stopped asking her about it. She got the feeling he hoped it would just go away and things between them would stay just like this. She admitted this was pretty damn good.

"Next comes the cattle. You'll get the other fields ready to plant. You'll have hay and alfalfa for the ranch and to sell. You'll be self-sufficient and making a profit in no time."

He rubbed his hand up and down her back. "Do you want to go riding later? I'd like to show you the rest of the property."

"I'd love to. But first I'm going to town."

"What for this time? More éclairs?"

"You ate most of them, Mister I-don't-really-like-chocolate."

"I never said that. I don't eat it a lot. That's not the same as not liking it. And those things were so good."

"I know. We're on the third batch. I eat any more and lie on top of you like this, I'm going to flatten you like a pancake."

"Sweetheart, with the way you run around this place doing everything, you're never going to gain an ounce. Even if you did, I wouldn't complain." He slid his hands down her back and over her ass.

"Mmm. Sweet-talking me. What do you want?"

"More of this." He rolled her to his side and kissed her long and deep, then held her close. "You didn't answer me. What are you doing in town?"

"I'm going to the courthouse to pull the land records."

His gaze locked with hers. "Why?"

"I want to know if they can tell me why your father wants this place so bad."

"You found the copy in my grandfather's papers."

"That was the tax assessment. I want the deed for the original purchase of the land."

"Actually, he inherited it from Great-grandpa Austin Jones."

"You're named after him." She liked that he'd gotten a family name. And not his dad's.

"My father wanted to name me after his father, Oliver. My mother refused to use that as my first name."

"You don't look like an Oliver." She made circles with her thumbs and index fingers and put them over his eyes. "Maybe if you had thick black glasses and were six inches shorter with a paunch belly."

Austin smacked her bottom. "Stop, or I'll insist we name our firstborn Oliver."

She caught her breath, then took the joke for what it was and said, "Our daughter would hate you forever for naming her that."

He laughed and the tension eased out of him, too.

This thing between them seemed to be going fast, but it also felt natural and like they'd known each other forever.

"We'll give her a beautiful name like her mother's."

She brushed her hand over his golden hair and wondered if their child would have his coloring or hers or something in between. She'd love a little girl with her dark hair and his brilliant blue eyes. "So you're Austin Oliver Hubbard."

"That's me. You know what? How do I not know your last name?"

"You never asked." She rolled to her back and stared up at the ceiling.

"What's wrong?"

"You never asked if one of my great-uncles is my father."

Austin levered himself up on his elbow and stared down at her. "I don't care who your father is one way or the other. It doesn't change who you are and how I feel about you."

She sighed, then opened up about her past. "My mother believes it's a boy who used to pay my great-uncles to let him be with her. He was in high school. He treated her well. He liked her, brought her little treats and presents. They used to sneak and see each other without my great-uncles knowing. She says I look like him."

"You look like your mother, but taller, and a lot less fragile."

She smiled at that. "Whether it's wishful thinking or true, I don't know." She sighed again, the pressure to hold all this in too great to bear. "When her father finally took her and me to the clinic after she gave birth, the doctor asked what name to put on the birth certificate. She told him she wasn't sure about the father. He said she could leave it blank, but

I needed a last name. She asked if she had to use hers. She didn't want me to have the same last name as her uncles. The doctor said she could give me any name, even though it would be harder to prove I'm her child in the future with our different names without the birth certificate. She didn't care. She named me what she wanted."

Austin brushed his fingers up and down her arm in a gentle caress that raised goose bumps on her skin. "What did she name you?"

Sonya gave a side-eye look and tried to hold back a smile. "Remember she was only fourteen."

His grin brightened his eyes with interest. "What is it?"

"Sonya Daphne Tucker. *Sonya* because the guy she really liked and believed could be my father had a sister with that name. *Daphne* from her favorite cartoon. She never saw the show, but a teacher gave her a book to help her improve her reading skills. She read it over and over again."

"*Scooby-Doo*." Austin chuckled. "One of my favorites, too. Daphne was hot."

Sonya smacked him on the shoulder and they laughed together.

"And Tucker?"

"Tanya Tucker. Her favorite country singer. She started singing when she was a teenager and my mother wanted her life."

"Being a superstar, singing and traveling, seemed like a much better life than the one she lived."

"Exactly. But Tanya's real life was a country song in and of itself with love and loss and drug and alcohol abuse. Like everyone, she lived through highs and lows. What my mother really wanted was a simple, carefree life."

"How come she didn't give you the boy's last name?"

"She didn't want to get him in trouble. What if I wasn't his? People would ask who got her pregnant. She couldn't say for sure one way or the other, but she could point the finger at a lot of people who would have wanted to shut her up. Several of them threatened her, so why say anything?"

"It's sad." Austin traced his finger down her shoulder and along her arm. "When I met her, I knew what happened, but all I saw was a loving mom who adored her daughter."

"She does. But the early years were hard. I have my resentments."

"How did she get away from her family?"

Sonya sighed. "Her mother had never crossed her father or stood up to the uncles, but she saw that even after I was born the uncles were never going to leave June be. Her mother hadn't saved June and tried to save me. She feared that in a few short years they'd start in on me the way they had with June. So she scraped together every dime and dollar she could for several months, pretended she needed June to help her do the grocery run, and put June and me on a bus when I was about eighteen months old. My mother ended up in Kansas City with ten dollars and a toddler. A cop busted her for panhandling. Instead of sticking her in foster care, which she vowed to run away from because to her families hurt kids, he took us to a shelter. It didn't take long for her to meet a guy who said he'd take care of her.

"Predators like that have an eye for finding vulnerable girls. He kept her so long as she turned tricks for him. When he got rough, she left him. Repeat that cycle a few more times and she's in Vegas with another loser with big promises but who is only using her.

"Big Mama found me panhandling on the sidewalk outside one of the big casinos. She wanted to know why I wasn't in school. I told her I was hungrier for food than book smarts. She asked if I had people and I told her enough about my mom for her to understand the situation. She asked if I wanted a real home where no one would ever hurt me or my mother and there was always food and I could go to school every day."

"I bet that sounded like heaven."

"It sounded like every other bullshit empty promise I'd ever heard. But then she handed me a fancy card with a vine of roses over the outline of a mansion."

Austin traced the vine tattoo winding its way over her hip and thigh. "The Wild Rose Ranch."

"I didn't know what kind of ranch, but I knew expensive when I saw it in the embossed card." Sonya sighed. "She made me believe her when she told me there was another girl living there who was just like me."

"Roxy."

"She promised me a friend and that my mother would never have to answer to a man ever again."

"Did June want to go?"

"I didn't give her a choice. She'd made all the decision for us up to that point. I told her either we went together, or I was going alone." Sonya saw the past so clearly. "We stood on the wide porch of that gorgeous house wearing discarded clothes from the Goodwill, paper sacks in our hands with our few belongings, stick thin, and praying for a miracle." Sonya choked back tears. "Big Mama opened those doors and changed our lives."

Austin traced the largest rose, a symbol for her, the smaller ones for her sisters, on the vine tattoo. "Were you happy there?"

"Yes. I mean, my mother was still selling herself for money, but we were safe and fed and had a family of sorts. I was behind in school, but Big Mama hired a tutor. I caught up and excelled, graduating top of my class in high school and college. I had every opportunity. I wanted that for my mother. But the life she was living in that mansion, making money that she got to keep, that's so much better than where she came from, she's content to take what she's been given and be grateful."

"How did her uncles find her?"

One of her few resentments toward her mother. Sonya tried to hold back the anger. "I want to blame her, but how can I fault her for wanting to stay in touch with her mom?"

"She called home," Austin guessed, shaking his head.

"A couple times a year. But this time she wanted her mom to know she lived in a big house and made lots of money."

"And your uncles couldn't wait to get a piece of that."

Sonya rolled over and laid her chin on her hand on his chest, her thoughts on the past and how her mother was doing now. She'd call her later.

Austin brushed his fingers through her hair. "Do you want to take that job and go back to the Ranch?"

She still hesitated when it came to rejecting the job offer, but, yes, she loved being with Austin. She picked at nonexistent lint on the sheet by his shoulder. "Not really. It's time for a change."

He gently tugged a lock of her hair. "Do you think you'd be happy living here?"

She met his earnest gaze. "I am happy here."

He leaned in and kissed her softly. "Good." He kissed her again, long and deep and filled with promise. He broke the kiss and groaned under his breath. "As much as I want to wallow away the day in bed with you . . ." He squeezed her ass to give her a hint of what he'd like to do again. "I need to go feed the horses."

She kissed him quick, then rolled off him. "I'll make breakfast for us before I head into town. Anything you want me to pick up while I'm gone?"

"I'll let you know before you go, but all I really want is you to hurry back to me."

She shifted back to him, put her hand on his cheek, and pressed her forehead to his. "People are always in such a hurry to go, go, go. Right here, right now, you and me, this is heaven."

"Let's stay in heaven a little while longer." His kiss sparked a fire that brought them together again in a passionate embrace that had their hearts beating as one as their bodies moved in perfect harmony until they reached an explosive crescendo and they lay content and wrapped in each other's arms once again.

Safe. Happy. Together.

Everything she'd ever wanted in her life.

Chapter Twenty

Sonya stood at the counter below the Records sign, waiting for the courthouse employee to finish her personal phone call.

"I'm telling you, she bought that cute little house on Pine Drive. She's setting up a place to run her girls. Every man for miles will be visiting that place the minute it's open for business. Moths to the flame. You'll see. People were talking about this happening when John made that woman come to town, but then we all thought she was legit, but turns out, not so much."

Sonya imagined her sharp gaze blasting the woman's head clean open like a laser strike. "That girl" had to be her sister Roxy, who hadn't told her anything about buying a place on Pine.

The woman turned and jumped back a step. Her hand flew to her chest. "Oh my God. I didn't see you there."

"Obviously. You're too busy talking out your ass and telling lies." Sonya leaned on the counter like she had all the time in the world for . . . Darla, according to her name tag, to get her shit together.

"Gotta go." She swiped her cell phone screen and stuffed the phone into her back pocket. "Uh, what can I do for you?"

"Stop talking about my sister. After that, I'd like you to pull the property records under Alan Jones and Austin Hubbard."

"Well, now, Austin inherited his granddaddy's ranch. Everyone knows that."

"If it's all the same, I'd like the records going back to when the property was originally purchased, handed down to Alan Jones, then turned over to Austin."

"Well, to go back that far I'll need to pull the microfiche. We've only got the records on computer going back to 1980. The rest are being added to the system, but it's a slow process."

"I'm happy to look through the microfiche if you pull them for me. Research is kind of my thing."

Darla tilted her head. "Really?"

Sonya nodded, confirming that even in jeans and a plaid button-down she remained a nerd. "I'm a forensic accountant."

"So you know how to hide all the money the brothel makes."

Sonya rolled her eyes. "It's a legitimate legal business. No hiding money. No hiding what the girls there do for a living. They pay federal taxes just like everyone else. Though most people think it's in Vegas, it's illegal to operate a brothel in Clark County. The mansion is located in Pahrump, which is in Nye County and is the closest to Vegas. Customers either drive out or are picked up at the airport or their hotel by limo and driven out."

"Really?"

"Really. It's a whole experience and people pay top dollar to visit the Ranch."

Darla leaned on the counter and said under her breath, "Women, too?"

"All kinds of people."

Darla stood and leaned back, surprise and acceptance in her nod and slight grin. "Wow."

"Which is why Roxy is not setting something up out here. That would be illegal and Wild Rose makes enough money she doesn't need to take the risk of setting up an illegal operation when she could simply open another site in another Nevada county that allows prostitution if she wanted to, which she doesn't."

"Huh. Okay." Darla typed into her computer and scribbled notes on a pad of paper. "If you want to look at the records yourself, come on back." She pressed a button under the counter and Sonya pushed open the gate. "Take a seat there. I'll get the films."

Sonya sat in the squeaky wood swivel chair and turned on the microfiche reader. It hummed to life. While she waited, she pulled out her cell and called Roxy.

"Hey, sis, how's that hunky cowboy you're shacking up with?"

Sonya smiled, happy Roxy had come around and accepted her relationship with Austin. "How's the one you're with?"

"Amazing." Roxy deserved the kind of happiness that put that sparkle in her voice.

"Mine, too."

"I can't wait to come over and see the new horses."

"Come to dinner tonight." Sonya could stop by the store and pick up some steaks to toss on the grill. Austin wouldn't mind having Noah and Roxy out to their place.

Huh. Their place?

Yeah, that felt right.

She'd had a possessive streak about the house when they began the renovation and all her ideas took shape, but living there with Austin really did make it feel more like hers. And theirs.

"Sonya?" The annoyance in Roxy's voice alerted her that she'd missed whatever Roxy said.

"Huh. Sorry. I got lost in thought."

"Do you want me to bring anything?"

"No. I've got dinner covered. But the reason I called is because I heard you bought a house on Pine Drive."

"How did you hear that?" More than surprise filled Roxy's voice.

"Gossip runs through this town like a raging river."

"That's for sure. Um, I did buy a place." A hint of deception filled her voice.

"Why? What do you need it for?"

"An investment. A rental. I need to do something with all the money I have now." It sounded good, but something still didn't ring true. "After you spent all that time fixing up Austin's place, I got the reno bug and thought I'd do my own project and fix the place up. You know how much I love to do that."

True. "Well, let me know if you need help. I can put together a rental contract, figure out rent and the deposit and advertising to get a renter."

"That's a little ways off. I'll let you know when I'm ready."

Darla set the films she needed next to the reader.

"Listen, Rox, I gotta go. See you tonight."

"Sonya."

"Yeah."

"I'm glad you're happy here. I love having you nearby and doing dinner night. We should make it a usual thing now that Austin's place is done."

"I'd like that." They were all going their separate ways, starting their own lives. But a standing weekly dinner together would keep them connected.

"We'll have Adria and Juliana out soon, too," Roxy added.

"About Juliana . . ." Her heart ached thinking about how Juliana was running down a path to self-destruction.

"She's got stuff going on. I know. Adria thinks we're going to have to step in and do something about it whether Juliana likes it or not."

"Keep me posted. I'm in when you need me." They'd always stuck together. Nothing would change that.

"See you tonight. We'll talk about it then." Roxy hung up.

Sonya glanced up at Darla. "Thanks for getting these for me."

Darla pointed to the two sets of films. "These are for the Jones men." She handed a printout to Sonya. "Those are the records for changing Mr. Jones's land over to Austin. There's a map included that shows the entire acreage."

"Got it. Thank you."

"If you print out the ones for the Joneses, make two copies. I'll scan them into the new system. One less thing to do as we work our way back in the records. And that way if you need them again, they'll be easier to find." Darla went back to her work area.

Sonya set aside Austin's records and slipped the first film in the reader and maneuvered the guide up, down, and sideways until she found the right ones. She printed out each page without really looking at them. She'd go through all of them once she got home.

Twenty minutes later, she handed the second set of copies to Darla. "Thanks for your help."

"No problem. That'll be thirty-five dollars for the copies."

Sonya couldn't believe the fee, but paid and accepted her receipt.

"If you need anything else, come on back."

Sonya smiled and waved goodbye. Despite Darla gossiping about things she knew nothing about, she was a nice lady. She wasn't trying to hurt anyone. Sonya needed to remember that the next time she overheard someone talking out of turn.

She walked outside and shielded her eyes from the bright sun. She jogged down the steps and headed for her truck, her hand deep in her bag as she rummaged for the keys. She pulled them out and tried to press the button on the key fob, but someone shoved her into the driver's door. Taken off guard, she cracked her head against the window frame. A blast of pain shot through her skull. A man put his hand over her face, covering her eyes so she couldn't see him. His body held her pinned against the door.

A shiver of fear went through her whole body at the intimate contact and her inability to see what happened next. Her mind veered into dark thoughts about him hurting or killing her.

She'd never see Austin again. That thought nearly stopped her heart.

He ripped the papers out of her hand and leaned into her ear. "If you know what's good for you, go back to Vegas where you belong."

No way she went down without a fight. She tried to elbow the guy in the gut to get him off her. She even tried to kick him with her heel, but nothing she did worked to overpower or back off the bigger stronger man.

The guy kicked her feet out from under her and shoved her down at the same time. She landed hard on her hands, scraping her palms and wrists. By the time she turned, her attacker took off around the back of the truck. But the glimpse she got of him reminded her of the guy who came to Austin's place with his father.

She rolled over onto her butt and brushed the pavement grit from her hands. She hissed in a breath when a particularly bloody scrape stung. She blew on the cut and took a few breaths to calm her racing heart.

She'd dropped her purse during the altercation and picked up her sunglasses, lip gloss, wallet, and two pens and stuffed them back in her brown leather bag.

She got up slowly. Her head throbbed and swelled where she'd hit it on the truck. Her body had taken quite a jarring with the guy slamming into her from behind and dumping her to the ground.

She stood, braced her hand on the truck hood, took a minute to let the shock wear off, and headed back into the courthouse.

Darla looked up when the doorbell dinged. "Back already." Darla's gaze shot to the side of her head. "What happened? Did you fall on the steps?"

"Nope. Someone wanted the records I printed out more than I did."

Darla picked up the phone. "I'm calling the cops."

Sonya took a seat by the window and waited for Darla to tell the dispatcher what happened.

"They're on the way."

Sonya tried to hold her trembling hands still. "Great. Until then, can you make me another copy of the documents?"

Darla nodded. "Yeah, sure, but it's going to cost you."

"It already has," she said under her breath. When Darla raised an eyebrow, she waved her on. "I'll pay the fee."

Darla laid her forearms on the counter and leaned over them. "If they wanted the papers so bad, why didn't they come in here and get them?"

"They just didn't want me to have them."

Darla narrowed her eyes. "But I can get them for you again."

Sonya's lips drew into a lopsided frown. "I know. Stupid, right?"

By the time Darla returned with the copies, a deputy sheriff arrived to take her statement about the assault and robbery, not that the papers were worth anything.

"So you think the guy works for Walter Hubbard."

"Yes. I recognized him from the night he and Walter came to Austin's house."

"You said the altercation happened so fast you only caught a glimpse of the man. Are you sure it was him?"

"As sure as I can be after having my head bashed in and the adrenaline rush of being scared out of my wits."

"You gave him what he wanted and survived. That's what counts." The deputy closed his notebook and handed her his card. "If you think of anything more, give me a call. I'll look into the matter and get back to you with what I find out."

"Thank you." Sonya stood, a little off balance on her shaky legs.

"Are you sure you don't want to go to the hospital and get that bump looked at?"

"I'll be okay." She touched the swollen lump. "It probably looks worse than it is."

The officer stuffed his notebook back in his shirt pocket. "Can I call someone to pick you up?"

"I'm fine. Really. Thank you for your assistance and taking the report."

"I'll do my best to put the guy away."

She appreciated his reassurance, though just like he did, she knew whoever did this would probably get away with it. She'd only gotten a glimpse of him. Mr. Hubbard would make sure his man had an alibi.

Her word against his.

The deputy patted her shoulder and headed back out to his cruiser to follow up on the lead she gave him. She paid Darla for the copies and headed out to her truck once again. She made herself drive over to the grocery store for steaks, keeping the papers tucked into her purse. She endured the stares from the other shoppers because of her injuries. Paranoid, she watched all the cars behind her as she drove out of town and back to the ranch.

Austin's truck wasn't in the driveway. He said he had fencing to put up and repair before the cattle arrived. She went into the house, locked the door, put the food in the fridge, and cleaned the cuts on her hands and the goose egg just above her temple.

Home and safe—she hoped—she went into the office, sorted the courthouse records and Grandpa Alan's files. Time to go through them and make sense of what seemed like a no-brainer. Austin inherited the property, but what else had Grandpa Alan brought into Austin's life?

Why steal public records from her?

Why did Mr. Hubbard want the land so badly?

The answers had to be here. She wouldn't quit until she found them.

Chapter Twenty-One

Austin hadn't worked this hard in longer than he could remember, and that included all the work he'd done on the house. His body ached with fatigue, but it only reminded him how much he'd accomplished since this project began. Every tight muscle told him he'd worked for each step forward. He'd take the pain and reap the benefits because he was damn proud of the effort he'd put into restoring the ranch.

Little by little his dream took shape into reality.

He pulled the last coil of barbed wire from the back of his truck, hung it on the hook in the barn, and pulled off his dusty work gloves. Done for the day, he rolled his sore shoulders and headed for the house. He couldn't wait to see Sonya and tell her about his day.

He loved their evenings together.

It made the house feel even more like a home.

And every sweet night with her made him want more.

The fact she hadn't said yes to the job made him think she wanted to stay. He hoped she felt safe enough to turn it down soon and find something here that made her happy, because the more he accomplished, the less she had to do. He didn't want idleness to drive her away.

His stomach grumbled, anticipating food. He hoped she'd cooked. If not, they'd make something together and have a beer to wind down for the day. Maybe they'd watch a movie or one of those home and garden shows she liked.

She wanted to put in some plants around the house. Another thing to add to the list, but if it made her happy, he was all in for digging holes.

Whatever made the house feel more like her home, the better.

Noah's truck came down the drive, headed for the house. Austin met Roxy and Noah and walked up the steps to the porch with them.

"What are you two doing here?"

Roxy looked up at him. "Sonya invited us to dinner."

"Cool. Who wants a beer?"

"Looks like you need one." Noah slapped him on the shoulder and sent up a cloud of dust around him. He coughed and waved his hand to clear the air.

"Right after I run through a quick shower and change." Austin reached for the door and nearly slammed into it when it didn't budge. He stared at the door, confused. "She locked the door."

Noah and Roxy gave him the same something-is-off look he felt speeding up his heart.

"She must not be used to living in the country." He knocked on the door, feeling silly because it was his house.

Sonya unlocked and opened the door with the phone to her ear. She turned immediately and walked back into the living room. "Of course he had an alibi. I expected nothing less."

Austin glanced to Roxy to see if she knew what Sonya was talking about. Roxy shook her head and touched her wrist, then pointed to Sonya.

He saw the bandage and took Sonya's arm and turned her to him. The bruise and lump on her head just above her temple made him see red. "What the hell happened to you?"

"Deputy, thank you for calling with the update." She planted her hand on Austin's chest to hold him off another minute. "Yes, I'll be careful. Goodbye."

Austin cupped her face and studied the brightly colored bruise. "Sweetheart, what happened? Are you okay?"

To his horror, tears welled in her eyes, though she tried hard to blink them away. "I'm fine."

Roxy came forward and stood next to them. "Who hit you?"

Sonya sucked in a breath and looked up at him. "I went to the courthouse to get the property records. I must have been followed."

"By whom?" He didn't need to ask. This had his father stamped all over it.

"That guy your father had with him the night he showed up here. I think."

"You think?" He knew, just as well as she did.

"He came up behind me and shoved me into the side of the truck. I hit my head." She touched her fingers to the edge of the wound. "He took the papers I got from the courthouse and basically told me to go back to Vegas."

"What happened to your hands?" Roxy gently held one, showing the scratches on the heel of Sonya's palm and wrist.

"He kicked my feet out from under me and pushed me to the ground so he could get away. Darla at Records called the cops. I filed a report, but it won't go anywhere because your father alibied his guy."

"Well, it's on record. If he tries something else, you've got a paper trail to establish a pattern." Roxy and Sonya gave each other a nod.

"A pattern. I'm going to fucking kill him for laying a hand on you." Austin spun around and got caught up short when Noah grabbed hold of his shoulders and stopped him. "Let me go."

Sonya wriggled between them and held his sides. "It won't do any good to go over there cussing and yelling. You'll only play right into his hands. He'll have *you* arrested. And while of course I'll bail you out, I'm kind of tired and would like to just have a nice dinner with our friends. Please."

The weariness in her eyes and words tore him to pieces and eased the rage roiling inside him. "Christ, Sonya. Come here." He wrapped her in a hug and held her close. He didn't like the tremble in her body one bit. Retelling what happened brought the fear back and he hated that she'd been scared and hurt and he hadn't been there to protect her. "Why didn't you call me and tell me what happened?"

"Because it was done and I knew you'd probably go after your father and that guy. Plus, I had to get another set of documents, which cost me another thirty-five bucks."

He liked that she'd shifted her anger from what happened to the expense. Back to her old self.

"Why take the papers in the first place when they are so easily replaced?" Roxy asked.

Sonya stepped back, but not out of his reach. He needed to touch her, feel her, know that she was okay.

"Why, indeed?" She took his hand. "Come see what I've put together so far." She pulled him toward the office.

Roxy and Noah followed. Austin stood in front of the desk with Roxy and Noah while Sonya went to the other side.

"Let me tell you a story about the Jones family." She picked up an old black-and-white photo of a family on the porch of a simple log cabin. The woman wore a long dress and held an infant in her arms. Beside her stood a man in a hat, wearing dark pants, worn work boots, a white shirt, and suspenders. Austin took after all the men in the Jones family. "Back in the day, Austin Jones came west from Missouri to build a better life for his family." She picked up a paper that had been under the photo. "According to property records, he bought a large parcel of land for a modest price. He built a home using timber from the land he owned." She picked up an old yellowed envelope. "He wrote to his wife in Missouri and told her he'd picked the perfect place. They had timber, running water, and grassy land. Enough to run a huge herd of fat cattle. He'll send for her and their child, your grandfather, as soon as he sells some of the timber and has the money."

"Okay, so my great-grandfather owned the land."

"Yes." She pointed to the map and the yellow highlighted area she'd colored. "He owned all of this."

"But—"

"Hold that thought. There's more." She held up another yellowed envelope. "A month after your great-grandfather wrote his wife the first time, he sent her another letter. In it he tells her he's struck it rich."

"How?" Roxy asked.

Sonya smiled. "He found a big-ass sapphire when one of the trees he was cutting down got away from him and fell, roots and all. There in the dirt, he found a treasure."

Roxy turned to him. "Didn't you say something to me about treasure when I made the offer to help you build the ranch?"

"Those were just bedtime stories my grandfather told me." He stared at the envelope Sonya held. "Unless they weren't. But everyone knows Montana is rich with sapphires. That's why my father started mining them."

"Wait. I've got more." Sonya held up another printout. "The local newspaper put their archive online a couple years ago. They're ahead of the courthouse in that respect." Sonya waved her hand. "Anyway, I found an old article. The sapphire your great-grandfather found was one of the largest ever discovered in the area. He took it to San Francisco and sold it for four hundred thousand dollars. A fortune back then. He could have lived a big life, but instead, he came back here and ranched and raised his son and was happy."

She spread the pictures out on the desk, showing a simple life here on the ranch.

"I don't have his financial records, but I'm guessing he had some lean years and used that nest egg to see the family through those rough times. He also bought another piece of land." She pointed to the blue highlighted area on the map.

He pointed to one of the photos of his grandfather atop a horse with the house in the background. "My great-grandparents added onto that small timber cabin and lived there until they passed. When Grandpa Alan married, he built this house for his bride. My mother grew up here. My great-grandparents' cabin and barn burned down in a wildfire when I was a teenager. No one had lived there in a long time."

"And when your mother married your father, your grandfather gifted them a piece of land." She pointed to the orange shaded area of the map.

"Yes, but the property is much larger than that."

Sonya eyed him. "What? Not according to the records."

He picked up the green highlighter and shaded in the area around the orange plot of land. "Blue Mining stretches out and around the property where the house, ranch, and original mining took place."

"Hmm. Okay, so your father mined the original property, found sapphires, and used the money from selling them to buy more land?"

Austin shrugged. "I guess so."

"Why didn't your grandfather and great-grandfather mine for sapphires when they knew there had to be more on the property?" Sonya stared at the map. "If there are sapphires here"—she pointed to the area his father now owned—"there had to be some here." She pointed to the yellow section of the original property his great-grandfather bought.

"Mining is an expensive undertaking with only the hope of a big payoff. These were simple ranching men. You said it yourself, the amount of money he got from that one score was a fortune. My grandfather always used to say, 'Count your blessings and be happy with what you have.'"

Roxy put her hand on the map. "So what you're saying is that Mr. Hubbard knows there are more sapphires on this land. That's why he wants it."

"It's the obvious answer," Sonya confirmed. "When Austin partnered with you, someone who's got a lot of money, Mr. Hubbard must have thought you'd go into the mining business and take what he feels should belong to him because he was married to Austin's mother. Had she survived her father, she, and Mr. Hubbard, in turn, would have inherited the land."

Roxy planted her hands on her hips. "Instead Austin owns it and Mr. Hubbard can't touch the land."

"What the hell does it matter? Mr. Hubbard has more money than he'll ever spend," Noah pointed out. "Is he that selfish and vindictive he wants it just because he thinks it should be his? Austin is his flesh and blood."

"I didn't say it made perfect sense. It's just the most logical answer based on the facts." Sonya held up a bank statement. "The thing I don't get is what happened to the money?"

"The four hundred grand?" Austin shook his head. "When my grandfather passed, he had a pittance in the bank. I used it and what I had to pay off his debt and the property taxes."

"Your grandfather kept everything, including years of bank statements. I'll go through them and see what they tell me."

"Let it go, Sonya. We know why he wants the land. Maybe in a few years I'll have the money to dig up some of the property. Maybe we'll get lucky and hit it big. Maybe all we'll end up with is a bunch of piles of dirt."

A buzzer went off in the kitchen.

Sonya sighed. "The baked potatoes should be done. Go take a shower. I'll put the steaks on the barbecue. Dinner will be ready when you join us."

Austin stared down at the stacks of papers and the map. "This is good work, but it's not worth you getting hurt. I'm really sorry."

Roxy and Noah left them to deal with the incessant buzzer and give Austin a moment alone with Sonya.

She walked around the desk and right into his arms. "I'm okay."

He held her tighter. "If something happened to you . . ." He leaned back, brushed his fingers through her hair, and kissed the spot just above the worst of the bruised lump. "If he touches you again, I'll kill him."

"Let's hope the cops persuaded him to stay away from now on."

"I don't like you feeling like you have to lock the doors to be safe here."

"I just got rattled. You're home now and I'm fine."

Austin kissed her forehead again. "I won't let anything else happen to you."

She knew he meant that all the way to his soul, but if Austin's father didn't give up his quest to get Austin to sell the land, she had a feeling he was coming back for more.

Chapter Twenty-Two

I told you to follow Sonya, not attack her."

Kelly's heart stopped at those angry words. She stood outside Walter's study, listening through the closed door.

Her behavior at the grocery store still embarrassed and shamed her. The more out of reach the things she wanted seemed, the more she acted like someone she didn't know. After growing up with modest means, all she wanted was security and a family of her own.

"She came out of the courthouse with the papers. I thought you'd want to know what she's up to and see them."

"If you'd simply reported that she went to the Records office I could have simply bribed that dimwit who works there to tell me what Sonya requested, confirming she didn't pull the documents she needs to prove—"

"What?" Walter's lackey asked.

"None of your damn business."

Kelly didn't understand what they were talking about, but no doubt her soon-to-be husband was trying to hide something. He liked to hide everything from her. Sometimes he treated her like a child, telling her not to worry, he'd take care of her. It didn't always bother her. But his obsession with getting back at Austin, for what, she didn't know, had made him short-tempered, and she didn't like it one bit.

What happened to the sweet generous man who'd swept her off her feet? She missed *him*. She wanted *him* back.

But it was starting to feel like one of those relationships where the abused wife states to the officer why she shot him instead of letting him abuse her again, *He wasn't like this before we got married. Two weeks into the marriage, everything changed. I married a monster.*

Maybe her imagination had gotten away from her. But Walter's behavior didn't match the man she'd fallen for even though she'd had her reservations about dating Austin's father.

If he'd just give this up so they could live their lives and let Austin live his.

"I'll keep my distance," Walter's man promised.

"You have two objectives. Follow her to determine if she goes to the bank. And given the chance, you're supposed to get into the house and search for that damn key."

"I'll try, but one of them is always around. If Austin hires help, it's going to be near impossible to get in there unseen."

"Keep trying."

"What about Kelly?" the man asked. "She got into it with Sonya and Austin right in the middle of the grocery store."

Kelly couldn't see what was happening in the room, but she bet that bit of news put a frown on Walter's face and narrowed his eyes with disapproval. "She won't be here much longer. Since she couldn't get Austin to impregnate her with my grandchild and she hasn't gotten pregnant with my child, I'll cut her loose. I'm thinking a surrogate is the better way to go. I get the child and save myself the trouble of a meddling mother." Those callous words cut deep.

"That's expensive, isn't it?"

"So is a wife," Walter snapped.

Kelly stepped back as if stricken. She couldn't believe the coldhearted way he talked about her and getting a child, like it was a to-do item on his list and not a precious gift.

Kelly held up the positive pregnancy test in her shaking hand she'd taken ten minutes ago upstairs. Her earlier exuberance and sheer joy faded to anger and worry. After what she'd heard, what happened now? Walter wasn't the man she believed him to be. She truly was a means to an end. He didn't care about her, only what he wanted from her.

Austin had tried to warn her, but she hadn't listened.

Rage and embarrassment heated her face and ears. She'd played right into Walter's hands. She'd left a good man, hurt him, for a dream and a promise that wasn't real.

Hurt, her heart aching, she fought back tears and quietly walked upstairs to the bedroom, pulled her cell phone out of her pocket, and called Austin.

"What do you want now? A kidney?"

His harsh words made her heart break even more, the sharp pieces knifing pain through her chest. "I deserve that after the deplorable way I acted. I'm truly sorry to you and Sonya. I'm calling with an olive branch. Keep your house locked. Make sure someone is always around your place. Your father is looking for a key he believes is in your house."

"A key to what?"

"That's all I know." She sighed, holding back tears, knowing she carried the baby she'd always wanted, but for the wrong man. "Austin."

"Yeah."

"I shouldn't have left you."

"I don't know what to say to that, Kelly. We had our problems before I went broke."

That was a truth she didn't want to face either. "Does she make you happy?"

"Extremely."

Kelly smiled sadly. He hadn't said that to hurt her. She'd seen it in his eyes when he looked at Sonya. He'd stood up for Sonya and defended her fiercely. He loved Sonya in a way he'd never loved her. "I'm happy for you." She meant it.

"I wish I could say the same to you, but I can hear it in your voice. Something's wrong."

"Every choice we make has consequences. I have to live with mine. Find the key. He won't stop until he gets it. Also, he said he didn't care about Sonya going to the courthouse, but he wanted to know if she went to the bank. She's smart. I'm sure she'll figure out why."

Sonya was smart enough to hold on to a good man.

Kelly hung up and wiped her eyes a split second before the bedroom door opened.

Walter stared at her, an accusation in his eyes. "Who were you talking to?"

"No one."

"I heard voices."

She held up her cell phone. "I was watching a show."

His eyes narrowed. "Why didn't you watch downstairs?"

"Why were the police here?" she shot back.

Annoyance replaced the suspicion in his eyes. She'd learned not to question him, but she refused to just go along anymore.

"Deputy sheriff," he corrected her. He loved to point out her mistakes, big, small, and inconsequential. "Someone scared that woman living with Austin. Of course, she blamed it on me."

"Did she get hurt?"

"Why would you care? She's turned Austin against you."

"I did that all on my own." She tightened her grip on the pregnancy test she kept hidden in her hand.

"You got out before he dragged you down with him." He undid his watch and set it on the bedside table. "Anyway, she's fine. And she'll stay that way so long as she keeps her nose out of my business." He issued that threat the same way he ordered lunch. Like it was nothing. Like it couldn't come back and hurt him.

"So you are responsible."

His head came around slowly and his gaze locked with hers. "Careful, Kelly. That sounds suspiciously like your loyalty lies with them and not me."

After what she'd overheard, she could no longer ignore that voice inside her that said she'd been taken in by a master manipulator and someone willing to hurt others to get what he wanted.

And one of the things he wanted was another child. What would he do to keep their child when she didn't stay with him? Because now that she'd seen this side of him, she wanted out. Now. For her sake, and her child's.

"Why are you doing this to Austin?" She'd asked that question a dozen times and numerous ways and never got a straight answer. "Why not talk to him and find a compromise? Work together, instead of pushing him away."

"You don't know what you're talking about."

"You're right. I don't get it. Austin doesn't get it."

"I don't owe you an explanation."

"Maybe if you explain it to Austin he'll be more agreeable about giving you what you want. Or at least working with you again."

Walter shook his head, his eyes dark with contempt. "I didn't work this hard for all these years, take the risks I've taken, all to lose control of the business."

That took a turn she hadn't expected. "Why would you lose control of the business?"

"Are you trying to start an argument by testing me? Is Austin more important to you than I am? Because it seems like you're taking his side when that ring on your finger means a promise that you're on my side no matter what."

She never thought the engagement ring symbolized her vow of blind faith and devotion. She'd done that to a degree. Up until now. "I'm trying to better understand your side."

"I own the company. What I say goes. That land should have come to me. Austin could have avoided all of this if he'd accepted my offer to buy it. He'd have had money and you. Instead, he chose the land over both. Maybe you've forgotten that."

True. And false. It went deeper than one or the other. Austin chose to stand up for himself against his father's authoritarian rule in his life.

Do as I say without question.

Not anymore.

Not for Austin or for her.

Walter closed the distance between them. She quelled the need to step back out of his reach. He brushed his hand through her hair and settled it on her shoulder in a practiced move meant to soothe her, but that now seemed calculated. "Stop worrying. This will all be over soon. Stress will only make it that much harder on your body to get pregnant. Focus on us, not someone who means nothing to you anymore."

She and Austin may not be together, but that didn't mean she didn't care about him. She regretted turning her back on what might have been. Maybe one day they could at least be friends again.

She wanted to believe telling Walter about the baby she now carried would change things between them. She thought he'd *focus on them.* But he'd made it clear he had no intention of letting the matter with Austin drop.

And thinking he'd change was another lie she'd told herself.

"I'm sorry I don't have good news for you yet." She could lie just as easily as he lied to her.

"It will happen. I always get what I want."

Yeah, even if he had to dump her and use a surrogate. Well, he'd get the child. She couldn't keep the baby a secret for long. But she wasn't sticking around for him to ruin her life. They'd share the child, but not a life.

She stepped around him and headed for the door.

He took her arm to stop her. "Where are you going?"

She pulled free. "Home. The apartment manager promised to fix my dishwasher first thing in the morning. I want everything in working order when I leave the apartment and move in here after we get married." She wanted away from him and time to think about her options. Maybe she'd move to Tucson and live closer to her parents. They'd love to spoil their grandchild.

New place. New people. New life.

Sounded good to her.

"He can get into your place and do it without you there."

"I don't want him alone in my apartment."

He brushed his hand up her arm. "I hoped you'd stay and we'd work on the baby."

She gave him a sad smile. "There's always tomorrow to try again."

Tomorrow was another day and another chance to make a better choice. For her and her child.

Chapter Twenty-Three

Austin folded up the last tarp and dropped it on top of the other four piled on the garage floor. After Kelly's call last night, he and Sonya made sure everything they'd taken out of the house was locked up tight. They still had a lot to donate, but not before they looked through everything and figured out if they had the right key.

Thanks to Sonya's obsessive need for organization, they had an old mayonnaise jar full of keys she found in the kitchen alone. They added eight more miscellaneous keys they'd unearthed in the other items from the house.

He could now count four sets of house keys, car keys to vehicles no longer on the property, and keys to his grandfather's old four-wheeler, which sat under a tarp behind the barn. Maybe he'd give it a once-over and get it working again.

The collection of various little keys could go to anything from a lockbox to a file cabinet. None of them stood out as the key to some hidden treasure.

If they had the key his father wanted, he didn't know it. With as much garbage as they threw out, it could be in the landfill by now. They'd been careful as they went through everything in the house. But let's face it, they couldn't possibly look in every nook and cranny.

"Hey, find anything else?"

He hooked his arm around Sonya's shoulders and hugged her close. "Nothing but the keys we already found."

She leaned into him. "Do we have the one? Or is it lost forever?"

He glanced down at her upturned face. "Your guess is as good as mine."

"If only Kelly knew what the key went to." Sonya turned to stand in front of him. "Why is she helping us?"

He shrugged. "I don't know." He'd been shocked to get the call from her at all last night. He almost didn't pick up after what she'd said to Sonya. But he remembered the devastated look in her eyes when she ran out of the grocery store and his guilt got the better of him. He didn't like being mean. "My father is all about loyalty, though he expects it instead of earning it. She stayed with him even after he sent her to me to . . . I don't even want to think about what he expected her to do."

"So something happened that turned her against him."

"Maybe." He shrugged. "Or maybe she just wanted to do something to make up for what she said to you."

"Kelly realized she made a mistake and left the right man for the wrong one."

Austin had put the call on speaker last night because he didn't want any secrets between him and Sonya. He didn't want even the appearance of his ex calling to make Sonya question why she called at all, and if he still had feelings for Kelly.

He didn't.

In fact, his feelings for Sonya grew each and every day.

In other relationships, his feelings were always something he'd put off to think about later. But with Sonya, the question of how he felt and how much he felt stayed front and center. It kept popping up in his mind, making him take notice and think about it. What it meant. How it impacted his future. What he wanted for the future. And ever present was the need to make her happy so she'd stay.

With him.

Because all those thoughts about his future included her. Every decision he made now, he thought about her or asked her to weigh in on the decision.

"Austin?"

"Yeah?"

"I lost you. What are you thinking about?"

"You. Always, you. I wasn't the right man for Kelly. She wasn't the right woman for me. You and me, we're the right fit. At least, that's how I feel."

She placed her hand on his chest. "I feel that way, too."

He pulled her into his arms and held her close. He raked his fingers through her soft hair and pulled the dark strands away from her face and looked down at the bright purple bruise on her head. "I can't believe he hurt you." He kissed her forehead and tamped down the renewed tide of anger washing through his system.

"I'm fine. The scare was worse than the knock to the head." She stepped out of his arms and took his hand. "Come on, there's nothing else to look through out here."

He walked out of the garage and pulled the door closed and locked it with the key they found among the many that matched the one on his grandfather's set of keys.

"You looked through all the toolboxes and cabinets in there, right?"

"Yes, dear. Just like you told me." Austin tried to hold back the grin, but ended up grunting when Sonya popped him in the gut with her fist. "Hey, you'll pay for that." He grabbed her wrist, pulled her toward him, dipped his shoulder, planted it into her waist, and hauled her up and over his shoulder.

She smacked his ass with both hands. "Put me down," she protested through her giggles.

"Not a chance." He walked toward the porch with her draped over him.

"You're going to hurt yourself."

His back hadn't stopped throbbing since they started all the work on the house. Carrying her didn't help, but it was a hell of a lot of fun. "You *are* kind of heavy."

That earned him a huffed-out gasp and her tickling both his sides. He had no choice but to swing her back over his shoulder and set her on the ground before they both fell in the dirt. Before she got away, he reached for her sides and tickled her right back. She laughed, squirmed away, and made a break for it and the house. He followed, leaping up the steps just as she made it through the front door and tried to slam it in his face.

He caught her in the living room and wrapped his arms around her waist and pulled her into his chest. He nibbled at her neck, making her squeal and laugh even more.

The silver spread across the coffee table caught his attention. Blackened utensils, picture frames, and a couple mirrors, bowls, and a large platter. "What's all this?"

"I need to polish them."

He let her go and tilted his head, a thought coming back to him.

"What is it?"

He spun on his heel and headed out to his truck, hoping he was right.

Sonya followed him out. "What's gotten into you?"

He unlocked the passenger door, leaned into the truck, and pulled the box out from under the seat. He held it up to Sonya.

"Oh. Your grandmother's jewelry box. I wondered where that went. I'll polish it with the other items. It'll look pretty on the mantel beside the picture of your grandparents."

"That's not why I came out here to get it. Remember what you said about Granddad protecting and storing important things in a way that they didn't get lost or damaged?"

"Like your grandmother's silverware alone in the drawer beneath the broken oven."

"Exactly. I didn't think anything of it, but when I opened the jewelry box"—he opened the lid so she could see in—"I wondered why she put a matchbox in here with her prized possessions." He nodded for Sonya to take the box out.

The same anticipation he felt brightened her eyes as she slid the matchbox out of the sleeve. They both sucked in a surprised gasp. "A safety-deposit box key."

"Which now makes sense that my father wanted to know if we went to the bank."

Sonya picked up the key to inspect it and the number on the other side. "What do you think is in the box?"

"Let's go find out."

Chapter Twenty-Four

Austin held Sonya's hand as they walked into the bank. For the first time, he had hope that they'd finally have an answer for his father's behavior about the property.

Mr. Foster, the bank manager, spotted him and met them in the wide lobby. "Mr. Hubbard. So nice to see you. My condolences on the loss of your grandfather."

"Thank you, Mr. Foster." Austin held his hand out. "This is my girlfriend, Sonya."

Mr. Foster shook her hand. "So nice to meet you."

"Likewise." Sonya's smile made the other man stand taller.

"I'm here about my grandfather's accounts."

"I wondered when you'd come in."

Austin tilted his head. "Why is that?"

"Well, of course as Mr. Jones's sole heir his checking and savings accounts were transferred to you, but there's also a safety-deposit box that you should check for important papers or items."

"I found the key today actually. Can I get into it?"

"Absolutely. Everything goes to you. Strangely, your father paid the fee on the account for the next five years."

Austin exchanged a look with Sonya. "That was very generous of him."

Or a devious plan. Pay the bill to keep Austin from receiving one and discovering the box, find the key, and make sure Austin never saw what was inside the box.

Mr. Foster frowned. "Well, he wanted to access the box."

"Did you let him?"

Mr. Foster furiously shook his head. "Absolutely not. Only you sign on it now."

So his father couldn't get in it, but keeping Austin out of it served his purpose. Which meant his father knew what was in the box.

Sonya pressed her lips together and eyed the banker. "Was Mr. Hubbard upset you wouldn't let him in the box?"

Mr. Foster's lips pressed flat. "He was . . . displeased."

"I'll bet." Austin had been on the receiving end of his father's displeasure all too often this past year. "I'd like to get into the box."

"This way." Mr. Foster waved his hand toward a high gate that led to the huge vault.

"Did Austin's father ask about anything besides the box?"

Mr. Foster unlocked the security door. Sonya entered the vault ahead of him.

Mr. Foster closed the gate behind them. "He asked if Austin had looked into his accounts."

Austin slipped his key into the lock on box 42. The banker inserted the master key.

Sonya leaned against the small table in the center of the vault. "After we finish with the box, can you pull up all accounts, opened or closed, in Austin's and his grandfather's names?"

Austin pulled the small box out of the wall and set it on the table next to Sonya. "We have the statements," he pointed out.

"I'd just like to see what the bank has on record, so we know we haven't missed anything." As a forensic accountant, Sonya's job meant digging deep into financial records. He liked that she was thorough, though he didn't think they'd find anything more than they already knew.

"I'd be happy to pull the records while you inspect the box." Mr. Foster went to the gate. "Take your time. When you've finished, I'll return to let you out and we'll discuss the accounts." Mr. Foster exited, giving them their privacy.

Austin unlatched the lid but hesitated and glanced at Sonya. "Whatever is in this box, my father wants it."

Sonya laid her hand on his arm, giving him the much-needed comfort and warmth he always craved from her. "Your grandfather hid so many things in the house to protect them. Whatever this is, he needed the added protection of a signature card and vault."

Austin eyed her. "Great. Thanks. That put my mind at ease."

Sonya squeezed his arm. "He wanted to protect you. He left you everything, knowing he could trust you to take care of it. For all we know, he put the matches from his favorite matchbox in there."

A laugh bubbled up his gut. "Let's hope he hadn't gone that crazy."

"You'll never know unless you open the box."

Austin sucked in a breath and held it. He opened the lid, stared at the innocuous papers, and exhaled.

Sonya didn't hesitate to pull them out and spread them open on the table.

Austin stared down at the deed to the ranch with Great-granddad's name. The brittle paper had faded over time, but it was quite a piece of history going back to when the west was settled.

"That matches the copy I got at the courthouse." Sonya tapped the next paper. "That one matches the property transfer to your grandfather when his parents passed away." She pulled the other paper closer. "This is the transfer of land to your father and mother."

"Their wedding gift from Grandpa."

"I pulled this record, too, but there's an attachment to the original I didn't get at the courthouse."

Austin read the contract and swore. "This is what my father stole."

"I don't get it. The land was given to your mother and father. Why did they need a contract?"

"Because my grandfather retained the mineral rights on the land. For me." He pointed to the contract. ". . . Alan Jones owner, or in the event of owner's death, divided equally by all children born to Annie Jones Hubbard."

"He never left the mineral rights to your mother. He always meant for them to go to you."

Austin rubbed at the back of his neck. "Because he didn't trust my father. And that proved right when my father started mining and kept the money."

"So you actually own all the sapphires Blue Mining found and sold."

Austin pointed to another contract. "This is a five-year lease. I own everything he dug up after this lease expired."

"Your grandfather wanted to give your father and mother a good start. Just like his father got when he found that first sapphire. He thought your father would find enough gems to give them a good life."

"But my father wasn't satisfied with enough money to make sure they'd never want for anything. He kept digging. He kept taking."

"Your grandfather wanted the mineral rights to go to your mother's children so they could do the same thing, pull from the land what they needed."

"A legacy that would spread across generations. I see now what my grandfather was trying to tell me. He used to say, 'Wanting more than you need can lead a man to ruin.'"

"Your grandfather filled the house and surrounded himself with more stuff than he needed." Sonya made the point that his grandfather knew what he was talking about.

Austin nodded. "My father chose wealth over his family. Without family, there's no love. Without love, you've got nothing."

Austin had learned that lesson well this past year. He'd had nothing. Then Sonya came into his life and made it worth living with an exuberance he'd never experienced because he was truly happy now.

He raked his fingers through his hair. "So my father didn't want me to find this because I could take his company and nearly all his wealth from him."

"Why didn't your grandfather put a stop to this years ago?"

"Probably because of my mother. As long as she was married to my father, Granddad didn't rock the boat. Maybe he even used this to keep my father in line." Austin rubbed two fingers over his brow. "Their marriage was tumultuous. If my mother ever decided to leave my father, I have no doubt Granddad would have given her this and let her take everything from my father in the divorce. When my mother died, my father and Granddad had several heated arguments over many days. I never knew about what. I was too caught up in my grief to really care. My guess is that Granddad wanted to tell me about this. My father persuaded—*threatened* is probably more accurate—Granddad to let it go. I worked for the company already. I'm my mother's only child. I'll inherit everything anyway."

Sonya laid her hand on his arm. "Except if your father has another child. If you didn't find these documents, he could have left everything to that child if you didn't claim what was rightfully yours."

"Which explains why he didn't want me to see these papers and he's trying to have another child. And it would have been all the better if that child was mine and rightfully heir to this." Austin tipped his head back, stared at the ceiling, and swore.

"It makes sense. He could simply bypass you and leave everything to his grandchild the way your grandfather left everything to you instead of your mother."

"As long as I didn't discover his deception." Austin slammed his fist down on the papers.

"Why not just let you share in the business and the wealth? Why go through all this? Disowning you. Kicking you out of the company. Insisting you sell the land to him. The land isn't as important as you discovering nearly everything your father has made belongs to you."

"He hoped to take over the property and gain the mineral rights and keep digging. Great-granddad found a huge sapphire. It's reasonable to assume there are more. If my dad got the land, he'd get the chance to be even richer. He'd keep me from finding the key that opened this Pandora's box."

"What are you going to do?"

"He's put me in the same position my grandfather was in. I don't have the money to hire an attorney to fight him."

"With this information, an attorney will do the work, knowing they'll get paid when you win. You could even use the property as collateral for a loan." She held his gaze. "Austin, technically, you're rich."

Austin planted his hands on the counter and hung his head. "I'm so tired of fighting with him." He turned his head and stared at her, the heaviness in his heart too much to carry. "None of this was necessary. If he or Granddad had simply told me I owned the mineral rights, I'd have come to a reasonable agreement with my father. He did the work. He built the company. But it was still my legacy." Austin pushed off the counter and fisted his hands, letting the anger rise again. "Greedy bastard. He had to have it all. The business. The money. The woman he thought I loved."

"He's jealous."

"Right." Austin rolled his eyes and huffed out a frustrated breath. "For the past year, I've had exactly nothing."

"That's not true, Austin. You've always had everything."

The words hit him hard, but the reality of it overwhelmed him. What did he do with the fact that he was wealthy beyond imagination on paper, but his life hadn't reflected that, especially this past year?

"You had your mother's love. Your granddad's devotion. Kelly's adoration. And everything your father's worked for really belongs to you. He kept it because of your grandfather's generosity and your mother's belief that her husband had your best interest in mind and you'd receive the benefit of all his hard work. Maybe it was your mother's letter, or the troubled marriage your mother couldn't hide from your grandfather, or that your grandfather knew he didn't have much time left to make things right, but something prompted him to go to your father on your behalf."

"Nothing changed after they argued. My grandfather didn't make my father give it all back to me."

"No. He left you this." Sonya held her hands up and over the papers. "For whatever reason, he couldn't fight your father, but he knew you would."

"Everything in me wants to take him down." He'd have the money to run the ranch without Roxy's help. He could provide for himself and Sonya.

They could have a life like nothing she'd ever experienced.

He'd had dreams of traveling. He'd like to tour Europe and especially Italy. He'd love to go to Mardi Gras and eat Louisiana gumbo. He'd never been to a big city. Maybe Sonya would like to visit New York or San Francisco.

They'd never have to worry about money.

Now that he knew what his father had done, how petty a reason he had for pushing Austin out of his life and treating him like shit, could they repair their relationship?

Would his father even want that?

Or would his father follow pattern and lash out? The fight had been his doing, not Austin's. His father only knew how to take. But he'd have to give if they even had a chance of fixing this.

Austin couldn't find any optimism that would happen. Not when it seemed beyond repair.

"Austin? What's wrong?"

"If I take back what's mine, then what? I push my father out of the company and run it myself? I'm not sure that's what I want to do. I like what I've got going now. My own ranch. A life I put together the way I want it." He cupped her face. "You." He kissed her, needing the connection they shared to settle him. "I want a future that isn't about the things I have but the people who make me happy and a life worth living and enjoying." Sometime over the last year he'd fundamentally changed. Money didn't mean as much to him as the people in his life. Friends like Noah, who had stood by his side. And Roxy, who took a chance on him.

Sonya, who saw potential in a broken man.

With no evidence that he could do it, she believed in him. He wanted to be the man she saw in him. The man she deserved.

And he wanted to give her everything.

Sonya hooked her hands over his wrists at her shoulders. "Before you talk to your father, I have a few more things I want to research. Let's go chat with Mr. Foster about the accounts." Sonya pressed her lips to his, not quick, but lingering for a few seconds to let him absorb her closeness. She fell back on her heels, gave him a reassuring smile, then gathered up the papers and handed them to him.

He tried to focus on what they needed to do and not giving in to his desire to pull her back into his arms. "What more are you looking for?"

"You're the one who knew about the mineral rights. I would have never thought about that when selling a piece of land. When I pulled the property records, I thought that was all the information. It wasn't. All I know is follow the money and you'll find the truth about how much someone is hiding."

Austin put the empty box back and locked it up. He waved to Mr. Foster to let them out of the vault.

"All finished, then. I've pulled the records for Alan Jones and Austin. Let's go to my office and review them."

They followed the bank manager and sat in front of his desk.

Mr. Foster turned the computer monitor toward them. "These are Alan Jones's accounts. Checking, savings, and the box. The financial accounts were closed by Austin." Mr. Foster clicked a few tabs and typed in Austin's name to bring up his accounts. "As you can see, Austin has an open checking and credit line account with the bank in his name only."

"I wish the numbers were flopped on the accounts and I had the amount I owe on the credit line in the checking account." He hated seeing that dismal amount in his checking account.

Mr. Foster pointed to the other checking account. "This is the account Roxy Cordero set up for the business partnership. Austin signs on it, along with you, Sonya. I assume you are this Sonya."

Sonya nodded. "That's right. What's that other savings account?" Sonya pointed to another block on the screen.

Mr. Foster clicked the account number and pulled up the information. "Strange. This is a custodial account. It should have been changed over to Austin on his eighteenth birthday. His parents are the custodians." Mr. Foster glanced at Austin. "I apologize for the oversight."

"No worries. Looks like there's a couple grand in the account." That would help him pay his credit card bill this month.

"I can change the account to your personal savings, or transfer the balance to your checking account."

"Hold on." Sonya held up her hand. "Can we see the activity on the account?"

Mr. Foster clicked on the statement tab. "There's been no recent activity."

Sonya pointed to the statement links going back years. "I want to see the opening statement."

Mr. Foster obliged.

The statement came up on the screen and Austin had to lean forward to be sure he saw the original deposit amount correctly. "Is that right?"

Mr. Foster adjusted his glasses and stared at the amount. "Yes."

"I started with one hundred and fifty grand and ended up with only about two grand. Where did the money go?"

Mr. Foster pulled up one statement after the next until they saw the withdrawal for all but fifteen hundred dollars. The account had been earning interest, which brought the balance up very slowly over the last twenty-plus years.

"Can you determine if the money was transferred to another account?" Sonya pulled a slip of paper and a pen from her purse and wrote down the amount and date of the transaction.

"The fee below the withdrawal amount indicates to me the money was paid out by cashier's check. This happened quite a long time ago. I'm not sure we have the records for who the cashier's check was made out to, but the money could only have been withdrawn by—"

"My father."

"Or your mother as custodians," Mr. Foster confirmed. "The thing is, once the money is put in a custodial account, the money irrevocably belongs to the child. A custodian can only withdraw money for you, the minor, for your direct benefit. They can't use it for themselves, say to buy a car."

Sonya turned to him. "The letter. What your father stole."

Austin nodded. "He took the money my grandfather put in my name to start the mining business."

Mr. Foster leaned forward. "Unless you own the business or a reasonable share of it, you have a case for him raiding your custodial account."

Austin clenched his fists. "My dad doesn't share, he takes."

Sonya shook her head. "Based on my research, he'd been mining his land long before this withdrawal. My guess, he didn't hit the mother lode he'd expected, so he bought the surrounding land." Sonya came to the same conclusion as Austin.

"In the early days I worked for the company, I remember him telling me the new land produced far more than he ever got from the original mining operation." That's when his father actually shared things with Austin.

Mr. Foster chimed in again. "Most of what he originally mined probably went right back into the business."

Austin had worked for his father as a teenager as his father drew him slowly into the business. But when he finished school and went to work full-time, he'd gone through some of the records to see where they'd found the biggest sapphire deposits, thinking it might be worth going back to those sites and looking for more. "He hit the big score on the new property about a year into mining the new land. Almost a year after he took the money from my account."

"Land that he bought with your money." Sonya stared at him, silently asking what he wanted to do next.

Austin never expected to find all this, his father's betrayal spelled out in land deeds, mineral rights, and bank accounts. "Can you make me copies of the records, please?"

Mr. Foster nodded, turned the monitor back to face him, and typed on the keyboard. The printer spit out pages of information that documented his father's theft and betrayal.

Mr. Foster peeked over his glasses and frowned. "I've found the original transfer of the one-fifty from your grandfather's savings account to the custodial account in your name as well. I'll include that for you."

"Thank you for all your help." Sonya stood and put her hand on Austin's shoulder. "The courthouse is a couple blocks up. I'm going to head up there and get the records for the purchase of that land."

He took her hand and held her still. "I don't want you going anywhere alone." He didn't want anything to happen to her like the last time. "What if he's still having you followed?"

Mr. Foster handed over the copies. "Is there anything else I can do for you?"

"Transfer the money from the custodial account to Austin's checking account and close it out."

Austin had already forgotten about that. His mind swirled with thoughts about what his father had done and what Austin should do now.

"Of course. Austin, if you'll give me a moment to complete the transaction and get your signature, I'll have you out of here in a few minutes." Mr. Foster went to work on his computer again.

Austin stared up at Sonya. "Wait for me."

She cupped his cheek and rubbed her thumb over his skin. "You can't let him get away with this. Your grandfather wanted that money to go to you."

He nodded and hooked his arm around her waist and pulled her close. "I'll take care of it."

This meant another confrontation with his father. The upcoming battle would be nothing compared to what he'd already endured listening to his father's harsh words and put-downs. Walter wouldn't go down without a fight.

If nothing else, he wanted his father to know that Austin knew what he'd done: cheating, stealing, and deceiving his only child.

He could forgive, but he'd never forget and allow his father to affect him the way he had this past year.

Austin was done taking it. For once, his father was going to know what it felt like to be at the mercy of someone who could take everything from him.

Chapter Twenty-Five

Austin followed Sonya into the courthouse, but swept his gaze over his shoulder and side to side, making sure no one had followed them from the bank. It seemed implausible and a little like some spy movie to even think his father had them under surveillance, but after Sonya's attack, Austin wasn't taking any chances.

"You're back." The woman behind the counter addressed Sonya. "Man, that looks even worse than when it happened." The woman pointed at Sonya's bruised forehead.

"Thank God it doesn't hurt anymore." Sonya folded her arms on the counter.

"What can I pull for you this time?"

Austin set the highlighter-colored map they'd brought with them on the tabletop. "We'd like a copy of the deed to this land." Austin pointed to the green highlighted area.

The woman took a defensive step back. Her gaze bounced from him to Sonya and back. "Um, why do you want that?"

Sonya shifted, setting her shoulders back and cocking her head. "Darla, it's a public record. Why can't we have it?"

Darla bit her lip and seemed to try to think of a logical reason. "Um . . ."

"Did my father, Walter Hubbard, tell you not to give us a copy of the deed?" Austin wouldn't put it past him.

"He did come in the day after Sonya got hurt." Darla's gaze did that tennis-match bob between them again.

"Darla, get the copy of the deed and the mineral rights. Now," Sonya ordered. "Don't make me go over your head to your boss."

Darla scrunched her lips, then spun on her heel and went to the computer on the desk behind her. "I don't know why he didn't want you to have it, but it can't be good if he came all the way down here to tell me not to give it to you, *or else*. You got your face bashed in. What's going to happen to me?" Darla snatched the papers off the printer and slapped them on the counter in front of Sonya. "You're putting me in jeopardy, you know."

"Oh, for the love of . . . Get over it. You did your job. That's all." Sonya turned her attention to the papers.

Austin read over her shoulder. "The land is in his name, but the mineral rights are in mine."

Sonya stared up at him. "Oh. My. God. This means . . ."

"Everything he ever pulled out of that land is mine." Austin swore and raked his hand over his head.

"Why would he put the mineral rights in your name?"

"Like Mr. Foster said, to use the money from the custodial account, I had to directly benefit. Legally, this satisfied that condition."

"But you didn't benefit. He kept it all."

"Which means I have to fight to get it back." Austin sighed. "But I think this has more to do with my mother. She probably insisted, since he stole the money from my account. She wanted to protect me and this did it. At the time, he thought I'd grow up and work beside him and worship him. I never did. Not the way he expected. I respected him as my father and boss, but we were never close. He kept a distance between us. The harder I tried to get close to him, the colder he got. I understood early on if I wanted a hug, I went to Mom. My father doled out unsympathetic lectures, not kind words or praise."

Sonya narrowed her gaze. "So he starts Blue Mining under the five-year lease on the property your grandfather gave him, then buys another piece of land with your money and puts the mineral rights in your name. Years later, you go to work for him. You help him run the company and the ranch. Your grandfather dies and all of a sudden your father wants to keep you from discovering this." She pointed to the papers. "What the hell? Yes, most of the wealth is yours, but he'd be compensated for starting the business and running it. So what? He just didn't want you to have any of it while he was alive? That doesn't make sense. As his only child, you'd inherit the company anyway. Everything he has would go to you."

"None of that accounts for the fact my father is an egotistical narcissist. He doesn't care about the law or hurting me or anyone else." He traced his finger lightly around the bruise on her head. "He doesn't have a conscience. He wants what he wants and he isn't going to give it up. He worked his whole life building that company and his wealth. In his mind, it's his. And he's not going to willingly share."

"You need a lawyer, Austin. This isn't right. You can't let him take what is rightfully yours. This came from your great-grandfather down to you and was meant to be shared by your whole family. Your mother knew that. It's why she made your father put the mineral rights in your name. Your grandfather wanted you to have it. They couldn't fight your father, but they knew you would because this is your birthright."

He'd been fighting his father a long time now. He didn't want to keep fighting. It drained him. He hated feeling like his father made him come down to his level. Even worse, he hated the way his father made him act. It wasn't him. It wasn't how he wanted to be, or how he treated people.

"Austin, if you don't take care of this, your father could cut you out completely and leave his estate to someone else. He's already trying to have another child. Short of that, he could donate everything. If you don't claim it, everything your family left you will be gone."

His anger boiled over. "Is that what this is about? If I take it back, I'll be rich. I won't need Roxy or anyone else to bail me out. I can bulldoze the house like you suggested and build a newer, better, grander one in its place. Money, a bigger house, is that what you need?"

Sonya stepped back like he'd struck her. "Your mother fought your father for years. Your grandfather tried to make him do the right thing *for you*. They were treated to his abuse for years. You were cast aside like trash and made to live on nothing and left out in the cold. And he's gotten away with it. No one stood up to him and put him in his place. He's never had to account for his behavior or his crimes. How can you possibly let him get away with that? Because you're tired of fighting with him. That's how he wins!"

Sonya raised her hands out to her sides and let them fall and slap her thighs. "If you're done and want to run your ranch and have your life, fine." She pointed her finger at him. "But don't put it on me that you think you're only worth being with if you have money." She pointed to herself. "That's not me talking, that's your father and Kelly in your head." That finger pointed right at his face this time. "*They* made you feel worthless. I only ever wanted you to believe you're the man I love because you're strong and resilient and kind and so much more than I ever thought possible."

He hooked his hand around the back of her head and drew her in for a long deep kiss. He put everything overflowing his heart into letting her know how sorry he was for letting his doubts creep in between them and how much her words meant to him.

Her initial hesitation faded and her arms wrapped around his neck. Her body pressed close. Not close enough. Never close enough.

He didn't want to ever give her a reason to leave. But she'd never do that. She'd stay by his side and have his back because Sonya didn't love or trust easily, but she did with him.

Over the last year he'd learned that things didn't hold as much value as those intangible things you couldn't buy. Like the love of a good woman.

A woman who'd seen too many people get away with being mean and breaking the law.

Her great-uncles had never answered for their crimes.

Her mother had never gotten justice.

Sonya spent her life trying to fight for her mother.

Now she fought for him to get what his father had stolen.

He kissed her one last time, holding her tight, and silently letting her know just how deeply she touched him. All the way to his soul.

He didn't deserve her. But he'd never give up trying to be worthy of her.

He cupped her face and ended the kiss. It took him a second to find his bearings, but then he opened his eyes and everything in his world aligned and centered on her. "I love you, too."

Her eyes went wide with surprise, then softened and filled with joy and wonder. "You do?"

"With every cell of my body and every breath of my life."

A phone clicked beside them. Austin glanced over at Darla, who snapped their photo.

She scooted a form across the counter toward them. "You guys might need this."

Austin smiled down at the marriage license. He kissed Sonya one more time, then grabbed the form and the copy of the property deed and mineral rights.

"You're taking that with you?" The surprise and shock in Sonya's voice only made him smile more.

"Yep."

"Why?"

"You never know when you'll need it."

Darla's smile filled her whole face. "That's ten dollars for the copies."

Austin pulled two fives from his pocket, which left him with two bucks, and slapped them on the counter.

He took Sonya's hand and headed for the door. He held it open for her. She slipped past him with a shy smile and a sideways glance. Yeah, he'd flustered her, but he also had her attention. He'd let her know with one move what he wanted.

And it was coming, because no way in hell he'd let her go. Ever.

Yes, he'd take back the sapphire mine and his family's legacy, but he didn't need it. He already had a gold mine, and Sonya's love was worth more than anything on earth.

Chapter Twenty-Six

Austin parked outside his father's house. The truck that followed them continued down the road and pulled into the driveway that led to the stables. Austin assumed the man who'd confronted Sonya had been following her everywhere, including here, where this would all finally end. His father had to know they'd gone to the bank and the courthouse again.

It didn't matter. Austin had come to talk terms.

He stared at the home he'd grown up in, where he'd felt safe and protected. He'd had a good childhood with the usual ups and downs. His mother took care of him. His father gave him a job and taught him responsibility. Neither of them taught him how to pick himself up after losing everything.

His father hadn't just kicked him off this land and out of his job, he'd gone out of his way to ruin him. Probably hoping Austin moved away and never came back.

He'd used Kelly to humiliate him and tried to steal his child.

All in the hopes of keeping Austin from discovering the truth.

And now Austin held the power and would have the money to do anything he wanted.

Part of him wanted to go back to the way things used to be when he and his father worked together. His father might have been an ass a lot of the time, but he'd never been this cruel.

But they couldn't go back. Not now. Too much happened to drive a wedge between them.

The family bond had stretched so tight, this would surely snap it.

He wanted to find a way to settle this matter amicably. But that wasn't his father's way.

His veneer had cracked, revealing the prosperous businessman and upstanding pillar of the community was really rotten to the core.

He called out the faults and misdeeds of others only because he wanted them to believe he was a good and decent man, but he wasn't. The finger he pointed at others left three pointed right back at himself.

Sonya's hand settled on his thigh. The warmth that always hit him when she touched him spread through his system, calming and exciting him all at once. "If you're not ready to do this, turn around and let's go home."

He wondered if she meant that the ranch had become her home, too. That she wasn't going to take that job and instead stay with him. But this wasn't the time to dive into those conversations. The gnawing need to know her decision grew more insistent with each passing day.

"I was just thinking about how I saw this place growing up and what it means to me now."

"Have you changed your mind?"

"No." He refused to let his father get away with robbing him blind. Austin wanted what was owed to him. He wanted to be financially secure. He never wanted to wake up again wondering if he'd have enough money for food and if the only thing he owned would be taken from him.

He wanted to pay Roxy back for taking a chance on him.

He wanted to carry on his family legacy and provide for his wife and children. He didn't need the whole damn thing. He just wanted enough to give his family a good life.

And yeah, that started with taking care of Sonya and taking those steps toward a life he wanted more each day.

He hoped she did, too.

Sonya took his hand. "I'm with you no matter what you decide to do."

For the first time, he turned his gaze from the home he'd known to the one that really mattered. Her. "I want to give you everything."

She leaned in close and held his gaze. "You give me everything that matters."

All those intangible things he'd been stripped of when his father turned his back and Kelly walked out.

Sonya would never leave him. She loved him.

"I can't tell you what it means to me that for you, I'm enough."

Sonya kissed the back of his hand. "You're more than just enough, Austin. You're my everything."

Austin didn't think. He went with his heart. "Right this minute, I barely have enough money in my account to pay my bills and take you to a nice dinner. All I can offer you is a promise that you and I will have a good life together. We haven't known each other long, but I know that for sure. I don't have a ring, but I want you to be my wife."

Sonya pressed her fingertips to her mouth. Her other hand squeezed his and held tight. Her eyes glassed over and filled with a mixture of joy and disbelief. "Austin."

"You like numbers. As I see it, you and me, we add up to forever. Don't think about all the details. Don't list the pros and cons. For once, go with your heart, knowing I want to be your husband more than I want anything else on this earth because you're my everything. I want to be your everything for the rest of my life. I'm yours, Sonya. Be mine. Marry me."

She dropped her fingers from her lips and cupped the side of his face. Her head tilted and one tear rolled down her soft cheek.

He held his breath and leaned into her palm and waited for that one word that would change his whole life.

"Yes." Sonya nodded, confirming he'd heard her right. "I will marry you."

Something shifted inside him. A piece of his broken battered heart moved into place, made it whole, and unlocked a wealth of love he didn't know he was capable of feeling. It ran deep and true and felt like the most raw and honest thing he'd ever experienced.

He'd taken the marriage license on impulse. Its presence sitting on the office desk kept popping into his head. He had it. Should he use it? Was it too soon? How long should he wait? Was this right, or was he just holding on to Sonya because he didn't want to lose one more good thing in his life?

Those worries all fell away.

This moment felt right. The elation and love that swept through him when she said yes solidified just how much he needed, wanted, and loved her. Her promise and commitment eased him in a way that went deep into his soul. He needed someone, her, to be honest and true.

She didn't want anything from him. She'd said yes with only his promise that he'd get back what belonged to him. Didn't matter to her. She'd given him an opening to turn his back on the coming fight and they'd live on the ranch they were building together and make the best of it.

He meant more to her than what he had now or in the future.

And that gave him the will to fight. For her. For them. For their future.

He hooked his hand around her head and drew her in for a long deep kiss. He took his time, letting her feel the difference in him. He hoped she understood all he didn't say because he didn't have the words to express how he felt in this moment.

Austin kissed her three more times, his excitement and exuberance spilling out. "All I want to do is take you home."

"But first, you need to do this." She finished his thought.

"I need to resolve this, so it doesn't spill into the life we'll have going forward."

"Then let's finish it, then go home and celebrate us."

"When I'm with you, that's all I want to do." He kissed her again, this time quick because he didn't want to spend a second longer than he had to here with his father when he could be alone with Sonya at home.

Chapter Twenty-Seven

Austin met Sonya at the front of the truck and took her hand. He paused before walking up the path. "You know I'll get you a ring and do the whole down-on-one-knee proposal you deserve, right?"

"I liked the spontaneous, from-the-heart proposal, but I look forward to you on bended knee." Her flirtatious smile lit up his heart.

"I'll be on my knees in front of you later tonight."

Her eyes darkened with desire. "Let's go." She tugged his hand to pull him back to the truck. Kidding, she came right back to him and kissed him.

He'd like nothing better than to take that spark in her eyes and turn it into a fire with them wrapped around each other all night, but he had unfinished business.

They walked to the porch and stood together, fingers linked. He knocked and waited for his father to answer the door. Sonya squeezed his hand to let him know she was right there beside him.

They both took a breath when the door creaked open and his father stood before them scowling. "What do you want?"

"Five minutes of your time." The less-than-warm welcome didn't faze him.

"Why would you bring *her* here?"

That tone and dismissive attitude pissed him off. "Get used to her. She's going to be your daughter-in-law whether you like it or not."

Kelly stood behind and to the left of his father. She gasped and locked eyes with Austin. Though they'd talked about getting married, he'd never actually asked her. Now he knew why. He didn't love her the way he loved Sonya.

He'd let Kelly walk away.

He'd asked Sonya to marry him because he couldn't live without her.

His father turned and pinned Kelly with a sharp glare. Kelly recovered quickly, placing her hand on her stomach and mumbling out, "Congratulations."

"It's one bad decision after the next." The disapproving glare had become his father's default when it came to Austin.

He didn't need his father's approval or even false well-wishes.

Asking Sonya to marry him had been the best decision Austin ever made. He'd never been this happy in his life.

And he wouldn't let his father ruin it.

Sonya hadn't done anything wrong or hurtful.

His father couldn't say the same.

Walter stepped aside and let them in. Austin didn't let go of Sonya. He led her to his father's office and let her take the seat in front of Walter's desk. He preferred to stand for this.

Walter went around the desk, sat, and leaned back like he had nothing to worry about and all the time in the world. "What's this about?"

"All your dirty deeds," Austin replied.

"That's her forte, I'm sure." His father challenged Sonya with one raised eyebrow.

Sonya didn't give the comeback Walter deserved. Instead she settled back, looking bored.

Kelly took the seat beside Sonya. "Walter, stop. She's not like that and you know it."

His dad didn't like being challenged by anyone, but especially the woman in his life. "This is family business. Wait upstairs for me."

Kelly sat back, linked her fingers over her belly, and settled in much like Sonya had done. "I'm your fiancée." She moved her fingers, playing with her ring. "I think that makes me family enough. I'll stay."

Walter eyed Sonya's fingers entwined with Austin's. "You can't even afford to buy her a ring."

"I'll make sure she gets everything her heart desires."

The eye roll annoyed Austin even more. "You're living off your best friend's girlfriend's ill-gotten money."

"I own the mineral rights on your property. *My* money paid for that land. Who's living off who?"

Everything about his father took on an air of intensity that filled the room. "So that's what this is about. You think you're owed something. Well, I'm not giving you a dime. *I* built the company. *I* dug every gem out of the ground."

"And all of them belong to *me*." Austin took a breath and tried to keep things civil. "I've turned over all the proof I've gathered from the bank statements, deeds, and mineral rights records to my lawyer, who will take them before a judge first thing tomorrow morning."

Thankfully, Roxy knew a sympathetic judge willing to hear his case immediately. The last thing he wanted to do was give his father a chance to . . . God knows what he'd do now that Austin had the upper hand.

Walter leaned over the desk. "You're coming after me and everything *I* worked for?"

"I'm taking back what's mine, so I can provide for me and my family."

His father grinned, but not in a nice way, and shook his head. "Family? So that's why you're marrying *her*."

One side of Sonya's mouth drew back. "I'm not pregnant."

"I'm marrying her because I love her and want to build a life with her, and yes, our children when we're lucky enough to have them." Austin focused on Kelly. "He only wanted the child so he could try to bypass me, but the documents are clear. Every single sapphire he pulled out of the ground, all the money he got from them, it's mine."

"Yours?" Walter slammed his hand down on the desk. "You didn't put your blood and sweat into building that company. You weren't there when nothing came out of the ground and the money ran out. You didn't sacrifice and worry how you were going to get by."

"No. But I can relate to having nothing and wishing you had the money to change your life. The difference is, you stole it and lied about it."

Walter pointed at him. "I used that money to give you a good life, and this is how you thank me for putting a roof over your head, educating you, and caring for you all these years. You want your hundred and fifty grand, fine, I'll give it to you, but you're not taking everything I earned. Blue Mining is mine. It's my legacy."

"What good is a legacy when you have no one to leave it to?" Austin shot back.

"I do. Kelly is pregnant with my baby." His father's predatory and triumphant smile didn't convey an ounce of joy that he was to be a father again. Instead, it showed how much his father wanted to win at any cost. Even a child he didn't know how to love and wanted to use as a means to an end.

Kelly gasped. "How did you know?"

"We've been working on this for months. You think I don't know your schedule. You're late, sweetheart, which leads me to the obvious conclusion."

The endearment sounded anything but sweet. It came out as an accusation Austin didn't quite get.

"I don't know why you've kept it to yourself. Doesn't matter. That baby is mine and he'll inherit the Hubbard fortune." His dad pinned him with a disgusted glare. "You were always more your mother's son than mine. You want the Jones legacy. Keep your land, build your ranch, and leave me and mine the hell alone."

Sonya reached over and placed her hand on Kelly's arm. "Congratulations. Austin told me how much you wanted to be a mother."

Kelly's face drained of all color. "Thank you. Yes. I can't wait to hold my baby in my arms."

The way she said "my baby" wasn't lost on Austin or his father.

"*Our* child will want for nothing."

"The baby changes nothing," Austin reminded his father, though he didn't seem to want to hear it. "The mineral rights are mine. They only get split if my mother had another child, not you. The only thing you have to leave Kelly's baby"—that pissed his father off—"is the land Granddad originally gave you and Mom. The land you bought with my money will come back to me when the judge sees things my way. Who knows, maybe my sister or brother will want to be a rancher. This place made a good profit when I was running it. You keep it going, he or she will have a good honest life."

His father shifted to the edge of his seat. "You are out of your mind if you think I'm not going to do everything in my power to stop you."

"You can try, but you put the mineral rights in my name. You bought the land with my money. Legally, I can claim it all. But I'm willing to make you a deal. We'll split the business seventy-thirty. In favor of me, but your share is more than you would have gotten by simply running the business. It's a generous deal. You should take it."

"You can shove it up your ass if you think I'll take anything less than the whole damn thing. I am willing to pay you a million dollars to go away before this gets ugly."

"You've already had your thug follow Sonya everywhere she goes and knock her around." He squeezed her hand to remind himself she was really okay.

"I had nothing to do with that." More lies. His father didn't know how to do anything else anymore.

"Right. We know the guy works for you. You've called her names and threatened her and me numerous times. This has gotten ugly enough. Bow out gracefully. Don't force me to be like you and take it all away just because I can."

"You were always weak. Just like you coming here to warn me what's in store. You won't beat me because you don't have what it takes. You want something, you take it. That's how people succeed in this life. That's how I took everything from you and how I'll hold on to it."

Austin shook his head and found that the only emotion he had left for his father was pity. "Maybe one day you'll figure out winning isn't everything. Not when you're alone with your regrets that you spent more time stepping on people than being a friend, husband, and a father." Austin turned to Kelly. "Get out while you can."

His father slammed his hand down on the desk. "Get out! Take that bitch with you. Don't ever step foot on my land again."

"Tomorrow I'll be saying the same thing to you about the Blue Mining land." Austin pulled Sonya up out of the chair and walked out of his father's office and his childhood home for what felt like the last time.

He held the truck door open for Sonya and waited for her to climb in. She sat and placed her hand on his chest as he stared back at the house. "I'm sorry, Austin. It can't be easy to fight your father and love and hate him at the same time."

"He made his choice, which made the choice for me. I hoped he'd take the deal and let it go, but I knew better."

"He's going to do something, you know that, right?"

Austin met her gaze. "Let him try. It's in the hands of my lawyer and a judge. It may get messy, but in the end he can't change what will happen. It'll all come to me. And if he's not careful, he'll end up in jail."

Chapter Twenty-Eight

Kelly took Austin's words to heart. She hated to admit she'd made a huge mistake. She'd been so obsessed with having a child and a family of her own, she'd mistaken Walter's attention as love instead of manipulation. But she saw his motives so clearly now.

He didn't care about her. He'd used her.

He just wanted to win.

And make sure Austin suffered.

Well, he'd made her suffer, too.

Austin had fallen in love with Sonya, who obviously loved him back. Just looking at them together, holding hands, exchanging knowing looks that spoke volumes about their connection and trust in each other, proved that he'd found something they'd never shared.

And Kelly didn't have anything like that with Walter.

He didn't look at her like he adored her. He just wanted to knock her up to prove he could and use the child as a means to get one over on Austin. He hoped that being with her would infuriate Austin and make him jealous. It hadn't. Austin saw through his father's plan and pitied her for falling for it.

"I'm so stupid."

"Smartest thing you ever did was leave him."

No, the smartest thing she could do right now was take Austin's advice and get out now before her child was born and twisted and used by the man sitting across from her. A man who'd strategically reeled her in with flowers, pretty words he didn't really mean, extravagant gifts, and promises to make her dreams come true.

Careful what you wish for.

She got the man who had wealth and prestige, a man who could take care of her, but didn't really want to. He didn't want a loving partner and a family to make beautiful, cherished memories with. No, he wanted a woman in his bed and an ornament in his home and on his arm. The only thing he wanted to make was more money. Whatever the cost to his heart and soul. If he even had those things.

Turning his back on Austin the way he did should have clued her in to just how ruthless and heartless he'd become.

But she'd wanted what she wanted. And now she had it: a child on the way and a responsibility to do her best every day to give him or her the best life possible. And that meant making hard decisions when the choices in front of her were all bad.

Walter would never let her walk away. He'd turn it into a fight. Like he did everything else.

Well, she was leaving. But not before she righted a few wrongs.

In her mind, she owed Austin. She should have never walked out on him the way she had. She should have believed in him. She'd taken Walter's side and told Austin to sell. She'd made it an ultimatum because she wanted a home and a family. What she'd really wanted was to be loved the way Austin loved Sonya.

She'd almost had that but let it go.

At this point, she didn't see anything in Walter's eyes or the way he treated her that pointed to any kind of deep affection.

"What are you going to do?"

"Hold on to what's mine." Walter picked up his cell from the desk and hit the speed dial. He waited for whomever he'd called to answer. "Come up to the house. I've got a job for you." He ended the call and dialed again. "Once I get my lawyer involved, Austin won't stand a chance."

Kelly didn't need to ask who he'd called first. Walter didn't do his own dirty work. He liked to order people to do his bidding.

It didn't start out that way, but now he treated her like the hired help, too.

Well, Kelly wasn't going to be one of the things Walter held on to anymore.

She stood and walked toward the door.

"Where are you going?"

"I'll leave you to your business. I'm tired. I think I'll go lie down upstairs."

"How long were you going to wait to tell me about the baby?"

She didn't really have an answer. She'd needed time to think about her options. "I was waiting for the right time to make it special."

Walter waved that away. "It's not much of a surprise. We were expecting it. I'll take care of this business with Austin, then we'll get married in the next week or two. A quick ceremony at the courthouse and it'll be done."

Right. Check it off the list like picking up the dry cleaning and feeding the horses. Not that Walter did either of those things. He had people to take care of the house and horses and cattle. Because Walter only cared for himself. He didn't care enough about anyone else to try to help or please them.

She'd talked to him about the wedding she'd dreamed of having on the property under one of the massive trees, an arbor bursting with flowers. Friends and family surrounding them to wish them well on their new life together. A lovely candlelit dinner under the stars and a beautifully decadent three-tier chocolate cake with chocolate mousse and raspberry filling with white chocolate frosting and a tiny-bride-and-groom-kissing topper.

Walter didn't want to give her the wedding of her dreams. He didn't want to do anything for her he didn't absolutely have to, to get what *he* wanted.

He thought her so malleable and easily manipulated. She'd fallen into his trap, but that didn't mean she had to stay stuck.

She may have lost her way in her quest to get what she wanted, but she hadn't lost sight of what really mattered. Being kind to others. Being the kind of friend others had been to her.

Austin may have had some harsh words for her, but he'd said them to get her to wake up to what was really going on. She'd turned her back on him then. Not now.

Walter grunted out a greeting to his lawyer, then started laying out his plan to crush Austin. She'd already been dismissed as far as he was concerned. Well, she knew her next move and Walter wouldn't like it one damn bit, but he deserved it.

She walked out just as his man walked in, giving her a leering once-over. She dismissed him the way Walter did her and walked up the stairs to the master bedroom. She bypassed the bed and headed for the massive walk-in closet, thanking God that she'd left the empty right side as it was and not moved in before the wedding that would never happen. She went to the cabinet that looked like four drawers, but was really just a secret door. She pushed the button behind the top hanging rod and the cabinet door swung open, revealing a secret vault. Walter's wife, Annie, had probably used it for her jewelry. Walter used it to hide all those things he didn't want Austin to discover.

She punched in the four-digit code Walter didn't bother to cover up the one time he allowed her in here with him while they were discussing all the medical options they had available to them to get pregnant. He'd been so distracted and agitated that it was taking so long to get pregnant, he simply went about stuffing folders into the safe and didn't think twice about her standing behind him.

She hadn't outright tried to get the combination, she just found it silly that he'd chosen such a simple one. So she started with two and went down the right side of the keypad and punched in three, six, and nine. The mechanism unlocked and she turned the handle and opened the door.

Annie's tray of jewelry sat on the top shelf. Beneath that were several large raw sapphires atop folders and six stacks of cash. She pulled out the folders and closed the door on the other items. Nothing was more valuable than the contents of the folders anyway.

She stuffed the papers into her overnight bag along with the few clothing items she had left on the dressing table and walked out of the bedroom.

At the bottom of the stairs, she momentarily stared at the closed office door, then retrieved her purse from the hall table, and walked out the door knowing whatever happened to Walter, he deserved it.

She was never coming back.

Chapter Twenty-Nine

Austin sat on the couch, his gaze on the fireplace in front of him but his mind a million miles away. Sonya fell into his lap and tried not to spill the double whiskeys in her hands. She gave him one and clinked her glass to his. "To us."

They both took a sip of the smooth twenty-year-old scotch they'd picked up on the way home. On her. This time. Because soon Austin would never have to worry about money again. She was so proud of him for standing up to his father, and for himself, even though it was hard.

Walter was his father after all.

They deserved to celebrate their engagement.

Austin smiled up at her. "You said yes."

She slipped her hand behind his neck and combed her fingers into his hair. "And I meant it. I hope you're sure, because I'm a yes-for-forever kind of woman."

"Exactly. That's why it was so easy to make the decision to ask, because you're the kind of woman I want. One who loves with her whole heart. One who sees the flaws and the potential. The kind of woman who works hard for what she wants, and even harder for the people she cares about. You don't back down. You don't give up. You stick."

She brushed her fingers through his hair and against his scalp, soothing him. "I know it feels like everyone in your life let you down. I can't promise we won't have our ups and downs, but as long as you want me to be your wife, I'll never leave you, Austin."

He clinked his glass to hers, took a sip of his drink, then set his glass on the table next to the sofa, wrapped his arm around her waist, and flipped her onto her back on the couch beside him. She nearly spilled her drink all over the floor and laughed at his audacious move.

He slid his hand down the center of her chest, over her belly, and right to the button on her jeans. "You might want to drink that before it spills all over you." He undid her jeans and tugged them down her thighs and right off her legs, taking her shoes and socks with them. He stared down at her burgundy lace panties.

His heated gaze acted like a laser, heating her core and making her hot and wet. "I want your hands on me."

He gave her exactly what she wanted and planted his hand over that swatch of lace and rubbed his thumb up and down her soft folds. She rocked her hips, needing more and wanting it rough to feed that urgent desire building inside her.

He leaned forward and kissed her belly. She melted, then came alive when his thumb swept inside her panties and slid into her wet core. She pressed into his hand, needing more, but he pulled away, stared up at her, and sucked the evidence of her desire for him right off his thumb.

"You taste so damn good."

Before her mind processed that sexy-as-hell move and his lust-filled words, he pulled her panties down her legs, propped her thighs over his wide shoulders, and licked her center in one long slow sweep. Her core tightened and she nearly leaped right over the edge, but Austin kept her hovering there as he made love to her, his lips pressing soft kisses, his tongue diving in, then circling her clit. Again and again, until she writhed against his mouth. He slipped in one finger and stroked inside and out, his tongue flicking and circling her clit until she climbed that peak and soared right off it, coming with intense spasms against his mouth.

He kissed a trail down her thigh and back up as she slowly came back to herself.

While he did that, he somehow managed to pull out his wallet, find the condom, undo his jeans, and shove them down to slide the condom on, then lever himself over her.

"God, you're beautiful." He leaned down and kissed her, sliding his tongue in for her to taste the passion he spilled out of her and the whiskey they'd shared.

He broke the kiss and met her gaze. "I meant to do this way better, but I want you so damn bad." He thrust into her hard and deep.

She grabbed his ass and pulled him closer.

His eyes rolled back and closed on a groan.

"Love me, Austin."

He pulled out nearly all the way, then thrust back in hard and deep again. "I do. So much." His hips pumped in long deep strokes, the tempo building.

She loved it. She wanted him deeper, closer, and wrapped her legs around his waist. He thrust deep and rocked his hips, creating that sweet friction she craved. Her core clamped onto his thick cock. Austin lost all finesse and control and pumped in and out of her, their hips slamming together in an urgent need for the release that came over both of them, bucking Austin's big body and tightening hers as waves of pleasure exploded through both of them.

Wrung out, her body went lax and Austin fell on top of her, his face in her hair, his breath sawing in and out at her ear.

Scrunched on the sofa, she tried to straighten her leg and found it pinned against the sofa back and hooked over Austin's arm. It made her laugh.

"What's so funny? I thought that was pretty damn fantastic."

She rubbed her hand under Austin's shirt and up his back. "You twisted me up like a pretzel."

He moved his arm and slid his hand down her thigh as she stretched out her leg. "Sorry. Did I hurt you?"

"I don't think I've ever felt better. *Ever.* Like you've set a new bar and I'm not sure how you're going to beat it."

His soft chuckle made her heart flutter. She loved that after all that happened today, he'd found a way to show her how much he loved and wanted her and could still laugh with her.

"You can bet I'm going to try. Every time I see you, even think about you, I want you. I thought it was bad those first few days you worked here with me, but it just keeps getting worse. So you're going to have to suffer through it."

She wrapped him in her arms and hooked her legs around him and held him close in a whole-body hug. "I can take it, if I get to feel like this every time I'm with you."

Austin leaned up on his forearms and stared down at her. His thumb brushed against her temple where the bruises had faded but not disappeared yet. "How'd I get this lucky?" He leaned down and kissed her softly. Sweetly. A kiss so filled with love, she wanted it to go on forever.

They lay like that, tangled around each other for a few minutes. But Austin's back got the better of him. He kissed her on the forehead, disentangled himself from her, stood up, and dragged his jeans up over his hips, but left the fly wide-open. "I'm going to get cleaned up." He headed to their room.

SONYA WALLOWED IN the afterglow of really great sex.

Austin's ringing phone disturbed the peaceful quiet. Sonya snagged his phone off the coffee table. She checked the caller ID and answered even though it wasn't for her.

"Hello."

"Oh, uh, hi. It's Kelly. I called Austin, but I really need your help."

Sonya played along. "What can I do for you?"

"I'm at the Blue Mining offices. I left Walter at home, talking with that man he sent after you. They're planning something. Before they go after Austin, I'm going to get the proof he needs to get what's his. I stole some files out of the safe at the house. Can you meet me here? I'll give you the documents and anything else I find. Some of the stuff is obvious, but you're an accountant, and I work for the heat treatment side of the business. You know what Austin needs. I don't want to miss anything."

Sonya rolled off the couch and grabbed her panties and started dressing.

"I'm on my way. Can you get into the computer system?"

"I'm in. I've pulled the inventory records. My guess is that the first thing he'll do is start moving the money out of the accounts as soon as the bank opens. What financial records do you need to prove Walter stole everything from Austin?"

"Hold on." She set the phone on the table, pulled on her pants, socks, and shoes, then grabbed the phone and went to find Austin. She entered their room, heard the shower, and walked into the bathroom. She smiled at the pile of clothes he left on the floor and the smell of her shampoo in the air. He liked her stuff because she told him it left his hair silky and soft. She loved to play with his hair when they snuggled on the couch and made love.

She opened the shower door and stared at her man. Sexy perfection. Ripped abs, sculpted chest and shoulders. And she wanted to bite that strong bicep that flexed as he massaged the soap into his hair. He tipped his head back and rinsed the suds away. She watched them slide down his chest and over his body. She'd like to follow that trail with her hands.

He opened his eyes and jolted when he saw her standing there watching him. But the wide smile he gave her was an invitation to join him. God, she wanted to, but she needed to help him finish this business with his father more.

"Ready for round two?"

He'd already gotten her off twice on the sofa. "I'm one up on you already. This would be round three for me."

"Then you need to catch me up, sweetheart."

"I'd love to, but"—she hid his phone behind her thigh—"the computer system at Wild Rose went down. They can't take any payments and I need to go over to Roxy's to see if I can fix the problem."

"Now? It's late."

"I know. I'm sorry. I'll be as quick as I can."

He came to her and kissed her softly. "Hurry back. I'm not done celebrating our engagement."

She traced her fingers along his strong jaw to his chin and let her hand drop. "I'll take care of this, and then we'll have nothing to worry about and we can focus on us."

He kissed her again, then slipped back under the spray.

She closed the shower door and headed for the front door and her truck. "Kelly, you still there?"

"Yeah. You guys are really great together."

Sonya stopped by the sofa and frowned. "I'm sorry you overheard all that." She didn't want to shove her happiness in Kelly's face.

"I'm happy for him. For both of you." The words sounded sincere.

Sonya grabbed her purse and pulled out her phone. "I need to leave Austin's phone here. I'll call you back on my phone." It only took a minute to hang up and use the number for Kelly on Austin's phone to call from hers. She didn't say hello, just headed for the door and voiced her concerns about doing this. "Walter is going to be furious when he finds out you're helping us."

"He deserves a lot worse."

She had a minor twinge of regret for lying to Austin about where she was going and why. But if she could get this done without adding more worries and stress in his life, then one little lie would be worth it.

Sonya jumped into her truck, started the engine, pulled out of the driveway, and headed for the Blue Mining offices. "You deserve a lot better."

"I'm really sorry about the things I said to you."

"That's all in the past. We both care about Austin. So let's do this together for him."

Kelly loved Austin. She'd never stopped loving him even though they'd split because Kelly wanted more than Austin had to give her at the time. But Kelly had come to realize what she'd had and given up.

Sonya had learned long ago that some things were worth more than any amount of money. Friends who were like sisters. A mother who loved her so much she'd do anything to keep Sonya safe and give her the life she'd never had. A man who loved her and put her first. A love that grew each and every day and felt so new and wondrous but at the same time safe and like it had always been there waiting for her.

She'd known for a long time now that she didn't want to take the job and move back to Nevada. She'd held on to the offer in case things didn't work out and she needed it. Austin had to have wondered why she hadn't said no. He didn't push one way or the other. He let her work it out her way and in her time. Saying yes to him meant no to the job and she was more than okay with that.

"I've found the electronic bank statements."

"We'll need those." Sonya pulled the truck over to the shoulder and grabbed her phone out of the holder. "Give me a second. I'm going to create a shared folder in my cloud service. You can copy all the files into there. What's your email address so I can send you the link?"

Kelly rattled off her email address.

"Okay, I sent you the link. Click it, then start dumping files into it. Inventory, bank statements, tax returns, any kind of reports that are surveys or estimates of what's not been mined." Sonya drove down the road again.

"Oh, I saw something like that."

"When I get there, I'll dig deeper into the system and paperwork to see if Walter is hiding anything else."

Chapter Thirty

Austin stood in front of the open fridge and surveyed its contents. Before Sonya, he'd survived on things he could cook quick in the toaster oven. Now he had so many choices, he didn't know what to make for his snack while he waited for her to come home.

His phone rang. He hoped it was Sonya, letting him know she was on her way back. Caller ID had him answering his best friend's call with, "I guess Sonya told you about the engagement."

"What?" Surprise filled Noah's voice. "How did you know Roxy and I got engaged today? We were calling to tell you guys."

"*You* got engaged? Sonya and I got engaged today, too. Oh my God, what are the odds?"

"Well, I guess congrats to you two, too," Roxy said. Noah must have had the phone on speaker. "Get her on the line so we can all celebrate this monumental day. Two wild roses tamed."

Austin's heart stuttered. "Isn't she with you guys?"

"No." Noah's voice held not even half the concern filling Austin's spinning mind.

"Roxy, did you call her about half an hour ago? Something about the Wild Rose computers going down?"

"No. Are you sure she said it was me and not Big Mama?"

"Hard to get those two names mixed up." He tried to think through the fear. Why the hell would she lie to him? They'd promised to be partners in everything today.

"Austin, what are you thinking?" Roxy asked.

"If she lied, it had to be for a good reason."

"To protect you," Roxy guessed. "Why? What's been going on with you two?"

"We saw my father tonight. I told him I'm taking control of the land and mine."

"I'm sure he didn't take that well." Noah made the understatement of the year.

"Do you think your father called her and is using her to get you to back off?"

"I'm sure as hell going to find out. I'll call you later." He hung up on his friends. Because of the nagging sensation of danger humming inside him, he grabbed his truck keys and wallet off the counter, and headed out to his truck. He drove down the driveway and hit the speed dial on his phone and prayed Sonya picked up and all his worries were nothing more than an echo of how he felt the last time his father hurt her.

Chapter Thirty-One

Sonya pulled into the lot in front of the metal-siding warehouse-style building. Spotlights on either end of the building lit up the small parking lot. She took the spot beside Kelly's and stared at the dark interior windows. The car door creaked when she opened it, the sound excessively loud in the quiet night.

An eerie ripple shivered up her spine as she approached the front door.

Kelly appeared out of nowhere behind the glass.

Sonya jumped back and put her hand to her chest. "Oh my God. Don't do that."

Kelly held the door open for her, then closed and relocked it. "Walter's office is over there. I've gone through most of the files and pulled things I think you'll need. I'm over here"—Kelly waved her hand to another office—"going through the accounting department's files. That's where I need your help."

Sonya followed Kelly into the office and stared at the number of folders stacked on the table.

"We need to hurry. As soon as Walter discovers I'm gone, he's going to suspect something. Take the computer. I'm logged in."

"He's going to know you helped us."

Kelly placed her hand over her still-flat belly. "It's the right thing to do. He's not the man I thought he was when all this started. I can't seem to reconcile the man who was sweet and funny and took me to dinner and sent me flowers and made promises to give me everything I wanted and deserved with who I've seen him be these last weeks." Kelly's eyes went flat with disillusionment. "He lied. He manipulated. He outright played me," she whispered.

Drawn to Kelly's sadness, Sonya stood and went to her. She held her shoulders at arm's length. "I'm sorry he hurt you. But he gave you a gift. You're going to be a great mother." Sonya hugged her.

Kelly held on for a moment. "I'm scared he'll try to take the child from me or ruin him with his self-serving manipulations and cruelty. He reels you in, makes you care, then shows how little you mean to him because he only cares about himself."

Sonya held Kelly away from her again and looked her in the eye. "He didn't ruin Austin. You won't let him ruin your baby." Sonya gave her a smile. "And big brother Austin will make sure of that."

Kelly's eyes shined with optimism. "I really screwed that one up."

"Live and learn. When the right man shows up, you'll know it. You won't second-guess it, the way you've probably been doing with Walter."

"There's always been this niggling feeling and whisper in the back of my mind."

"Intuition. Listen to it next time." It was what made Sonya say yes to marrying Austin even though they'd only known each other a short time.

Kelly squeezed Sonya's arm and nodded. "He never looked at me the way he looks at you."

"He" was Austin.

"I'm glad he has you. He's happy. I want that for him. For both of you."

"Thank you. We want you to be happy, too." Sonya went back to the desk. "Let's get moving on this. We don't want to get caught."

Famous last words. Ten minutes later, Sonya had enough evidence to bury Walter. Her phone vibrated on the desk. She swiped her finger across the screen to accept the call, but never got a chance to say hello.

Walter walked in the office door and pointed a gun right in her face.

Chapter Thirty-Two

"Move and I'll shoot you."

The words Austin intended to tell Sonya—about how mad he was that she'd lied and left without telling him what was really going on—lodged in his throat the millisecond his dad's words penetrated his brain.

He wanted to yell at his father, *Leave her alone. Touch her and I'll kill you.*

But he didn't want to give away the fact he could hear everything. He wanted to hang up and call the police, but he didn't know where to send them.

"How did you know we'd be here at the office?"

Thank you, Sonya!

He'd been headed there but the confirmation he was going in the right direction eased a tiny bit of his all-encompassing worry. He planted his foot over the gas pedal and all the way to the floor. He prayed he got there in time to stop his father from doing something even crazier than he'd already done.

If he hurt Sonya . . . if Austin lost her . . . his father would really wish Austin had never been born.

"Kelly told me when she flattened my man's tire to slow him down."

"Because I knew you were sending him here to gather all the evidence."

"This is my business. My money. My gems. You think I'm going to let you or that asshole son of mine take it away?"

"Austin offered you a fair deal." Sonya's calm voice only infuriated his father more.

"Thirty percent of everything I built. That's not an offer, that's a slap in the face of everything I did for him."

"You did it for you."

Austin wanted to tell Sonya not to antagonize him. But all he could do was steer the truck down the road and closer to her. He needed to get there before this volatile situation exploded.

"Maybe in the beginning you thought using his money to buy the land and keep the mining operation up and running was your way of providing for your family. But mining became your obsession."

Gold fever. Austin read about it in the fourth grade when he did his gold rush project. He'd never attributed the affliction to his father, but it did explain why what started as a means to build the ranch turned into something that eventually alienated everyone he cared about.

Austin understood what drove his father now, but it didn't excuse his behavior. Especially when he had no remorse. And held a gun on Sonya and the woman carrying his brother or sister.

"You have no idea what it takes to run this business, to see all those little pebbles add up to nothing but enough to keep your employees paid and the lights on. But then you find one, two, a dozen gems that are worth more than the buckets you've found before and you have to keep digging because there's more out there."

Austin had never heard his dad talk with that kind of intensity. Obsession and greed tainted the drive Austin admired in his father. Yes, he worked hard, but the motive behind it made it all so irrational.

"I will never let Austin shut me down. That land is filled with gems. And I intend to find them."

Austin pulled into the lot, threw the truck in Park, shut it off, and leaped out on the run for the door.

"Talk to Austin, Walter," Sonya pleaded. "He'll listen. He'll come to an agreement you can both live with and be happy. It doesn't have to be all or nothing."

"Right now, I have everything. The business. The land. The gems. The money. His ex."

Austin paused with his hand on the door and stared at his cell. His father's obsession to possess had spread and twisted into a need to take everything from Austin.

Sonya had been right. His father wanted to keep everything that belonged to Austin.

Austin opened the door, careful not to make a sound, and made his way toward the office, the security lights at the front of the building casting a glow over the room and highlighting his father's back.

"You used me. You don't care about me." Kelly's voice trembled with anger. "You were ready to get rid of me because I hadn't gotten pregnant and was no use to you."

"But you are pregnant. That child is mine. You might be thinking about leaving, but I'll never let you get away with my child."

"Maybe there won't be a child," Kelly threatened, though Austin didn't believe she'd harm the baby she wanted more than anything. "I hate you. I hate even more that you're this child's father. You ruined everything! I loved Austin. We were supposed to get married. He was going to be such an amazing father. He's a better man than you'll ever be!"

Austin saw his father swing the gun and turn toward Kelly's voice. He grabbed a palm-sized, round, cut-glass, sapphire paperweight with the Blue Mining name and logo on it off a desk. His father fired a split second before Austin slammed the fake gem into the back of his father's head, sending him to the ground.

He was too late.

Austin looked up and stared in horror when he saw Kelly on the floor, blood splattered on her face and shirt, and Sonya lying in front of her, blood pouring out a gunshot wound on his fiancée's side.

"Sonya!" He rushed to her, placed his hand on the wound, and pushed hard to stop the bleeding. "No, no, no, no, no." He didn't want to believe what his eyes saw.

Kelly stared at him wide-eyed and trembling. "She ran for me and pushed me down toward the table."

Sonya moaned and grabbed his hand, trying to get him to stop pushing on her. "I couldn't let him shoot you. You're carrying Austin's sibling."

Austin leaned down and pressed his forehead to Sonya's. "Damnit, sweetheart, why didn't you tell me you were coming here? You scared the life out of me."

Kelly touched his shoulder. "I was trying to get everything you'd need against Walter before he hid or deleted it. I wanted to show you how sorry I am for all I did. But I needed Sonya's help to go through the files. I wanted to make it right."

"You got my fiancée shot!" Fear and anger overrode sense and reality.

Sonya reached up and grabbed a handful of his shirt. "She wanted to help you, Austin. We both did. It's not her fault."

Austin let out a frustrated breath and handed his phone to Kelly. "Call an ambulance."

"They broke in to steal documents and the gems out of the safe. It's dark. I thought they had a weapon and defended myself." His father lay on his side, propped on his elbow, his hand on the back of his head.

Austin turned, spotted the gun on the floor a few feet from his father, and scrambled to get it just as his father dove for it. Austin beat him to it and shoved his father back with a boot to the chest. He barely contained the urge to kick him while he was down.

Austin stared down at the man who had turned into a stranger. He didn't recognize the man who'd spoiled him at Christmas growing up and taught him how to drive, run the business, and work hard for what he wanted.

"Austin," Sonya called, her voice weak. "My phone. The app I use for reminders."

Austin stared down his nose at his father, not caring one bit about the blood running down his head and neck. "You're fucked. She recorded everything."

Sonya's obsessive list making would take down his father once and for all. Walter deserved every bad thing coming his way.

Behind him, Kelly spoke frantically to the 911 dispatcher. "She's bleeding a lot."

Austin worked quickly so he could take care of Sonya. He tucked the gun at his back and grabbed the lamp off the desk. He yanked the cord from the wall and right out of the base. His father tried to stand, but his legs wobbled and he pressed the heel of his hand to his head.

"Dizzy. I'm betting concussion."

"You hit me." Surprise and sadness filled Walter's voice.

Austin didn't have an ounce of sympathy. "You tried to kill Kelly and shot my fiancée. Be grateful you're still breathing." Austin yanked his father's hands behind his back and tightly wrapped the cord around his wrists.

His father tried to fight him off and get free. "Let me go. You can't do this."

"I just did." Austin shoved his father into a chair. "Stay there or I'll knock you out again and this time you'll wake up with a busted nose."

His father leaned back and closed his eyes. The head wound must be pretty bad, but it was nothing compared to what he deserved.

Austin kneeled beside Sonya and wiped the tears from her cheeks. "Can you hold on a little longer? The ambulance will be here soon."

Kelly ran back into the office with handfuls of paper towels from the bathroom. He hadn't even realized she'd left. She dropped to her knees on the other side of Sonya. "The bullet went right through her. I'm pushing the towels to both sides of her now," she said to the dispatcher.

Sonya tried to hold back the worst of her scream, but the piercing sound broke Austin's heart and echoed through his head. He wondered if he'd ever stop hearing it. He wished he could take away her pain. He wished he hadn't brought this into her life.

"This is not your fault." She took his hand, but her weak grip didn't ease his mind or heart.

"I'm so sorry, sweetheart. We'll get you to the hospital. You're going to be okay."

"O . . ." Sonya went limp.

He brushed his fingers over her hair. "Sweetheart, come on, wake up. Stay with me."

Kelly kept pressing on Sonya's wounds but the bleeding didn't stop. "It's just the pain and blood loss. She passed out. She'll be okay." Kelly sucked in a ragged breath. "She has to be okay. If she hadn't pushed me out of the way, he'd have shot me in the stomach." A torrent of tears cascaded down Kelly's cheeks but she never stopped helping Sonya.

He cupped Kelly's face. "Take a breath. Stay calm. You and your baby are fine."

The sirens grew louder outside and multiplied.

He kept brushing his hand over Sonya's hair, hoping she knew he was there with her.

The cops rushed in first, guns drawn. They quickly assessed the situation and took his father into custody, replacing the lamp cord around his father's wrists with handcuffs.

One officer read his rights, but his father refused to remain silent.

"They broke into my place of business. I had every right to protect my property."

"I'm an employee and your fiancée," Kelly pointed out, pulling herself together enough to put some oomph in her voice. "I didn't break in. I used my key."

His father struggled to get to Kelly, but the cop held him back. "You do something to my baby, I'll kill you. I'll kill you!" The officer dragged Austin's irrational father out of the office to make room for the paramedics who *finally* arrived.

He hated to let go of Sonya and reluctantly stepped back to let them work. He watched her face, looking for any sign she was waking up, or needed him. His gut knotted with tension and all he thought about was the future he wanted with her.

Kelly stood beside him, her shaking hands covered in Sonya's blood just like his. He hooked his arm around her shoulders and pulled her close. "Thank you for helping us."

"I shouldn't have asked her to come. I just wanted to find all the accounts before he transferred the money out of them and cut you out of what belongs to you."

"She's more important than any amount of money. You both are." His heart lurched when the paramedics rolled Sonya onto a backboard, strapped her down, picked her up, and put her on the gurney and she mumbled out his name.

He couldn't stand idly by any longer and took her hand. "I'm here, sweetheart. You're going to be okay. We're on the way to the hospital."

"Mr. Hubbard, we need to get your statement about what happened here."

"Sonya's phone on the desk recorded everything. Kelly can answer your questions. You can send an officer to get my statement at the hospital, but I'm going with my fiancée." He didn't give the officer a chance to waylay him and walked out with the paramedics to the ambulance.

He settled in next to Sonya, held her hand to his heart, and gave her a reason to hold on and come back to him. "We need to set a wedding date. It has to be soon. No more than six months. We need to decide on the cake. Or our favorite éclairs. What about the flowers? My mother loved lilies."

"White roses. Classic," Sonya whispered. "Where's my phone? We'll make a list." A soft smile touched her lips.

He kissed her, taking in that small bit of joy she'd shown him and letting it sink in and take over the overwhelming dread that gripped him the second she'd passed out and he feared she'd never wake up, that she'd leave him the way his mother and grandfather had.

"You're back." His voice shook with the emotions clogging his throat.

"I'm not going anywhere. I love you."

"I love you, too."

"Now, about the wedding, do you have a black suit? Not a tux. That's too stuffy for us."

He found a halfhearted smile for her. "I'll buy a new suit."

"Noah will be your best man. Roxy my . . ." Tired and hurting, her soft voice faded away.

He squeezed her hand. "I didn't get a chance to tell you. Noah and Roxy called the house. That's how I knew you weren't with Roxy. They got engaged."

"They . . . did?"

"Yes, sweetheart, so you need to recover from this so we can all celebrate together."

"I love celebrating with you."

He kissed her palm and held her hand to his cheek the rest of the ride, giving her a break. His mind didn't rest. He worried about her serious injury and recovery. He needed to call her mother and sisters.

Not once did he think about his father and what he'd done. He let that rage simmer in the background because the only thing that mattered now was getting Sonya to the hospital and the doctors she needed.

He couldn't live without her.

Chapter Thirty-Three

Sonya woke up the second day in the hospital with a dull ache in her side and the sun in her eyes. She rolled her head away from the light and found a smile for her mom. "Hey, what are you doing here?"

June set aside the romance novel she'd been reading, stood, and kissed her on the head. "Austin called and told me what happened. You saved that woman's life and her baby's. I'm so proud of you. But you scared me."

"I'm sorry, Mama. But I'm so glad you're here."

"Well, I had to move up my schedule, but I'm here for good."

Sonya hit the button to raise the top of the bed and held her breath as the movement sent a sharp pain through her side.

She'd first woken up in recovery after surgery, with Austin holding her hand, his face a mask of concern and so much love it melted her heart.

"Where's Austin?"

"Out in the hall talking to Roxy and Noah. They didn't want to wake you."

Yeah, it'd been hard to sleep with the noise in the hospital, nurses checking on her through the night, and nightmares about what happened. She'd acted without really thinking, pushing Kelly out of harm's way. The second the bullet hit her, she'd screamed from the shocking pain, and panicked that the life she'd imagined with Austin would never come true.

Her mother's words came back around and hit her. "Wait, did you say you're here for good?" The pain meds slowed her mind.

June squeezed her hand. "I wanted to surprise you."

"I'm shocked. I never thought you'd leave the Wild Rose Ranch. At least, not for several more years."

June squeezed her hand. "This isn't a good time to explain."

"Mama, spit it out." She rubbed the heel of her hand over her brow. "Did you really quit the Ranch?"

"I took your advice and a good long look at myself and my life. I . . . uh, don't like the way you look at me sometimes." June's gaze dropped to the bedsheet.

"Mama. I love you."

June's lips pinched together. "I disappoint you sometimes. Like with what happened with your great-uncles."

Sonya shook her head. "That was not your fault."

"I know. And I've heard you every time you've begged me to do something about it. I just couldn't. Until now." June looked her in the eye. "I didn't want to tell you in case I couldn't go through with it. I didn't want to disappoint you again. But I contacted the police. A nice detective came to talk to me and I told him I want to press charges against those bastards." June swearing and calling people names, that was new. So was the vehemence in her voice.

Tears filled her eyes. "You did?"

"They arrested my uncles two days ago. I'll have to testify against them." June squeezed her hand. "It's too late to get them for what they did when I was a child, but I can make them pay for what they did this time and make sure they never do it again."

Tears stung her eyes. "Mama, I'm so proud of you." She held tight to her mom's hand and kissed the back of it. "I'll be right there with you in the courtroom."

"The detective thinks they'll make some sort of deal. But the prosecutor said she'll fight to get the most she can. Justice for what they did to me all those years. She'll want to talk to you and hear your side of things. It will help my case."

Sonya couldn't believe all her mother had done—on her own—to change her life. But she wondered if she meant it. "So you've decided to leave the Ranch until this is over?"

June's smile bloomed with delight. "Oh no, I bought a place here."

The lights were starting to come on in her mind. "The house on Pine Drive." She remembered Darla gossiping about Roxy buying a place in town. But not Roxy. June.

"How did you know?"

"Through the grapevine. Everyone knows everything in a small town. So Roxy's been helping you get a place here? Why didn't you ask me?"

"You seemed to have your hands full with Austin's place."

"Mama, I'm never too busy to help you."

"I wanted to surprise you. I wanted you to see me stand up for myself." A soft blush pinked June's cheeks and made her look even younger. "You dreamed of a different kind of life, and you found it here. I once dared to dream of another kind of life when I was pregnant with you. But it never came true. I don't want to find myself at the end of my life wishing I'd had the courage to at least try. So I bought a house and hired a contractor. He put in this adorable white picket fence, excavated the yard, except for the trees, so I can put in a garden, and is currently finishing the renovations. For the first time in my life, I'll have my very own house."

"But, Mama, there's just one thing."

"What's that?"

Sonya gave her a mischievous grin. "You don't know how to garden."

June giggled. "I'll learn. I've already signed up for a cooking class at this cute Kitchen Clutter place in town where I bought my very first set of dishes and pots and pans." The exuberant smile and joy in her eyes lightened Sonya's heart. "I'm not so old I can't still have a normal life. Maybe even another child, this time with a loving husband to go with it." June's gaze fell away again with that whispered admission.

Sonya tugged her mother's hand and waited for June to meet her gaze. "I hope you have all of that."

June played with a lock of Sonya's hair. "You mean that? You don't think it's silly to want to have a family now?"

"I think you get one life, Mama, and you should have everything your heart desires."

June hugged her tight, held on for an extra-long moment, then leaned back. "I'd never have had the courage to do this if not for you. You always believed in me. You saw more in me than I ever saw in myself. I needed your strength and confidence."

"Mama, you instilled that strength and confidence in me."

"I tried to be a good mother."

"You are a great mother. Maybe we didn't have the house with the picket fence and a husband and father to love us, but we always had each other."

June cupped her cheek. "And now you'll have that with Austin."

"She'll have everything she wants with me." Austin stood in the open doorway and smiled at her. "I'll even build you a picket fence if you want one."

"Right now, I just want a hug."

June let her go and smiled like an indulgent mother.

Austin wrapped his arms around her and gently held her close. He kissed her cheek, then whispered in her ear, "You okay, sweetheart?"

"So much better now."

Austin carefully released her. "I'm sorry I wasn't here when you woke up."

"Mama watched over me the way she's always done." Sonya smiled for her mother, letting her know she had no regrets or resentments about how she'd grown up. Her mom did the best she could under the circumstances.

Austin laid his hand on her thigh. "We've been invited to dinner at her place when you're feeling up to it."

"I can't wait. But right now, all I want to do is go home."

Roxy and Noah walked into the room. Roxy came to stand beside Sonya's mother and wrapped an arm around June's waist. "Did you tell her?" she asked June.

"I did. I'm going to be living close to my girl again."

Roxy's lips drew back in a lopsided frown and she met Sonya's gaze. "I'm sorry I didn't tell you I've been working with June."

"Don't worry about it. What do we need to do to get her house ready?"

Roxy shrugged. "It's almost done. I'm taking her to the bank later to set up her accounts here. I've got some work to do later, so Noah is going to take her for her first driving lesson."

Sonya's eyes went wide with the surprise she couldn't help but show. "You're going to learn to drive?"

"Roxy found a house close to downtown and shopping, but I'll need a car in winter and to drive out to see you."

"This is a lot of firsts for you. Are you sure you're not taking on too much?"

June patted her leg. "It's long overdue. I've been afraid for so long to step out of what I've known, even though it wasn't a healthy life for me. I see you, so happy and in love, and I can't help but see your example and want that for myself."

Sonya reached out and took Roxy's left hand and held her fingers so she could inspect the gorgeous diamond engagement ring. "Congratulations, sis. I can't tell you how happy I am for you." She glanced at Noah. "I've never seen her as happy as she is with you."

Noah winked at Roxy. "I plan to make her happy the rest of her life."

Sonya squeezed Roxy's hand. "When's the wedding?"

"Soon." Noah eyed Roxy, letting her know he didn't want to wait.

"We could make it a double wedding," Roxy suggested.

Sonya didn't believe she truly meant it. Though the idea appealed. A lot. Roxy probably wanted to have her special day all to herself. Truthfully, Sonya hadn't had time to think about the engagement or the wedding. After being shot, her thoughts were consumed with replaying the event and thinking about what happened next.

She glanced up at Austin. "Have you checked on Kelly? How is she?"

"I spoke to her this morning. She's okay. Still shaken but getting better. She's worried about you. I told her to come by the house tomorrow so she can see you and know you're okay."

It touched Sonya that Kelly worried about her. "What's going on with your dad?"

"His ass is sitting in a cell where he belongs." Austin bit out the words, a fresh wave of anger flattening his lips into a tight line.

"What happens now?" She hoped Walter got everything he deserved.

"His lawyer's left half a dozen messages."

Sonya didn't like the sound of that. "You haven't spoken to him?"

"Not yet." Austin sat on the edge of her bed and laid his hand on her stomach. "I need time to calm down and think clearly. I can't do that without you home with me."

Roxy stepped past June and kissed Sonya on the forehead. "We'll talk later about June's move, the possible trial, and"—Roxy waved her hand—"everything else going on."

"Thanks for being here, Rox."

"That's what sisters are for." Roxy reached across her and squeezed Austin's shoulder. "Take care of her."

"I will," he vowed.

June kissed Sonya on the forehead, too. "I'm going with them, unless you want me to stay a little longer."

"No, Mama. I have everything I need." Sonya brushed her fingers down Austin's arm and gave him a smile, hoping to see some of the darkness leave his eyes. Today they were blue for a whole other reason than the brilliant azure she liked so much.

Sonya nodded to Noah in goodbye and waited for everyone to leave. Austin still didn't speak, so she started the conversation. "What should we do for dinner tonight?"

Austin stared at her. "Three hours in surgery. Thirty minutes in recovery before they'd let me see you." He glanced down at his hand on her belly, then back at her. "Your blood on my hands and spilling out on the floor. I can't stop seeing it. I can't stop thinking about how I almost lost you."

It cost her, but she sat up, hid the pain, and wrapped her arms around his neck. "I'm right here. I'm not going anywhere. There is nothing standing in our way. Let's get back to the business of getting the ranch up and running and planning our wedding."

"I still haven't gotten you a ring."

"You've been kind of busy stressing over the fact your fiancée is in the hospital and your father tried to kill your ex-girlfriend and her unborn child. You get a pass," she teased. "I'll take life with you over a ring any day."

Austin pulled her into a light hug. "I came so close to losing you. Twice. I don't think I can go through that again. Noah gave Roxy six months, but I'm asking you to make it as soon as possible." He brushed his hand through her hair, fisted a lock, and held tight, not hurting her, just needing to hold tight to her.

She'd left him after that confrontation with his father outside the restaurant, and then she'd gotten shot. All he wanted was for them to be together without all the drama and trauma. They needed time to get past what happened with his father and live their lives together, building on the joy they felt when they were with each other.

"Let's settle this business with your father, then we'll set a date. Something soon. I don't need or want a big wedding. Something simple. Our family and friends. You and me."

"I don't really have much family left."

"You have a sister or brother on the way. You have Noah. You have my mother and sisters. You and me, we aren't alone." She put her hand to his face and looked him in the eye. "We will always have each other."

Austin kissed her softly. He tried to be gentle and soothing, but she wanted him to know how much she loved him. How much she needed him to let go of what happened and believe that she was still his. She'd always be his.

So she took the kiss deeper, pressing her chest to his, holding him closer, and sliding her tongue along his in one long deep sweep that made him growl low in his throat. He tried to pull back to say something to her, but she dove in for another sexy kiss that warmed her from the inside out. She slid her hand over his shoulder and down his bicep. All those restrained muscles. All that man at her fingertips made her forget about her wound and pull him closer.

"I guess you're feeling better," the doctor said from behind Austin.

They broke apart, but Sonya didn't let Austin go. She hugged him close and laid her chin on his shoulder and stared at the doctor. "He's the best medicine I could get."

"I prescribe a daily dose of him, then." The doctor winked and patted her leg. "Let's check that wound and get you out of here."

Austin helped her lie back on the pillow. The doctor lifted her gown and pulled the bandage off to check the incisions, front and back.

"How does it look? Is she going to be okay?" The concern and fear in Austin's voice made her sad. She didn't want him to worry about her anymore.

"It looks great. Healing well. How's your pain level?"

"About a four. Tolerable."

"I'll send you home with pain meds and antibiotics. You'll need to take it easy for a couple of weeks, but I don't think you'll have any complications."

A nurse walked in with a clean dressing for her side.

"Any questions?"

"How much do I need to restrict her activity?" Austin asked.

"Due to the muscle damage, don't carry anything heavier than five pounds for the next couple of weeks. Keep your activities light. Rest when you get sore. Over time, the muscles will heal and you'll need to work them again to build them up. You'll have a scar on your abdomen and lower back, but you were very lucky. The bullet didn't hit any organs. We'll reevaluate in ten days at your checkup."

Sonya held her hand out and took the doctor's hand. "Thank you for everything."

"If you have any questions, get a fever, or increased pain, contact me immediately."

"I will, but I have a feeling Austin will be sure I don't do anything to mess up my recovery."

"Hell no. You get the couch, the remote, and as many desserts as you want."

The doctor smiled, gave Austin an approving nod, and left so the nurse could rebandage her wounds.

True to his word, Austin drove her home three hours later because it takes forever to be discharged from the hospital. He settled her on the couch, then went out, fed the livestock, came back in, and made her dinner. As promised, he delivered on dessert with her favorite rocky road ice cream.

He ignored calls from Walter's lawyer and cuddled with her on the sofa. But still she felt a distance in him, like he couldn't get out of his head and believe that everything really was going to be all right now.

She'd just have to show him that nothing would come between them again.

Chapter Thirty-Four

Sonya woke up the same way she fell asleep: with Austin kissing her shoulder and neck, his arms wrapped around her. He'd held her through the night and the nightmare that woke her with a jolt. But she'd immediately let go of the fear when Austin distracted her from the past and anchored her in the present with his strength and love.

"Morning."

"How's your side?"

"Fine." Nothing but a dull ache he didn't need to know about because she was a pain med away from making it disappear. Another day or two of taking it easy, giving it time to heal, and all she'd be left with was the scar and a bad memory. She could live with that because she had the man she loved and a bright future with him on their ranch.

"You don't need to hold back just to make me feel better."

She rolled over and faced him. He combed the hair from her face and traced his fingers down her arm and settled his big hand on her hip.

She put her hand on his face. His scruffy jaw scraped her palm. She stared into his blue eyes and saw the depth of emotion he tried so hard to keep contained. "You need to find a way to let this go."

His eyes narrowed. "I want to kill him."

"This anger is going to eat you alive. Just like it did when he kicked you out. Please, Austin, I don't want to see you fall back into that kind of despair."

"Or a bottle?" He gripped her hip. "I won't. This is different. I know what I have to do, it's just not what I thought my future would be."

"What are you talking about?"

"Someone has to run the mining business. I can't lay off all those workers or turn away the customers who rely on the heat-treating operation. All I wanted to do was run this ranch with you."

"You don't have to do this alone."

"You've got enough on your plate with the Ranch, Roxy and Noah's ranch, and the investments you oversee. You're taking care of the accounting for our ranch, too."

"First, it means everything to me to hear you call it our ranch. Yes, I have a lot on my plate, but—"

"Your mother is going to need you to get through this thing with her uncles."

"And I'll be there for her. But none of that means I can't be here for you. You don't have to give up everything you want to clean up your father's mess and take back what's yours."

"Who else is going to do it? And you still haven't decided if you're going to take the job back in Vegas." Resentment and fear filled those last words.

She'd put off that decision and left him hanging and thinking that she might actually choose the job over him. She never meant to do that and it made her heart ache to know she'd hurt him. "I'm not taking that job. I've known that for a while but was afraid to let it go. After all we've been through, it's so easy to see now exactly what I want. And that's my life here with you."

"Do you mean that?"

"Yes. Absolutely. And I have a plan I think will work for you and me. Hear me out because it may not seem like the logical thing to do, but I think once you consider it, you'll see the benefits for everyone involved."

Austin held her gaze and nodded. "Okay, let's hear it."

IT TOOK AUSTIN a minute to digest Sonya's plan. First he thought of all the complications it could cause, which included hurt feelings and jealousies he didn't want to deal with or have infect what he and Sonya had together and wanted to build on for their future. Anything that jeopardized that got a hard no. But the more he listened to her plan, thought it over, and played it out, he had to admit, it just might work and make everyone happy.

If Sonya could live with it—it was her plan after all—then he would give it a try.

But the second he even smelled something sour, he'd put an end to it.

The doorbell rang and he took a deep breath and sighed, hoping this went well.

Sonya opened the door and Kelly stepped inside and immediately broke down in tears.

Austin's gut went tight. He didn't know what to do, but this wasn't a great start to the conversation he needed to have with Kelly about the future and his father.

Kelly wrapped Sonya in a hug and rocked her back and forth.

Austin stepped forward to pull her away before she hurt Sonya's side, but Sonya held up her hand and stopped the rocking motion, holding Kelly still.

"I'm so sorry. It's all my fault. I shouldn't have asked you to meet me at the mining office. I should have just gotten the files and brought them to you."

His sweet Sonya held Kelly tight with one arm and rubbed her other hand up and down Kelly's back. "I'm glad you reached out. We needed your help to prove how much Walter stole and where he'd stashed the money."

Kelly held Sonya at arm's length and glanced down at her belly, then back up. "Are you okay? You look good."

Sonya squeezed Kelly's sides. "I'm fine." She waved her hand toward the sofa. "Come, sit down."

Kelly glanced at him, then looked away, embarrassed and unsure of him. "Hi, Austin."

"How are you feeling?"

Kelly sat on the edge of the couch, clutching her purse on her lap. "I'm trying to wrap my head around what happened and figure out what to do next."

Austin sat in the chair beside the sofa and Kelly. Sonya sat on the chair arm beside him.

He hooked his arm around her waist. "I asked you here today so you could see that Sonya is healing."

"I shouldn't have taunted Walter. I shouldn't have said what I said." Her lips trembled but she held back a fresh wave of tears. Thank God. Austin didn't know what to do with an emotional woman.

Austin reached out, giving comfort the only way he knew how, and laid his hand on her knee. "Stop. You're not to blame. He refused to see reason and compromise. We could have settled the matter at the house, but he didn't want to give up anything. He wanted to control you, me, the business, every damn thing." Austin sat back and tried to calm his growing anger. "We need to talk about the baby and the future of the company."

"I know what I said about the baby, but I didn't mean it. I want to have this baby."

Austin nodded. "I never believed you'd hurt the baby. This may not be how you want things to happen, but Sonya and I want to help."

Kelly's gaze shot to his. "You do?"

"Yes. You're carrying my brother or sister. A Hubbard. A child who won't have a father for a long time because my dad will be locked up."

Kelly leaned forward. "Do you have any idea what is going to happen to him?"

"I spoke with his lawyer this morning. My father wants to fight my taking back what he stole from me. His lawyer is going to discuss with him how fighting me and the charges against him will only extend the inevitable outcome. I will get back what is mine and take over Blue Mining. I've offered to make a deal with my father. The same one I offered him at the house with a few changes."

"What changes?" Kelly wiped her nose with a tissue she took from her purse.

"Thanks to the documents you took from the safe and the others you got from the office for us, we know the net worth of the business and its holdings. I will pay out thirty percent to my father, cutting him out of the business from now on. He'll keep ownership of the land my grandfather gave him when he married my mother. As your child is his heir, I will ask him to leave it to the baby. I don't see why he wouldn't. But you and the child won't need it."

"What do you mean?"

"I'm taking ownership of the land he purchased for Blue Mining. Sonya and I discussed it, and we agreed that the baby should benefit from my father's hard work and the business he started. So, from now on, the baby will receive twenty percent of the profits."

"Austin, you don't have to do that."

"I want to. But I need your help."

Kelly tilted her head. "What can I possibly do for you?"

"Help Sonya run the company."

Kelly's gaze shot to Sonya, then back to him. "You want us to work together?"

This is where things got tricky. Kelly still had feelings for him. They all knew it, even Sonya. But she'd come up with this plan and believed they could all work together without jealousy and hurt getting in the way. Austin hoped so.

"We're going to pull back the mining business and focus on the heat-treating operation. You will organize and run that while Sonya will oversee the finances. You will receive a good salary to care for your child. The baby will benefit from your hard work and maybe one day run the company. It always was and will continue to be a family business."

Kelly's eyes sprung another leak. Tears cascaded down her cheeks again, dabbed away by another tissue but not fast enough for the stream that overtook her again. "You think of me as family."

"That baby may not have a present father, but he or she is going to have a big brother looking out for him or her."

Kelly glanced up at Sonya who sat beside him, quietly backing him up. "Do you agree to this? You and me working together?"

"Austin and I aren't going to let Walter get away with what he did and leave you and your baby abandoned. Austin cares about family. Though your relationship ended and things have been difficult because of Walter's interference, Austin and I believe we can all be friends."

"Is that your polite way of letting me know this offer is a business deal, not an opening for me to hope Austin and I will get back together?"

Austin wanted to be sure everything was clear. "Kelly, I—"

"You love Sonya." Kelly cut him off from saying that very thing. "I know that, Austin. I can see the way you love her. It's in the way you look at her, the way you touch her, and even how you've changed. You're . . . happy. At ease. Connected to her in a way that just never happened between us. While I wish things turned out differently for us, I want what you two have and know I won't get it by trying to take you away from her. So neither of you has to worry that I'll cause trouble. I'm going to focus on this baby." She put her hand over her belly. "And I'll take the job and your support as we all move forward with our lives as a family. Who knows, maybe soon this baby will be an aunt or uncle to your baby."

Sonya ran her hand over Austin's head and smiled down at him. "Let's do the whole wedding and living together thing without all the drama for a while."

Austin hugged Sonya to his side. "Whatever you want, sweetheart." He focused on Kelly once again. "We'd like you to close up my father's house. He can decide what he wants to do with it once his fate is determined. As part of your benefits, there's a cottage on the Blue Mining land."

"The property and mining manager lived there. He moved out a couple months ago. I think one of the security guards took over the place."

"We'll make other arrangements for security. You can take over the cottage. Sonya's great at renovations and decorating, so if we need to make some improvements and changes to the property, we'll work it out."

Kelly pressed her hand to her chest. "You guys really mean this. I'm going to have a place to raise the baby, a good job, and security for my child."

Austin glanced up at Sonya, got a smile from her, and looked at Kelly. "Yes. We're going to make this work and give you and this baby a good life. The life my father promised you both. It may not include him, but I don't think you'll have any trouble finding a man who sees what I saw in you and wants to be everything you deserve."

Kelly's lips pressed into a wobbly grin as her eyes filled with tears again. "Thank you, Austin. That means a lot to me."

"Then it's settled and you can stop crying."

"It's the hormones," she assured him.

He wanted as far away from any more crying as possible. Lucky for him, Kelly and Sonya would work together with minimal help from him. If they could be friends, or at least business partners, then he didn't have to worry about things getting messy. It seemed that Kelly didn't harbor any notions that they'd eventually get back together or that this was an opening for that to happen.

Kelly stood. "Thank you both. Walter may end up behind bars, but I plan to make sure he doesn't forget his child. With a job and a place to live, I can focus on getting my life in order, starting with getting a lawyer and child support. I appreciate what you're doing, but Walter needs to be held accountable, too."

"Go after him," Austin encouraged.

Sonya stood to see Kelly out, wincing when the movement hurt. "Meet me at the cottage tomorrow. We'll take a look at the place and see what needs to be done to get you settled in there."

Kelly gave Sonya a quick hug. "Thank you. I'll see you there. If the place turns out half as good as this," Kelly said, glancing around the renovated house, "I'm sure I'll love it."

"Leave it to Sonya. She'll make a list tomorrow and the work will be done before you know it."

Kelly headed for the door. "I'll be in touch."

Sonya showed her out, came back, and sat on the coffee table facing him. She put her hands on his knees and squeezed, making him jerk when it tickled him. The grin said one thing, but her words conveyed another. "Sorry."

"No you're not."

She squeezed his legs again and he took her hands to stop her from tickling him again.

"You're playing with fire, sweetheart."

Sonya leaned in and kissed him. "Trust me, Austin, it's going to be all right. Kelly and I have an understanding now. We can work together. Once she settles in to the job and the house, she'll be focused on work and the baby. Having your ex around all the time isn't exactly ideal, but I think we can be friends and a family for the baby."

"I think so, too. I just don't want you to ever think or suspect something is going on, because I love you, not her. I want to be there for the baby, but I'm dedicated to you."

She cupped his face. "I know. I'm okay with this. That's why I suggested it. Your father tore this family apart. We are going to hold it together."

He sighed out his relief that the meeting went so well. But the stress tightening his shoulders didn't ease, because he still had to face his dad.

Chapter Thirty-Five

Four days later, Austin sat in the hard plastic chair facing the glass and waited for Walter to be brought in from his cell to speak to him. Gray cinder-block walls, high barred windows, locked doors, the stale air tinged with sweat and desperation, and armed guards. This was the life his father faced for years to come if convicted. In Austin's opinion, he got off easy after shooting Sonya.

The door in the opposite room buzzed, then opened. His father walked in ahead of a guard, who pointed to the seat in front of Austin. No need. Walter rushed over, sat down, and picked up the phone on his side of the divider.

Austin took his time and looked his fill at the man in front of him. A man he'd loved and admired. A man he thought he'd grow to become.

Somewhere along the way, he'd shot higher.

Now he couldn't stand the sight of the pale, unshaven, desperate man before him. Even the bandage around his head from the knock Austin gave him didn't soften Austin's heart.

He wanted his father to suffer a thousand times over for the intense fear and despair Austin felt in those moments he thought Sonya might be dead, or would die if he didn't get her help in time. His whole lonely life flashed in his mind and he'd known what his father had taken from him.

He wouldn't let his father take anything else.

Walter pounded on the glass with his fist, then furiously pointed at the phone. The guard slammed a hand down on his shoulder to make him settle down. From now into the foreseeable future his father would be corralled and commanded by guards and the system.

Subdued, Walter gave him a pleading look.

Austin reluctantly picked up the phone next to him. He'd come with a purpose and he'd have his say.

Walter flattened his hand against the glass, the plea in his eyes turning to desperation again. "You gotta get me out of here."

Austin sat back, not swayed by his father's selfish need. "The judge denied you bail. What do you think I can do about it?"

"Tom is worthless. I need a criminal attorney. Get me another lawyer."

"You should have fired Tom when he revealed Roxy's privileged information to you and others in town months ago."

"I was getting to it."

"Well, the court can assign a public defender, or you can find a new lawyer on your own."

"From here?" Walter glanced around the dismal room.

"I'm not here to help you. I came to discuss what happens next."

"If you won't help me, I'll find someone who will. Someone who knows what the hell they're doing and can get these ridiculous charges dropped."

Austin rolled his eyes. "Good luck with that. You can't stop what's coming, because you deserve it and a hell of a lot worse."

Pure rage filled Walter's eyes. "You're loving this, aren't you?"

"I tried to get you to see reason. I offered you a deal that would have left you rich and free to do whatever the hell you want. But that wasn't good enough for you. You had to have it all, by any means necessary, including hurting everyone close to you."

"I'm not letting *you*"—Walter jabbed his pointed finger into the glass—"take everything I've built. I'll be out of here soon enough. You'll see." Maybe Walter needed to hear it out loud so he could believe that lie instead of facing the cold hard truth.

"You've been charged with attempted murder and you're implicated in sending that guy to hurt Sonya at the courthouse."

"I never told him to hurt her."

Austin held back his temper because he needed to get through this meeting because he didn't plan on ever coming back. "But she did get hurt because of you. You threatened her, said nasty things to her that were not only untrue but deeply hurtful. You have no compassion or empathy for anyone, yet you want me to show that to you and help you out of this mess." Austin shrugged and frowned at his father. "None of this would have happened if you'd simply done the right thing. Since you didn't, I'm forced to make you do it. So here's the deal: I'm taking over Blue Mining. Kelly and Sonya will run it, though they'll do it my way. As per the judge's order you received a copy of today, you've been allowed to keep thirty percent of the total profits made by the company to date. Compensation for starting the business and running it all these years. You will not receive a dime more. You keep your home and land. I've asked Kelly to close up your house. She reluctantly agreed, though I'm surprised she'd do you any favors after the way you treated her."

Walter grinned, though his eyes held contempt. "She wanted me. Not you. I gave her what you couldn't. No one forced her to do anything. She wanted it."

Walter made everything someone else's fault, their own doing, never his father's dirty work.

Austin didn't take the bait and rail against his father for being with his ex. None of that mattered now. "If you want to continue to pay the manager to run Hubbard Ranch, that's up to you to work out with him. If you don't, I'll buy the horses and cattle at a reasonable price."

Walter fell back in his chair and crossed his arms like a petulant child. "What will I have left?"

Austin leaned forward. "Your life." This time Austin punched his finger into the glass. "You're lucky I didn't kill you when you shot my fiancée."

Walter leaned forward and spread his arms wide. "I wasn't trying to shoot *her*."

"No, you wanted to kill the mother of your baby. What the hell is wrong with you?"

His father glommed on to the one thing that had a glimmer of hope of getting Austin to help him. "This is about family. I need to get out of here so I can save my child." Walter didn't care about the baby. He cared about saving his own ass.

"You're not getting out for a long time. As for your child, well, you tried to steal my baby from me, but it looks like I'll be raising yours."

What a twist of fate.

"What?" Shock filled Walter's eyes. "You and Kelly?"

"Are friends. Unlike you, I don't turn my back on family. Kelly will have the income she needs from Blue Mining in addition to the child support *you will* pay. The baby will collect twenty percent of the profits from Blue Mining. I will be the guardian over the account so you can't do to him what you did to me. That kid will never have to rely on you to take care of him. He or she will know what a good man looks like and how he treats others with respect, kindness, and love. By the time you get out of here, the baby will be grown, and I will be the only father figure that child has ever known."

Maybe it was petty, but Austin hung up on whatever his father had to say and walked out. He wanted his father to know he couldn't have his way anymore. He couldn't manipulate people and not suffer the consequences. He couldn't hurt people and reap rewards that didn't belong to him.

He couldn't hurt Austin anymore.

And Austin was done.

He'd held on to hope this past year that his father would change, but his selfish nature grew and infected everything in his life.

Austin refused to participate in his father's twisted games anymore.

He had a life with Sonya that had him anxious to get home to her where he could breathe and be himself and love and be loved with an open, honest heart.

Chapter Thirty-Six

Austin pulled into the drive and stared at the woman who made everything in his life better. She'd turned the run-down house into their home. She'd fixed his broken heart. With her, he was safe.

Yes, they'd face some hard times. He didn't expect the rest of his life to be carefree, but there was nothing they couldn't face together and work out.

He stepped out of the truck. She smiled down at him from the porch steps, so pretty in a floral dress that barely reached her knees, bare feet, sexy legs, her long dark hair draped down her back.

He liked coming home to her, seeing her here waiting for him.

He glanced around the yard, noticing the flowers and plants she'd added to the landscape. Horses roamed in the field to the left of the house. Cattle grazed the property, fat and happy.

The wasteland this place once was had been transformed into the home and ranch of his dreams. But none of that mattered as much as having the woman waiting for him to come to her.

Life didn't get better than this.

He went to the back of the truck, lowered the tailgate, and pulled out the surprise he stopped off in town to pick up just for him and Sonya and the house they rebuilt. He hefted the heavy weight in both hands and carried it across the drive and up the steps to where Sonya stood, a pretty smile lighting up her face.

"A bench swing."

He set it down where he'd bolted in two hooks before he'd left to see his father this morning. He pulled one side up by the attached chain and hooked it in place, then did the same with the other side. Finished, he glanced from the bench and out to the yard and ranch spreading out before them.

Sonya touched her hand to his chest to get his attention. She reached up, cupped his face, and brushed her thumbs over his cheeks. "I missed you today."

He gripped her hips. "Not as much as I missed you." He kissed her softly, needing some of her sweetness to wash away his sour morning.

"How did it go?"

"As expected. He refuses to take responsibility, so I'm done. I said what I wanted to say. I can't fix him. I can't make him care. So I'm going to live my life and not think about him anymore." He nodded toward the swing. "What do you think?"

"It's perfect."

Austin turned to her, dipped his hand in his front pocket, and pulled out the other surprise he had made for her. "You're perfect." He took her left hand, went down on bended knee, and stared up at her.

She pressed her fingertips to her mouth to cover the gasp and her eyes shined bright with unshed tears.

"I thought about taking you on a trip, getting away from here for some fun and sun, so I could do what I promised. But then I thought about how we met and how much things have changed and decided this was the spot for the swing and for me to do this." He held the ring between them. "I met you right here on this porch. Best thing that ever happened to me was a water bucket wake-up call from an angel who saved my life and gave me a purpose. I want to spend the rest of my life loving you."

Sonya brushed her hand over the side of his head, her fingers raking through his hair.

"I had nothing when you met me. Now I have everything I need because I have you in my life."

"I feel the same way."

"Live the dream we turned this ranch into these past weeks with me. Let's turn this amazing connection between us that has been such a gift in our lives into a lifetime of memories. Be my wife." The waning sun caught the brilliant cushion-cut blue sapphire between trillion-cut diamonds and made the stones sparkle. "This stone came from the land that is my legacy. It's a piece of my history and a promise for our future. I swear I'll love you the rest of my life. Will you marry me?"

She nodded, then got the word he wanted to hear again out past her choked-up throat. "Yes."

He slid the ring on her finger, thankful it fit.

She stared down at it through watery eyes. "It's beautiful, Austin. More than I expected."

He stood and kept her hand in his. "You're not disappointed it isn't a big-ass diamond?"

"The ones on the sides put together are as big as the sapphire, which is gorgeous. It's perfect, Austin. It's you and me and the gift of this land."

"I knew you'd get it."

"I love you. I can't wait to be your wife." She cupped his face and kissed him. He sank into her sweetness and the soft press of her lips against his.

He took her head in both hands and stared into her beautiful eyes. "I can't wait to celebrate the way we did last time I proposed."

"I think I can help you with that." She kissed him again, but this time she infused the kiss with all the heat and passion they'd kept banked the last several days as she healed.

He broke the kiss that had his heart pounding and his body demanding to be closer to hers. He'd held her every night, keeping the nightmares at bay and letting her know how happy he was to still have her by his side and in his arms. "Are you sure you're up to turning me on like this?"

"I can't wait anymore." She proved it by kissing him again and sliding her tongue along his. Her hands slipped up under his shirt and caressed his back, her nails biting in as she dragged them down along his spine, sending a shiver of desire across every nerve.

Careful of her side, he hooked his arm around and under her bottom, picked her up, and carried her through the open front door. He kicked it shut and walked through the living room, down the hall, and into their room without stopping kissing her.

She slid down his body as he set her on her feet. Her hands stopped roaming over his chest and abs and grabbed hold of his shirt and pulled it up and off over his head. She sent it sailing across the room.

The sweet smile he came home to turned into a sexy knowing one that heated his blood as she took in his bare chest. Her hands spread wide over his pecs, went up his shoulders, and down over his biceps.

"I have really missed you."

He swooped in and kissed her again, sweeping his hands up her sides and around her back. He unzipped her dress, his fingers caressing her silky skin. He pulled the material down her shoulders and arms and let it fall and puddle at her feet.

She stepped into him, her bare breasts pressing against his chest. He swept his hands over her hips and up her sides. "You weren't wearing anything under that dress," he said against her lips, amazed she'd planned this sexy encounter.

"You're overdressed." She tackled his button and zipper and dragged his jeans and boxers down his hips. He stopped kissing her long enough to take over and pull off his boots and the rest of his clothes.

Sonya threw the bedcovers back and climbed up on the mattress. She didn't lie down, but kneeled in front of him, hooked her hand at the back of his neck, and pulled him in for another searing kiss.

He cupped her breasts in his hands and rubbed his palms against her tight nipples. She arched into his hands. He squeezed her breasts and brushed his thumbs over the hard peaks, making her moan against his lips.

He slid one hand down her belly and over her mound to her soft folds. He traced one finger over her center, then sank it deep into her wet core. She rocked her hips into his hand as he caressed and kissed her senseless.

Her fingers wrapped around his hard shaft, and her thumb circled the bead of moisture on the head, tightening his balls. He desperately wanted to sink into her welcoming heat but he also wanted to take his time loving her. Though he didn't know how long he'd last if she kept stroking her hand up and down his cock, her fingers caressing his balls, and her hot mouth and tongue simulating what he wanted to do with his dick.

"Damn, baby."

She stared into his eyes. Desire danced in hers. He wanted that flame to burn brighter and hotter and he thrust two fingers into her this time. Her eyes went wide even as she sank down onto his hand. When he pulled out, she backed away, leaned over on her hands, and took his aching shaft into her mouth.

All the breath rushed out of him. Seeing her on all fours, her rosy lips wrapped around his cock, her head bobbing up and down over his flesh, sent a blast of heat through his system. He combed one hand through her long hair and held her head as she made him feel nothing but pure pleasure and drove his need for her to new heights.

Unable to endure the sweet torture for long, he grabbed a condom from the drawer beside him, cupped her face, and pulled her off him and up for another mind-blowing kiss. She leaned back and fell to the bed, taking him with her.

He hated to wait another second but kept his head long enough to roll on the condom before he thrust into her. Seated deep, he paused and stared down at her. "I love you." The words burst out of him, and now he needed to pour every bit of that feeling spilling from his heart and every fiber of his being into her.

His body rocked in and out and over hers in long soft strokes that attuned their heartbeats and connected his soul to hers until he breathed with her and felt every wave of pleasure wash through her body and his at the same time. He stopped thinking and just let himself feel.

The tempo changed as their need grew and the demands of their bodies took over until they were both moving toward each other, pressing close, rocking their hips harder and faster into each other until they both reached the point of no return, and her body locked around his and squeezed every ounce of pleasure from him. Her body quaked around his pulsing shaft as she settled into the bed and he fell on top of her, their breaths sawing in and out, their arms around each other.

He didn't want to crush her, but when he tried to rise and shift off her, she wrapped her arms around his back and held him close.

"I love the weight of you on me."

He rested most of his weight on his forearms and looked down at her. "That was . . ."

"Amazing." Tears swam in her eyes. She reached up and touched his face. "I can't believe we almost lost this."

He'd hoped what happened had faded over the last few days, but their raw lovemaking had released her emotions. She needed time to deal with it, but right now she needed his reassurance.

"It's over now, sweetheart." He brushed his fingers through her hair. "This is how things will be between us from now on. I promise. Actually, it's only going to get better. You're going to be my wife. I'll be your husband. It's you and me and anything we want now."

He had the money and means to give her anything she wanted, but it had become crystal clear when she got shot that what they really wanted was each other.

That was enough.

That was everything.

Chapter Thirty-Seven

Sonya held Austin's hand in the front seat of the truck and stared out the windshield at her mother's beautiful little house with the white picket fence, towering trees, and the turquoise pots overflowing with ivy on the porch. Two navy blue rocking chairs sat in front of the window with a table between. She had no trouble imagining her mother sitting on the porch enjoying the peace and tranquility of the work-in-progress yard.

"Don't forget the strawberry plants."

Sonya picked up the six-pack by the handle from the floorboard. "She's done a great job putting in bushes around the garden that will thrive and live through winter."

"With summer just around the corner, she can fill in with flowers to give it some more color. The strawberries will be a nice addition to what she's started."

"Roxy and Noah are already here. Whose car is that?" Sonya didn't recognize the silver sedan.

"I don't know. Maybe June made a new friend."

She hoped her mother had settled in and found peace here.

Her uncles were in jail after accepting a deal from the prosecutor. Ten years for kidnapping, beating, raping, and extorting money from her mother. Her mother got the justice she deserved even if her uncles didn't get the life sentence her mother did having to live with what they'd done to her.

It made Sonya angry that they'd gotten away with so much. But her mother's relief that they were behind bars and she didn't have to testify in open court made her happy to see June so carefree and embracing a new life.

Austin brought their joined hands up and kissed the back of hers below her gorgeous engagement ring. "Let's go see everyone."

Sonya had visited her mother several times over the last month. Since she and Austin had gotten engaged and taken over Blue Mining, things had been crazy busy. Austin focused on the ranch. She helped the prosecutor, gathering all the records to make the case against Walter.

Again, a deal had been struck. Walter didn't want to air all his dirty deeds in open court. Instead, his lawyer pleaded the case down to lesser charges and Walter would ultimately serve far less time in jail than he deserved. Again, justice had been served. Everyone in town followed the story in the local paper. The man they knew and respected had fallen from grace. His true character had been revealed. Walter Hubbard no longer held sway over this town or its residents.

Those who had shunned Austin in some way or talked behind his back now held him in high regard.

Kelly was doing well. She'd moved into the cottage. Sonya caught her flirting with the contractor doing the repairs and renovation on the small house. Maybe it would turn into something, maybe not, but Kelly had put what happened with Walter behind her and focused on her new management role at work, the baby on the way, and the life she wanted for both of them.

They were all settled and living their lives. And as part of living a normal happy life, her mother had decided to put her new cooking skills to use and start a new tradition: Sunday dinner.

Sonya slid out of the truck behind Austin. Their relationship had grown closer these last weeks as they spent their days taking care of business and their nights getting to know each other better. They took long rides at dusk, enjoying the horses and seeing the changes on the ranch that now had more animals than Austin could handle on his own because his father had closed down Hubbard Ranch and sold the livestock to them.

Austin had hired three full-time guys to help out and would probably bring on a couple more part-time during the calving and harvest seasons.

She and Austin stood together on the porch at her mother's door.

He smiled down at her. "This is nice. Dinner with friends and family."

She squeezed his hand. "I'm so happy she moved here."

Austin knocked. "I like it that your trips to the Ranch to take care of business are short because you're not staying to visit her."

"You just want to keep me all to yourself."

"Guilty." Austin leaned down and kissed her right when the door opened.

Sonya turned to her mother.

June's smile had never been more radiant. "You two are so good together." Her mother held her arms out. "Come here, Angel."

Sonya released Austin and hugged her mom. "Hey, Mama, how are you?"

"So happy to have my girl here."

Sonya stepped back and held up the strawberry plants bursting with dark green leaves, pretty white flowers, and a few green berries that promised a bounty of bright red fruit to come.

"Oh, I love them. Thank you. I'll plant them tomorrow."

Sonya glanced past her mother to a man she hadn't seen in a while. "Mr. Foster. What are you doing here?"

June stepped back and hooked her arm through Mr. Foster's. June's shy smile still lit up her eyes with joy. "I invited him. Tim and I met at the bank weeks ago and haven't gone a day without seeing each other since."

Sonya glanced up at Austin to gauge his reaction because she didn't know how to feel about her mother dating the bank manager.

Austin winked at her, held out his hand to Mr. Foster, and said, "I know just how you feel. The second I set eyes on Sonya I didn't want to spend a day without her."

Mr. Foster relaxed and shook Austin's hand and smiled at Sonya. "What can I say, she captured my heart with her sweet charm and pretty smile."

June hooked her arm around Sonya's shoulders and they walked through the entry and into the open main living space. June held her back a few paces and whispered in her ear, "I really like Tim. He's kind and funny and doesn't care about my past. He's a couple years older than me and has never been married. He wants a wife and a family. And I just love being with him, talking about his work, how he grew up in this town, and the heartache he suffered when his fiancée died in a car accident. He closed himself off to another chance at happiness. But then we met and hit it off, and all of a sudden, we discovered we both wanted a shot at a second chance at happiness."

Sonya wrapped her mother in a hug. "I'm happy for you, Mama. You deserve love and happiness and a husband and children."

"Good, because if my suspicions are correct, you're going to be a big sister."

Sonya held June at arm's length and glanced down at her belly, then back up to her face. "Really?" Tears sprang to her eyes.

"We didn't want to wait. I'm no spring chicken. At my age, we thought it might take a while, but I guess not."

To show her mother how excited and happy she was for her, she turned to Austin, Noah, Roxy, and Mr. Foster in the kitchen. "I'm going to be a big sister!" She hugged June again.

Everyone in the kitchen held up their beers.

Austin made the toast. "To another Wild Rose."

That made Sonya and Roxy laugh.

While the guys drank and Austin and Noah slapped Mr. Foster on the back, Roxy joined her and June. They shared a group hug.

"I'm so happy for you, June." Roxy smiled but it didn't quite reach her eyes.

June laid her hand on Roxy's shoulder. "Thank you, sweetheart. I wish, for your sake, your mother was different."

"I wish she had your strength and guts. You're going to be a great mom. You already know how to be one. Look how great Sonya turned out." Roxy hooked her arm over Sonya's shoulders and hugged her to her side. "I love you, sis."

"Love you, too, Rox."

June gave them another shy smile and held out her hand, showing off the simple diamond solitaire.

Sonya pressed her fingers to her lips, then gasped. “Mama, it’s gorgeous.”

The doorbell rang. “That’s Tim’s friend. He did this thing on the internet to do the ceremony.”

“What ceremony?” Sonya asked, taking in her mother’s pretty, white, lace shift dress.

“To marry us.”

“You’re getting married right now?” Sonya tried to keep up with all the changes in her mother’s life. She and Austin’s relationship happened quickly, but this was meteorically fast.

“Yes, Angel. Don’t worry. I know what I’m doing. Tim is a good man. But I know how you worry, so I had him sign one of those agreements so that what’s mine stays mine.”

Shocked, Sonya spit out, “You have a prenup?”

“I have a lot of money. While I don’t believe for a second that Tim cares one bit about that—he’s financially secure on his own—I wanted the insurance because, you know, men.” June added an eye roll to go with that “men.”

She’d known a lot of men in her life.

Sonya had to hand it to June for looking out for herself.

“I need to protect this baby the way I protected you. Though I hope I do a better job this time around.”

Sonya hugged June. “You did great with me, Mama. This baby is lucky to have you. And so is Tim. He’s not like those other men. He’ll treat you the way you deserve.”

“He already does.”

“And if he doesn’t, we’ll have Austin and Noah kill him,” Roxy teased.

“You don’t need us.” Austin brushed his hand down Sonya’s hair. “Sonya’s got you covered.”

“Shoot, shovel, shut up.” She winked at Austin, who laughed with her because they’d gotten through the ordeal with his father and could look back without all the anger and pain.

Tim stood in the entry next to his friend, looking nervous.

Sonya shrugged and said, "Welcome to the family. You'll get used to us."

Tim laughed with all of them and showed his friend into the living room.

Noah walked out of the kitchen holding a beautiful bouquet of white roses and handed them to June. "Congratulations."

"Thank you, Noah." June laid her hand over her belly. "Oh wow. I'm nervous."

"Don't be. This is everything you wanted," Sonya reminded her. "You're a beautiful bride."

Austin and Noah pulled out their phones and became the official wedding photographers. She and Roxy stood beside her mother as June and Tim exchanged vows. June teared up when Tim promised to love, honor, and cherish her forever. Other than Sonya, no one had ever done that for June.

The vows were followed by Tim's beautiful declaration. "I will always take care of you." He kissed his bride with such tenderness, Sonya's heart melted, and she knew Tim meant every promise he'd made.

She didn't need to worry about her mother anymore.

They clapped for the happy couple and took more pictures. Noah popped the cork on a bottle of champagne and poured for everyone.

Sonya held up her glass. "To the happy couple. May you always have love and joy and each other."

Everyone drank the bubbly.

June took a tiny sip, kissed her husband again, then set her glass aside. "Just a sip for me and the baby. Thank you, Angel, for all your love and support."

"Always, Mama."

"Let's sit at the table. My cooking class made the meal. I'll just get it from the kitchen."

"Let us." Roxy grabbed Sonya by the arm and pulled her into the kitchen. "I'm so happy for them."

"Me, too. I've never seen her look this happy." Sonya stared at her mother as she sat with the men at the table. "She's radiant."

"I don't know about you, but between work and spending time with Noah and Annabelle, I barely have a minute to plan our wedding."

"I know what you mean. Maybe Mama's got the right idea—keep it short and simple."

"This was lovely, but I'd like a little more. The dress. Flowers. Our friends."

"Adria and Juliana," Sonya added. "They missed this."

"Adria graduates next week. Who knows what trouble Juliana's in right now."

Sonya took the foil pans out of the oven, set them on the stovetop, and uncovered them. "Hand me that platter." Sonya piled the garlic-and-mushroom chicken on the plate then poured the gravy over it.

Roxy spooned the vegetable medley into a huge bowl. The broccoli, carrots, and cauliflower steamed.

Sonya took thc final baking dish from the oven and peeled back the foil cover. "Oh God, that smells good."

Roxy took a whiff of the scalloped potatoes au gratin. "Maybe we need to take this cooking class."

Austin came into the kitchen. "Need some help?"

Sonya handed him the hot potatoes using the oven mitts. Roxy took the vegetables. Sonya carried in the huge platter of chicken. They placed the food on the beautiful table decorated with a dozen votive candles and three pretty white flower bouquets. The new china and silverware June bought sparkled along with the crystal glasses in the soft candlelight.

She and Roxy took their seats.

Before they ate, Tim looked at all of them from the head of the table. "I'm glad you're all here. Family is everything." He turned to June. "We're just starting our family, but I'm so glad to celebrate this wonderful day with yours."

"Ours," June reminded him.

Sonya met Roxy's gaze across the table and they said in unison, "Double wedding."

They didn't need two separate weddings, they just needed their family around them on their special day.

Austin and Noah fist-bumped across the table, agreeing with them on the double wedding ceremony.

They ate the scrumptious meal and talked about the baby and the upcoming weddings. Sonya and Roxy couldn't wait to help her mother turn the spare room into the baby's room. Roxy talked about a gorgeous dress she saw in one of the bridal magazines she thought would be perfect for Sonya. The guys talked about horses, cows, ranching, and baseball.

Sonya ate two slices of the amazing white chocolate and raspberry mousse wedding cake her mother ordered and slid into bed later that night full to the brim and happier than she could remember.

Austin took her in his arms like he always did and nuzzled his nose into her neck, kissed her softly, then whispered, "When do you want to have a baby?"

They'd talked about wanting to start a family sooner rather than later.

She turned into him and pressed her hand to his chest over his heart. "Wanna start now?"

Austin dove in, taking her mouth in a searing kiss that spun out and made her forget everything but the feel of him against her.

His hand slid down her side and stopped on her hip the second her phone rang. He broke the kiss and stared down at her, his body tense with concern. "Who'd call this late?"

Sonya rolled out from under Austin, sat on the edge of the bed, and picked up her phone from the bedside table. "Hello."

She barely registered the words spilling out of Roxy, but the gist of what she said and what it meant hit her heart and made it clench and bleed. She hung up after only saying, "I'll meet you there."

Austin's chest pressed against her back. His chin rested on her shoulder. "What's wrong?"

"Roxy and I have to go back to Vegas. Juliana overdosed."

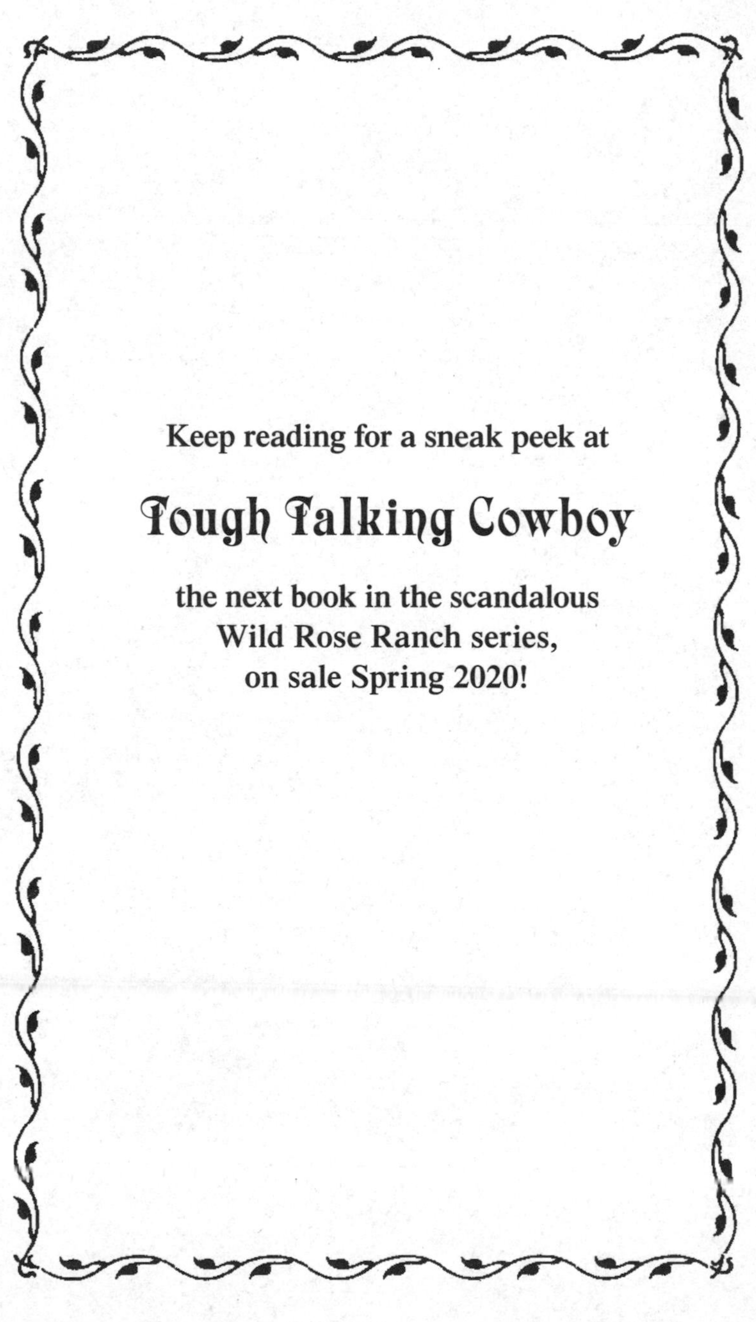

Keep reading for a sneak peek at

Tough Talking Cowboy

the next book in the scandalous
Wild Rose Ranch series,
on sale Spring 2020!

Chapter One

Adria unlocked the front door and stood in the opening feeling the stillness and quiet as intensely as the prickle of awareness that something was wrong. Without thought, her hand dipped into her purse and her fingers closed over her phone and the bag she pulled out. Her purse slid off her shoulder and dropped to the floor as she moved toward the hallway and the call she clearly heard but didn't make a sound.

She felt her sister's need in every fiber of her being. She couldn't ignore that primal call and the connection they shared.

Adria's heart raced as the quiet coming from the bathroom seemed to thicken the air until she could barely draw a breath. Every step toward the door felt like it took forever. Her mind shouted to hurry, but her heart warned of heartbreak beyond the closed door. She pushed it open against the barrier on the other side, found her identical twin lying motionless on the floor, her lips tinged blue.

Adria's stomach pitched, sour bile rising to her throat.

She swallowed hard and tried to think through the dizzying shock.

Nothing, not even her resigned heart, could prepare her for this.

She dropped to her knees and shook Juliana. "Wake up!"

No response. Not even a flutter of her eyes.

Adria's heart jackhammered. Her mind skittered from one thought to the next, all of them scary and filled with denials and rationales for what was so obvious.

She leaned down, tilted her sister's head back, pressed her lips to Juliana's, and gave her mouth-to-mouth. They'd breathed as one in utero, but she never expected she'd have to take over for her beautiful, broken sister like this. "Come on, Jules, I can't live without you. Don't do this to me."

She gave her three more breaths, then had to use drastic measures to bring her back.

She flipped her phone over, dialed 911, put the phone on speaker, and left it on the floor next to her dying sister.

"911, what is the emergency?"

"My sister overdosed. Heroin. I'm administering naloxone." Adria unzipped the cosmetic bag she'd instinctively pulled from her purse, pulled out the syringe, and unwrapped it. She broke open the glass ampule, used her teeth to pull the cap off the needle, and filled the syringe despite how much her hands shook.

"What is the address of the emergency?"

She rattled off the house number and street for Wild Rose Ranch as she jabbed the needle into her sister's bare thigh and pushed the plunger.

Waiting for a response stopped Adria's heart. She held her breath. The world around her paused.

And nothing happened.

Fear squeezed her heart. Hope made her send up another prayer.

Juliana didn't miraculously wake up, but her barely-there breaths deepened and evened out.

"Paramedics are three minutes out. Have you administered the naloxone?"

"Yes. She's breathing. Shallow, but even."

The terrifying blue in Juliana's lips faded as they turned pink once again.

"Roll her to her side if she's not already in that position."

Adria turned her sister and brushed the blond hair from her face, relieved but still worried sick. "Why, Jules?" Of the two of them, Adria had reason to want to escape and numb her emotions and drown out her nightmares.

Yes, their childhood sucked. They'd grown up with a drug-addicted mother who prostituted herself out for drugs, and money to buy more drugs.

She always needed more.

She'd done a lot worse than sell herself to get them.

Mom—Christie, now Crystal since she started working at the Wild Rose Ranch—had done so many drugs she'd short-wired her reasoning, judgment, and empathy. She only cared about herself and proved it to her young twins too many times to count.

Adria hated seeing her sister do the same thing she'd watched their mother do their whole lives and self-destruct.

It broke her heart to pieces.

"I'm not going to let you do this to yourself." She combed her fingers through Juliana's hair and tried to breathe through the fear and heartache.

"Paramedics and police have arrived." Focused on Juliana and making sure she kept breathing, she'd forgotten about the dispatcher on the phone.

"The door is open. We're in the bathroom." She checked the urge to hide Juliana's drug paraphernalia. Even though her stomach knotted at the thought of the police seeing the evidence of Juliana's drug use and possibly arresting her, she didn't hesitate to invite them in because Juliana needed help. And Adria would make sure she got it.

They weren't alone in the world anymore. They had their sisters, Roxy and Sonya. Without them, without the Wild Rose Ranch, they'd probably both be dead by now.

"Miss, we're here to help. Please step back."

Adria leaned down and kissed her sister on the forehead. "Hold on. You're going to be okay now. I love you."

The paramedic held his hand out to help her up off the floor. She appreciated the gesture, because even though he was there for her sister, he took the time to help her, too. His presence eased her mind.

But her heart still clenched when he put his dark hand on her sister's deathly pale wrist to check her pulse. The wild rose tattoo that started at her sister's shoulder and wrapped around her arm stood out dark green and pink against her translucent white skin. Four roses. Juliana, Adria, Roxy, and Sonya.

Her imagination had one of those roses shriveling and dying. She pushed the nightmare image out of her mind. She couldn't even conceive of her sister leaving her.

An officer's radio squawked behind her, the dispatcher relaying information about a burglary in progress. All Adria wanted was for these guys to care about her sister more than anything else, because right now, nothing mattered more than saving Juliana's life.

"Miss, can you answer some questions for me?"

She didn't turn to the officer, but watched the paramedic check her sister's blood pressure. "What do you want to know?"

"Let's start with your name."

"Adria Holloway. That's my sister Juliana."

"Twins?"

Usually that was so obvious, but Juliana had lost weight the last many months she'd been partying away her days and nights instead of attending school. Adria had just graduated. Juliana, for all intents and purposes, dropped out because as far as Adria knew she hadn't attended classes since the first week of the semester. She gave up last year asking if Juliana actually earned her credits the last two semesters. And it pissed Adria off to see her sister waste the opportunity to do and be something better than this: a drug addict, looking for her next score instead of living the life they'd been given here on the Ranch.

A second chance Adria tried hard every day to embrace instead of her own demons.

"Identical," she confirmed, though not in every way.

"Can you tell me what happened tonight?"

Adria wished she knew what possessed her sister to think getting high and putting her life at risk was a good idea. Or that it solved anything.

"I'm not sure. I was on a blind date." *From hell.*

More than a year after her last dating debacle, she'd wanted to try again. Another chance to see if she could get past her hang-ups and connect with a man and not see him as the monster from her nightmares.

Lonely, she'd wanted to connect with someone. She wanted some physical contact, to feel a man's hands run over her skin and feel the pleasure in his touch.

She'd never use one of those stupid apps again. "I ended the date early and came home." Because she'd gotten a bad feeling and an urgent need to get to Juliana overtook her.

Not because her date talked about sports for nearly an hour, forgot to stop at the bank for cash to pay the tab—who didn't have a credit card for that very reason?—told her he had cash at home and would pay her back once they got there. Like she'd go to his place after swiping on his picture and messaging him twice to set up the date. She knew nothing about him, except for his favorite football team and that he wanted her to give him head before they had sex.

He preferred it that way.

She left him with a big "Fuck you" and hauled ass home, her mind on her sister and not the Raiders' biggest fan.

"I walked in the door and knew something was wrong." She'd felt Juliana slipping away. Like a piece of her that Adria carried in her soul evaporated. The echo of fear and desolation swamped her system again. She wrapped her arms around her middle, wishing her sister would wake up and hug her. "I grabbed the naloxone and my phone out of my purse and ran to her."

"Has she overdosed before?"

"Once." She never wanted to receive that call from the hospital again. Another shot of pure terror raced through her. For a split second, she'd thought her sister had died. Just like tonight when she saw her passed out on the floor, her face gray, lips blue, and barely an ounce of life left in her.

"Looks like she was getting ready for bed." The officer pointed his pen at Juliana's state of undress.

In her red lace bra and a black leather skirt that barely covered her ass, maybe it looked like she'd been undressing to go to bed. But Adria knew better. "She was getting ready to go out."

"It's late."

Juliana had taken to coming home in the morning, sleeping the day away, and spending her nights out partying.

Because of Juliana's unpredictable schedule, Adria started sleeping in Roxy's room. Their sister hardly ever came home to visit now that she'd moved to her inherited ranch in Montana with her new family. Roxy was raising her adopted stepsister, Annabelle, and got engaged to Noah.

She'd found her home. Love. Family. A life that made her happy.

Adria was working on finding hers while Juliana played Russian Roulette with her life.

"She likes the night life." Juliana liked driving into Vegas. So many strangers looking for a good time. Fun. Frivolous. No strings. No expectations. Just go with it.

What happens in Vegas stays in Vegas.

Juliana thought that suited her. She thought she could escape whatever drove her.

All it did was make her worse because when you're that high and out of it, you can't feel. Not really.

And when you wake up, you still have the same problems and that just bums you out more.

You still can't escape yourself, because in the end it's just you and your thoughts and your past and the decision you have to make every day to either leave it behind and move on, or don't.

The fact that Big Mama and security at the Wild Rose Ranch brothel caught Juliana selling herself with the other prostitutes who worked at the legal whorehouse only showed how far off the rails Juliana had gone these last few months. They'd sworn to each other that they'd never end up like their mother. But Juliana spent more time with Crystal these days than she did with Adria.

Some form of self-punishment? Adria didn't know. She'd begged Juliana to talk to her. But Juliana shut her down and pushed her out of her life.

She missed Juliana and the closeness they'd always shared.

The closer Adria got to graduation and starting her life and hopefully her own business, the more self-destructive Juliana became.

It felt like her fault. But didn't she deserve her own life and successes?

It meant they were slowly going in different directions. At some point, they needed to live their lives. They couldn't always do everything together and the same.

It hurt Adria's heart to think that life would take them down separate roads when they'd spent their whole lives not just traveling the same path but holding hands as one. But Adria couldn't follow her sister or even stand beside her down this path of destruction Juliana continued to take despite the risks and how miserable it made her. And it tore them apart a little at a time.

Adria could only hope that what happened tonight woke her sister up and made her want to change her ways before things got worse. Because, yes, Adria knew from experience, things can always get worse.

"Do you guys work up at the Wild Rose Ranch?" The officer held her gaze, a look of interest in his eyes.

"No. Our mother does."

That raised a few eyebrows among the three men there to take care of her sister.

The paramedics did their job, efficiently stabilizing her sister, putting in an IV line, and getting her settled on the gurney. They covered her with a blanket and strapped her in. Seeing her covered marginally warmed Adria even though goose bumps still covered every inch of her skin.

The paramedics rolled Juliana down the hallway. The officer took pictures of the bathroom, including the mirror sitting precariously on the edge of the counter with the remnants of powder on it, along with the cut straw her sister used to snort the heroin.

Adria stood on the porch while they loaded her sister into the back of the ambulance.

Big Mama pulled into the driveway in her Cadillac from the mansion across the wide pasture. Someone up at the brothel must have seen the flashing lights. She slipped out of the front seat dressed in a black skirt, black bustier, red stilettos, her red hair curled in waves, and her black lined eyes glassed over with sadness and filled with fear. "Is she . . ."

Adria shook her head, unable to speak for fear her sister would prove her wrong and die on the spot.

"What happened?"

Adria ran into the Madam's arms and ample breasts and hugged her close, relieved she'd come and Adria wasn't alone.

Big Mama had been the only real mother figure she'd had since Big Mama rescued Crystal from a shelter and gave them a home before child protective services took her and Juliana away to a foster home. Big Mama took care of them. She cared about them. She kept Crystal from hurting them anymore.

"She overdosed. I gave her the naloxone just like the doctor showed us after the last time."

Big Mama squeezed her tight. "Good girl. You saved her."

"I can't do this again." The tears clogging her throat burst free on a ragged sob and her sadness and anger poured out.

"I hope you don't have to."

Adria stepped back and tried to rein in her wild emotions. "I won't because whether she likes it or not, I'm getting her the help she needs."

Big Mama nodded. "Call Roxy. It's time to intervene." Big Mama swept her gaze over Adria. "Change into something more comfortable. I'll drive you to the hospital."

The ambulance pulled out. Big Mama went to talk to the officer who walked out of the house. Adria's mind caught up to the fact that she was standing in the too-tight, low-cut, electric blue tank dress and four-inch strappy heels Juliana insisted she wear on her date. Not Adria's style or comfort zone, but Juliana coaxed her to be bold and give her date a reason to come back for more. Too bad the only message her date got was that she was easy and the officer and paramedics thought she worked at the Ranch.

Not the image she wanted.

She needed to stop experimenting and trying to figure men out and just be herself and focus on her future. Something broke inside her when that man . . . Well, it happened, and she didn't know how to fix it. Dating random men wasn't the answer.

But God, how she dreamed of a real relationship with a guy who knew how to be kind and made her burn.

She left her nonexistent love life on the back burner. She ignored the heavy, sour ball of dread in her gut and the whisper in her heart that spoke her worst fear, *You will always be alone*.

She ran into the house, peeled off the too-sexy-for-her dress, tossed the uncomfortable heels, pulled on a pair of jeans, a tank top, and a comfy shrug. She slipped her feet into a pair of Keds and left her hair in wild disarray as she grabbed her cell from the bathroom floor and her purse off the tile entry and met Big Mama at her car.

She dialed Roxy as Big Mama drove and followed the ambulance to the hospital.

Roxy picked up on the first ring. "What's wrong?"

This late at night, of course Roxy expected trouble. "Juliana overdosed again. She's in an ambulance on the way to the hospital. I need you to make that call."

"On it. Want Sonya and me to meet you in Vegas?" They'd come running the last time, too.

"No. I want her to see us all supporting her at the rehab. I don't care what it takes, but I'm getting her on the plane and to the rehab center whether she likes it or not."

"I'll make it happen."

Adria sighed out her relief. "Roxy."

"Yeah, honey."

"Thank you."

"What are sisters for?"

In this case, to pick up the pieces when everything fell apart. And to pick up the tab. When Roxy found out she owned the Wild Rose Ranch, she'd made it clear that she meant to use the enormous amount of money she earned to help her sisters. She'd paid for Adria and Juliana to finish school and eliminated all their debt. Now, Adria needed Roxy to pay for the astronomically expensive rehab her sister needed to save her life.

"I love you, Adria. You're not alone. Sonya and I will be there."

"Thank you." The simple but heartfelt words didn't seem enough to convey to Roxy how much she appreciated what she was about to do. Because saving Juliana meant saving Adria.

She could live without a man, but she couldn't live without her twin.